MW01330003

An Heir of Realms

Book One of the Realm Riders Series

Heather Ashle

First published in the United States 2022

HB Ink, LLC
979-8-9866515-0-7
Young adult fantasy: age 14 and up.

Custom cover art by Rob Carlos
www.colorsmith.com

No dragons were harmed in the creation of this tale.
No such vow can be made for Narxon.

RADAR O'REILLY

I'll dedicate my first book after you.

COLONEL POTTER

Eh, better let me read it first.

- *M*A*S*H*, season 5, episode 15

For Moo and Did.

Sorry I didn't let you read it first.

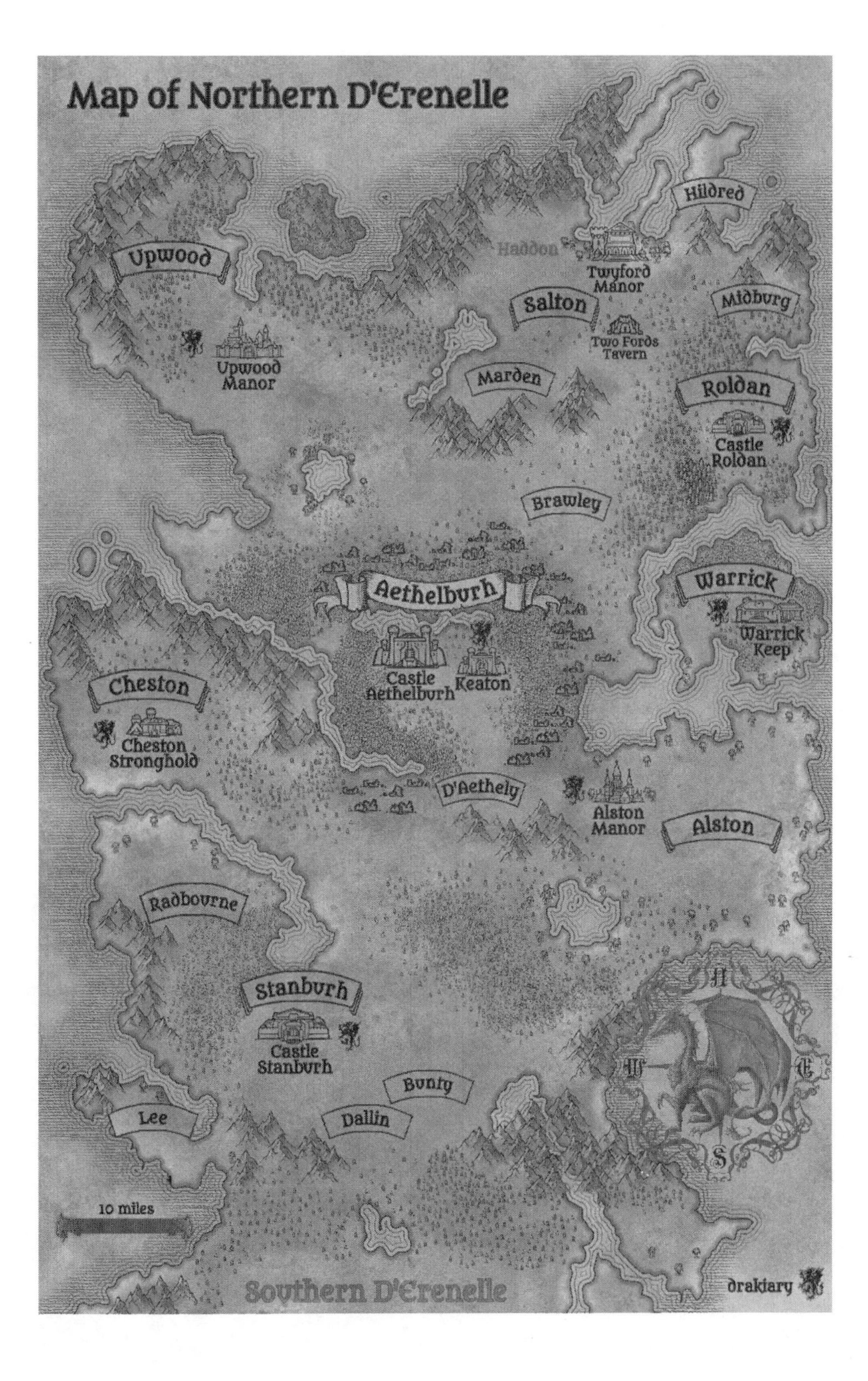
Map of Northern D'Erenelle
Upwood
Upwood Manor
Haddon
Twyford Manor
Hildred
Salton
Two Fords Tavern
Midburg
Marden
Roldan
Castle Roldan
Brawley
Aethelburh
Warrick
Warrick Keep
Castle Aethelburh
Keaton
Cheston
Cheston Stronghold
D'Aethely
Alston Manor
Alston
Radbourne
Stanburh
Castle Stanburh
Bunty
Lee
Dallin
N
W
E
S
10 miles
Southern D'Erenelle
drakiary

FOR thousands of years and hundreds of recorded Movements, the Realm Riders and their Dragons have secured our Realms from harm. In all that time, a Cycle has developed that has come to describe our Realm System and the journey our Riders take within it.

A new Cycle begins when the Queen Dragon opens a Portal into a Realm uninhabited by Riders and Dragons. But in this beginning, we also find the end of the Realm she leaves behind—one that was rife with abundance and prosperity but has fallen into disrepair, abandoned to regeneration in the hopes that it may, one day, flourish again.

- an excerpt, *From Those Outlying*

Prologue

Stanburh

Allistair of Stanburh made his way down the ladder-like stirrups of his green dragon's saddle, and his boots stuck firmly in the thick mud below. Rain slapped against his already drenched riding leathers and ricocheted off Cahal's emerald scales as lightning sliced through the night sky. Four sluggish stable hands bit down on yawns as they dragged themselves out into the rain to usher Rider and beast under the stable's awning. Allistair patted Cahal's hide with a gloved hand as another flash transformed the beast's scales into shimmering gemstones before they faded in a wash of darkness.

The Rider twisted his boots in the muck to dislodge them and made his way to the castle's entrance. He let himself in—the staff inside was not moving as quickly as the stable hands—and shut the storm out, muffling its roar behind the thick stone walls and heavy wooden door.

An older man approached from the other end of the dim hall. He was fending off a young waiting-woman, who kept pace beside him and peppered him with questions. He flung his arm wildly toward a hallway, and she scurried off out of sight.

Allistair tugged off his wet gloves and shoved them into the pocket of his water-logged jacket. He looked to his boots. He wished he could be rid of them, but he knew he would never get back into them wet, and he didn't intend to stay long enough for them to dry. Instead, he smiled at the gentleman bustling toward him. The man's beard seemed grayer now, but his kind eyes were the same watery blue that Allistair remembered.

"Father," Allistair said, stepping forward to embrace the man.

"Allistair." Eamon of Stanburh withdrew from his son to study him at arm's length.

Soaked tendrils of Allistair's golden hair clung to his face, and he watched his father from behind the darkened strands that had fallen into his eyes. Eamon brushed the hair away, and water drained down Allistair's neck in small rivulets. He suppressed a shiver.

"You must tell me everything," Eamon said.

Allistair laughed. "May I come in first, Father? Or must we discuss this in the trail of mud I've tracked onto your floors?"

"Aye, forget the floors, lad! Give me your co—" He stopped, his eyes catching on a rent in the leather of Allistair's sleeve. He angled his son's arm to inspect the flesh beneath. A fresh gray scar caught the dim light. The discolored skin was still dimpled and bubbly like flatbread freshly pulled from the fire. He met Allistair's eyes, his own narrowed in concern. "When?"

"Right after the Royal Flight," Allistair replied softly. The timing of the Descent had felt ominous enough when it happened, and he did not wish to welcome in any ghosts with its retelling.

"It must have been bad if you were hit."

Allistair remembered the smoky beast careening toward him, his forearm the only protection he'd had from taking the brunt of the attack in the face. It would have killed him instantly. He shook the memory from his head before he could re-watch the black wretch burn across his leathers and turn his skin to ash. "Two Narxon hurled themselves at us at once. Cahal did his best to evade them."

Eamon let go of his arm, gingerly removed his son's coat, and hung it over a hook in the wall. "That could use some balm," he said.

"The rain did its job," Allistair protested. As his flesh had burned from his brush with the creature, healing rain had washed away the ash and scarred over the wound. Already, the burning sensation had dulled to an ignorable prickle.

His father grunted. "I've sent that bothersome girl for some libations, but she can bring you some balm when she returns. Hungry?"

"Mostly wet," Allistair replied wryly as they walked deeper into his boyhood home. They moved into his father's study, and Eamon handed him the quilt that always covered the back of the chair nearest the door. Since he was a boy, their home—and its staff—had barely changed. "She's a new one," Allistair said, referring to the busy little maid his father had just shooed away.

"Annice. Greener than your Cahal," Eamon grumbled. "Good old Gunnhild retired when her grandson's child was born. Wanted to live out her final years with her own family."

"Have I been gone that long?" Allistair asked, shaking his head. Gunnhild had practically raised him. He unfolded the blanket and spread it over the chair so he could sit in his wet leathers.

"Four years, my boy," Eamon said.

Allistair had been in Keaton for the first two, but after he had tethered to Cahal, he'd opted for freedom of transfer with his girlfriend, Magge. They'd been stationed in several territories and towns since then, but the

Royal Flight had called him back. Magge had chosen not to join him in Aethelburh for it. He ignored the knot that twisted his stomach at the memory of her refusal.

"A lot can happen in such time. And much has...." Eamon stole a glance at his son's injured arm and raised his eyebrows inquisitively.

Allistair usually enjoyed teasing his father with suspense, but his news didn't warrant playfulness. "Badrick won," he admitted, slumping into the chair. "Blaxton out-flew every other beast in the Flight for Deowynn. Badrick and Orla will be wed tomorrow—our new king and queen Riders, the rulers of this realm." His despair reflected in his father's face.

"Realm it all!" Eamon threw himself into a wingback chair and covered his eyes with a large, weathered hand. "Not that I'm surprised...." He took a deep, steadying breath. "Then, the Narxon came?"

"As soon as Deowynn and Blaxton parted in midair, the sky split open," Allistair answered with a nod. He couldn't bear to tell his father how big the tear had been—how many Narxon had poured through it. After a brief silence, he added, "I could never have matched Orla, Father."

Eamon snorted to the contrary but did not look at his son.

Allistair's tone grew sterner than he intended. "You cannot say I should have allowed it to be otherwise. Not using the method the Triars suggested."

Eamon waved him off. "No, no, I can't. What they suggested might not have even worked."

"Worked?!" Allistair replied in disbelief. "Father, Badrick is your *son*! You couldn't have considered allowing them to—"

"Of course not!" Eamon conceded, struggling to smooth the gruffness from his voice. "Of course not. There was nothing good about their plan. I didn't condone it." Thunder rumbled overhead, and they both looked to the window in time to see a bolt of lightning streak through the sky. Eamon turned a sad but reassuring gaze on his son. "This is not your fault, Allistair."

"That's the problem," Allistair replied. He knew the truth of his father's words, but he felt defeated, unable to celebrate his own brother's achievement.

Eamon shook his head. "In truth, it is a good thing, lad. You know that. Orla's a good woman—*too* good. And you would have had to be much crueler to have matched her." His eyes wandered to the bookcase across the room and lost their focus. "Even if your sister had lived, I fear Badrick would still have grown into our rightful king."

"Arietta had a way with him," Allistair said, his response rehearsed and repeated through the years.

"You were so small, then—you don't remember her. Not enough to know." Eamon's tone was gentle and betrayed no trace of malice or accusation.

Badrick could never have said that so placidly, Allistair thought.

"She might have soothed him from time to time, but there was no balancing that boy. He was born dark. She was his tether to the light. And when the sickness took her, that tether just... snapped."

That much Allistair remembered. Not from experience but from the stories he'd been told time and again—as if reliving the memories could someday reverse his sister's fate. Badrick would never let anyone forget Arietta's death—would never let anyone misremember whose fault it was that his prized sibling, whom he'd loved above all else, had perished. The family held no one responsible for her death. Badrick blamed himself.

Their mother, Cerelia, had been fighting to get Allistair's eagerly squirming—and steadily growing—feet into galoshes when his older siblings rushed from Castle Stanburh without him. From light-gray skies—the kind that only half-heartedly suggest a coming shower—rain had suddenly poured onto the field where Badrick and Arietta were playing, drenching them. They had barely turned for home before their garments were soaked through. Arietta's fever began that night, and it didn't take long for her to succumb.

Allistair grimaced at the vivid memory of his brother's self-perpetuated grief. *That* he had witnessed firsthand for *years* after her passing. Badrick would sit for hours, staring into the sky, cursing the clouds—and himself for ignoring their vague threats. When it rained, he would run out into the storm in only his trousers, desperate to catch the cold that had stolen away his sister.

Badrick's grief over her loss consumed him. He was inconsolable, unreachable, and *unkind*. The family was at a loss until a package, delivered to them upon the death of Eamon's father, distracted Badrick from his grief.

Eamon cleared his throat as he wiped the butt of a hand over his eye, and Allistair shook the memory from his head. He studied his father's beleaguered face. "He asked for grandfather's maps."

"No," Eamon barked.

"Father," Allistair blurted in surprise, "you can't deny him—they're *his!* Grandfather bequeathed them to him."

"Realm it!" Eamon cursed again. Before Allistair could question his father, the double doors to the study opened, and the young waiting-woman backed into the room, a laden tea tray in her hands.

"Coming through, Darrs!" Annice announced altogether too cheerfully for the middle of the night. Blonde wisps frayed out at all angles from the frazzled bun at the back of her head. Her young cheeks were rosy, and her eyes were bright. "I have everything you'll need right here," she continued. "Do you take cream and sugar, like your father? Not too much sugar, mind you, but enough to kill the bitterness—"

"Tea?!" Eamon cried in despair. "At this hour, woman? It's the middle of the night! I don't want any realming *tea*—"

"Rootwine, then?" she offered.

"ALE!" Eamon bellowed, thrusting his spread-fingered hands into the air.

Annice looked as though she had been struck. Her pretty face bloomed with shock that soured into dismay. She was so young—too young to have hardened to Eamon's gruff impatience… *yet.*

Allistair smiled, thinking of how "No-Nonsense Gunnhild" would have left Eamon cowed and grumbling into his mug if he had tried that outburst with her. "Don't mind him," he told Annice and reached for the tray. "The tea will be fine. We'll prepare it ourselves. Thank you."

Annice gave him a weak smile in return, her fingers absently touching a familiar, odd-shaped pendant hanging from a thin chain around her neck. It resembled a small key at the bow, but instead of a single bit, there were several, as though a sun sat perpendicular to the end of the shank, its crooked rays pushing the pendant away from her skin. It was exactly like a necklace Gunnhild had worn. The girl's eyes traveled to the gray patch on his arm, and her expression pinched in worry.

"Bring him some balm for that scar, Annice," Eamon ordered. "And see to his jacket. That sleeve will need patching."

"She doesn't need to—" Allistair began, but the waiting-woman was already mid-curtsy.

"Of course. Right away, Darr Eamon," she squeaked and slipped from the room. Eamon rolled his eyes at the closed door.

When Allistair held up a mug in offering, his father waved him off. Allistair smiled and drank with relish from the warm cup. "Where did you find her?"

"Recommendation from Gunnhild—although not an altogether satisfactory one." Eamon's countenance darkened. "Did he really ask for the maps?"

"He did."

"I will never know why my father gave them to him. But we still have recourse…." Eamon crossed to the bookshelves. He reached for two fat, leather-bound tomes, their tall, thick spines overhanging the shelf. He pulled them out together with one hand as though they weighed nothing. With his other hand, he reached into the shelf and withdrew a plain wooden box the size of his palm. He replaced the books and offered the box to his son.

Allistair lifted the lid. Inside, an ornate compass indented the satin-lined cushion. He held the device toward the dim light of the lantern nearby. He recognized the artistic rendering of the compass rose that seemed to come alive below the needle. The ornate, curling font of the old-style letters at each cardinal direction were carved with unimaginable precision, dating the compass by centuries. The needle was made with similar curls and twists that resembled the styling of elaborate wrought-iron gates. On its reverse, the silvery metal case was engraved with a queen dragon in profile, her wings outstretched behind her. The bones in the underside of her wing were delicately etched, and not a scale was missing from her hide. Talons could be seen at the end of each tiny toe; in their grasp, she held a chain from which a round object dangled.

"The compass," Eamon said, watching his son squint at the queen's treasure. "She holds that very compass."

"I never noticed that before," Allistair mumbled. He could never get close enough to the thing to inspect it. "Which queen is she?"

"Any of them," Eamon replied. "She stands for them all."

Old as it was, the metal remained polished and undented. Allistair tore his eyes from the flawless artifact to gaze at his father. "You still have this?"

Eamon nodded. "Your brother left the maps here for safekeeping when he went to train in Keaton. You know, long before this compass was Badrick's, it was your grandfather's—and his father's before him. Do you remember it? It mirrors the compass rose in the corners of your brother's maps."

Allistair remembered stealing glimpses of the maps his brother used to play with—that is, until Badrick inevitably shooed him away. The topography was not well preserved in those memories, but the colorful compass rose in the lower corner of each map could not be forgotten. Its arms extended toward four cardinal letters that were surrounded by intertwining ribbons of brilliant purples, reds, blues, and greens. A queen dragon, identical to the one etched into the metal resting in his palm, stood in profile, obscuring the middle of the cross, her radiant hide an almost indescribable mix of silver, white, and gold. The whole compass rose was rendered so artfully that it appeared to hover over the parchment. As a boy, Allistair had once tried to lift it from the map's surface. "You will honor his request for the maps?"

"Yes," Eamon replied. "But I will not include the compass. He knows its importance—at least in part. And I'm certain he will balk at its absence."

"Then why deny it him?"

"Without this compass," his father continued, "Badrick's maps are just renderings of the realm." He tapped the metal semblance of a queen dragon in his son's hands. "*With it,* in the right hands, there is a chance that D'Erenelle will not be lost to Queen Orla's unfortunate pairing."

Allistair stared at his father. "What do I need to do?" he breathed.

Eamon's eyes sparkled. "Listen."

I

The Exchange

Emmelyn's visits to the Exchange always began the same way.

She could be out with friends, busy at her internship, or doing homework—and the next moment, she would find herself standing outside that seedy club in the heart of downtown Detroit, unaware of how she had arrived there. She could only liken it to the jarring immediacy of a vision, like in the movies when the heroine touches a powerful object and sees its past. The sky would take on that weirdly bright, overcast gray of early spring, regardless of the season she had left behind moments ago; and the street would be deserted, the occasional abandoned car parked along the curb. Even in broad daylight, she would never dream of entering this kind of place, especially alone.

The first time she appeared on the empty Detroit street—when she didn't understand how or why she was suddenly there—she found herself shuffling toward the club's entrance. Seconds earlier, she had been eating lunch at a picnic table in the university quad, setting down the peanut-butter-and-jelly sandwich she had just taken too big a bite of. Then, all of a sudden, she found herself here, mouth full and entirely alone. This club was not just a place she would never go; it was a place she had never *been*. If not for the familiarly named crossroads, she wouldn't have even known if she were still in Michigan. Still, her feet edged her toward the club. *Who wouldn't go in, under such circumstances?* she reassured herself. *I mean, this is all a dream, right? Or maybe I'm in a coma?*

She looked past the long black awning overhanging the sidewalk to a black screen-printed tarp plastered to the weathered brick above. The sign announced the club's name in hot pink letters made to look like they had been spray-painted: DISSONANCE.

She had heard of this nightclub before—had even been invited to join a group of people headed there one night—but it wasn't her scene. Now, she stood before it, contemplating the door. *I wonder if this dream club is what the real Dissonance looks like. Someday, I'll have to go there to see.*

Unless I'm in a coma.

And that's when she caught herself working to melt the last of the peanut butter still clinging to the roof of her mouth. *If I were comatose, I wouldn't know I had peanut butter in my mouth, would I? And I wouldn't be able to taste it... right?* But she did—on both counts. She felt her heartrate increase. *Really* felt it. She placed her fingers against the quickening pulse in her neck. This was no dream. She was outside a dingy club, in an unsavory part of town, and had no clue how she had arrived there.

It would take about forty minutes to drive here from the university, she calculated. *If I had been knocked unconscious and dumped here, the peanut butter would be gone, and I'd have a headache.* But neither was the case.

Okaaay....

She pulled out her cell phone from the cross-body bag resting against her hip. No service. *I have to call someone,* she thought, glancing toward the door again. She didn't know whether her desire to go in stemmed from a need to use their phone or genuine curiosity. With a habitual glance to either side for nonexistent traffic, she made her way from the pothole-riddled street to the door under the awning and went inside.

But this was *not* Dissonance.

It couldn't be. From what she had heard, Dissonance was a one-story dance club with sticky floors, thumping music, and handsy men—and women.

The massive space before her was easily three stories high and bigger than an entire house in the richest Metro Detroit subdivisions. This lobby couldn't have fit inside the dirty, one-story club she'd seen outside if she'd washed it on hot—*twice.*

The place looked like it had been carved out of cream-colored marble in the fifteenth century. Gothic ceilings overhead and polished, compass-point tile floors beneath her feet led her eyes past massive pillars to the opposite end of the lobby. A wide reception counter stood in front of an expansive, marble-tiled wall the same cream color as everything else.

In stark contrast to the endless off-white stone, shady-looking characters wearing black leather jackets over black shirts, black slacks, and black boots watched her as she made her way toward the reception desk. They would have been right at home in the club she was supposed to have walked into, but she couldn't understand their presence in a spotless cathedral like this. She glanced down at her particolored canvas sneakers, blue jean capris, and oversized T-shirt. *Perhaps I shouldn't judge.*

At the end of her arm, she noticed a square white tube the length of a ruler had appeared in her left hand. As she turned it over, she saw one side of its smooth surface was marked near the end with a simple shape: thin, metallic-red lines formed something akin to a child's rendering of a house, and in the middle of this pentagon was a capital E. Rather than a fancy, scrolling font, the E was a typical block letter, like it had been printed by a large typewriter. She ran her thumb over the mark to find it had been indented into the plastic—if that's what this baton thing was made of. It looked like something you might pass to another person in a relay race. It weighed almost nothing. *I'd bobble it in the handoff,* she thought with a roll of her eyes.

Up ahead, two receptionists stood behind the counter. The tall, thin man to the left was helping another tall, thin man in a well-tailored royal blue suit and blue suede Oxfords. The shorter woman to the right stared at Emmelyn, her expression grim. Her brown hair was pulled up in an excruciating-looking bun, and her crisp white suit with angular black piping was so stiff that it did not pucker *anywhere*. Her style made Emmelyn uncomfortable, and she was not the one who had been over-starched from head to toe.

Emmelyn approached the woman, the eyes of the suspicious, black-clad onlookers following her as she passed. Her skin prickled, but she tried to ignore it. "Hi, I'm—"

The woman behind the desk held out her hand, palm upturned. "The Transitor," she snapped, her eyes fixating on the baton in Emmelyn's grasp. "Give me the Transitor."

"Oh." Emmelyn handed it over. "I'm sorry, but I was hoping to borrow—"

"Name?" the woman asked, tapping away on something below counter-level. Emmelyn heard no telltale clicking of a keyboard and suspected it was a touchscreen.

"Uh, sorry," she replied. "Emmelyn Darrow. Could I just—"

"Darrow… " the woman repeated, searching her screen. "Transfer…." She squinted at the screen below the counter and made a face like she smelled something sour. "First time."

"I'm sorry?" Emmelyn asked. The man in the blue suit next to her finished up at the counter, walked up four wide stairs to the left of the reception desk, and disappeared behind the marble-tiled wall. Emmelyn thought she could hear the distant clinking of cutlery coming from that direction. Waiters in tuxedos bustled back and forth from a set of double doors farther to the left, their trays held aloft. "Look, I don't know how I got here or what is going on, but I was hoping to use your phone—*please*—so I can have someone pick me up."

The receptionist did something that made a *click* behind the counter and handed the Transitor back to Emmelyn. On the side opposite the red insignia, the woman had punctured the baton with a small hole that had five squiggly rays shooting outward from it. It looked like a sun. Emmelyn ran her finger over the mysterious cutout. When she looked back up, the woman was holding out her hand again. *Is she expecting a tip?*

"Give me your wrist," the woman demanded.

Emmelyn didn't like the sound of that. "Which one?" she asked, stalling.

The woman rolled her eyes. "Your non-dominant one."

"Why?"

The woman's eyebrows fell flat above her eyes, giving her general look of annoyance an added boost. In response, she held up a round stamp and an ink pad. "Timestamp," was all she said by way of explanation.

"But I don't plan to stay—"

"No one does." She continued to stare, unmoving, until Emmelyn laid her left arm on the counter, palm up, fingers curled. The woman dabbed the ink pad forcefully and stamped a single red insignia on Emmelyn's forearm, two inches from the base of her hand. It was the same pentagonal emblem as on the Transitor but circumscribed by a thin circle.

"Your first one is delivery only," the woman said, snapping the ink pad shut. She pointed to her left, where an endless marble staircase ascended past a Gothic arch and out of sight. "Get this to Lorelle."

"Lorelle?"

"Maid's outfit," the woman said with a dismissive wave. She began doing something below the counter again. "Can't miss."

"Look, I just wanted to make a call, so I could get back to—"

"You will—*afterward*."

"After *what?*" Emmelyn replied, her voice rising.

One of the watchful lurkers slid a hand into his jacket pocket and edged in her direction. The receptionist held up an index finger to him, and he stopped. "After you deliver that to Lorelle," she said, her eyes on the Transitor.

Emmelyn didn't want to know what the man could be reaching for. "Right," she said, taking a step back from the counter and turning toward the huge staircase. Even from this distance, she could see dips in the stone stairs where they had been worn down by the passage of countless feet. It was the only place in the lobby that didn't gleam with polish.

She glanced over at the restaurant area behind the marble wall that was only four *stairs* up from the lobby, not four *flights*. "You're sure Lorelle isn't over there?" she asked.

"You have two options," the woman said, her gaze cold. "You can leave, or you can deliver that Transitor to Lorelle." She pointed a finger toward the huge staircase again. The onlookers in black were frozen in place, watching for a signal to intercede.

Emmelyn nodded and stepped back from the desk. *If it gets me a phone call....* With one final glance to her left, she trudged toward the stairs.

She paused at the bottom of the steps and looked up. It was the longest staircase she had ever seen—easily four stories and *steep*. At the top was a small landing with black walls around it and a neon-green arrow pointing to the left. A man was coming down the stairs at a run, and Emmelyn jumped aside. He slowed his pace as he reached the final step, walked briskly to the other side of the lobby, and disappeared into the restaurant. Emmelyn gazed back up the staircase, which was not comfortably wide enough to pass someone, and set her foot on the first step.

She had never heard any accounts of an unusual entrance to the night-club, but she couldn't imagine anyone scaling these stairs and not talking about it.

Or complaining *about it,* she thought as her breathing grew labored about halfway up. She paused, pressing her shoulder blades against the wall. The railing pushed at a diagonal across the small of her back. She could just make out the rhythmic thudding of a bassline. *So, the club is here after all. Maybe they'll have a phone I can use.* Her legs and lungs protesting, she forced herself up the second half of the staircase—before someone might need to pass her.

Loud music thumped from behind a black door to the left of the neon sign. Emmelyn groaned. It would be deafening inside. *No way to make a call in there.* She glanced down the long staircase toward the black-jacketed thugs and then stared at the door handle.

As she finally reached for it, the door swung open, and another man outfitted in black burst through. He was hustling someone in plain clothes out of the club with him, his grip buckling the fabric of the man's shirt. Emmelyn retreated a step, and her hands shot up over her ears to block out the thundering music as the two pounded past her down the stairs. She watched them for a moment and then reached for the closing door, forcing herself to slip inside.

The club was packed. Vertical stacks of swirling, multicolored lights illuminated little, and a swarm of undulating clubgoers danced like a rippling mass in the shifting shadows. They were not rowdy, and she saw no sign of a recent squabble. She wondered what the guy had done to warrant such a hasty—and *indifferent*—removal.

Someone tapped her shoulder. A man with the stature of a bouncer uncrossed one of his massive arms and held out a small packet to her. She almost backed away from him. *I haven't been in here a full minute, and I'm already being offered drugs,* she thought. The man shifted the packet so it sat flat against his outstretched palm, and she saw two orange pellets inside the clear plastic. *Earplugs!* She mouthed her appreciation and ripped into them. The foam saviors squished easily between her fingers, and she jammed them into her ears, sighing as the music faded. These were heavy duty. She smiled. The bouncer nodded once, his face stoic.

Emmelyn skirted the mass of bodies in front of her and followed along the bar as she made her way further into the room. Opposite the counter, on the other side of the dancers, were circular seating areas made up of leather couches and chairs and mismatched coffee tables. From the look of it, the second-hand, wood-and-leather furniture could have been assembled from the lodges of various defunct ski resorts.

A woman in a long-sleeved sundress passed her, and Emmelyn realized that not everyone was dressed in typical club attire. She surveyed the bodies that were visible in the swirling lights. This was not some ridiculous theme night. The costumes around her were from too many different time periods—some she recognized and a few she was fairly certain had never existed. Genies danced beside hippies, longshoremen beside renaissance courtiers, and the matte drapes of white togas clashed with tight, metallic fabrics in passing bursts of light. It was like walking into a cast party for a night of wildly different one-acts. She felt almost out of place by being dressed so *normally*.

She turned back to the bar. *I need a drink.* She rested her hand on the bag at her hip and felt the bulge of her wallet inside. Having just turned twenty-two, there wasn't a bar in existence that wouldn't card her before she made it through the doors. Yet, the bouncer had simply offered her ear protection. She scanned the bottles against the mirrored wall. She could really go for a beer, but she didn't trust that the lines were clean in a place like this, and she preferred drafts to bottled. *Liquor it is.*

"What can I get you?" the lips of a nice-looking bartender appeared to ask her. He was probably around thirty and had short brown hair, a clean-shaven face, and a black button-down shirt with the sleeves rolled up to his elbows. His shiny metal name tag read, *Trevor.*

"Amaretto sour," Emmelyn leaned in to yell. The order was more complicated to lipread than to make. *Maybe I should have ordered beer after all.*

Trevor nodded and reached for the amaretto. Emmelyn shoved the Transitor inside her purse and pawed around for her wallet. Even diagonally, the white baton was too long and poked out of the top of her bag. Trevor rapped his knuckles on the counter in front of her to get her attention. He shook his head, eyeing her purse. She held up a hand and rubbed two fingers and a thumb together in what she hoped was a universal gesture for money, but Trevor smiled and shook his head again.

"You don't pay," he mouthed. In all fairness, he might have vocalized it, but she didn't know why he would bother. She thanked him as she snapped down the flap on her purse.

Armed with her free drink, she stepped away from the bar to make room for the next patron. His frilly white cuffs peeked out from the sleeves of his well-tailored jacket, and a tall white wig towered over his head, like one of the great composers of the 1700s. As she passed him, though, a flash of light caught his pants. They shined like patent leather. The outer seams were lined with gromets that stretched the full length of his legs, displaying little circles of flesh all the way down to his boots. She didn't remember seeing those on the actor playing Mozart....

Emmelyn remembered what the woman behind the desk had told her about Lorelle: "maid's outfit." *Yes, but from what century?* she wondered as she looked around. *Or are we talking French maid?* It wouldn't surprise her after seeing Amadeus' pants. She continued through the club, discreetly scoping out the crowd. She might not have been a regular club-goer, but others' experiences had told her the wrong eye contact was a sure way to invite a fight.

The clientele here didn't seem remotely agitated, though. *And why should they be, if they're drinking for free?* She glanced toward the seating area—and walked headlong into the chest of another leather-jacketed man. She ricocheted off him into a circle of chairs and couches, where her hip bumped the shoulder of a man holding a rocks glass. He jumped to his feet and hollered at her in an unrecognizable language as he struggled to right the glass before more of its contents could spill over his rust-colored sharkskin pants.

"Sorry! Sorry!" she yelped to both the man hurling foreign insults and the black-jacketed one glaring at her. She stepped away from them, glancing around herself to avoid bumping into anything else, and noticed a woman waving at her from the next chair circle over. Emmelyn rushed toward her as both men ignored her apologies and returned to their business.

"It's okay, sweetie," the woman called to her in a high-pitched, Jersey accent. She looked like a burlesque dancer from the '50s. Her short brown hair was styled in finger waves, and she was smacking her gum. A pink bubble grew from her rounded lips before she popped it with her teeth. "Accidents happen. Anyway, the ones in the jackets always look miserable. Ya get used tuh it."

"Who are they?" Emmelyn called back. She moved in closer and pulled out one of her earplugs to better hear the response. It was a *painful* sacrifice.

"You're new," a guy on the other end of the couch announced. Thick black liner ringed his eyes, and his spikey black hair ended in frosted blue tips.

"Obviously she's new," the burlesque dancer snapped at him. She must have been in her mid-thirties, from the look of her. And there was a lot to look at in that tiny, sequined dress. "I'm Bernadette," she called.

Of course you are. "Emmelyn," she called back, wondering if she should have been using a false name all this time. *Too late.*

"Foist time, huh?" Bernadette asked.

Emmelyn nodded. "I guess. I just... ended up here. I'm trying to get out."

Bernadette's eyes moved to her stamped wrist. "Ya won't be heah long, hun," she noted. "Who ya lookin' foah?"

"Someone named Lorelle," Emmelyn replied, glancing around the group. No one wore anything remotely resembling a maid's outfit.

Bernadette looked thoughtful, or at least that was how Emmelyn interpreted the expression. Her eyebrows sort of crinkled, and her mouth fell slightly ajar—the combination reminiscent of a confused fish. She shrugged. "I dunno 'er." She looked around the group inquisitively, but everyone shook their heads.

"For whom are we looking?" a man with a hint of an accent called from behind Emmelyn. He had four drinks in mismatched glasses balanced between his fingers. How he carried that many was a mystery to Emmelyn. She stepped aside so he could pass them out and tried not to let her jaw drop.

He is gorgeous!

He had that thick, perfectly feathered, brown hair from the '70s that could be brushed back in place—if it ever moved—with a quick finger comb. It was the kind of look that made women of her mother's generation both jealous and terribly excited. His strong jaw and bright-green eyes didn't hurt either. But he wasn't in bell-bottoms. He wore a fitted tan sports jacket over a white button-down shirt and dark jeans. Emmelyn guessed he was edging on forty, but in this lighting, it was hard to tell. She smiled at the hearty approval her mother would extend if she brought him home. Of course, there was no chance of that: he was *definitely* out of her league. And very probably gay—all the best-looking ones were.

"Someone named Lorelle," the punk-goth guy on the couch yelled, glowering.

"A new one foah ya, Vonn," Bernadette hollered to the handsome newcomer with a wink in Emmelyn's direction.

"The waiting-woman in D'Erenelle?" Vonn asked. He sounded vaguely French, but it was hard to tell over the music.

Emmelyn shrugged. "If by 'waiting-woman,' you mean 'maid,' very possibly," she yelled in his ear. He smelled wonderful, which seemed like a feat in this place.

Vonn assessed her before flashing her a knowing smile. "You got Janelle."

The others made a revelatory "ahhh" sound.

"I'm sorry?" Emmelyn asked.

"Janelle," Vonn repeated, somehow boosting his volume, "at the front desk. Cold like something from the depths of the sea but with an even saltier disposition?"

Emmelyn nodded.

He flashed her a broad smile, and his straight white teeth gleamed between his perfect lips. "Yeah. She's not exactly what anyone would call... forthcoming. Don't worry. You'll figure it out." He handed off the last drink to the middle-aged ranch hand in the overstuffed armchair. "Hold this, will you, Randy?"

The glass was filled with two fingers of a rich brown liquid Emmelyn guessed was bourbon. Randy sniffed the bouquet with relish and grinned up at his benefactor. "No promises it'll be here when ya get back," he drawled.

Vonn patted Randy's shoulder. "I know Lorelle," he yelled in Emmelyn's ear. "I can take you to her. She's over there." He thumbed a spot over his shoulder farther within the club.

"Uh, thank you. Can you also help me get out of here so I can go home?" Emmelyn asked.

He smiled and took her hand to guide her through the crowd.

As she squeezed between groups of dancers and inaudibly excused herself, someone bumped into her, breaking Vonn's hold and spilling her drink. The amber liquid narrowly missed her shoes. "'Scuse me," the man droned. He flashed her a slimy smile and sidled in closer. He was dressed in unremarkable jeans and a T-shirt, and from the way he was swaying, it was clear he had been in the club quite a while longer than she had. "Lemme replace that for you," he schmoozed in her ear. She could have gotten buzzed off his breath.

"That's okay," she replied, trying to slip away from him, but he snaked an arm around her waist.

"I must insist," he slurred and pulled her closer. She considered splashing the dregs from her glass in his face, but she didn't have the chance. Two fingers slid in between their faces as someone tapped the man on the shoulder. The drunk's swagger fell away, and Emmelyn turned toward the source of the hand: Vonn had come back to rescue her.

"She's with me, *Jet*," he yelled with an emphasis of disapproval on the man's name.

"Sorry, Vonn; I didn't know!" Jet replied, stepping away from Emmelyn and raising his hands as if Vonn were holding him at gunpoint. Emmelyn slid toward Vonn, and he put a protective arm around her shoulders. He nodded at Jet in that way men do when an understanding has been reached and led her away.

"Thank you," she hollered in his ear.

"He's not as bad as he seems," Vonn replied. "He's just drunk."

"Is he as *disgusting* as he seems?" Emmelyn asked.

Vonn laughed. "Yes," he replied, "whether he is drunk or not." He scanned the room, peering over the heads and shoulders crowded in around them. "Lorelle is right over there," he said in her ear and cut a path through a group of people chatting, or rather, *yelling* at one another over the pounding techno. He brought Emmelyn up to another occupied ring of mismatched furniture. No one wore a maid's outfit. "Well, she *was*...."

"Who ya lookin' for, Vonn?" asked a man with the accent of a mobster and the pinstripe suit to match.

"Lorelle," Vonn called back.

"I'm right here," came an accented voice from behind them. A petite, curvaceous woman approached with a drink in each hand. Her delicate features were offset by her large brown eyes, which popped against her light-brown skin. Her black hair was confined in a long, thick braid that snaked down over her shoulder, and she was clad in the drab gray maid's outfit Janelle had promised. Lorelle passed a glass off to a beautiful woman with dark skin, close-cropped hair, and a brightly colored muumuu before giving them her attention. "What is it, Vonn?"

Vonn turned to his charge and dropped his arm from her back. "This is...."

"Emmelyn Darrow." She offered her hand to Lorelle.

Lorelle grasped the inside of Emmelyn's arm near the elbow and held on for a moment, their forearms touching along their lengths. It was not the handshake Emmelyn had expected, and she barely had time to grasp the woman's elbow in return before the maid pulled away.

Lorelle seemed to recognize Emmelyn's foreign reaction to the greeting and gave her a weak smile. "You're my new Transfer?" Her Rs had a slight roll to them, like her first tongue could be one of the romance languages.

"I have no idea," Emmelyn replied. She slipped the Transitor from her purse and placed it into Lorelle's hand. "But I think I'm supposed to give you this."

"Thank you," Lorelle yelled. "No trouble finding me?"

"None, thanks to Vonn here," Emmelyn called back, but as she turned to gesture to him, she realized he was gone.

Lorelle smiled. "He's a good guy."

"Where did he go?" Emmelyn asked. "I didn't get to thank him...."

"He's a Runner, like I am," Lorelle replied, as if that explained everything. She tipped up her glass and downed her drink in one long gulp. Emmelyn noticed a peculiar pendant gleaming at the end of her necklace. The handle of a metal skeleton key ended in a thin cylinder with several perpendicular rays emanating from it where the bit should have been. The short rays pushed the pendant away from her flesh, and it hung awkwardly below her collarbone. Something about it felt oddly familiar. Lorelle set her glass on the table in the middle of their seating area and waved at the group. "He probably had to go, as I do now. Nice to meet you," she yelled and moved toward the back of the club.

How much more of this place is there? "Wait!" Emmelyn called and jogged to catch up with her. "Wait, what do I do now? How do I get out of here?"

Lorelle had disconnected the key from a clasp on her necklace and was fitting it into the hole with the squiggly offshoots that Janelle had put in the back of the Transitor. *That's why it felt familiar.* When Lorelle turned the key, one of the ends of the baton popped open, and she fished out a rolled-up piece of paper with one finger.

"I have to go," Lorelle insisted, tucking the paper into the front pocket of her calf-length dress. She turned to a hip-high receptacle that stood against a nearby wall and slipped the Transitor into a square slot on the top. It disappeared from view. "I'll see you next time. Thanks again."

"Next time?" Emmelyn called back, but Lorelle had already stepped up to a knob-less door ahead of them and fitted the key into a barely visible, sun-shaped hole. The word "D'Erenelle" materialized on the door. She turned the key, and the wood disappeared, replaced by a black void. Lorelle walked into it as she replaced the key on her chain. She, too, disappeared, and the door rematerialized behind her.

"Whoa," Emmelyn breathed. She stepped forward and placed her palm against the door. It was unyielding. Her fingers groped around until they brushed the small, sun-shaped indentation that Lorelle's key had fit into. "What the hell is this?" she wondered aloud.

"It ain't Hell, honey," a familiar voice called from beside her.

Emmelyn looked over to see Bernadette eyeing her with motherly concern.

The burlesque dancer smiled. "It's the Exchange."

TRAINEES—those who have reached the minimum age of half eighteen—flock to the Royal Drakiary with the aspiration of joining the next generation of Realm Riders. The propensity to become a Realm Rider tends to run in families; however, the first Rider of a family can surface anywhere in its lineage.

A Trainee can only become a Realm Rider when he or she Tethers to a Dragon. Tethering creates a bond between Rider and Beast that cannot be broken, except in death or under the most extreme and unlikely circumstances (to be discussed in another chapter).

Dragons communicate telepathically among themselves, unheard by non-Dragons universally. Realm Riders can also communicate to their Beasts in this way through a process called Nexing. A Rider can hear only the private Nexing of his or her Dragon. The exception to this rule, of course, is the Heir Rider, who can Nex with any and all Dragons or even broadcast a communication to all Dragons within an indefinite vicinity.

- an excerpt, *Wanderer the Realm*

II

Aethelburh

The map's rustling broke their wearied silence.

"How much farther, Rose?" Thane asked again.

Rhoswen glanced at the parchment she had just crumpled against her saddle to keep the wind from stealing it. She tried to smooth it out against her leg. "You know it's almost half a day's journey, even at the pace we've kept," she reminded him for the fourth or fifth time. Her rear ached from the endless galloping.

"Well, we must have done that by now! You're the cartographer of the family. Just tell me how close we are."

Rhoswen snorted. In an attempt to affect maturity beyond his years, Thane had begun feigning a general ambivalence to all events, large and small. Lately, however, his indifference had become so convincing that Rhoswen had begun to believe he had lost interest in everything, including their training. That is, until he started whining that their journey to Castle Aethelburh was taking too long. "Not far… probably," she guessed.

Thane sighed and turned his head to stare at the grove of unusual trees nearby, and Rhoswen followed his gaze. Their silvery bark had a greenish cast to it, and their branches, low and sprawling, were covered with delicate, long leaves of a darker silver-green. Sitting Trees, they were often called. Most grew wider than they grew tall, their thick branches dipping low and stretching outward as if to reach beyond those above them. Despite their length, the lowest limbs were strong enough to support one's weight, even at their outermost ends. Rhoswen could not remember their real name; they didn't have many Sitting Trees back home.

She looked at her brother. His head was turned away from her as he studied the sprawling limbs. Thane's cropped, muddied-blond hair shone like brass in the midday sunlight. The sway of his body as his horse plodded forward gave him a lazy look, despite his obvious irritation. Rhoswen remembered how edgy she, too, had been at their dawn departure. Now, she relished the leisurely pace that had allowed the tension to slip from her muscles and her shoulders to drop out of their anxious hunch.

"You will be careful," her father had said. It had not been phrased as a question.

"Of course we will, Father," Rhoswen had assured him.

Allistair had stared at each of his children in turn. "Very careful," he had repeated. "Protect each other." His words had been tinged with something more than mere fatherly concern. "We didn't hold you back a year, Thane, so you two could blunder about. Aethelburh is a dangerous place—especially for our family."

"A year and a half," Thane had joked. He would occasionally confide in Rhoswen his frustration for being held back, but he rarely made any comments about it to their parents. His smile had faded as their father shot him a withering gaze.

"We will protect each other," Rhoswen had insisted.

Allistair's mistrust of his brother was rooted more deeply than most of his longest-held convictions. The two had not gotten along since childhood, and King Badrick's lopsided rule in the wake of Queen Orla's death had done little to improve Allistair's opinion. So, sending his children to live under his brother's royal roof to train with his dragons was profoundly unsettling. Given that Realm Rider training was an exclusive privilege of the king and queen's drakiary, however, alternatives were nonexistent. Only after months of constant debate was their grandfather, Eamon, able to convince Allistair to allow his children to fulfill their potential as Realm Riders—when Rhoswen had come of age and both could go together.

Their mother, Magge, had stepped into the kitchen, then, cheeks flushed and hair—the same color as Thane's—tangled by the wind. "Macon saddled your horses, and we loaded your bags. Are you ready to go?"

Macon had entered the kitchen behind her, wearing a tired—*or was it sad?*—expression. The stable hand would not have needed their mother's assistance, but Magge had not stopped bustling about since the night before. Rhoswen and Thane had stood at once, eager to escape the turmoil.

Rhoswen blew at a lock of light-brown hair—the same color as her father's—willing it away from its unwelcome perch against her right eyelashes. Sun blinded her where her hair had provided cover, and she sighed in exasperation. The shade beneath the shaggy, silver-green foliage of the Sitting Trees beckoned. "Do you want to put one of those trees to good use and let the horses rest?"

Thane held a hand above his eyes to shade his view. "Perhaps we should," he agreed. "But I don't want to stop for long. The sun is getting hot."

Rhoswen nodded, and her hair fell back onto her eyelashes. She dismounted and stepped into the shade. She considered hacking the lock off above eye level with her knife but remembered that such an act had shortened it in the first place. Resigning herself once more to let the hair grow out, she did her best to tuck it behind her ear. She retrieved a water skin from their packs and drank deeply from it before offering it to her brother. "What do you think it will be like?" she asked.

Thane shrugged. "Probably like it is with Cahal," he said, his nonchalance returning.

Rhoswen nudged him. "Don't pretend you're not excited. It has to be even better than old Cahal! These dragons will be *ours*."

"Not at first, they won't," Thane said. "Until we tether, if we even do, they will be just like Cahal—someone else's dragons letting us take them for a ride."

"We'll tether," Rhoswen said. "It's in our blood." She snapped off a long, thin leaf from the branch above her head and twined it around her fingers. Its surface was soft and fuzzy. "Anyway, you're a natural. I had good luck with Cahal, but you practiced well with him *and* Kuney. So, what color do you think you'll get?"

"I don't know," Thane said, chuckling. "Color doesn't matter. It's about temperament."

"I know," she muttered. "It's just for fun, Thane."

A sigh escaped his lips. "What color do you think you'll get?"

"A tawny," she replied without hesitation.

Thane laughed at her ready answer. "Why a tawny?"

"Why not?" she asked.

He rolled his eyes. "How do you figure?"

"Well, Kuney is a tawny… " she said, envisioning her mother's tan dragon.

"So, I will get a green, then?"

"No," Rhoswen said definitively. "Red for you, I think."

"And why is that?" he asked, his amusement plain.

"Because you are brave."

"Father is brave, and Cahal is green."

"I know." She offered no further explanation than a sideways smirk.

Thane laughed again, and Rhoswen was pleased to see him abandon his uncaring façade. "Let's go," he said, grinning. "I'll race you!"

"We're lost."

"We are not!" Rhoswen laughed and shook her head at her brother.

Not long into their race, Rhoswen's map had caught in the wind and flown from her hands into a small pond. Although the path she had plotted was now an unreadable blur, she vaguely remembered tracing the outline of a river in the King's Forest that would guide them to the castle. She pulled a compass from her pocket and edged her horse closer to her brother's. "The river should be nearby. Listen for it."

Thane pulled on the reins, bringing his horse to a stop. He cupped a hand around one ear and cocked his head to the right. Rhoswen took quiet, shallow breaths beside him.

"I may hear it!" Thane said and urged his horse forward. Rhoswen shoved the compass in her pocket and followed. The trees began to thicken around them, and before long, they found themselves in a forest at the water's edge.

"You're certain this is the river we're looking for?" Thane asked as his horse dipped his nose into the clear water.

"I am, if this is the King's Forest," Rhoswen replied. An image of the map she had copied from flashed across her mind's eye; the castle should not be far ahead. "Let's follow this north. The shade feels good, anyway."

Their horses plodded along the moist ground, nibbling grass as they went. The temperature cooled below the trees' canopy. Small gaps in the leaves overhead sprinkled the forest floor with bright flecks of dancing light. The brush rustled anonymously around them, and birds called to one another, their songs reaching a deafening volume as they vied to be heard.

The trees thinned once more, making the water sparkle and churn busily in the sunlight. Rhoswen was watching a school of tiny moss-green fish dart around near the water's edge when Thane called out to her. He pointed to the sky.

Overhead, a vertical silver slash hung in the air. It was almost invisible in the bright sunlight, but as she rode up beside her brother, it seemed to darken against the light-blue sky. "A Narxon tear," she breathed. They had seen plenty in their time, but all the exposure in the realm couldn't prevent a chill from running up her spine.

Thane nodded. "Looks like a big one. Not that high up, either," he noted.

That must have been a nightmare, Rhoswen thought, unable to suppress a shudder as the chill zipped up to the base of her skull. She looked down from the silvery scar to the cleared area below it. Nothing taller than grass grew beneath the tear; the soil was still too contaminated to sustain shrubs or trees. "I don't see any ash."

Thane shrugged. "Maybe Riders were already nearby, and they caught it in time. Or maybe it's old. It takes a long time for trees to grow back."

Rhoswen urged her horse past the hanging scar and glanced up the hill that had been obscured by the forest. "There it is," she said. A turret of the castle peeked up over the rise, beckoning them onward.

Even from the side, Castle Aethelburh was more impressive than their father had described. Its weather-beaten stone walls were the color of storm clouds. Great round turrets stood at the four main corners of the structure, their crenelated tops contrasting with the peaked roofs of the slimmer turrets near the main entrance. As they drew nearer, a massive wrought-iron gate came into view before the great front doors. A walkway lined with squat stone walls the same stormy gray as the castle led from the gate and over the river where a small bridge connected the castle grounds and a dirt road snaking through the common land. Rhoswen recognized the hoof-worn road as the one they would have traversed had the map not taken flight.

Thane stopped his horse at the foot of the bridge. "It's not exactly a humble home, is it?"

Apropos of its status, Castle Aethelburh sat high on the upward slope of its expansive grounds. To its right, where the land fell off again, a similar structure stood in the deep valley: the drakiary. Its four corners were also marked by crenelated turrets—the only parts that were visible from this angle. A black dragon shot upward through the air from the valley, its wings beating effortlessly as it soared toward one of the great castle's turrets. The dragon slowed itself, and the talons of its back feet grasped the crenelated surface. It turned to face the valley below and curled its front toes around the edge of the stone. Someone waved from the saddle on the beast's back, and a great deal of cheering sounded from below.

"Is that Blaxton?" Rhoswen asked, watching the beast glide back down from its perch.

"They're training!" Thane exclaimed, ignoring her question. He lifted himself up from the saddle, craning his neck to get a better view of the drakiary. Finally, he urged his horse forward and galloped over the bridge toward the celebrating students below.

As they passed the gate, Rhoswen could finally make out its design. Each side bore a dragon in profile, with wings outstretched behind them and a forefoot reaching forward. In their claws, they held between them a snake-like dragon biting its own tail to form a ring. The dragon-ring broke cleanly down the middle, and the gates opened, revealing their cousin and four waitmen dressed in gray livery behind him.

"Prince Gethin!" Thane pulled on the reins and dismounted to bow before their cousin. Rhoswen did the same.

"Cousin Thane, Cousin Rhoswen," Gethin replied with equal formality. "Welcome to Castle Aethelburh." His wavy dark hair fell down the back of his head to his shoulders, an oil of some kind pulling it away from his face. The style emphasized his angular features, which cast unflattering shadows on his face under the high sun. He looked about as pleased to see them as

Rhoswen would be to find a slug on her new riding boots.

Gethin gestured to his staff, and they jumped forward to tend to the horses and luggage. "Father thought you might like to stay in the castle rather than in the dormitories of Keaton with the other trainees."

Rhoswen looked down the hill toward the drakiary in the valley below. *Keaton.* Along with the training arena, the stone walls held stables and supplies for the dragons and classrooms and lodgings for the students and trainers. From what her parents had told her, Rhoswen would have much preferred to stay there.

Gethin sneered at them. "You are *family,*" he added with poorly masked contempt.

"Either would have suited us," Thane replied in a gracious tone she had never heard him use, "but we appreciate our *uncle's* hospitality." Rhoswen smiled as she watched her cousin for a sign that he had caught Thane's sleight.

Gethin raised a patronizing eyebrow and turned from them, his cape flourishing outward behind him. "The waitmen will take your things to your rooms. Meanwhile, I am to give you a tour of the castle and drakiary." He began walking toward the great doors before them.

"We'd be delighted," Thane called after him. He glanced at Rhoswen, a smirk playing on his lips.

She grinned and slid her arm through his with mock ceremony. "Come, Brother," she whispered. "We are to be shown the castle by the prince himself!"

It took some doing, but Rhoswen convinced their cousin to let them unpack before their tour. She did not relish the idea of having to search for her belongings after waiting-women had distributed them throughout her new chambers.

Outside her door, the balcony that overlooked the high-ceilinged court below doubled as a reminder of the distance between her and Thane's rooms. She could see his door from hers, but reaching it required circumnavigating half the entire floor, for their rooms were centered on opposite sides of the opening. Rhoswen eyed the gap. They were as close and as far apart as they could possibly be. Thoughts of her parents' concerns for their safety echoed in Rhoswen's mind, but she pushed them away and headed inside.

As she scanned her room—a light coating of dust exaggerating its vacant feel—Rhoswen briefly questioned the need to unpack. She could not imagine how distributing her belongings among foreign dressers and cupboards could dispel her sense of detachment.

Across from her bed stood a tall, wooden wardrobe on four carved dragon feet with gold-tipped talons. She dragged her bag to its dark, imposing doors and opened them. Instead of finding it emptied for her use, she found gorgeous gowns—some sleek, others puffy and massive—all made of sumptuous fabrics that she had never dreamed of touching in her lifetime. Metallic threads were woven into ornate patterns on vibrant silks and satins, all of which would have taken small eternities to stitch into place. Rhoswen glanced around as though she would be reproached for her prying eyes and fingers. She forced layers of escaping fabric back into the wardrobe and hastily closed the doors. Her eyes moved to the dresser along the wall. She slid open the top drawer, half disappointed to find it empty, and tossed her belongings inside.

That done, she moved to the window. She had a perfect view of Keaton. Her heart swelled with excitement—and her stomach rumbled. She eyed a small tray of food on a nearby table. Dinner would not be served for some time yet. She tucked an apple into her pocket and nibbled on a piece of soft, oozing cheese as she made her way around the balcony to her brother's room.

The cheese was gone by the time she knocked on Thane's door. "You've unpacked already?" he asked, letting her in.

Rhoswen nodded. "Why have they placed us so far apart?"

Thane shook his head. "I don't know. Does it matter?"

"What if something happens, and we need to reach each other?"

Thane looked at her as though she were paranoid, delusional, or both. "What could happen?"

Rhoswen shrugged, her father's warnings repeating through her mind. "Nothing. Just struck me as odd." She tried to sound unconcerned.

Thane nodded, his expression turning mock serious. "You're right. We must always be together. Let's move into your room—all I have is a view of the forest...." Thane's eyes sparkled with amusement in much the same way their father's did when he teased his children.

Rhoswen shoved him lightly and flung herself onto his bed. "Will you stop kidding around? Something about this feels wrong. Don't you sense it?"

Thane dropped his half-emptied bag in a chair and studied his lunch tray. "It's a new place; it can't possibly feel right yet."

Rhoswen sighed. This conversation was going nowhere. She glanced at his wardrobe, which was identical to hers in placement and detail. "Did you open that yet?"

"Yes. Pretty fancy attire. Yours has the same?"

She nodded. "Whose do you think they are?"

"I think they're ours."

Rhoswen's jaw dropped. "No."

Thane laughed. "Why not? You think we can just show up to dinner with the king, dressed like wandering beggars?"

"We look fine!" Rhoswen's eyes darted from her brother's leathers to her own. Their parents had spared no expense on their new training gear. Their vests and pants were made of a soft, durable hide, the only wear on them the permanent creases behind their knees. Rhoswen had chosen a brown leather lighter than Thane's and cream-colored linen shirts that wouldn't show dirt as easily as her brother's stark white ones. She smiled as she remembered Thane's overly masculine rationale for choosing leathers darker than hers. Their parents also furnished her with new boots; Thane's year-old pair showed no more wear than hers and still fit him. "Our father, *Lord* of Stanburh, is the king's brother, and our parents are Realm Riders! They've dressed us better than most could afford!"

"Compared to the contents of that closet, we might as well be wearing sacks."

"Thane!" Rhoswen snapped.

He held up his hands. "We are very well dressed to train, but we could not eat with his majesty in our leathers, smelling of dragons and wind. No one could."

"Do you think we'll have to dine with Uncle Badrick often?" she asked. Her face scrunched up in distaste.

He shrugged. "Probably." He applied himself to the food tray in much the same way she had, secreting the apple in his pocket as he took a bite of the cheese. Someone knocked on the door.

"Cousin!" Gethin yelled from the other side. "Are you ready for your tour?"

Thane stepped to the door. Gethin stood outside, his hands clasped behind his back and his black cape hanging around him like a threat. His features were forced into a strange grimace as if he had never smiled before and were trying it out for the first time. "Ah, you're both here. Shall we, then?"

They descended to the first floor and walked along behind Gethin, uttering lackluster responses as he pointed out objects of decadence. In the king's study, Rhoswen's gaze drifted to the windows over Gethin's shoulder. She could see Keaton below. It was so close. If they could only conclude the castle tour, the drakiary would be their next stop....

As if on cue, a lanky, middle-aged waitman in gray Aethelburh livery interrupted their tour to call Gethin away on some whispered duty. Once Gethin was well out of sight, Thane raised an eyebrow at Rhoswen to mimic their cousin's condescending expression. "Shall we finish our tour on our own, Sister Rhoswen?" he asked in an exaggerated, regal tone. She chuckled, and he dropped the pretense. "I am dying to get down to Keaton," he admitted.

"Let's go," she replied.

III

The Exchange

"The Exchange?" Emmelyn called back.

Bernadette held out her arm and ushered Emmelyn back to their circle of mismatched, overstuffed furniture. "Vonn had tuh go. His Transfuh found 'im while ya were meetin' with Lorelle. He told me tuh tell ya goodbye and then portaled back tuh Welsamar."

Emmelyn stared at Bernadette, unsure which of her three-thousand questions to ask first. The woman smiled and directed Emmelyn to the middle of the couch. Punk Guy begrudgingly slid over, and Bernadette plunked down beside her. "Why don't ya staht by tellin' us what *you* know."

I materialized outside a club called Dissonance and am now sitting with a bunch of costumed eccentrics, one of whom just walked through a disappearing door, Emmelyn thought. "I don't think that will get us very far," she replied.

"Think!" Punk Guy barked like a moody teen. Emmelyn blinked at him.

"Shut up, Kyle," Bernadette snapped and waved him off. "It's easiuh if ya staht piecin' together what ya understand tuh be true, Emmelyn. You'll wanna hold on tuh what ya do know... 'cause we're about tuh tell ya a whole bunch uh stuff ya don't."

Emmelyn slammed back what little was left of her amaretto sour. Bernadette grabbed up her glass and shook it at Randy, who left to refill it before Emmelyn could protest. She took a deep breath. "I was eating a sandwich at school, and then I was here—well, outside this club. But when I walked in, it wasn't a club. It was an ornate, marble lobby with a chilly receptionist, a long staircase on one side, and a restaurant on the other. I had a white block—*Transitor*—in my hand, and Janelle put a sun-shaped keyhole into it. Oh, and she stamped my—hey! Where did the stamp go?" Emmelyn could only see the very edge of the stamp on her left wrist, and it seemed to be fading away as she watched.

"You completed your Transfer," Kyle sulked. "The stamps disappear when you're done."

"I'm sorry?" Emmelyn asked.

The burlesque dancer nodded. Randy returned with another drink, which Bernadette accepted and shoved into Emmelyn's hand. "Yuh doin' fine," she yelled. "Keep goin' 'til ya get to now."

Emmelyn shrugged. "Well, then, I met all of you, and Vonn took me to Lorelle, who opened the Transitor with the sun-key on her necklace. Then, she took out a piece of paper from it and walked through a door labeled 'Darnell' or something."

"D'Erenelle," Kyle corrected.

Bernadette nodded. "Lorelle and Vonn are Runnuhs. We all are—well, except Kyle."

"I'm a Transfer, like you," Kyle explained. He did not appear thrilled by their shared position.

"What do you mean, 'like me?' What is a Transfer?" Emmelyn asked.

"Transfers do what their name implies," Randy yelled across the circle, his voice twangy, like he had just ridden in off a ranch in the deep South. "Y'all take messages from the front desk and pass 'em on to us Runners, and we take 'em back with us to our realms."

"To your realms," Emmelyn repeated.

Randy nodded. "I'm from Tallulahdur."

Of course you are, Emmelyn thought again. "And you, Bernadette?"

"Dellatees," she replied.

Yup.

"I'm from Chicago, in case you were wondering," Kyle offered before she could turn to him.

"Detroit," Emmelyn called back. "Well, a suburb north of the city."

"Well, now yuh also a paht uh the Exchange," Bernadette told her. She smiled. "Get comfy, sweetie. We don't got long, but this'll take a minute."

To understand the Exchange, one had to understand how everything around the Exchange worked. The world Emmelyn knew was actually one of many realms, all of which coexisted simultaneously on various planes of existence. The physics behind it proved far too complex for the group to explain in any detail, but one commonly believed distinction bore mentioning: unlike all the other realms, the Exchange was *not* a realm. It was a place tangential to all the realms and was considered "realmless" because it occupied this separate space. The only way to pass from one realm to another was through the Exchange.

For hundreds of years, the number of realms remained steady. Occasionally, a new realm might blink into existence, or an existing one might blink out of it, but the numbers remained fairly constant. In the last century, however, more realms blinked out than in, decreasing their numbers over time.

The means to a realm's creation might have been up for debate—and one began between Kyle and Randy before Bernadette could prevent it—but the cause of a realm's destruction warranted no dispute: realms were destroyed by a parasite called Narxon.

Every realm held theories about what the Narxon were, some more believable than others, but it all sounded like science fiction to Emmelyn. Narxon were dark smoke creatures that sucked the soul out of everything they touched. If a realm were deemed imbalanced by its queen dragon, that decision would end its lifecycle, and the Narxon would enter the realm to deplete its lifeforce. Then, things called Quaerlithe would replenish the realm, so it could begin anew.

"A Quaerlith is the soul of a dead dragon," Bernadette explained.

"I'm sorry?" Emmelyn asked.

"You heard her," Kyle replied.

But the Narxon didn't only infiltrate a realm *at the end* of its life cycle; they could also make their way into a realm *throughout* its life cycle. The Narxon entered realms through tears—sudden breaks in the existential fabric of a realm. Any time a tear formed, the Narxon would pile through it, as if they had been waiting hungrily on the other side for the opportunity.

To combat the parasites, dragons would burn the Narxon with their fire, destroying them before they could destroy the infiltrated realm, and cauterize the tears. This was what made the Realm Riders and their dragons so revered in the Exchange and the realms they inhabited.

But it was also what made the Narxon so unnerving—besides the whole soul-sucking thing: Narxon took the form of adolescent, malformed dragons with black misty hides. Riders and their dragons found it unsettling to fight an enemy that looked so much like a broken ally. Many of the various theories about Narxon hinged upon this odd similarity, but there was no way to study the Narxon closely enough to draw any real conclusions—you know, without getting your soul sucked out and having your body reduced to ash.

Emmelyn left the sci-fi parasites alone and protested, instead, that dragons were not real. She didn't get very far before Bernadette and the others assured her otherwise.

"We don't have dragons *yet*," Kyle explained as if he were addressing a tiresome little sister. "Some realms don't."

"But what about the Narxon?" she asked.

"We don't have those yet either," Kyle replied, adding gravely, "*thank the realm*."

It wasn't a familiar saying to Emmelyn, but she got the idea. Her skin prickled. "So, no one on Earth knows about any of this? The realms, the dragons, the Narxon...."

Kyle shook his head. "Only the Exchangers from our realm. Until we get dragons—or the Narxon come, realm forbid—there's no need for the inhabitants to know." He smirked. "Do you think they'd believe us anyway?"

"How would we get dragons?" Emmelyn asked.

"At the end of a realm's lifecycle, the dragons open a portal and travel with their Riders to another realm, abandoning their old realm and everything in it," Kyle yelled. "Our realm could be that new home to them. Or not. Who knows when or if we'll ever get Riders and dragons?"

"But it's the unprotected realms like yours that ah dyin' out befoah their time," Bernadette explained.

Randy nodded. "Without dragons to burn 'em away, the Narxon infiltrate the realms and decimate 'em."

"You're saying our realm—and everyone in it—could be destroyed by these things simply because we don't have dragons?" Emmelyn asked. The group nodded. Terror ripped through her as she considered the decimation of the billions of people in her realm alone. "And we're just going to sit around and play the odds?"

"What do you suggest we do about it?" Kyle asked haughtily. "In the five minutes you've been here, have you figured out a way to bring the dragons to our realm?"

Emmelyn scowled at him. "Well, how about tackling this from another angle? How do the tears form in the first place? Can they be prevented somehow?"

Bernadette grimaced. "Not really. Ya see, the teahs form when a rule changes in a realm. Rules change—that's not something ya can prevent."

"Explain," Emmelyn barked.

"Realms have rules," Kyle began. "Most rules have to do with how a realm is managed by its governing body or bodies, but they can also define what can and can't happen within a realm—you know, like physics. You can't stop the rules from changing—nor would you want to; a rule change is what allows for dragons and Riders to inhabit a realm."

"Different combinations uh rules can lead to the continuation or end of a realm's lifecycle," Randy added. "You can't avoid the rule changes, but you can try to *nudge* 'em in a certain direction, so they're less frequent and destructive in the long run."

That was what Runners were for. The energy that rule changes created also allowed a Runner to activate a portal into or out of a realm. Runners—like Bernadette, Randy, Vonn, and Lorelle—used these portals to travel between realms and the Exchange.

"The Exchange isn't just tryin' tuh figuh out why the Narxon have gained such an advantage ovah the realms," Bernadette explained. "It's also usin' Runnahs to bring back infuhmation about what's goin' on in each realm, so the rule changes can be tracked and studied by the Datists."

"The eggheads upstairs, who crunch numbers for the Exchange," Kyle explained.

"Don't be such a snit, Kyle," Bernadette chided before she turned back to Emmelyn. "Datists use that data tuh figuh out how tuh *nudge* realms in line so their rules aren't broken enough tuh end a Realm Cycle. It's called tweaking. They do it for all the realms, whether they have dragons or not."

"And that's important because some uh the realms are connected," Randy yelled. "If the rules change, tears form, and the Narxon come sailin' on through. But sometimes, a tear in one can create a mirrored tear in another."

"So, Narxon enter both?" Emmelyn asked.

Randy nodded. "More changes means more tears, and more tears means—"

"More Narxon," Kyle interjected with dark theatricality. Randy glared at him.

Emmelyn's head began to spin. She thought she might faint.

Bernadette scooted forward to put a hand on Emmelyn's knee. Her expression softened. "I know this is scary, and ya think we're all numb tuh the reality uh the Realm System, but we take comfort in knowin' we're doin' ah paht. Every position within the Exchange is woikin' tuh save the realms. Ya can't save a realm in a day."

"But the Narxon can destroy a realm in one." Emmelyn stared at them.

"That's why the Exchange is so important," Kyle hollered. "The Datists are trying to figure out how to protect the realms from extinction. Every Transitor that moves through this place brings us one step closer to the answers."

Emmelyn took a slow, steadying breath. "So, if Runners bring information *back,* what did I just deliver to Lorelle?" Emmelyn asked, trying to track their conversation instead of losing herself in the terrifying logistics. It felt like being alone on her side of the rope in a tug-of-war match against an entire football team. She pushed her heels against the floor.

"Her next mission to help her realm," Randy explained. "Or so we hope...."

Emmelyn looked at him with renewed horror and confusion. "We *hope*...?"

Bernadette removed her hand from Emmelyn's knee. "There's... a lot uh politics behind it all, honey," she explained. "But you'll hafta figuh all uh that out on yuh own. You gotta get goin'."

"Going?"

"Home. To our realm," Kyle yelled. "Out of the club, down to the lobby, out the front doors, and back to your sandwich."

"And ya bettah hurry, hun," Bernadette continued. "Ya only had one stamp tuh begin with, and it's long gone."

Emmelyn glanced down at Bernadette's wrist, where four red stamps made an uneven V pattern. "But I have so many more questions! Why me? How did I get chosen to be a Transfer? Why not a Runner? You can't tell me *anything*?"

"We ain't got time," Randy yelled back with a nod at her wrist. His expression was sympathetic but urgent.

She looked back to the clean skin above her left hand and felt a sudden wave of panic rise within her. "What happens if I don't leave in time?"

"Best not tuh find out, honey," Bernadette replied.

Emmelyn shot to her feet. She maneuvered around the water-ringed wooden coffee table to the edge of their circle of seats and turned back. *This can't be real.* "So—what—I'll just show up here again sometime? What if I don't want to do this?"

"Could you really walk away from this now that you know about it?" Kyle yelled to her. "Now that you know you can help save our realm?"

Emmelyn bit her lip. "But will you be here? Will I ever see any of you again?"

"Ya might, hun," Bernadette called. "We hope so, at least."

"Just depends on how our schedules line up," Kyle explained with a shrug.

Emmelyn thanked them and ran back to the door at the top of the endless staircase. Between Bernadette, Randy, and even Kyle, she had received quite an education—at least, as much of one as she could withstand in a single sitting.

She stepped into the blinding light of the landing and waited for a man in a white linen kurta and matching pants to pass her before she sped down the stairs. When her feet hit the first compass-point tile, two Ministers slid out in front of her from behind a nearby pillar, palms raised to halt her.

"You're late leaving," the woman said. She grabbed Emmelyn's wrists and turned them up to show her unstamped flesh. "You should disappear by the time the stamps do."

Emmelyn's heart hammered in her chest. The woman's grip was firm, but her tone and expression remained flat. Emmelyn didn't know whether to feel threatened or cowed like a penitent child. She glanced at the silent man, who stood as still as a statue, his features equally unreadable. "I—I didn't realize," she stammered, neglecting to mention she had just been given the same warning by a much warmer group of people—Kyle included. "It's my first time."

"So we'd noticed," the woman replied. She must have been watching Emmelyn's exchange with Janelle when she walked in. The woman released Emmelyn's wrists and stepped aside to open a straight path to the lobby doors. "Next time won't be your first. And we don't warn Transfers twice."

Emmelyn had half a mind to ask what they did instead but thought better of it. "Got it," she said, her voice low. The pair continued to stare at her until she dipped her head, strode to the doors, and stepped through them—onto the bench of the picnic table in the university quad.

IV

Keaton

Thane and Rhoswen stepped into the sunshine and made their way to the east side of the castle. From the top of the valley, they could see the entire drakiary below. "Aethelburh in miniature," it was coined.

Keaton was a two-story castle, but it was otherwise designed to match its big sister on the hill with the addition of two long wings that trailed out from either end of the back wall toward the north. These created the boundaries of the U-shaped training arena at the rear of the drakiary; the northern end remained open for takeoffs and landings. On the ground floor, these annexes held the dragon stables. Above them were the Riders' rooms, except for the head Riders, who occupied apartments in the four crenelated towers that dotted the corners of the arena. Two more towers flanked the castle's formal southern entrance. Additional massive wooden doors at the sides of the arena provided easy access to the dining hall, classrooms, and dormitories within.

The pair headed down to one of these side doors and stepped inside. Keaton buzzed with activity. All along the outer edge of the arena, trainers and students gathered in bunches, dwarfed by the dragons standing in their midst.

The adult beasts stood two to three times as tall as the men and women huddled around them, their four massive legs anchored to the ground by bony feet and sharp talons. Some sat like cats with long tails curled around their bodies or thudding on the ground behind them. The tops of their folded wings sat higher than their heads and would span the full length of the beasts from nose to tail were they unfurled. Horned heads sat atop long, regal necks as large, slit-pupil eyes took in the scene around them. The only thing that reduced their magnificence was the dimming of their gem-colored scales in the shadow of the upper floor of the annex.

A gasp escaped Rhoswen as everything suddenly felt real: she was here to become a Realm Rider. She would join the ranks of her fellow trainees and learn how to care for and fly on a dragon of her own. And if she were deemed worthy enough for a dragon to choose her as a partner for life, she would tether. This was her only ambition—her greatest dream—and she was finally here to achieve it. She followed Thane toward the arena, eyes scanning and heart pounding.

A tall man in black leathers clapped steadily as a trainee-dragon pair descended to the sandy arena floor. He caught sight of the newcomers and crossed to them, his eyes still trained on the landing. He was probably in his mid-forties, with shoulders so broad that he appeared top-heavy. His long, wavy dark hair was pulled back and tied with a thin strap of leather behind his neck. He reached them as the student dismounted and the clapping died down.

"We have visitors," the man bellowed, his voice deep and clear. He turned to Thane and extended his hand. "Darr Thorndon," he said, using his formal Realm Rider title. His accent held the harsh foreignness of the far northern region of the realm.

"Thane and Rhoswen of Stanburh," Thane said. He grasped the inside of the Rider's arm at the elbow, as their father had taught them.

Darr Thorndon did little to hide his surprise. "You're Darr Allistair's children."

They nodded. "We're here to train with you," Rhoswen said, taking the Rider's arm in turn.

Darr Thorndon inclined his head and half-smiled. "We were not told to expect you."

"Welcome!" another Rider called as he approached. "I am Darr Beval."

"My Riding partner," Darr Thorndon added.

Darr Beval was maybe ten years his partner's junior and in every way his opposite. Dressed in tan leathers, his layered blond hair shined brighter than Thane's in the sunlight. Whereas Darr Thorndon's pale, pockmarked skin had seen many hours in the sun, Darr Beval's tan complexion seemed impervious to the damage that endless training had inflicted on his fellow Rider. And while Darr Thorndon had a narrow, dark beard edging his jaw and mouth, the entire lower half of Darr Beval's face was shadowed with a mess of two-day stubble.

The newcomer extended his arm to Rhoswen first. His grip was firm but gentle, and as his fingers curled around her arm, she found herself transfixed by his eyes. His dark amber irises made his hair appear even lighter where it fell around his temples. She swallowed hard. He was lovely. His fingers shifted against her skin, and she realized she had forgotten to let go. "Rhoswen of Stanburh," she blurted, loosening her grip and forcing her lips up into a smile. His eyes widened at her surname.

As Darr Beval turned toward Thane, Darr Thorndon's clear blue eyes caught Rhoswen's, and he smiled at her knowingly. She felt her cheeks warm, and the older Rider winked at her before turning back to the arena. "Everyone!" he called out. "Please welcome two new trainees, Thane and Rhoswen of Stanburh." Riders and trainees clapped politely before returning to their various discussions.

"When did you arrive?" Darr Beval asked.

"Just now," Rhoswen replied.

"And you are unaccompanied?" Darr Thorndon asked.

"Our cousin was called away on... royal business before he could give this part of the tour," Thane replied.

Darrs Thorndon and Beval exchanged unreadable glances.

"If you will allow me, I'll show you Keaton while Darr Thorndon continues with the others," Darr Beval offered. His partner nodded and returned to the arena, arms raised and voice booming.

"It was not our intention to interrupt training—" Thane began.

Darr Beval held up a hand. "It was time to switch lessons anyway. Besides," he added with a conspiratorial grin, "Prince Gethin could not have done this part of the tour justice."

Rhoswen giggled. She was surprised to hear the girlish laugh come out of her. "We would be honored," she said quickly.

Darr Beval gave a small bow. "Come with me."

They followed the split-rail fence along the edge of the arena and down the line of stalls across the back wall. The doors of the stalls were made of wood and did not touch the stone floor. Different-colored heads, tails, feet, noses, and wing tips peaked out above and below, teasing the imagination. The stone walls between stalls stood short enough for dragons to socialize over the top but also tall enough to provide privacy. Several stalls lay empty, their owners probably hunting or working in the arena.

Darr Beval led them toward the southeast corner of the drakiary. "You'll meet the dragons as you work with them, but I can introduce you to mine now. She is off-duty today." He pulled open the door to a stall near the corner turret. "This is my beloved Fleta."

A large tawny raised her head from where it had lain on her forefeet, her eyes half-opening to take in the visitors. Darr Beval stepped forward and stroked her long snout. Rhoswen had to fight the urge to do the same. "Fleta trained with the recruits yesterday," Darr Beval explained. "We try not to work them twice in a row. Darr Thorndon's green, Merry, is out instead."

A clipped yelp drew their attention back to the arena. A trainee straddled the back of a red dragon, holding on for dear life. The beast jerked around beneath her with all the madness of an enraged bull.

"Turbulence practice," Darr Beval explained when Rhoswen glanced at him with wide, terrified eyes. "She'll be fine—she's one of our most promising trainees."

When the red settled down once more, Rhoswen turned back around.

To the left of Fleta's stall stood the entrance to the corner tower. The knocker on the door was a smaller copy of the ouroboros on the Aethelburh gates.

"My rooms," Darr Beval said, following Rhoswen's gaze. "Darr Thorndon's is on the other end, closer to Aethelburh." He patted Fleta and made to close the stall door when he halted, mid-step. He turned back to the dragon, listening as she conveyed something to him through their telepathic connection. Finally, the tawny dropped her head back onto her forefeet, but her eyes remained intent upon her Rider. Darr Beval nodded and tried to smother a look of confusion as he closed her door. "You're not staying in Keaton, then?" Something about the way he asked the question told Rhoswen it had nothing to do with what Fleta had just nexed to him.

Thane shook his head. "Our uncle has invited us to stay in Aethelburh," he admitted with unmasked disappointment.

"Then we'll skip the dormitories," Darr Beval said. "But it appears we have another stop to make before we take the tour inside." He led them farther around the arena to the stalls along its eastern wing.

Rhoswen peeked around him and down the length of the annex ahead of them. "If you and Darr Thorndon live in those two towers," she asked, gesturing behind her with a thumb, "who lives in the towers at the open ends of the arena?"

Darr Beval stopped and pointed at the tower ahead of them. "That one is empty. Our other two senior Riders were more advanced in age and left to be stationed in their hometowns. The king has yet to assign their replacements." He pointed at the far tower on the other side of the arena. "That tower is home to Aelfraed, our caretaker. He should actually be in one of the caretaker apartments beside the supply rooms, but they are filled with additional supplies." He grinned. "We need to reorganize."

"You have only one caretaker for all these dragons?" Thane asked. There must have been well over a hundred beasts housed in the stables of Keaton.

"Aelfraed's son was working with him, and the two of them could handle the lot with the stable hands," Darr Beval explained. "Dragons rarely take sick. And everyone here must do their share of the work. Riders tend their own dragons, but we all pull together to help with the untethered beasts until a connection is made and the new Rider can take over." His brow furrowed, and his dark amber irises appeared brown. "Aelfraed's son fell ill some years ago and passed away. Since then, apprentices who have tried to train with Aelfraed were all rejected by our caretaker for... *deficiencies* of one kind or another." He shrugged. "Two of them became Riders after he cast them off. Perhaps he knew they were destined for a different path." He looked about to say more but seemed to think better of it. "Along this wall are the royal dragons' quarters. Would you like to meet the queen dragon?"

Rhoswen was struck dumb by the offer.

"Is that allowed?" Thane asked, wide-eyed.

"Normally, it would not be a trainee's privilege to meet the royal dragons," Darr Beval admitted. "But you are blood relatives to the royal family. I am certain Prince Gethin would have shown you his parents' beasts had he not been whisked away."

Thane's glance at Rhoswen told her that their cousin would most certainly not have bothered.

Darr Beval's earlier confusion returned. "Besides, Fleta told me Deowynn wants to meet you."

Rhoswen's jaw dropped, but Darr Beval had already turned away to knock on the queen dragon's stall door. In an instant, he swung back around to face them, his gaze steady and serious.

"One rule: do exactly as I say—nothing more, nothing less," he warned. "Bow low and avert your eyes until I tell you to do otherwise. The queen dragon must be handled with care. If you wish to leave her stall after this audience, you would do well not to upset her."

MANY generations of Royal Riders can rule a Realm before one pair leads it to ruination. A Realm can only endure when its rulers lead in a well-balanced fashion, or in the plainest of terms: when their qualities of benevolence are in equal measure to their qualities of malevolence.

Contrary to the Realm-tale nature of this reductive description, the definitions of good and evil are by no means black and white. In addition to those obviously moral and amoral qualities that perhaps need no elucidation, such polarities can take on grayer forms. Goodness can be seen in a ruler's discriminating common sense, whereas evil can take the shape of a ruler's naivety. Regardless of their faults and strengths, the King and Queen Riders must provide balance to each other's natural inclinations.

(Note: Given the subjective and highly dependent nature of this balance, the definitions of what might be considered "good" or "evil" are far too expansive to conclusively detail here or in any volume.)

Should the Royal Riders be deemed irretrievably imbalanced by their Queen Dragon during their rule, their children shall not succeed the throne within their Realm. Instead, the process of the Realm Cycle will begin anew.

This ongoing threat of extinction can have the outcome of illuminating the rulers' deficiencies, so they may correct them and maintain their Realm, but some pairings can break beyond correction. In such a case, their Realm is forfeit, abandoned to destruction by Narxon. After Judgment, the Queen Dragon initiates a Movement, herding her Dragons and Riders to a new Realm with a new line of Royal Riders to rule them.

- an excerpt, *From Those Outlying*

V

Aethelburh

Prince Gethin was shown into his father's apartments by the king's waitman, Delwyn. The servant shut the double doors behind the prince, divorcing him from the rest of the castle with a wooden *thud*. King Badrick's rooms were dark. Half-closed oil lamps cast the occasional dim glow, but the walls were swathed in crimson curtains that sucked at the light and exuded only shadows. Scattered chalices, jewels, and other riches, all dulled and tarnished with disuse, reflected little of the meager lamplight.

Gethin's eyes adjusted to the gloom with a sluggishness he deemed unbefitting a prince. He squinted, unable to locate his father, and decided to wait for the man to speak.

"Your eyes are failing you," the darkness growled. "How else are you blind?"

Gethin turned toward the voice. "I am not old enough to be blind. Turn on a realm-ridden light, and you will find me full-sighted," Gethin snapped.

"You are *your mother's* child." His father's tone was not complimentary. Finally, a flash of the golden threads in the king's cape caught in the light. He loomed on the opposite side of the room from where his voice had first sounded.

Gethin had not heard him cross. *Is my hearing also failing me?* "Her light is my strength; your darkness simply makes you weak," he boasted.

A low rumble of laughter emanated from Badrick's throat. "Her light makes you *useful*," he corrected. "You are not stronger than I because of that good-natured streak Orla bred in you."

"I am the balance," the prince argued. His vehemence unmasked his doubt.

Badrick laughed heartily this time, and the whites of his eyes glinted in the dim light. "You are no balance, boy. Your mother died before she could balance you. Being born to her is not enough. You are no Heir to save this realm. D'Erenelle would fall with either of us on the throne."

Gethin seethed at his father's words. Childbirth had not been easy for Queen Orla; she had died before her son's third birthday, and her goodness had gone with her. Badrick—who had been covetous, feudal, and disinterested in the needs of his subjects even when Orla was alive—learned nothing from her virtue after her passing.

An imbalance of power and resources that Badrick had nurtured in Gethin's youth had grown to favor northern D'Erenelle over the south, misinformation over truth, and Riders over the untethered. Left to its own devices, the south's lawless territorial battles resulted in persistent and inescapable disorder. In the north, where territories were rigidly defined, five titled Riders enjoyed privilege over the others, creating tiers of wealth among their lands. Soon, Badrick's court sessions dwindled into obscurity, leaving a gathering of long-unheard misfortunates to assemble into a permanent settlement around Aethelburh's grounds. The dilapidated ring-town, dubbed D'Aethely, drew criminals and grifters, who stalled into residency and, despite their proximity to the royal castle, lived meager, dangerous lives.

Fortifying this legacy of inequity, however deliberately, Badrick's bitterness infiltrated his every action, including the lopsided upbringing of his son. As a child, the prince would escape his father's moods in the castle libraries. He found greater comfort in reading about others' interactions than experiencing his own. Among the histories and reference materials, he stumbled upon the graver details of the Realm System. Before the tutors his father had hired could convince him otherwise, he realized Badrick's unchecked callousness would condemn the realm if Gethin did not balance himself and take over. But the prince struggled to remember his mother's teachings over his father's. He stood little chance of saving D'Erenelle either.

Gethin resented his father for this disinheritance, unaware that animosity only compounded the damage that Badrick was inflicting. By his thirteenth birthday, Gethin was so much his father's creature that he rarely thought to behave more like his mother until he had already made a mess of things. Now, the prince's only hope was to tether and Ride out with the rest during the inevitable Movement. Once the queen dragon passed imbalanced Judgment on D'Erenelle, the Aethelburh legacy would be irrevocably destroyed. Gethin's fingers fidgeted in agitation and regret.

"Your cousins have arrived?" Badrick asked, peering into a jewelry box on the small table in front of him. His curly jet hair hung about his face and shoulders. It made the pale skin around his eyes appear to float above the thick facial hair that anchored his jaw to the darkness.

"I was giving them a tour when you summoned me."

The king smiled, and his teeth gleamed unnaturally. "Now that you are no longer under the blissful delusion that you could somehow play the hero of D'Erenelle, perhaps it is time to train you as my successor."

Gethin scrunched up his face in disbelief. "You contradict yourself. If I cannot be D'Erenelle's hero, what have I to succeed to?" His fidgeting increased. "Please, Father, explain it to me. Because you keep letting Blaxton fly Deowynn as if you *want* her pregnant. How do you think Heirs are made and realms abandoned?"

Badrick dropped the lid of the jewelry box with a *thunk* and stepped into the light. His gaze was venomous. "Sadly, I am well aware of *how*," he seethed. "Only a fool would keep a dragon in heat from flying her mate—especially a *royal* mate. Dissatisfied queen dragons are the most dangerous. If you would attend a lesson or two, you would also know why her repeated flying is irrelevant. No *fool* could outwit the realms, but I am not a fool, Gethin, and I have done it. I have discovered how to protect our realm from this pathetic, grasping need for *balance*." The last word took on a vile shape, as if it were imbued with a truly detestable quality. "Your lessons begin tomorrow."

"I do not understand."

"That is why *you* are the fool, Gethin." Badrick stepped forward, and his son fought the urge to retreat. "Tomorrow, you must entertain your cousins over dinner."

Gethin scowled. "I would rather starve," he spat.

A frightening sneer distorted Badrick's angular features. "A tempting alternative."

In his own room, Gethin leaned over the end of his bed, arms outstretched and hands braced against the footboard. His fingers rapped on the wood, but they could not drown out his father's words. They mocked him, over and over, as he failed, once again, to surmise the king's plan.

Gethin could almost recite from memory the histories that spelled the fate of the realm. Upon imbalanced Judgment, Deowynn would become pregnant and lead her whelp and the rest of the dragons and Riders out of D'Erenelle. Then, Narxon would seep into the skies through proliferating portals and drain the life from the realm. No man—fool *or* king—could alter this age-old path. For all his power in D'Erenelle, Badrick could not change the workings of the system that affected every realm in existence.

So, what did he mean about Deowynn's mating flights being irrelevant? For once, Gethin wondered whether his absences from lecture had finally proven regrettable. He never dreamed he could somehow use his training down in Keaton *against* the Realm Cycle.... He cleared his throat as it began to tighten with anxiety. It wasn't what his mother would do, but that dragon had long since flown.

The light from the open window faltered as an average-sized green swooped up to land on a castle turret high above Gethin's window. Cheering reached the prince's ears, and he moved from his bedside to look down on the drakiary below. As the dragon glided back down, Gethin remembered his abandoned cousins—and his father's promise that he would entertain them again at dinner that night. He did not understand why he had to act as their keeper, but he had better things to do than ponder his father's whims. *Let's get this over with,* he thought and headed for the door.

VI

Keaton

Gethin arrived at the drakiary as a dragon lurched into the air under an unsteady trainee. The prince rolled his eyes. *Even if my father* has *discovered how to prevent the Movement, this realm will be reduced to ash before he'll get the chance.*

The Stanburhs were nowhere to be seen. Darr Thorndon caught Gethin's eye and jerked his head in the direction of the back wall. *Meeting dragons,* Gethin translated. *As if they will ever tether!* The prince circled the arena, a smirk curling his lips, but it faded when muffled voices caught his attention near Deowynn's stall. He padded toward her door and pressed his ear against it.

"She's beautiful," Gethin heard a female voice coo. He had not spent enough time with his cousins to recognize their muddied voices from behind thick, wooden doors, but who else could have gained access to the queen dragon? The Stanburhs held high status in the realm, whether Gethin liked it or not, and they probably thought that warranted a special audience. What floored Gethin was Deowynn's willingness to grant it. Had *he* tried to visit her, he would have been reduced to a puddle of molten prince in the hay at her feet.

He strained to make out the next speaker's words. "She wants... stroke... snout." It was Darr Beval. Gethin's knees buckled. *She is letting Rhoswen* touch *her?!* Deowynn had forbidden anyone other than Aelfraed to come near her, let alone *touch* her, since Queen Orla had passed away... at least, as far as he knew.

"—scales... smooth," Rhoswen replied. Her awestruck voice rang low, and Gethin could only catch a few syllables. "Never... white dragon... scales with gold...."

"That was not...." Gethin thought it was Thane's voice, but he could not make out the words. "You... think... attack us on sight." *She should have attacked you!* Gethin thought, finally getting the gist of Thane's comment.

"—a possibility," Darr Beval admitted. "Rhoswen... first... touch... passing... Orla."

"What does that mean?" Thane asked, his volume rising in disbelief.

Unable to make out a response, Gethin imagined Darr Beval shrugging with uncertainty. Indeed, he saw no justification for Deowynn's special treatment of Rhoswen. The prince's eyes traveled down to his forearm where the aftermath of his last visit to the queen dragon's stall had left a long, straight scar. It gleamed a livid white against the surrounding skin. He grimaced at the memory of her sharp talons.

A door opened down the hall. Gethin darted away from the stable door toward the arena and leaned against the fence, out of sight behind a pillar. The footsteps grew louder and finally stopped outside of Deowynn's stall. Gethin peeked around the pillar to see Aelfraed disappear inside and then returned to the stall door to press his ear against the wood once more.

"Remarkable!" Aelfraed exclaimed. "You have your father's affinity for dragons, my dear. Perhaps even more so. Deowynn does not normally take to strangers."

When Aelfraed spoke again, his voice was quieter than before. "—queen dragon... bond so strongly... suddenly... a stranger... indicative of...."

Gethin couldn't make out the rest. He cursed his luck... *aloud.*

The voices inside ceased. Gethin straightened up and raised a fist to the wood as though he were about to knock on it. A moment later, Darr Beval appeared before him and bent into an automatic bow. "My prince?"

"You have saved me the trouble of knocking, Darr Beval; I thank you," Gethin said with a transparent excess of courtesy.

The Rider stepped aside. Thane and Aelfraed flanked the door, and Rhoswen stood within an arm's reach of Deowynn. The queen dragon snorted at Gethin for his intrusion. The sound seemed to jar the others back to their senses, and they bowed to the prince. Deowynn just glared at him.

Gethin made his obligatory bow to the queen dragon as an uncomfortable silence fell. "My apologies for leaving you to your own devices, Cousins. We have made special arrangements to present you at a dinner party tomorrow night. I hope you will allow me to entertain you to make amends for my rudeness."

Rhoswen blinked at him, and Thane had to clear his throat to utter a coherent reply. "The honor would be ours, my prince. Thank you."

"Excellent," Gethin said, backstepping toward the door. *No use enabling any more of this nonsense,* he thought with a sneer at the queen dragon. "Shall we resume our tour?" he asked his cousins and stepped from the stall, desperate to distance himself from the unsettling feeling Deowynn always gave him.

"Of course, my prince," Thane and Rhoswen muttered as they shuffled out after him.

THERE is no prescribed schedule for the completion of a student's training, and training can, indeed, continue for years before a trainee finally Tethers.

Trainees must Tether by age two-and-twenty, as it is universally acknowledged that a trainee will not make a connection with a Dragon after that age. Trainees who remain Untethered by their two-and-twentieth year must remove themselves graciously from the Royal Drakiary and surrender themselves to the lives of non-Riders.

- an excerpt, *From Those Outlying*

VII

Tendalar

Emile Illisan walked up the lush but well-manicured path toward the gazebo, where the baby would be named before his family and their numerous acquaintances. It had been many years since he had attended one of these ceremonies. His family remained relatively small, and no infants had come into it since his youngest nephew had been born twenty-two years ago.

In typical Tendalarian fashion, a gigantic heptagonal pergola overhung the seating area. It was strewn with panels of pale-yellow tulle that draped across it and pooled luxuriously at the base of each column. Enormous bows of the same material hung at the backs of each thin-cushioned chair. Emile sighed. At least there would be plenty of leg room to accommodate the bows' extravagant bulk. The place looked like it had been outfitted for a wedding, although everyone was wearing white—but for the parents. They were dressed in a light yellow, only slightly darker than the gazebo fabric. Emile thanked the realm he didn't have to wear that color—jaundice was not his best look.

Of all the places in Welsamar he could go, Tendalar was one of the wealthiest and most beautiful. This made his visit home somewhat less agonizing—except for the presence of his family, of course, who could taint any occasion. To make matters worse, the gardens were filled with friends of the family, most of whom Emile knew well enough to know he didn't want to know them. He glanced around for his sister and found his youngest nephew, Jerold, in olive-green leathers beside her.

Ah, the Rider's privilege, he mused. The leathers of a Rider were their all-time uniform, almost always acceptable, regardless of the expected dress code for everyone else. Beside the young Rider, Emile's sister, Talena, stood beaming at her new grandmotherly status in a flattering white frock. This was her first grandchild, but if Corsol and Andlie's groping of each other near the naming altar offered any indication, it would most certainly not be her last.

"Talena," Emile crooned. He planted a kiss on her cheek.

"Emile," his sister replied with practiced obsequiousness. She flashed an apologetic glance at the couple she had been conversing with, and they moved along to gossip elsewhere. "We're so glad you could make it," she told him. "You've been so busy since the wedding; it seems like we only see you at these milestone events anymore!"

Considering the wedding had only been last year, and they had celebrated three holidays together since, it really hadn't been that long since they'd seen each other. He would have to draw out his next absence just to give her words some validity. "Duty calls," he pandered with a wink. He reached across his sister to shake the hand of her husband, Diron, who looked about as pained as Emile felt.

Finally, he turned to his nephew. "Jerold!" he exclaimed, taking the young man's elbow in his hand in true Rider tradition. "Congratulations on tethering, my boy! You have honored your family transcendently."

Jerold inclined his head and thanked his uncle before falling silent once more. Unlike Talena and her other children, Jerold was a modest young man of few words.

"You tethered to a young beast, I believe?" Emile asked, trying to draw him out on the subject so he wouldn't have to hear about it from Talena.

Jerold nodded. "A young green named Kipling. I call him Kip." His excitement was almost evident beneath his unwavering austerity.

"How marvelous," Emile replied. "You must be proud."

"I am always proud of Kip."

Emile nodded and searched for his next question. "So, where is he? Green foliage or no, a dragon can't be easy to hide...."

"He's gone off to the stream nearby," Jerold replied.

The officiant scuttled around behind Talena, eager to interrupt. Capitalizing on a break in conversation, he leaned in close to her ear, his hand perching gently on the small of her back. He was bald but for light-blond fuzz along the sides of his head. He wore the obligatory dark-yellow cassock, which bulged at his midsection and did his pudgy frame no favors. Emile would normally have indulged himself in mentally redressing the man—even though the costume was not his choice—but he couldn't enjoy the cerebral exercise. Something about the man's touch and Talena's eager response to it felt sickeningly intimate. *Come on,* Emile thought with a glance at Diron. Talena's husband seemed unaffected by the gesture. Emile scoffed. He had always liked Diron, but the man was a bit of a pushover, especially where his wife was concerned.

Talena flapped her hands at everyone, signalling them to find their seats before taking her own in the front row. Emile found an empty chair in the row behind Jerold and leaned his ruby-studded cane against his leg. He didn't like wearing hats, even if they did tend to look spectacular on him.

Instead, his collection of canes provided the finishing touches to his already distinguished look. *The expensively tailored, three-piece suit doesn't hurt either,* he mused, unbuttoning the white jacket.

The boy was named Wallen in a blissfully short ceremony by the—it turns out—*oddly charming* officiant. Emile could see why Talena had taken a shine to the man.... Why Diron wasn't perturbed by it defied understanding.

Strolling appetizers followed the ritual. Guests were expected to wind their way through the maze-like gardens, which were punctuated by tables of bite-sized goodies. Signage at each station indicated another trope along the journey from infancy to adulthood, but Emile didn't care to give it as much attention as the caterers had. He extended brief congratulations to his niece and nephew and looked around for Jerold. The Rider was alone at the head of the procession, making his way briskly along the path. Emile could appreciate his nephew's desire to escape on dragonback unnoticed. *I would do the same if I had a winged beast nearby,* he thought.

Emile caught up to his nephew and snuck an inconspicuous silver flask out of his vest pocket. He offered it first to Jerold, who smiled with one corner of his mouth and accepted it. They continued onward, several steps ahead of the other guests, their privacy ensured by the party's disinterest in either of them.

"Do you remember what we discussed at your sister's wedding before you became a Rider?" Emile asked, keeping his voice low.

Jerold nodded. "I do, but I've tethered now. None of it applies."

"Yes," Emile said with a smile, "the first Realm Rider of the family! You know, it's not often a Rider emerges from a line entirely devoid of them. Why did you reject your mother's offer to put on a celebration in your honor?"

"Being a Rider is honor enough," Jerold said, shuffling his feet. "I don't need to—"

"Sully it with an afternoon of pretentious fawning from your mother's high-society friends?" Emile suggested. He flashed his nephew a sideways glance.

Jerold blew air through his nose and grinned. "It seemed best not to go to all that trouble."

"I appreciate your choice," Emile replied earnestly. He abhorred spending time with Talena's pathetic acquaintances, as well. "I only ask to make sure you have not regretted your choice in becoming a Rider."

Jerold looked at his uncle as if he had made the tragic decision to pair a sapphire-studded cane with a maroon suit. "Does anyone regret that?"

Emile smiled again. "Probably not."

They continued through the shrub-lined labyrinth and happened upon another table. Emile gestured toward it, and they paused to grab something representative of one's teenage years on a cracker. Emile selected one with an artful pyramid of caviar and tried to ignore the allusion. "The lifestyle here in Welsamar can be rather… *limiting* for a Rider. Especially for one with *your* family," Emile suggested.

Both corners of Jerold's mouth quirked upward, and he shrugged. "I can't complain."

"No," Emile agreed, "but you can do better."

Jerold squinted at his uncle. "I'm sorry?"

"You are in the unique position of having an Arbiter for an uncle, Jerold."

Emile's work was not something he could broadcast *anywhere*. Few people outside Emile's family knew about his profession or the Exchange. Most, like Talena's ignorant friends, believed him to be some sort of all-important ambassador. The status rather than the details of his job was what these people found most intriguing—and glamorous when they advertised their distant association to him.

Realm Riders were usually the last to know about the Exchange. Jerold's unique connection to an Exchange family gave him knowledge of both worlds—and his parentage gave him *access* to both. "Have you ever thought you might like to travel as a Rider?"

"We travel all the time to fight the Narxon," Jerold replied. "And—don't tell my mom—but I've put in for freedom of transfer, so they can send me wherever they need to protect Welsamar at large, not just my hometown of Tendalar."

"Good for you, my boy!" Emile exclaimed. He caught himself and mimed the turning of a key at his lips. "I shan't say a word." He glanced over his shoulder to verify their continued privacy. It seemed most of their followers had paused at the teen angst table behind them. "What about going… farther than Welsamar?"

Jerold laughed. "Farther than Welsamar? I'm a Rider, Uncle Emile. I can't do the Exchange thing."

"*You* can," Emile replied.

Jerold stared at his uncle. "What?"

"Jerold, I wasn't kidding when I said Riders seldom come out of thin air," Emile said. "We don't have a single Rider in the long lineage of our family, and your parents' families are two of the oldest in this realm. Haven't you ever wondered how you stumbled upon the aptitude for—or even the *interest* in—Riding?"

His nephew just stared at him. His thick, dark eyebrows furrowed like cliffs overhanging his sunken hazel eyes. "Riders can emerge from anywhere in a family line," he recited, presumably from an old history text.

"That doesn't make it a common occurrence." Emile sighed. "*You* have Rider blood, Jerold. On your father's side."

"What are you talking about?" Jerold asked.

"Haven't you ever noticed how different you look from your siblings?" Emile asked. Jerold began to protest, but Emile cut him off. "You look like your mother, that much is true. And your father probably looks a lot like Diron—your mother had a type," he glanced over his shoulder at the handsy officiant, "*once*."

"What do you mean, 'my father *looks like* Diron?'"

Emile sighed. "There's no easy way to say this. Diron raised you, but he is not your birth father, Jerold. Your father is a D'Erenellean man. That's where you get your Rider blood." Emile watched his nephew for signs of impending violence or outburst. None were forthcoming. The young man looked numb—not at peace with this information but numb. *Anyone else in his family would have caused a scene,* Emile thought.

Instead, Jerold's eyes lost their focus as he considered the concept. "Who was he?" His voice sounded hollow.

Emile shrugged. "Don't trouble yourself with that. What I can tell you, however, is that you belong to two realms: Welsamar and D'Erenelle, and I believe you can travel between both."

"D'Erenelle? How is that even possible?" Jerold asked, locking eyes with his uncle.

"Your mother used to be a Runner," Emile explained. Jerold looked surprised, and Emile mirrored the expression. "She never told you?"

Jerold shook his head.

Emile groaned at the inconvenience. *Of course, the* one *thing she keeps to herself.* "Your mother stopped Running shortly before you were born," he explained.

"Why?"

"Because she disgraced her post and was relieved of it," Emile replied. "Runners are not permitted to share details of the Exchange and the greater Realm System with the common folk in their realm—let alone have their *children*. Your mother was already being watched for her loose tongue.... When she became pregnant with you, the Exchange exiled her." Emile remembered it like it was yesterday. "Under normal circumstances, she would have been abandoned in D'Erenelle, but I was able to pull some strings to get her back home. Your brother and sister were too young to be motherless, and Diron did not deserve the hardship of raising them on his own."

"Do my brother and sister know our mother was a Runner?"

Emile shrugged again.

"And my father? Does he know about me?"

"Which one?" Emile asked, instantly regretting the callousness of the question. It was not Jerold's fault his mother was a tramp. "Forgive me. Your D'Erenellean father? Not likely. Diron, I'm not sure about. But Diron loves you—of that, I'm positive. It would seem, for once, that I cannot be certain of what your mother has *or hasn't* shared. I had no idea she could keep a secret."

Jerold was silent as they walked down the path. They ambled up to another table, this one replete with champagne flutes. It was the final stop on the stroll before the party would disband with a toast and disintegrate into memory.

"I don't understand how you think I could travel between the realms," Jerold said. He grabbed up a flute of champagne, downed it in one gulp, and continued toward the forest beyond the gardens. The stream trickled nearby. Kipling was likely in the vicinity, drawing Jerold in. Emile didn't mind; it had been a while since he had seen one of the gorgeous beasts up close.

"Frankly, I don't understand it either," Emile replied. He took a sip from his flute. "The twenty-second birthday seems to be the sweet spot. Riders are only eligible to tether on or before it, and Exchangers can only be initiated on or after it. If memory serves, you tethered precisely on that birthday, yes?" Jerold nodded. "So, twenty-two years later, at the same moment of your birth, you tethered, *and* the Exchange suggested you as a candidate Runner. I expected this anomaly to sort itself out once it realized you had tethered, but it never did." He emptied his flute and tossed it into the grass, uninterested in returning it to the table. "You qualified for both positions simultaneously, Jerold, and neither system has figured it out since."

VIII

Aethelburh

"Why can't I dress as you do?" Rhoswen whined to her brother.

Elsie, one of Rhoswen's two appointed waiting-women, stood behind her and pulled taught the strings that corseted down the back of a shiny sapphire dress she had selected for Rhoswen to wear to the dinner party.

"Because I would look ridiculous in a dress," Thane joked. He was leaning against her bedpost, one ankle crossed over the other—the picture of comfort in his elegant suit of black satin. His long-tailed, double-breasted jacket bore the traditional white lapels of the untethered. They were glaring. Eventually, they would be made to match the color of his dragon—if he ever bothered with such formal wear again. Rhoswen's attire would also change when she tethered, but without Rider status, she was simply another lady of the court—in a puffy blue dress.

"Oh, hush!" Rhoswen made a face at odds with her regal-looking gown. "Dresses simply do not suit me."

Her brother grinned and shook his head. "You do not allow them to, Rose. Tomorrow, you can dress like a boy again."

"I do not dress like a boy!" Rhoswen snapped. "I dress like any other trainee."

The other waiting-woman—whose name Rhoswen had embarrassingly forgotten—held out two pairs of dainty heeled shoes for Rhoswen to choose from, and Thane howled with laughter again. "The sparklier the better!" he hooted.

"To the Narxon with you, Thane Stanburh!" Rhoswen yelled. She huffed and pointed at the less ostentatious pair of blue satin ankle boots.

Thane pushed himself away from the bed, still holding his sides. "Surely you do not mean that, my precious Rose," he cooed. "A lady as beautiful as you could never say something so foul to someone she loves so dearly."

"Beauty can be deceptively dangerous, *brother dear*," she retorted with mock sweetness.

"Not *so* deceptive," he replied and flashed his most annoying smile. Rhoswen punched his arm before he could dodge her. "Ow!" he cried, rubbing the spot for effect.

Before Rhoswen could assure him that he was unharmed, someone rapped on the door. Elsie admitted their cousin into the room. Gethin was dressed as Thane was, but his lapels were a deep purple to denote his royal status. The purple would eventually be made to swirl with the color of his dragon's hide when he tethered. Such complexly patterned fabric, even in quantities meager enough for lapels, would triple the garment's price. "Nearly ready?" he asked politely. Civility was not a quality Rhoswen associated with her cousin. She froze the muscles along her spine to suppress a shiver.

Elsie draped a large, droplet-shaped jewel on a twisty black chain around Rhoswen's neck to fill the void above the low-cut bodice. The fuchsia gem and blue dress made for a gaudy combination, but Rhoswen did not wish to offend anyone by saying so. A pair of long, matching earrings sat in the velvet-lined box from which Elsie had pulled the necklace. "Milady, are your ears pierced?" the waiting-woman asked.

Rhoswen shook her head fervently. "No!"

Elsie made a soft, disappointed click with her tongue and teeth. "Then she is ready, your highness," she announced with a curtsey.

Rhoswen and Thane entered the Great Hall behind their cousin. The scene was overwhelming. High over their heads, the famed thousand-candle chandelier hung just below the open balcony near their rooms. At their feet, the floor was mosaicked with reenactments of dragons and their Riders in historical Descents. Before them, in a particolored sea of satin and tulle, aristocrats mingled feverishly as if on a tight schedule to visit everyone in attendance. Starched and sleek lords accompanying ladies in tulle-expanded gowns wove themselves into and out of groups.

Rhoswen's gaze drifted toward the resistant clusters of high-ranking Realm Riders, whose shiny hide-colored lapels looked livelier than their wearers. The stationary Riders kept mainly to themselves, unless briefly accosted by aristocratic couples, who ultimately excused themselves in favor of more engaging company. Rhoswen could not understand why the lords and ladies even bothered approaching the Riders, given their disinterest. She searched the area for Darrs Thorndon and Beval but could locate neither. *Shouldn't the two head Riders of Keaton be here?* She ignored the thought that her parents probably should be, too.

Everyone bowed and curtsied to the prince before resuming their conversations. No one engaged him. The three progressed quickly through the crowd and into the empty dining hall.

"We'll sit down there," Gethin instructed, guiding his cousins to the far end of the table. Rhoswen moved to take a seat beside her brother, but Gethin stopped her. "No," he barked, forgetting his feigned courtesy. He cleared his throat and adopted a sweeter tone. "Dear cousin, you shall sit on my other side. You both deserve places of honor."

"You flatter me, my prince," Rhoswen replied, remembering Thane's coaching. She wondered whether she had sounded convincing. Her brother's smirk told her that she had not.

"You flatter us both, my prince," Thane added with a slight bow—mostly to hide his grin.

Rhoswen moved to the seat across from her brother and stood behind her chair. The prince's entrance into the dining hall had opened the room to the other guests, but no one would sit before King Badrick arrived. Men and women poured in to select their seats, their eyes darting around the room. It felt like the first day of school, when students sized each other up and tried to maneuver into ideal spots around one another. Rhoswen wondered at their strategies for selection.

Spying someone of interest near the door, Gethin excused himself. He walked the length of the table to approach a woman with long blonde hair and a form-fitting, seafoam-green satin dress. She had delicate features and cool green-blue eyes. Her every move was graceful, and her gestures seemed both natural and calculated. No one could deny her beauty, and there wasn't a single man—or woman—in the room who was unaware of her. Gethin escorted her to his end of the table, whispering in her ear as they walked. Whatever his words, her expression did not waver. She looked quietly amused, with one eyebrow quirked upward and her mouth a relaxed line that picked up at the corners. As they neared the open seat beside Rhoswen, their conversation ceased, and Gethin abandoned his charge to resume his place at the head of the table. He did not introduce the woman to the Stanburhs. Rhoswen flashed her a weak smile and received a single, polite nod in return.

After most of the aristocrats had taken their places behind their selected chairs, the Riders filed in and assumed whatever empty spots they could find. Finally, Darrs Thorndon and Beval sped into the dining hall and stood behind the last pair of chairs on either side of the king's empty seat. They exchanged harried expressions, and Rhoswen wondered at their tardiness. She glanced down at them, but several Riders at their end of the table had already captured their attention.

"Quite an audience the queen dragon gave you yesterday, Cousin Rhoswen," Gethin said with undisguised venom. Thane's glance shifted between them.

"Yet another honor bestowed upon me in my short time here, my prince," Rhoswen replied stiffly.

Gethin's jaw clenched. "Yes, it would seem you have been heaped with honors since your arrival—" He was cut off by a hush that overtook the room from one end to the other, like the tide rolling over the shore. The king had arrived.

King Badrick's satin suit seemed somehow blacker than those of the men around him, as if light fled from him, save for his lapels. They swirled with onyx, purple, and gold, as did the cape that hung from his shoulders and fastened before his collar with a large ball-and-claw clasp. The bauble dwarfed the massive purply jewel hanging from Rhoswen's own neck. The pale skin of his face was obscured by his long black hair, the mustache anchoring his upper lip, and his intricately carved beard that scalloped under his cheeks like dragon's wings.

He extended his arms outward, as if to embrace the room. "My worthy guests: be welcome. Please sit," the king offered, lifting his cape over the arms of his chair. Guests scrambled into their seats as if in a race. Only the Stanburhs, the Riders, and the beautiful blonde woman were in no hurry to sit.

Rhoswen looked down the long table at her uncle. His dark form was framed in the brilliant gold of his ornate, high-backed chair. Indeed, the late Queen Orla's elegant throne had been moved to the head of the table from its raised platform in the Great Hall. On the tour, their cousin had said it was to remind them of her once-lively presence at every event, but Rhoswen didn't know whether her cousin actually believed the justification. The guests' seats—including Gethin's—were less ornate than her bedposts upstairs. The king seemed to be making a very different statement.

"Let us begin," Badrick announced without preamble.

Waitmen flowed into the room from all angles. With astonishingly swift precision, food was piled onto plates from each man's tureen. Before Rhoswen could take stock of what had been set before her, the waitmen had disappeared, and the king was speaking again. His slick, smooth voice was a threatening bass that made Rhoswen's skin crawl.

"You will have to forgive me, Darrs, Lords, and Ladies. I am out of love with decorum this evening. I have opted for one large course rather than several smaller ones that stilt conversation and hinder the general enjoyment of my chefs' hard work." Ignoring the low rumble of surprise emitted by his guests, the king held up his large pewter goblet for a toast. Rhoswen could just make out the black, embossed likeness of a dragon between his fingers—presumably an homage to his own beast, Blaxton. "To D'Erenelle," he said tonelessly.

The guests echoed his toast, and goblets clinked around the table. Unlike Badrick's chalice, the guests' were made of glass to display a colorless liquid. The drink was so delicate that it hardly tasted of anything at all, except for a barely discernible finish of fruit and flowers. Rhoswen set down her drink and glanced around the table. Beside each goblet sat a small pewter chalice embossed with an ornate vine pattern. She watched her neighbors empty the contents of the tiny cups into their wine goblets, their attention rapt on the mixture.

Rhoswen tipped the tiny cup of burgundy liquid into her glass goblet. Instantly, the colorless wine began to swirl with little crimson spheres of incandescent liquid that danced under the surface. The spheres melded together and separated again before bursting and turning the colorless wine a deep crimson. When the liquid stilled, Rhoswen looked up from her glass in astonishment. Thane, too, seemed pleasantly surprised.

Gethin smirked. "Realm Water. The first sip—for the toast—is devoid of alcohol to symbolize the realm's purity. Then, the impure, or alcoholic, active wine is added." The prince laughed as Rhoswen's expression shifted to one of horror. "*Active* because it moves within the Realm Water, not because it is alive, dear cousin. They swirl together in a display of balance. Some call it 'Dancing Wine.'"

Rhoswen sighed with relief and lifted her now-still cup. "Well, I call it beautiful." She took a sip of the new drink. Fiery acid hit her tongue, setting her mouth and the back of her throat aflame. Then, the fire was replaced with a soothing coolness reminiscent of the original, virgin liquid. She blinked in an effort not to grimace and set the goblet back on the table. Gethin and Thane laughed.

Everyone had already begun eating and chatting, their conversations comingling nonsensically. Rhoswen peered at Darr Beval again from the corner of her eye. He was engrossed in his plate. She found herself confined to making small talk with her brother and cousin, neither of whom had much to say. The woman in green beside her was enduring the endless, high-pitched chatter of a woman in bright pink on her other side. Rhoswen grimaced at the nasally whine and fussed with her worthless cutlery. It had little effect on a stringy, greenish vegetable that resembled asparagus but had a texture more akin to the leather laces on her riding gear. She glanced up at Thane to see if he were having any more luck, but his eyes were fixed on the lovely woman in green beside her.

Rhoswen cleared her throat. "We are excited to begin our training next week, my prince," she said. Thane blinked and returned his attention to their conversation.

Gethin nodded. "I should expect so."

Thane smiled weakly, and they descended into another silence. The woman in pink continued to drone on, but Rhoswen could not bring herself to make sense of her screechy words. The guests around the woman poked at their food and sipped from their goblets, their gazes directed away from her to avoid the responsibility of responding.

Rhoswen's dress crunched around her as she shifted in her seat. She finally surrendered her mangled vegetable to the side of her plate and tried the mahogany-colored meat. At least *that* fell apart with the slightest prod of her knife. It tasted oddly of beef *and* poultry but was not unpleasant.

Suddenly, she sensed the tingle of eyes on her. She looked hopefully toward Darr Beval. Instead, she found King Badrick staring at her, unperturbed by her returned gaze. Her eyes snapped back to her plate, and her breath hitched in surprise. She could almost feel his prolonged, blistering glare from across the room.

"Cousin Rhoswen, I am most intrigued by your recent experience with Deowynn," Gethin said, interrupting her forced focus on her plate. "She seemed to take to you with such ease. Did it take long to win her over?"

Rhoswen did not know the correct answer, so she opted for the truth. "Not long, my prince."

"No?" Gethin asked. He wiped his mouth with the corner of his napkin and stared at her. His interest was disturbing. Perhaps the truth had not been her best option. "She tends to require an inordinate amount of bowing and scraping when making any acquaintance."

A commonality among the royal family members, Rhoswen thought. She decided not to voice any more truths and simply nodded.

"Such a lengthy process for so little return," Gethin grumbled. "And what good does it do anyone?"

"I am sure she must miss Queen Orla very dearly," Thane offered.

Gethin snorted. His tone began to fray with agitation. "She was always that way, even before my mother died. And to what end? She—" The prince's eyes caught at the other end of the table, and his voice fell flat. "She was very dear to us all, my mother," he amended.

Thane stole a glance at what had silenced their cousin. When his eyes shot back to his plate, Rhoswen resisted also peering at the king.

Badrick's cool scrutiny fostered a sort of sympathy in Rhoswen, and she ventured to comfort her cousin. "Deowynn is a magnificent and devoted dragon," she said. "It must be in her nature to choose the subjects of her affection carefully." As the last words fell from her mouth, she realized they would have the opposite effect she had hoped for: the prince was clearly not one of those chosen few. She popped another bite of meat into her mouth and flashed Gethin a closed-lipped smile before returning her gaze to her plate. The woman in green beside her chuckled, but Rhoswen didn't dare look at her.

Gethin glowered at Rhoswen for some time before he spoke again. "Did Aelfraed say anything about why she chose *you* as a subject for her affection?"

Aelfraed had had little opportunity to say much of anything before the prince had interrupted their discussion in the stall, but Rhoswen would have kept the caretaker's thoughts from her cousin anyway. She shook her head. "I'm afraid not, my prince."

Gethin's lip curled in a sneer. "Nonsense! After nearly two decades, I know the tone of voice he uses when he has an idea about something. Now, what did he tell you?"

The prince's outburst caught the attention of everyone at their end of the table, including the woman in pink, who paused her babbling long enough to look in his direction. Thane bristled, perhaps deciding whether to handle the situation verbally or bodily. Rhoswen hoped for the former. She peeked toward the far end of the table to see if the king meant to intervene. This time, Darr Beval was the one watching her. Her pulse quickened, and she turned back to her cousin with a smile. "He was as surprised as you, my prince."

Anger flashed in Gethin's eyes, but his gaze darted to his father and transformed his fury into sulky resignation. "Aelfraed never was the most communicative of servants," Gethin mumbled and studied his inadequate knife.

The woman in pink picked up her story once more. Her chatter had finally reduced itself to an ignorable hum, and random words from other conversations filtered into Rhoswen's consciousness. She hoped that what Gethin had said about Aelfraed had merely been a dodge. The wizened caretaker did not strike her as being at a loss for words but rather at a loss for privacy. If her meddlesome cousin had not shown up, she felt certain the old man would have explained exactly why he thought the queen dragon had shown her such kindness.

Inwardly cursing the prince, she lay her utensils across her plate. The meat had grown cold, and she could not bring herself to make another attempt at cutting the fibrous green leatherstrings again. She shifted noisily in her seat and suppressed a groan. She wanted out of this ridiculous dress and away from royal scrutiny.

As servants cleared the dinner plates, smaller bone-white plates filled their vacancies and goblets swelled again, this time with a pale-green liquid that smelled of savory herbs. In the center of each dessert plate lay a large, purple flower, the likes of which Rhoswen had never seen. Its five long petals ruffled at the edges and came to a pointed tip that curled in on itself like a ribbon pulled across a blade. Its deep amethyst surface paled with a fine dusting of sugar crystals. The stamens were pushed outward to cradle a clear, glasslike sphere that Rhoswen guessed was made of jelly. She noticed Thane raising an eyebrow at her. He had no more experience eating candied blossoms than she did. She smothered a laugh.

The king raised his goblet once more. "Aethelia, the Flower of Aethelburh," he explained to his guests, the first words he had spoken since his toast. "Grown only in our fair countrylands and unseen by many, it is a delicacy rarely enjoyed by the eyes and even more seldomly by the tongue. But we have cause to celebrate.

"New trainees are among us, and they are of particular note, for they are family. I am certain you remember their father, Allistair.... I hope you will extend that same regard to his children. Please welcome my nephew and niece: Lord Thane and Lady Rhoswen of Stanburh."

Something about their uncle's speech did not inspire much warmth. The guests clapped and murmured greetings, but they seemed ill at ease. Rhoswen gazed at the Darrs on either side of the king. They looked like they wanted to crawl out of their skin.

The king fixed each of his relatives with an intense stare. "My son has dominated his cousins' attention all evening, but you will surely find the time to get acquainted, as the Stanburhs will be with us while they train in Keaton. So, please: enjoy these magnificent new blooms—*and* our dessert, of course."

Polite laugher filled the room as glasses clinked in another toast, but the king's words had left Rhoswen cold. She was startled from her distraction by a waitman, who proffered a thin pair of white gloves to her over her right shoulder. Confused, she slid the garments up to her wrists and watched as her neighbors began picking delicately at the blossoms before them. She tugged a petal from her own flower with her forefinger and thumb and nibbled at its base, as others did. She continued to chew closer to the curled end, when the tip began unfurling itself away from her. She pulled the petal from her mouth in surprise. "Is this active, too?" she asked.

Gethin sneered. "The Realm Water is a chemical reaction, Cousin. Liquids do not live. This is a plant. Plants *do*."

Rhoswen nearly dropped the petal back onto her plate, her shock further diminishing her tenuous grasp of decorum. She looked down at the withering flower. "So, what is this gelatinous sphere? Its brain?" Around her, guests were dipping the base of their petals into the balls of clear gel, which broke and oozed thickly across their plates. Gethin sneered at her and laughed. She clenched at the napkin in her lap to stop herself from recoiling.

The prince's laughter seemed to catch everyone in the vicinity off guard—except for the woman in green. She flashed the prince a brilliant smile. The guests eased themselves back into hushed conversation. Rhoswen glanced at her brother, but he was grinning at the lovely woman in green, who paid him no mind.

"An intriguing thought, Cousin Rhoswen—very good," Gethin praised her slimily. "But I must disappoint you; the gel is merely nectar from the flower itself. Flowers lack brains—and your cleverness."

Rhoswen did not feel clever. "How is it still... alive?" She almost couldn't get the question out.

"Aethelia are rare not only because they grow solely in the Aethelburh countrylands but because they are also eaten by nearly every wild animal that happens upon them. In the wild, if the flowers are disturbed, poisoned nectar is released to cover the petals, and the tips unfurl to be coated, as well. But the flower must be alive to release the toxin. Aethelia can survive for a substantial period of time after dismemberment." Gethin smirked. "Of course, these blooms have been specially prepared for our consumption, so the nectar stays in the center until you eat it."

"But the nectar is poisonous?" Rhoswen confirmed.

Gethin smiled and nodded.

"And you're feeding this to your guests?" Thane asked, placing a petal back onto his plate.

Gethin's smirk remained. "Of course. The Aethelia's poison is so weak that it does little to protect the flowers from anything larger than a rabbit. They are so readily eaten that their numbers would probably near extinction if they didn't spread like wildfire. It's a delicate balance."

Rhoswen did not know whether to believe her cousin and eat the flower or feign illness and excuse herself for the night. She glanced down at the other end of the table. The head Riders did not appear to be partaking in the dessert. She swallowed uneasily.

Gethin ignored her obvious discomfort. "Allow me," he said and demonstratively touched the curl of a petal to the nectar ball in the center of his flower. It unfurled into the delicate gel, which broke open into a puddle. He bit off the pointy end and dipped the petal in the gel a second time before consuming the rest of it. His eyes lit up as he swallowed the second half. "It is a marvelous sensation. Try it."

Rhoswen did not like the sound of that, but their conversation had attracted some attention, and she did not wish to appear impolite at the king's table. She did as her cousin had, dipping the point into the gel. When it hit her tongue, it immediately set her taste buds aflame with a numbing fire. The sugary coating melted on contact and left a sweet finish in her throat like burnt sugar. Desensitized by the rush, her empty mouth grew cold and lifeless. The remainder of the petal began to gray in her hand.

Gethin watched the hues muddy with a sickening grin. "Most people start with the base of the petal. Once the point is detached, it begins to die, so you have to eat it quickly—if you want it fresh, that is."

You mean alive, Rhoswen realized. Her gums grew numb, and her tongue felt like it was made of cloth. "What does it matter?" she managed to ask, astonished by her ability to form words with a fabric tongue. "My mouth feels deathly already."

"Exactly." Gethin smiled.

Rhoswen's eyebrows had begun to crease when the sensation in her mouth changed again: the numbness dissipated, leaving her flesh feeling light and alive. She could taste flowers, sugar, warmth; even the air she inhaled in a gasp of surprise was palatable: it tasted of the meat and stringy vegetables from dinner—although she could no longer smell either in the room—and hung heavy with the perfume of the woman in green. Her eyes popped wide.

She turned to her cousin, remembering his almost immediate reaction. "You experienced that sooner than I did," she said.

"I did not." Gethin's eyebrows fell flat to match the line of his fading grin.

He's serious, Rhoswen realized. Her eyes returned to her discolored flower petal, and her stomach flipped. It was not the bright, vivid rush that had awakened the prince's senses but the dull sensation of mortality he'd relished.

No one else seemed bothered by the deathly feeling that preceded the bright and lively one, and Rhoswen realized that nibbling the petal from the base must preclude the negative sensation altogether. She glared at her cousin.

Thane had not picked up a petal again. His brows knitted in concern. *Do I dare?* his eyes asked. Rhoswen could not politely convey to him the proper way to eat the dessert, so she just shrugged. It had not killed her—*yet.* With a fleeting glance at the oblivious lady in green, he grabbed up a petal and dipped the tip into the gel as Gethin had.

Rhoswen smothered a laugh. Thane's bug-eyed expression as he chewed resembled a man possessed. As she watched her brother, a papery feeling coated her mouth, and she wondered if she should take another bite—properly this time—to try to clear it out. *What if that makes it worse?*

She glanced unhappily down the table to see if the Darrs had made any more headway with their flowers—and she met the eager eyes of Darr Beval. She almost looked away again, but he picked up his goblet of pale-green liquid and lifted it to her, his gaze intent. He wanted her to follow suit. She raised her own goblet in return and took a sip. The herbal liquid flooded her mouth with a taste she could only describe as "green." It was refreshing—and *cleansing*: all the strange tastes and sensations left her mouth as she swallowed. She turned a grateful smile on him, and he nodded, replacing his goblet on the table.

Next to him, the king observed their exchange with an unpleasant expression. Rhoswen looked down at her plate, her relief quashed by her uncle's threatening attention. With her appetite now completely diminished, she slipped off her gloves. Gethin made no comment at her surrender.

Dessert took almost as long as dinner. The guests savored each oral reincarnation as if it were their first encounter with the plant. It was the quietest Rhoswen had seen the woman in pink, who closed her eyes and puckered her lips with every bite. Thane managed to finish an entire petal, but he, too, appeared overwhelmed by the experience and removed his gloves.

Rhoswen gestured to the green liquid in front of him and smiled as his shoulders dropped from their hunch after his first sip.

When the mostly apetalous plates were replaced by thin, glass flutes of unanimated dessert wine, all attention shifted to Allistair's kin and their "secret visit." Gethin yawned as the woman in pink fixated on why the Stanburhs' coming had not been announced by the king; the rest seemed more intent on grilling the siblings about their father and what had occupied him since leaving Keaton. The pair gave vague answers about raising children and protecting Stanburh from the Narxon. Every detail was scrutinized and judged, birthing only more inquiries.

As questions began repeating and answers were shouted down to the far end of the table—mostly by the woman in pink, who had appointed herself their go-between—King Badrick stood. Everyone lurched to their feet, chairs scraping and conversations ceasing.

The king held up a hand. "You'll excuse me once again, my honored guests. I grow prematurely weary this night and fear I must retire before you. Do be seated. Enjoy your wine and your company. Gethin will act as suitable host in my stead." With a flourish of his grand, swirling cape, he left as abruptly as he had arrived. Rhoswen wished she could do likewise.

Clearly ill-at-ease with his father's abandonment and his newly appointed status as grand host to the aristocracy, Gethin remained silent, shifting in his seat and watching his guests' glasses like a hawk. As soon as the last one emptied, the prince pronounced the dinner a success and ended the evening with gracious and seemingly genuine appreciation for his guests' attendance. It was far more tactful behavior than Rhoswen would have expected from her cousin. The woman in green smiled demurely at the Stanburhs and the prince before stepping aside to allow her neighbor in pink to approach them. Red curls bouncing, the woman grasped Rhoswen's elbow and exclaimed, at length, what a pleasure it had been to spend an evening with the extended royal family. Eventually, Gethin shot her a look that could have made the dye in her dress run, and she bid them all a hasty goodnight.

Trapped by their location in the dining hall, the Stanburhs had little choice but to assist the prince in seeing the guests out. Rhoswen craned her neck to search for Darr Beval. She had hoped to thank him for his assistance during dessert. Her eyes finally locked on his golden hair. He and Darr Thorndon were surrounded by the other Riders, who moved in a tight group toward the doors. A few Darrs nodded at the prince in weak appreciation as the rest laughed at something one of the head Riders had said. It was the first time any of them had expressed delight all evening. At the main entrance, they turned in the direction of the drakiary and disappeared into the night. Rhoswen frowned. She would have to thank him later.

As soon as the doors closed on the final guests, Gethin escorted his cousins back to their rooms. Rhoswen half expected him to return Thane to his room first so he could plague her with more questions about Deowynn. Surprisingly, however, either due to some residual decorum or exhausted indifference, the two young gentlemen saw Rhoswen to her chambers first.

Although she did not particularly wish to part from Thane after such an evening, Rhoswen was grateful to be away from everyone else. She wasted no time in removing the dress and dismissing her waiting-women. Alone, in her nightgown, she stood for a moment, soaking in the blissful quiet. But she was too wound up to sleep. She shimmied back into her leathers and moved toward the door to visit Thane. As she reached for the handle, she heard a faint knock on the opposite side and someone begging entrance in a theatrical whisper.

"What are you doing in your leathers?" Thane asked as he entered the room. He still wore his dress pants and shirt, but he had left his jacket behind.

"Coming to see you," Rhoswen replied, scanning the hall and latching the door.

"I already looked." Thane threw himself onto her bed.

"It doesn't hurt to double check."

"You may not be wrong." He looked exhausted. "What a dinner! I wouldn't be surprised if they torture us in our sleep, too."

Rhoswen leaned against the tall post at the foot of her bed. It was carved to resemble the scales of dragon hide but held none of the creatures' comforting warmth. "I don't think we're important enough for them to bother," she said, her fingers tracing the detailed etching.

"What do you mean?"

"You heard them tonight. No one knew we were coming. *Guests of honor!* The King hid our visit until our presence made it impossible to do so. His speech after dinner barely explained our anonymous attendance at the far end of the table, and the guests were shocked. This is clearly unusual behavior." She swung herself around the bedpost and sat beside her brother. "What have we walked into?"

Thane's eyebrows furrowed as his sister spoke. "I'm not sure. But we're public knowledge now. They can't do anything to us and think it would go unnoticed."

"No one at *that* table would protest."

"Except the Darrs," Thane corrected.

"Except the Darrs," she agreed. "I couldn't possibly sleep now."

A smile crept across Thane's lips, as though his cheek muscles knew better than to grin but failed to resist. "Then let's go on a tour of our own," he suggested.

Gethin strode into his father's chambers without waiting for Delwyn to show him in. The waitman blustered helplessly behind the prince, but Badrick dismissed him before he could formulate coherent apologies.

Gethin was breathing hard. He had leapt up the stairs in twos, eager to reprimand his father for his early exit. Despite having changed into his dressing gown, the king looked just as formidable as he had in his cape. Gethin ignored the knot mangling his stomach and pushed his anger forward.

"Why did you abandon me at dinner tonight?" When no answer escaped the gloom, Gethin filled the void. "Did you have something better to do than hosting your own guests? Or perhaps you simply found it amusing to leave them with your undertrained son—a circumstance for which you are also to blame!"

Badrick's guttural intake of breath sounded like a growl. "*Perhaps*," he replied, "you could suggest how one should train the untrainable."

"You're the first to say I am too much like you, Father; if I am not trainable, who better than you to understand my plight?" Gethin declared, his voice stronger than he had expected.

"I *understand* one needs a brain to interpret instruction, Gethin," Badrick sneered. "I left to show my disinterest in our familial guests."

Gethin rolled his eyes, wondering as he did if it were dark enough to conceal the insolent gesture. His tongue did not exhibit such caution. "Idiocy. Dismissing their importance only made them more tantalizing fare for those shallow gossips."

The whites of Badrick's eyes flashed as he emerged from the darkness in one great stride to stand nose-to-nose with his son. "The only *idiot* here is the one calling the *king* an idiot." Gethin could still smell the Aethelia nectar on his father's breath: tangy, sweet, and ending in a dull note of rot. Gethin generally savored that last bit, but it lost some of its charm under these circumstances. "Those aristocratic nincompoops cannot remember anything that does not have a masquerade preceding it. No pomp? No circumstance. If I don't care, they will not bother to care either."

Gethin's breathing grew shallow as his father stood a nose-length away from his face. "And what do we gain from my cousins' professed insignificance?" Gethin asked, his voice thin.

Badrick exhaled his impatience and turned away from his son. The prince's tensed shoulders dropped a fraction. "We could not hide them forever," the king explained. "Eventually, word would get out once they began training. And if they have any of their parents' aptitude for Riding, word will travel quickly. By minimizing their presence now, whatever filters out to the masses will seem less wonderful."

"Like the fact that she had an audience with the queen dragon today?"

His father's eyes widened. Clearly, he had not overheard their conversation at dinner.

"Why would Deowynn have allowed such a thing? That beast doesn't want to see anyone—even me, and I am Orla's son," Gethin added unnecessarily.

Badrick paced in the dim light, and the pale flesh of his exposed face flashed in and out of sight. "Like Orla, the Stanburhs harbor a detestable streak of morality—much more than *you* do," he added as Gethin began to protest his lineage once more. "Your uncle and aunt have always been meddlesome; their *conscience* seems to supersede all sense in complex matters. I cannot imagine their offspring would be any different. If your cousins discovered my plan to save this realm from Movement, they would feel some insidious need to tell their parents, and then we would have the *four* of them to deal with." He mumbled something else that Gethin could not catch.

"What *is* your plan, Father?" the prince coaxed. "You said my lessons would begin today, so tell me."

In a rare act of agreeableness, Badrick nodded. "The only way to maintain my rule over this realm is to deny Deowynn the Realm Portal object that she needs to Move to the next."

"You have it?" Gethin asked, wide-eyed. Few in D'Erenelle even knew what shape the object took.

"I do. And my brother would happily liberate it from my care if he knew my intentions."

"Where is it?"

Badrick shot his son a practiced glare that implied Gethin's stupidity. "As if I would tell you."

The prince had expected that look *and* that answer. "How do we know that is all it takes, hiding the portal? Do you think you're the first to consider such action?"

"Well, we would have no way of knowing, would we? If it proved successful in another realm, the Riders would not have Moved to tell the tale. Their histories would not have traveled with them to the next realm—to ours, had D'Erenelle been next in line." Badrick's almost imperceptible patience was wearing ever thinner. Gethin bit his tongue.

"Deowynn cannot initiate the Movement without the Realm Portal in her possession," Badrick continued. "That is why it does not matter if Blaxton—*or any other realmed beast*—flies her. Pregnant or no, she knows she cannot Move without the ring. Therefore, it is unlikely that she will even bother to conceive."

Gethin nodded. Badrick may not have told his son where the Realm Portal object was hidden, but he had just divulged that it was a ring. "But all would not be lost if your plan failed, Father. I could Move with the other Riders, regardless of the verdict here in D'Erenelle. Our line would continue."

"*Realm* our line, you moronic twit! *I* am king, and *I* cannot leave here. I will not give up D'Erenelle because of your mother's choices, and I'll be *realmed* if I fall prey to a bunch of soulless, life-sucking portal beasts for her!"

Gethin shuddered, whether from the mention of the Narxon, his father's icy selfishness, or the cryptic comment about his mother's "choices." "She did not choose to die," he murmured.

Badrick froze but said nothing.

Anger helped Gethin find his voice again. "And what about after *you* die?" he asked more harshly than he had intended. "Of natural causes, surely," he added.

Badrick composed himself. "Do whatever you like. You are my successor. When you are king, you are more than welcome to hand the Realm Portal object back over to the dragons and have your life force sucked slowly and painfully from your body. I do not care. Now get out."

IX

Tendalar

"No."

Emile frowned. "Jerold, you don't understand what a mess that could create." The partygoers' volume increased as more of them congregated in the final clearing for the champagne toast. He tried to edge Jerold farther into the woods, but his nephew wasn't budging—physically or mentally.

"The answer is no," Jerold repeated for the fourth time, his feet planted. "I've effectively just lost a father. I'm not losing what's left of the only family I've ever known—regardless of how annoying they can be—by being declared dead in Welsamar."

"One might argue that you have just *gained* a father," Emile quipped, but Jerold was unamused. Emile sighed. "Stay alive for the family, then. But don't come back to Welsamar with your dragon after you start Running. Just sneak in, say hello, and sneak out. It's not like the green could fit in your mother's kitchen anyway."

"No," Jerold replied. "I'm not going anywhere without Kip."

"What if you're recognized by someone from the Exchange as you sneak back into Welsamar? They would know you as a Runner. Runners don't have dragons." Emile raised an eyebrow. "Or were you planning to grow a mustache between each visit as a disguise?"

Jerold rolled his eyes. "That my mother was a Runner and never told me is a wonder. But she has never befriended a discreet person in her life, and I don't expect her to now. If I were declared dead and her friends happened to stumble upon me as I snuck in and out of this realm, the rest of Welsamar would know I was alive by the following morning. I would be realmed either way."

"So, you can see my wariness on all fronts," Emile replied.

"You're the one who wants me to live a double life. Surely, you've put more thought into it than this," Jerold said.

Emile's fingers tapped on the head of his cane. "Well, you've certainly made the mustache idea obsolete.... All right. I'll find some way to leave your picture off your shrine."

"My shrine?" Jerold asked in mounting concern.

"The death shrine they'll create in the Exchange for you," Emile replied with a dismissive wave. "Here's how we'll play it: as far as our family knows, you will be reassigned to a remote region of Welsamar—Sullinar perhaps—and you'll come home—*with Kip*—for the holidays whenever possible. But in the Exchange, Jerold Illisan will be dead. I'll make it valiant... a Narxon Descent gone awry. You'll need a new name as a Runner—no one can know our connection." He looked around them at the green foliage. "How about Denver?"

"Just one name?"

"How many could you possibly want?"

"But Riders only use one name," Jerold replied, "with their title."

Emile nodded. "And you're going to live and Ride in D'Erenelle. Anyway, no one in the club is on a last-name basis, but they may ask where you're from. Denver is also a name in another realm, so if anyone asks, tell them you're French. The accents are close enough."

"Frrriiinch?" Jerold asked, mangling the foreign word. "And if they ask in D'Erenelle?"

Emile's fingers rapped on his cane again as he considered an answer. "Just try not to speak too much."

Jerold did not find the humor in his uncle's suggestion. "How would I return for holidays?" he asked.

"I would give you a special key, like this." Emile switched his cane to his other hand and pulled his own key from his vest pocket, where it was attached to the watch chain. "You'll need a modified one anyway if we want to be sure your dragon can come through."

"We want to be sure of that," Jerold replied. His eyes grew unfocused, and his stony features barely shifted as he considered his uncle's offer.

Emile struggled to read the expression, and for a moment, he wondered if his nephew would bite. Were he Jerold's age and newly tethered, the thrill of Riding for another realm and—let's face it—getting away from the family would have had his palm outstretched for that key before he could give it a second thought. But Jerold had already expressed his unwillingness to give up his family through the ruse Emile had devised. *He wants to come home for the holidays,* he reminded himself with a grimace.

A single voice emanated from the champagne area. Emile could tell from its cadence that the final toasts were underway. Traditionally, he and Jerold would each be expected to make one as uncle and brother to the new parents, but neither headed back toward the party.

Finally, Jerold looked up. "When will I start?"

Emile eased his breath through his nose to mask his relief and shifted his fingers to display a second key on the chain. "How about now?"

X

Aethelburh

Oil lamps in hand, Rhoswen and Thane traversed the dark, abandoned halls of the castle. The sconces along the walls had been clamped low after the dinner party, and the pair had grabbed lamps from their own chambers to help light their way. They kept their fingers near the knobs to close them at a moment's notice, but no one seemed to be around to catch them wandering.

A spiral staircase traversed each of the castle's six turrets. When they located one that went below ground, they padded downward until they stepped into a hall of doors at the bottom.

"Where are we?" Rhoswen whispered. Gethin hadn't bothered to take them below ground level in the castle.

"The cellar?" Thane suggested. He turned up his lamp and held it out before him as he rounded the circle of doors. "Shall we go in?"

"To which one?" she asked.

Thane turned back to her, and even in the dim light, she could see he was excited. "Let's split up."

"No," she hissed.

Thane held a finger to his lips. "Rose, who would be down here at this hour? We haven't run into a soul."

"Anyone. Spies."

Thane smirked. "I doubt that."

Rhoswen stamped her foot in protest and immediately regretted how childish it made her feel. She tried to smooth her voice so it would sound more adult and authoritative. "Something could happen, and we would have no way of contacting each other."

"I know what our parents told us, Rose, but I've seen little more threat than our family's inhospitality." Thane went to the nearest door and pulled at it. It hardly budged. He set down his lamp and yanked on the curved, vertical handle with both hands until a single person could slip through. "These doors are heavy. We'll leave them open, and we won't go far into the rooms. That way, we can call out if we need to." He picked up his lamp and disappeared inside before she could protest.

Rhoswen screwed up her face in dissatisfaction. Leaving doors open would create a trail that led directly to them, and yelling out in the middle of the night seemed like an equally terrible idea. She stared at the door. Following him would only incite a noisy argument. She sighed.

Something told her to go three doors to the left. She pulled on the handle, but it wouldn't budge. After setting her lamp out of harm's way, she placed a foot against the wall and yanked hard. The door flew open—rather than being heavy, it had simply been wedged in the frame—and Rhoswen careened backwards, clinging to the door handle as she tried to catch herself. When both feet were steady on the floor again, she let go of the door and gathered up her lamp. Her heart thudded in her chest as she eyed the threshold of the dark room and crossed over it alone.

Only somewhat anticlimactically, Thane found himself in a larder. He held out his lamp to survey the room. It was so tightly packed with food that he could barely discern a path through the bags, barrels, and crates. *This could come in handy,* he thought with a smirk. Wading in past the sacks of flour and meal, he neared the far side of the room, where he could make out open archways into other sections of storage. After the baking goods came meats and cheeses, a gargantuan and well-stocked wine cellar, and floor-to-ceiling shelves of jarred produce. One wall still had room for more stock: the summer was running long, and some late-harvest vegetables had not yet come in season.

Loud, clacking footsteps approached in the hallway outside. During the day, the halls rang with these metallic clanks: the king had outfitted all his waitstaff with metal-soled shoes so they could be heard coming and going at all times. Gethin had explained that it allowed for more privacy—a warning of intrusion if they were discussing something confidential—but Rhoswen saw it as a symptom of their uncle's controlling paranoia. Thane had to agree with her.

He shut the lamp and dropped to his knees, feeling like a child who had snuck into a cupboard to hunt for sweets. He slid behind two upright barrels stacked high with wheels of cheese. As the clanking drew nearer, he thought he could discern *two* sets of footsteps. He peered around the barrel but saw no one in the darkness; they had clearly stayed in the front area of the larder with the baking goods. Muffled voices barked out ingredients to each other as they were accounted for and lugged toward the door. *Don't need cheese,* he prayed.

One pair of footsteps drew closer, and Thane scooted deeper into the maze of ornately wrapped wheels and blocks. Fragrant wedges covered in cornflower blue cloth were piled beside hunks in purple-brown burlap that smelled strongly of feet. He pressed the back of his hand to his nose and ducked down behind them.

A gap in the stack caught his attention. He pried it wider for a better look, and the wedge at the top of the pile wobbled dangerously on its round edge. He froze. When it finally stilled, he peeked through the gap, and his eyes landed on the oil lamp he had left behind. His heart flew into his mouth.

A crown of dark-brown hair under a chef's hat came into view through the gap. Thane barely breathed. The cook grumbled as he rummaged around, drawing nearer with every step. Now, Thane could smell him—a feat, considering his proximity to the overpowering cheese. The man reeked of the Dancing Wine everyone had enjoyed with dinner. Thane was shocked and amused by the cook's impudence, and he hoped, for the sake of all the staff, that King Badrick never found out.

The man picked through the wedges nearby as someone might a trash heap and plucked a sapphire-wrapped block from the gaudy assortment. He lifted it to his nose and screwed up his face, almost dropping it. He was still sputtering curses when he exchanged the hunk for another wrapped in bright-orange cloth. This one passed the sniff test. As he turned to leave, the other man who had been helping him appeared once more in the doorway.

"Done yet?" he asked. He wore the drab livery of a waitman. Thane recognized him as the one who had summoned Gethin away upon their arrival. He was grumbling about how this was not his job when his eyes fell on the abandoned lamp. Thane held his breath. The waitman glanced at the cook. "Did you leave this here?"

The cook peered at the lamp and shook his head. "Mine's outside the door."

"What's this, then?" the waitman asked. "If this had been burning, the whole place could have gone up in flames!"

The cook shrugged. "Help me lift this last bag of flour."

The waitman took to griping again and moved the lamp outside the door of the larder before returning to help. After much uncoordinated struggling and cursing, the pair managed to hoist the sack out of the room, their shoes clacking heavily on the stone floor. Finally, the door closed behind them, and the room fell to darkness.

Thane exhaled and cursed himself for the loss of his lamp. How would he find Rhoswen now? *What if she has already been found?*

He stood and stretched his hands out ahead of him as he groped his way back toward the door. He knocked over a crate of something lumpy and stubbed his toe on a fallen sack of sugar, but his fingers finally collided with the wooden surface.

He peeked out to find an empty hall, but his progress was halted when his foot landed on something small and unyielding. A nearby wall sconce identified it as a bracelet; on it hung a metal key with a sun-like array of bits. He slid the jewelry into his pocket and looked down the hall to where another door stood ajar. Thane chided himself for not waiting long enough to find out whether this had been the room his sister had selected. It was pitch black inside. With another muttered curse, he slipped through the crack and into the darkness beyond.

Rhoswen held her oil lamp out before her and made her way down a narrow hallway. It opened onto a small library. Every wall was covered with books. She moved toward the shelves, her fingers trailing on the spines as she inspected them. This section held the classics—complete with books she had seen on her own parents' shelves: *Wanderer the Realm*, *Riders through the Ages*, and *From Those Outlying*. Rhoswen recognized the mottled dark-brown binding of the epic poem, *The Darrs Evernelle*, and the smooth navy cover of *An Index of Realms: Judged and Unjudged* with its hyper-italicized silver title sprawling the spine. She had never read it, but the name suddenly struck her as hyperbolic—the only unjudged realm it could possibly list would be D'Erenelle… *right?* The urge to slide the tome from the shelf and verify her hypothesis gripped her, but she could do that in the daylight, when poking around the castle might seem less like snooping.

As she surveyed titles, her hand grasped at the outside edge of the cabinet for stability—and found none. The floor-to-ceiling shelving full of leatherbound tomes began pulling away from the wall. She scrambled backward, prepared for the whole cabinet of books to rain down on her, but when it didn't topple over, she stepped forward again and tugged on the outer edge of the shelf. As if it weighed nothing, the wall of spines swung outward to reveal hinges at the far corner and yet another wall of book-lined shelving behind it.

She set her lamp on the table in the center of the room and turned up the flame. With the first wall of books pulled out of her way, she tugged at the wall behind it and dragged it out from a third. This last wall was immobile but just as full as the others before it.

She eyed the layers, her mind reeling. These numerous texts had been compiled through the ages by Realm Riders and historians alike. She glanced around at the other walls. *How many layers were in this place? How many* books*?*

As she escorted the walls back into place, her gaze fell on unfamiliar symbols on the spines at eye level. Titles on the shelf seemed to alternate between a recognizable language and an inscrutable one, and the bindings of every two books were matched in color and style: pairs of blue sat beside pairs of brown beside pairs of tan. Although not always perfect, the attempt at coordination was unmistakable. *They are translations of each other.*

She closed the walls and made her way around the room, checking for more layers. The adjacent walls also had three sets of shelves stacked along them, but the wall opposite the first did not budge. Ironically, she found herself more surprised by its *lack* of layers and searched for something to explain its normalcy. A glaringly empty section of one shelf—the only barren spot in the whole room—caught her eye. She examined the books beside the gap to try to guess what was missing and noticed dust on the wood. Nothing had disturbed this space in some time—including the cleaning staff.

Rhoswen reached for the volume nearest the gap, and as she tipped the spine forward, she heard a soft *click*. She drew her hand back in surprise and gawked. The book remained tipped out at a forward angle. *That's not possible,* she thought.

She tugged at the askew spine and felt the shelf shift into motion, as if that book were drawing out the entire wall with it. She eased the shelving outward and watched as the dark shadow of a gap grew at a break in the middle of the wall. Soon, she had exposed not another layer of books but an opening into darkness behind the shelves. *Another room?* With one final glance into the layered library, she grabbed up her lamp and slipped inside.

This smaller room was lined with old, rickety shelves piled with long rolls of parchment. Upright barrels held more of the same, the rolls poking out at all angles. The center of the room held a large table with mismatched paperweights, a magnifying glass, an inkwell, and a pointy metal object that was hinged in the middle and had needle-like points at the end of each arm. Rhoswen had never seen such an instrument before. Lifting it in her hands, she then pulled both arms away from each other, widening the angle between them. She placed the thing back on the table and moved toward a shelf. Her toe knocked into a barrel on the floor. She selected a long scroll from its wide mouth and took it to the table.

The roll contained several sheets of parchment. After a struggle with paperweights and curling corners, she forced the stack open. As she smoothed out the bottom-left corner to put the final weight in place, her fingers brushed over a familiar symbol.

Rhoswen reached into her pocket and pulled out the compass her father had given her. It matched the compass rose at the bottom of the maps perfectly. The curling arms, the four ornate letters marking each cardinal direction, the queen dragon—*everything* was the same.

The map displayed a floorplan, and the faded names that labeled each room were scrawled in the same cursive as her compass. The script was so old and elaborate that the words were almost inscrutable.

As she searched for an intelligible name, Rhoswen's eyes landed on a room with layered walls. Three layers on each—except one. She parsed out the words "Overflow Library" at its center. This was a map of the cellar. She traced her fingers down the hall from the layered library to the small foyer of many doors, where she and her brother had parted. She located the room Thane had chosen: "Larder." *Of course,* she thought with a smirk, *Thane will have lost himself in there.*

Now, with more than a dozen identifiable letters at her disposal, she lifted up the paperweights on one side of the map and flipped through the parchment sheets beneath. She found the Great Hall and Dining Hall, guest rooms, and royal quarters.... This set of maps comprised Castle Aethelburh's entire floorplan.

She replaced the paperweights and looked back to the outline of the layered library, to where this secret maps room ought to be. Although no room was denoted on the map, three small dots, like an ellipsis, floated in the empty space beside the library. Other than that tiny and easily overlooked symbol, the map suggested that the hidden room beyond the library did not exist at all. *Why would someone hide maps away like contraband?*

Rhoswen's skin crawled with uneasiness, and her mind raced toward her absent brother. *How long have we been at this? Is he still exploring the larder? Could he have been discovered?* She steadied herself before her thoughts could grow darker. *Has he simply found something worth eating?*

The dark hallway Thane had entered made an abrupt turn to the right, as evidenced by the wall he walked into. He padded on soundlessly through the darkness, his fingers now trailing the wall beside him. Some yards ahead, the sound of a cabinet closing alerted him to another's presence. He took one more step forward before realizing it might not be Rhoswen. With nowhere to hide, he turned to go back the way he had come, but the hallway brightened with the light of a lantern, and someone's throat cleared behind him. "Out for a bit of a late-night stroll, are we?"

Thane recognized that throaty accent immediately. He did not know whether to be relieved or mortified. He turned to face the voice. "Darr Thorndon. I—"

The Realm Rider chuckled. "Couldn't sleep, right?"

"You could say that."

"Not surprised after a party like that." He held out his lamp to better illuminate Thane's face and displayed a thick stack of rough leather garments slung over his arm. *This must be the leathers storage,* Thane realized.

"Garb for you and your sister. Can't have the Stanburhs using the communal Keaton sets."

"Yes, you could," Thane protested.

Darr Thorndon flashed him a look like the choice was neither of theirs to make. "You're up terribly late." Thane began to mumble an excuse, and the Rider nodded, his eyebrows pulling together in a look of mock seriousness. He leaned in toward Thane. "A word of caution, young Stanburh: the king has many eyes about this castle, and you would be wise to avoid them outside your chambers this late at night."

Thane nodded, swallowing hard.

Darr Thorndon smiled. "Come. I will escort you back to your room to quell suspicion. Besides, I can leave you with these garments instead of lugging them back to Keaton." He split the pile and handed half to Thane, whose arms buckled a little under the unexpected weight. "I can trust you to give these to your sister, I hope?" It was a rhetorical question, but Thane nodded. "Good. Let's go."

Thane's mind raced as he walked one step behind the Rider in the narrow hallway. Rhoswen was right—they really were being watched. His heartrate increased. Who knew where Rhoswen was? And now, he couldn't look for her. *How can I signal to her that I've been discovered without drawing attention to her?*

After they stepped out into the foyer, Thane gave the door a hard shove, and it slammed shut. Darr Thorndon wheeled on him, and Thane hunched up his shoulders in a wince. "Sorry," he whispered. "Slipped."

The Rider shook his head and motioned Thane up the stairs ahead of him. As they ascended, he prayed his sister had heard the slam and would make her way back to her room on her own. *If she's even still down here,* he thought, wondering if she, too, might have been found. *Perhaps splitting up hadn't been such a good idea,* he admitted, his balance faltering as he reached the main floor.

Darr Thorndon grabbed his arm to steady him. "A bit jumpy tonight," he said. "Good. You should not be out exploring. The king dislikes spies he has not himself employed."

BANG!

A door slammed in the distant hallway, and even behind layers of books in the secret maps room, Rhoswen heard it. She froze, certain her heart was beating as loudly as that door had shut. When no one appeared in the gap in the shelving, she returned the maps to their barrel, grabbed her lamp, and stepped out into the still-vacant library. She closed the shelving behind her with the same soft *click* it had made when opened and padded down the hallway to peek into the empty foyer. Two distant pairs of footsteps were nearing the top of the stairs. One set seemed to trip, briefly halting both before they continued on their way. These were not the clacking shoes of servants. *Had Thane been found?* She dimmed her light and followed them.

At the next floor, Rhoswen looked around for waitstaff before continuing upward. The pair above her headed toward the floor that held her chambers. She followed quickly and soundlessly, hoping to catch a glimpse of them. A nervous misstep halfway up sent her grasping for the wall and juggling her lamp, but she righted herself, took a deep breath, and continued. The other two had made it far enough down the hall not to have heard her stumble (and curse). *Thane would have chided me for that word,* she mused as she peeked around the corner of the stairwell.

Halfway down the hall, Thane and Darr Thorndon stood outside her brother's room with leathers draped over their arms. A wave of relief came over Rhoswen, but she clamped her lamp shut and darted into the alcove in front of the nearest doorway. *If Thane is in trouble,* she thought with a smirk, *he can tell me about the lecture he's getting later.* She peeked around the wall and slipped to the next alcove, listening for a sign that they'd noticed her. As she peered around the stone wall again, she watched Darr Thorndon hand his load to Thane and open the door for him. Thane hobbled into his room, and Rhoswen made a dash for her own chambers. She swung her door open and slipped inside, shutting it behind her without risking a glance across the hall.

She leaned her back against the door, her heart racing, and waited for her breathing to steady. Finally, she relit her lamp and changed into her abandoned nightgown, which had grown chilly on the stone floor. If she had been seen, no one was bothering to confront her. She slid into bed, and her fingers had barely left the switch on the lamp before she fell asleep.

XI

The Exchange

Emile traversed his usual path through the Atrium to the half-moon table he often shared with Olivia. She was easy to spot in her typical monochromatic attire and oversize hat, but he wouldn't have needed to see her to locate his seat; he rarely occupied a different table during his Atrium shifts.

He smiled at Olivia as he leaned his cane against the table, threw the tails of his jacket out behind him, and lowered himself into the seat beside her. He had always found her choice of headwear laughable; it seemed to draw as much attention as it deflected. But the wide brim shadowed her expressive eyebrows that rendered her mute opinions transparent. Their ability to read each other afforded them more privacy than whispering. He had to admit, it was hard to eavesdrop on a wink. Especially a wink obscured by a large hat.

"You're on edge," Olivia noted, her voice low.

Emile gave her a single nod, his own back stiff against the chair's. "The first of my new team starts her doubles today."

"You'll wear them all in," she replied.

"I have no doubt of that," he agreed.

"What then?"

"The old team." He stared at her and widened his eyes.

She waved him off. "They won't pass a word. The Exchange's many levels can occasionally be useful. Why would a Runner convey conspiracy theories about an old Arbiter to a new one?"

"You think that's how it would be interpreted? As baseless conspiracy?"

"Don't you? Arbiters and Runners are kept at such a distance from each other that it would be hard for one to know for certain what the other was doing."

"I suppose it would depend on where the Runner *went*." Emile's head did not move, but his eyes darted to one side in the direction of a table over his shoulder.

Olivia followed his gaze, and her eyes meandered across the Atrium before casually returning to his. "No," she breathed, having identified the red-headed Arbiter he had indicated. Her voice was barely audible. "Your Runners will be reassigned to *her?*"

"At least one will," he replied.

She sighed. "What is it you say? 'Irony is the spice of life?'"

"In this case, I think it's the bitter, charred crumbs one scrapes off burnt toast."

She rolled her eyes. "Is this Runner likely to tell—"

"I have no idea." The thought chilled Emile's spine. He suppressed a shiver that even his friend's huge hat could not possibly have hidden.

Olivia rubbed at a smudge near the wrist of her long white glove. "Well, you will just have to limit what that Runner does before he or she trades teams."

He stared at her.

Her eyes widened in alarm. "It's not *Lorelle…?*"

"Sometimes all the scraping in the realm can't save that piece of toast…."

Olivia tutted. She was the only being Emile had ever known who made a noise that he could genuinely describe as a "tut." "There's no other Runner who could put our plan into motion?"

He shook his head and stared off over her shoulder. She afforded him a moment's contemplation before she cleared her throat. He blinked. "Apologies. Shall we compare notes?"

"After we order." She nodded toward the approaching waiter. Once the man was out of earshot again, Olivia unfurled her napkin and laid it over her lap. "How kind of Turbalen to have us researching Triar activity throughout D'Erenelle," she said with a raised eyebrow.

"It is convenient," Emile agreed, unwrapping his own cutlery. "I only hope it will give us enough notice, so we can tweak things before Turbalen's plans are enacted. What have you learned?"

"It would appear there is no Triar activity in Upwood," she told him.

His eyebrows lifted in surprise. "You're certain?"

"Would I have declared that if I weren't?" Olivia asked, taken aback.

"It's just hard to believe. They were stationed all over northern D'Erenelle. Their presence was like a bad acne outbreak on the forehead of the realm. *None?*"

She shrugged, but a crease between her eyebrows betrayed her displeasure at being questioned. "Not *yet*, I suppose."

"Well, Dallin will be rife with them, given its proximity to Stanburh."

"And its Rider in charge."

Emile waved her off. "Ravinger's a turncoat."

"Not anymore," Olivia insisted. Emile hummed his skepticism, but she ignored him. "What about in Alston?"

"Probably," he said. "It's close to Aethelburh."

"But Lord Alston—"

"Has retired and left his estate in his daughter's care. I don't believe Lady Ethelinda is as tightly aligned with the Pentagraphs as her father—"

"*Still* is," she finished for him.

"It doesn't matter. She has the reins... and a vendetta," he added. "Such a combination always makes for an interesting twist in character."

"So, nothing confirmed in Alston?"

Emile shook his head. "It's too early." He sighed. "It's too early *everywhere.*"

Olivia looked brim-ward. "But the Stanburhs *know*. They've *always* known. Surely they won't wait until the last minute to put out the call."

The waiter returned with their drinks. The staff moved so quickly up and down all those stairs that it was a wonder they weren't constantly winded. *But it certainly does wonders for the glutes,* Emile thought as he watched the man retreat toward the kitchen.

Olivia cleared her throat again.

"My sources can't get close enough to be sure," he said finally.

"I suppose neither can mine," she replied with a shrug. "Maybe the shakeup will help after all. New faces...."

"That's the plan," Emile said. He took a sip of his floral iced tea. It faded from rose to lavender at the bottom of the glass. As a rule, he never stirred it, prefering the gradual change in taste as he drank.

Olivia's eyes swept over his face. He tilted the glass a little more to obscure his expression, little good as that would do. "How did it go with...?" She trailed off, so he could supply whatever name they had selected.

"Denver? Oh, you know how family is," he replied airily, but he didn't want to talk about that here. His voice grew stern. "We're going to need the information about the Triars if we want to act on this, Olivia. If the realm fractions like it did before, Deowynn will Move. And sooner than later."

Olivia's eyebrows crumpled in dismay. "But your theory—"

"Won't hold up against that kind of divisiveness," he interjected.

"We have a lot riding on this, Emile," she reminded him. "What will you do?"

Emile's face went blank. "Whatever I have to."

NARXON are parasites that slip through tears in the fabric of realms to drain the soul, or lifeforce, from everything they touch. As they enter through a tear, in what has come to be termed a "Descent," they take on the form of ink-black, smoky, malformed, adolescent dragons and fall heavily toward the ground. Their maneuverability is limited only by their inability to soar upward.

As the Narxon reach the ground, they stampede across it like a herd, turning everything to ash in their wake. While fast-moving in air and along land, Narxon move fastest through water and are almost impossible to stop once waterborne. Those that are not destroyed before landing must be hunted and irradicated with utmost speed.

With the help of their Riders, dragons must burn the parasites and cauterize the tear to prevent more Narxon from passing through it, lest the realm should be destroyed.

- an excerpt from the *Datist Handbook*

XII

The Exchange

To this day, Emmelyn wondered what would have happened to her if Bernadette, Randy, Kyle, and Vonn—or "the Crew," as she liked to call them—hadn't taken her under their wings. They continued to further her education every time she ran into them. The five of them were not always together, but at least one or two at a time, along with other members of the group she came to know and love.

It turned out Emmelyn's realm knowledge, although off to a good start after she met the Crew on her first Transfer, was still significantly lacking. She spent most of her visits grilling the others about the Realm System and trying to act as casual about it as they did. Whereas they appeared content with their limited contributions to the wellbeing of their realms, she was not so easily placated.

Bernadette had warned her of the many politics behind the Exchange, which had proven a considerable understatement. And, interestingly enough, one could say the same for the politics of the Crew. Unlike Emmelyn's last two visits, this time, the five of them were together again. From what she could tell, Vonn provided all the latest gossip, and Randy consistently disputed whatever "news" Vonn brought to the circle. Kyle liked to play devil's advocate to both, just to stir things up. Bernadette could only struggle to act as peacekeeper.

"I don't believe that fer a second!" Randy drawled emphatically over the thumping bassline. Tonight's music seemed akin to a bluesy version of electronic dance music, which Emmelyn had never before experienced. She couldn't decide whether she ever wanted to again either.

"Now, boys… " Bernadette cautioned in a maternal tone.

Vonn's face was awash with glee; he loved the debate. "It's true!" he insisted. "But there is more than politics changing around here! *Rules* are the driving force behind everything!"

"Don't start that again! The rules don't change *here*!" Randy countered. "The Exchange ain't a realm!"

Emmelyn's face scrunched up at the familiar assertion. "The Exchange isn't a realm?" Had they discussed this on her first visit?

Kyle shook his head. "It's 'realmless.'" He used two fingers from each hand to bend quotation marks around the term.

Bernadette leaned in toward Emmelyn. "Most Exchangers think it's untouchable. Narxon don't enter heah, so no Riduhs or dragons are needed."

"It has its own set uh rules," Randy added with a nod. "Except, unlike the realms, the rules uh the Exchange never change."

"What if we're wrong about that? What if they *do* change?" Vonn protested. "Or what if we've never fully understood the rules here at all?"

"We ain't wrong about the rules," Randy insisted. "The Exchange has been termed a 'non-realm' fer hundreds uh years."

"But what if it's just that? A *term*," Vonn replied. "They haven't figured out the Narxon yet—what if they haven't figured out the Exchange either?"

Randy shook his head. "I don't want to have the rules debate again!"

Bernadette rolled her eyes. "That untouchable feelin' that so many Exchangers have heah has created a...." She searched for the right word.

"Disconnect," Kyle supplied.

She nodded at him and turned back to Emmelyn. "The Datists have it woise than anybody because they nevah leave. Ovuh time, they needed some kind uh diversion from the daily grind uh crunchin' numbahs. So, they created the underground gamblin' ring known as the G'Ambit."

"It's a geeky portmanteau: 'ambit,' as in, the bounds of a place, and 'gambit,' like a calculated move that weighs risk against reward—a *place* to *gamble*, if you will." Kyle accented the explanation with one of his signature eyerolls. Emmelyn was beginning to find his theatrics oddly endearing. Perhaps this punk was more than just some hanger-on that the Crew couldn't shake. "They're sort of synonyms for 'realm' and 'gambling.' Datists love wordplay." Emmelyn thought she saw him mouth the word "nerds" disparagingly under his breath.

"Kyle would know. He's got a Datist goilfriend." Bernadette added a conspiratorial wink.

"She isn't my *girlfriend*," Kyle insisted. "We just date from time to time."

Emmelyn chewed her lip to avoid laughing out loud. She couldn't envision black-clad Kyle dating a hardcore bookworm. (At least, that's how she envisioned Datists; she had never met one in person.)

Bernadette flashed Emmelyn a disbelieving glance. Kyle's expression darkened more than his excessive guyliner, and Emmelyn's struggle for composure continued.

"What ya said before—*that* suggests the Exchange *politics* are splittin' in two," Randy drawled to Vonn. "But no one'd believe the Narxon could be *beneficial* when the realms are *disappearin'*! Where do ya get all this hogwash?"

It amazed Emmelyn that they could hold such discussions in the Exchange. Given the almost cult-like and secretive nature of the place—not to mention the black-jacketed security guards staring everyone down—she imagined a list of topics ruled off-limits. Of course, Exchangers could barely communicate through the blaring music and near darkness, so perhaps such rules seemed superfluous. She'd once asked Bernadette if they could go to a quieter area within the bar to chat, but the dancer had assured her that no such place existed.

Regardless of *what* they were discussing, the real marvel here was that they could *understand* each other. Like the others, Emmelyn had become adept at lip reading—in dim light, no less—but often, she figured everyone just caught bits and pieces of their conversations and knew enough to fill in the blanks.

Emmelyn, however, *did not* know enough to fill in the blanks.

"But that's exactly what they're saying," Vonn called back. "Some Exchangers believe we should let the Narxon destroy all the realms, so the parasites have nothing left to feed on. That way, the Narxon will die out, and the realms could regenerate without further threat of predation."

Emmelyn's jaw dropped open. *What would happen to the inhabitants if the realms were allowed to die out? Had anyone even considered that when they started throwing this idea around? Wouldn't her own realm be in danger of extinction if this were allowed to pass?* She turned to Bernadette, her mouth moving in silent entreaty as words refused to form.

The dancer waved her off. "There's always theories flyin' around this place," she yelled. A flash of light revealed her unperturbed expression.

Emmelyn nodded as Randy and Vonn continued refuting each other's arguments. Perhaps this was nothing more than watercooler chit chat. She looked down at the four—*now two*—stamps disappearing from her wrist. Almost time to find Lorelle and leave the Exchange. She and her Runner had learned where they each liked to hang out in the club, so they had little trouble finding each other. While Emmelyn appreciated having the extra time with the Crew, she wasn't used to this much waiting. She had performed Transfers a few times now, all with no more than two stamps on her wrist, but today marked her first double delivery, so she wanted the extra time after meeting with Lorelle to get the second half right.

"That's not how it woiks," Bernadette yelled, leaning across the narrow coffee table to get closer to Emmelyn's orange-plugged ear. "By the time yuh Runnah shows up, yuh'll always be down tuh one stamp or less."

"What happens if I don't have enough time to finish my double?" Emmelyn had no desire to find out from personal experience.

"You will." Kyle waved to someone behind her—presumably his

Runner. "The second half doesn't take long." He hollered goodbye and disappeared from the circle.

"Are you sure?" Emmelyn asked Bernadette.

The dancer waved away the concerns once more. Today, she was wearing a flapper dress made entirely of tassels, which danced with her every move. "It's easy, hun. We do those every time. Ya just go ovah tuh the othuh side when yuh done with Lorelle heah."

"The restaurant side?"

Bernadette giggled. "So *you* call it. It's the Arbituhs' side. They call it the Atrium. I hear it's really somethin' ovah there."

"Why?"

"Yuh'll see."

Bernadette wasn't usually coy, but she was smiling, so Emmelyn figured whatever it was had to be safe. "How do I know whom to give it to?" she asked.

"Lorelle'll give ya the name of 'er Arbituh."

Emmelyn nodded.

On her second visit to the Exchange, the chain of information had been explained to her like this: Runners collect data in their realms to give to Transfers (in the club), who pass that data along to the Arbiters (in the Atrium). Then, Arbiters give that data to the Datists. The Datists, or "nerdy number crunchers," as Kyle often called them, process all that data to create some sort of report for their superiors to sift through. The superiors make the final decisions on tweaks the Runners will make and pass down their orders to the Arbiters to give to the Transfers to give to the Runners, and the whole process starts over again.

"What are the people above the Datists and Arbiters called again?" Emmelyn asked.

"Universals," Bernadette replied with a Kyle-like eyeroll, but it was not meant for Emmelyn. "It's such a grandiose title. We all just refuh tuh them as Ivuhs."

"And the Ivers make all the big decisions?" Emmelyn asked.

"The Ivers are primarily to blame fer all this unrest in the G'Ambit!" Randy interjected, having somehow overheard their conversation. Vonn instantly argued against the sentiment, and off they went again.

Emmelyn smiled at Bernadette and tried to circle back to their previous conversation. "You were explaining the G'Ambit," she glanced at the empty spot on the couch, "before Kyle got defensive when you mentioned his girlfriend."

Bernadette laughed. "Right. Being a Datist is hard. They woik long hours, and they sift through endless amounts uh data. The suicide rate was gettin' stahtlingly high. That's when the gamblin' stahted up. All that knowledge.... Datists would bet each othuh on what moves the Ivuhs would make next or what would happen in a realm aftuh a Runnah carried out his or her ordahs. It wasn't long befoah Arbituhs were eager tuh get in on the bettin', so Datists took up positions as bookies, and the G'Ambit was born."

"But didn't you say it was illegal?" Emmelyn asked, glancing around again for Lorelle.

"It is," Bernadette replied with a nod. "Those guys in the black jackets who stopped ya on yuh way outta heah that foist time? They're called Administratuhs. Ministuhs for short. They're technically patrollin' tuh intercept G'Ambit activity, but it's not all black and white."

"Not even close!" Randy interjected, listening in again. "The *biggest problem—*" and here, he stole an argumentative glance at Vonn, "—is how the Arbiters meddle to get a better payout. If the Ministers are after anyone, it's the rotten Arbiters skewin' the G'Ambit, not the Datists gamblin' all their hard-earned cash away."

Emmelyn's expression betrayed her confusion. *If the Ministers were after the Arbiters, why weren't they in the Atrium...?*

Vonn smiled at her and held up a finger to Randy as if to say they would be discussing that further after he explained something to the new kid. "The gambling that the Datists do isn't all bad," he explained. "Not only is it a way of reducing stress—suicides and depression have decreased sharply since the advent of the G'Ambit—but sometimes, the Datists will find patterns or have breakthroughs that they simply couldn't have managed, mired and overworked at their desks." He pointed downwards. "The Datists used to work in cubicles in the basement of the Exchange. When the Exchange started losing them to the stress, they built on an airy top floor entirely of windows—like the Atri—"

Bernadette shushed him. "Don't ruin it fuh her!" she screeched.

Vonn threw up his palms in apology. "Anyway, the basement was relegated exclusively to storage after that, but the bright, new conditions upstairs simply weren't enough.... The G'Ambit soon followed."

"I'll admit, it ain't somethin' the Ivers can just shut down," Randy added. "The Arbiters' only job in the Atrium is to pass messages through Transitors, so it's impossible to catch 'em gamblin' there. Instead, they brought in the Ministers and tasked 'em with findin' the gamblers in the club. Then, they follow the chain uh bets all the way up to the Arbiters who manipulate the G'Ambit to their advantage—and often to the *disadvantage* uh the realms. 'Course, it's easy to say ya can't fix a problem when you're turnin' a blind eye to it...."

Vonn's mouth fell open, but before he could embark on another argument, something behind Emmelyn distracted him.

"Emmelyn," Lorelle called, tapping her on the shoulder. The maid had a skinny roll of paper—no, it was colored more like *parchment*—in one hand and her Transitor key in the other. "Been waiting long? Sorry, I needed the break."

Another stamp disappeared from Emmelyn's wrist. "It's fine," she replied, handing Lorelle the Transitor.

Lorelle unlocked the white block, removed the parchment inside, stuffed a new roll in its place, and handed the Transitor back to Emmelyn. She read the slip she had removed, and her expression morphed into something akin to despair. "I have to go. Get that to Emile!" she ordered and turned on her heel, disappearing into the darkness.

In the last couple visits, Emmelyn began to get a feel for Lorelle's mild personality, and she was relieved to be paired with a Runner who was kind, like the Crew. Although, she still knew little about the waiting-woman, her obvious distress on this Run—Emmelyn's first double—made Emmelyn uneasy.

Not half as uneasy as the wide-eyed stares she found the Crew giving her when she turned back around, though. "What's wrong?" she asked them, frozen in place as if any sudden movement might be her last.

"Ya got 'er update—unlocked—open—in yer hands," Randy spluttered.

Emmelyn glanced down at the open Transitor. "So?" she asked the incredulous Crew.

"Ya could read it!" Bernadette exclaimed.

"Lorelle was supposed to lock it up before giving it back to you," Vonn offered, finally putting the last piece of the puzzle into place.

"But I shouldn't read it, right?" Emmelyn replied, snapping the lid shut.

The Crew unanimously drew in a sharp breath.

She might want to learn everything she could to save her realm, but it would not be at the expense of her relationship with her Runner, which might prove beneficial someday. "If Lorelle trusted me not to read it, I won't."

Vonn shook his head and smiled. "Astonishing. You are something else, Emmelyn," he announced, standing. "I see my Transfer. Till next time—Randy!" He pointed at the cowboy in playful challenge, waved to the others, and stepped out of their circle of mismatched chairs.

"Ya'd best be goin', too, hun," Bernadette yelled. "Ya still got one moah stop tuh make."

Emmelyn jumped to her feet, said her goodbyes, and wove her way toward the door. It closed heavily behind her, muffling the loud music. She removed her earplugs with a sigh and squinted at her wrist in the blinding brightness of the well-lit staircase. Less than one full stamp left, and she had no idea how to find Emile. She grabbed onto the railing and bolted down the stairs into the lobby.

XIII

Aethelburh

When the knock on her door awoke Rhoswen, she knew she hadn't gotten enough sleep. Her joints ached, and she tried to ignore the sensation as she dragged herself out from under the covers to answer the door. Her waiting-women would have infiltrated her chambers without knocking. Fearing her cousin might be outside, she opened the door a crack and peeked around it, steeling herself for an unpleasant start to her day. Instead, she found Thane with an armful of leathers, rubbing his eyes with his free hand. He did not appear to be in much better condition than she.

"I've forgotten to give these to you for days, but you'll need them today." He grinned and thrust the heavy stack of leathers at her as she pulled the door wide.

The reminder of the first day of training helped clear the fog from her head. "Where are yours?" she asked, eyeing his normal leathers.

"We'll get into them after breakfast."

Rhoswen heaved the pile up onto the corner of her vanity and moved behind her changing screen. Her waiting-women would normally have been here to help her into her leathers by now. She wondered where they were—not that she needed the assistance. The bulky new leathers Thane had delivered would be unwieldy, though. She privately hoped the ladies would show up when she returned to change.

Thane yawned. "Apparently, Gethin is the only one joining us for breakfast. He told my waitmen not to overdress me."

"How thoughtful," Rhoswen replied flatly.

Gethin was already at the breakfast table when Thane and Rhoswen arrived.

"I hope we have not kept you waiting, my prince," Thane dissembled.

Rhoswen was not certain she had the strength for sycophancy this morning.

"Not at all." The prince smiled and leaned back in his seat. He had his leg bent out in front of him, his left ankle resting on his right knee. No one, in Rhoswen's recollection, had ever looked like they were working so hard at being comfortable. The charade made her feel as uneasy as her cousin looked. "I woke early. First day of training for you both! Wanted to be here to see you off."

"That is very kind of you, my prince," Thane said. Rhoswen dipped in a shallow curtsey.

"Not at all." Gethin gestured to the food, and the two began gathering things onto their plates. "Were you given your roughs yet?" he asked as they assumed seats on either side of him.

Rhoswen paused, butter-covered knife and toast in hand, and cocked her head at her brother. Thane nodded to the prince. "Yes, Darr Thorndon delivered them to us." He failed to mention *when* the Rider had done this.

The heavy leathers, Rhoswen realized groggily. She had never worn roughs before.

"Indeed. Uncomfortable, roughs. But you will not be wearing them for long—just a novice precaution. Undoubtedly, you two possess your parents' deftness with dragons and will not require the added protection."

Rhoswen balked at the idea of needing additional protection for even a single training session. Her brother must have noticed her distaste, for he replied hastily, "Thank you. We appreciate the extra care."

Something about Gethin's smile increased Rhoswen's uneasiness. Rather than sneering at them with general distaste, he seemed *supportive* on their first day of training, and she couldn't believe he cared enough about them—or anyone—to act so selflessly. *Did Uncle Badrick force him to join us?* she wondered. *Is he trying to endear himself to us for a purpose?*

She noticed the steaming mug in front of her cousin and reached for the pitcher in the center of the table. She filled a cup with a milky brown liquid that smelled more of flowers and fruit than the roots and soil of the brew she enjoyed in the mornings at home. She lifted the mug to her lips. Her mouth filled with a bitter taste that sweetened on the back of her tongue as she swallowed. It was no replacement for her rootwine, but it was oddly delicious. "What is this?"

Gethin shrugged. "We call it vine water, but it isn't made with vines anymore—just flowers, herbs, and fruit."

Rhoswen nodded. "We drink a much stronger brew of roots, nuts, and seeds at home, but it doesn't change flavors as so many of your drinks do. Who knew such different foods could exist in so short a distance from each other? Aethelburh is like another realm."

"Entirely," Gethin replied, his tone as insincere as his smile.

If Rhoswen thought the roughs were heavy to hold, she should have considered maneuvering them onto her body, let alone walking around in them. For once, Rhoswen appreciated the assistance of her waiting-women, who seemed somewhat at odds with one another when they arrived after breakfast to help her change. Elsie's pointed apology for their earlier absence seemed to hint that she was not to blame for it.

Rhoswen waddled in the bulky, rust-colored tunic and pants. In the future, she could look forward to the addition of pads to protect her in case she fell from dragonback, but today held no threat of flying practice. She hobbled from her room in time to see Thane emerging across the hall. His roughs were dark green and looked equally uncomfortable. Rhoswen giggled.

"Wonder why Mother and Father never told us about this part of training, eh?" he quipped.

XIV

The Exchange

Emmelyn made her way briskly across the lobby. She fixed her eyes on the four wide stairs that led into the Atrium to avoid making eye contact with any skulking Ministers.

As she reached the top of the steps, she understood why Bernadette didn't want Vonn to ruin the surprise: the Atrium was perhaps the most beautiful "restaurant" she had ever seen.

The eating area was enclosed by a half-dome of glass, made up of octagonal panes. Double doors at the base of the dome led out into a lush garden, replete with colorful flowers, palm leaves, vines, and cascading water features. Overlooking the gardens, half-moon tables draped in white linen peppered a series of platforms that rose upward toward the back wall, like a maze of stadium seating. The platforms were connected by small sets of stairs, and waiters bustled up and down them as they delivered food to the patrons. The chairs lined only the tables' outer curve, so occupants, alone or in pairs, could look out at the foliage.

Like a restaurant on bleachers in an open clam shell overlooking a jungle behind glass. Emmelyn's jaw dropped as she took in the scene—which likely explained the bored look the waiter gave her when he approached.

"Who?" he asked tersely.

"E-Emile," she stammered.

The waiter nodded and gestured for her to follow him. He turned on his heel, his chest puffed and feet traveling quickly along a well-practiced path toward the middle of the space. It took Emmelyn some careful maneuvering up and down the steps to keep up with him. On the tables all around her, tiny, colorful delicacies—like those served at overpriced restaurants in the big cities of her realm—sat in the centers of unnecessarily large plates. People she guessed were Arbiters picked at the artful piles as if dismantling bombs. Emmelyn was distracted by a well-dressed man lifting a single, tiny sprout on the tine of his fork, and her foot slipped on a step. Her waiter-escort sneered at her with disapproval. He had stopped beside a table, at which two people, one male and one female, stared at her with silent interest. *Am I supposed to bow?*

"Thank you, Dartan," the man said. Emmelyn recognized his accent: similar to Vonn's vaguely French-sounding one but more prominent, and it prevented him from fully pronouncing the N at the end of the waiter's name. Emmelyn thought it sounded infinitely better than how she would have said it. "For whom are you here?" the man asked her kindly.

"Emile, sir. I have a Transitor from—"

"Lorelle," the man interrupted. "Yes. I am Emile. I'll take that." He pulled a sun-shaped key on a watch chain out of his vest pocket and opened the Transitor with the deft ceremony of someone dissecting the daily newspaper at the breakfast table.

Uncertain of her duties now, Emmelyn backed away, down the few stairs that led up to Emile's table.

"One moment," Emile said, not looking up from the parchment. He wore a well-tailored navy three-piece suit, and his dark hair was slicked back into a small ponytail. He looked like a maître de. From a pocket inside his jacket, he pulled two rolls of parchment and inspected them both. One, he laid on the table, and the other, he replaced in his pocket. Then he picked up the one from the table and slid it into the Transitor, locking it shut before returning it to her.

Emmelyn looked at the white baton now back in her possession. "Lorelle has already gone," she said.

The woman beside Emile tittered. She wore long white gloves, a heavily ruffled black-and-white dress with a high collar, and a gauzy oversize hat with satin flowers. She had the haughty look of someone attending a horse race.

Emile held up a hand to beg the woman's patience. "Hold on, Olivia. She *is* new." He turned his attention back to Emmelyn and reached for her left wrist, which he gently pulled up to the table. The final stamp had almost disappeared; only the left edge of the outer ring remained. He nodded at it. "Take the Transitor to the front desk. Janelle or Stuart will help you," he said with a smile that did not seem entirely genuine.

"Thank you," Emmelyn replied before turning to navigate the maze of stairs and platforms.

Admittedly, she had never done a double delivery before, but she had not been made aware of this third step, which was making it feel much more like a *triple* delivery—if there were such a thing. *Of course, I am rarely made aware of* anything *in this place,* she mused. She approached the front desk; Janelle was the only unoccupied receptionist. Emmelyn cursed her luck and smiled at the woman.

"Um, hi," Emmelyn mumbled, "I've completed—well, I thought I'd completed a double, but then Emile gave me this again and told me to—"

"Give it to me," Janelle snapped.

"Right, exactly," Emmelyn replied, handing over the Transitor. "That's precisely what he told me to do." She wondered if Janelle *ever* laughed. Or smiled.

With an audible click, Janelle unlocked the Transitor below the level of the counter and continued to interact with it out of Emmelyn's line of sight. As Emmelyn waited for further instructions, she glanced around at the tall, Gothic arches and worried at the inside of her mouth with her right incisors. Janelle did not appear to appreciate the nervous habit, for when Emmelyn looked back to her, the receptionist stared at her with flat eyebrows and unsmiling eyes. Emmelyn ceased her chewing.

"You can go," Janelle said.

"But my stamp—" Emmelyn began, holding out her wrist. It was clean. Her job was complete. Janelle stared at her. "Excellent," Emmelyn blurted, smiling weakly at Janelle once more. "Bye, then." She turned away from the desk to walk out the front doors—

—and into Jeremy's backyard. She had been at her friend's summer party when she had blinked and found herself outside Dissonance.

Emmelyn was beginning to believe the hardest part of being a Transfer was having no one to confide in back in her own realm. Whatever had just happened in the Exchange did not feel normal, and she had no one here she could discuss it with. In fact, nothing would make her sound more delusional to her non-Exchange friends, or "realm friends," as the Crew called them. The only people she could ask about the "triple" would be inaccessible to her until she suddenly wound up in the Exchange again. And who knew when that would happen? In a momentary lapse of aloofness, Kyle had recently told her that she would begin to sense her approaching trips to the Exchange before she found herself on the street in front of the nightclub. So far, not the case.

"Hey, Em!" Josie called, coming over to her with the lemonade she had promised before Emmelyn's Transfer. Josie's dark hair was pulled up into a high ponytail, the ends curling in as though she had abandoned a styled look for something more functional in the heat. Her green eyes, much like Emmelyn's own—the one feature they shared—sparkled in the sunlight, and she handed off a cup so she could lower her sunglasses from the top of her head. "You okay? You look kind of dazed."

Josie was her best friend, and it killed Emmelyn not to tell her everything she was experiencing. But how could you tell someone that you'd suddenly become an agent in a parallel realm… that was sort of *not* a realm?

Over obscenely loud music in a seedy bar at the top of an excruciatingly tall staircase—that's how.

In other words: *you didn't.*

"Yeah, I'm fine—thank you," Emmelyn replied.

Josie sniffed the air a bit. "Did you have a drink while I was gone?"

As if learning about the Exchange weren't enough, Vonn had begun augmenting Emmelyn's education with the finer points of gin. With some effort, she was starting to appreciate his fondness for the liquor—at least in club soda. Tonic was still a bit of a stretch.

"Ah, yeah—Jere came by and wanted me to try a sip of whatever punch he was drinking," Emmelyn replied. She *hated* lying to Josie. It made her skin crawl.

Josie rolled her eyes. "Oh, gross; I'm so sorry. Those college punches are the worst. Why must they feature at every gathering?"

"Rite of passage, I think," Emmelyn said.

"Maybe I should have spiked this," Josie said, peering into her cup of yellow liquid.

"I believe vodka is used in those vile college swills," Emmelyn replied and put her arm through her friend's. "Let's go see if there's any left in the bottle to make a punch *worth* drinking."

XV

Keaton

Rhoswen and Thane shuffled into Keaton and met up with a group of similarly attired—and uncomfortable—new students. Apparently, she and her brother were not the only ones abiding by these excessive "safety precautions." But they seemed like the only ones who could barely move their limbs.

"Our roughs are stiffer than everyone else's," Rhoswen whispered into her brother's ear.

Thane appraised the other students' movements and nodded. "Theirs are more broken in."

Rhoswen cursed her cousin and uncle for their "thoughtfulness" at providing them with roughs from the royal supplies. "They did this on purpose," she hissed.

Thane waved her off as Darr Thorndon stepped into the arena and held up his hands. "Welcome, all!" the Rider called, his voice loud and clear. "Today begins another cycle. We are joined by a new batch of trainees, all aspiring to the honor-bound tradition of Realm Riding." Everyone applauded.

"Becoming a Realm Rider is not simply about tethering to a dragon and flying around the realm," he continued. "It is about fighting a threat more insidious than most of you can imagine. It is about survival—not only yours or your fellow D'Erenelleans'—and not even the realm's, for it, too, is impermanent. It is about the survival of *our kind*. Realm Riders do not merely protect *one* realm. They protect *all* the realms. If we fail to keep the Narxon at bay, the very souls you have come to love—and those you have yet to meet—will cease to exist.

"It is imperative that you understand this is more than a game of saddle-the-beast. What you learn here, whether you tether or not, will teach you about life for the rest of yours. What you learn here will change you, and there will be no changing back, even if you do not emerge with a dragon on the other side. What you learn *here* is fraught with risk—and with the possibility of extraordinary reward. If this doesn't sound like the calling of your soul, now is the time to leave."

He paused for effect, but his words did not require more dramatic emphasis. No one moved—or perhaps even breathed. One could have heard a dragon shed a scale onto the hay-strewn floor in the silence.

Finally, his face broke into a conspiratorial grin. "But we can still have a little fun with these beasts, aye?" The established trainees hooted jovially while the bundled novices flashed nervous smiles at one another as if belatedly catching a joke. "Let us begin!" the Rider hollered with a clap of his hands.

Darr Thorndon dismissed the older students and set to the task of separating the new trainees into groups by size. Trainers emerged from nearby stalls, each with a dragon, to join a group of trainees. A large red the size of Cahal was brought to Thane's group of tall, young men, whereas a medium-sized tawny walked toward Rhoswen's group.

"She's beautiful," Rhoswen breathed as the dragon drew near. Despite her experience with dragons, Rhoswen couldn't help but feel awed by the beasts' magnificence. A few students within hearing range nodded in wide-eyed agreement.

The slim trainer accompanying the tawny had white-blonde hair that curved around her chin and cut sharply upwards toward the middle of the back of her head. She wore black leathers and thick coal around her eyes. The combination gave her a severe and imposing look, regardless of her average height.

"My name is Maven," she said, her voice deeper than Rhoswen had expected. "I will be training you today. And this is Rusalka, Darr Elmina's dragon."

Upon hearing her name, the tawny cooed and bobbed her head.

"Wood sprite," Rhoswen whispered to herself.

Both Rusalka and the trainer looked at her. "What did you say?" Maven asked.

Rhoswen shook her head and apologized. "'Rusalka' is the olden word for 'wood sprite,'" she repeated.

The tawny stepped forward with overeager haste, and Rhoswen took a step back, more out of instinct than fear. Rusalka stopped short and stared at Rhoswen for a small eternity before edging toward her again. Finally, she extended her snout, and Rhoswen stroked it easily, as if they had been friends forever.

Maven looked positively bewildered by the exchange and had to work to compose herself. "Rusalka seems to appreciate your knowledge," she said and turned to address the group again. "While those two get acquainted, I'll explain what you have to look forward to. You are in your roughs today because our lesson covers general dragon care, and none of you have worked with these particular beasts before. As you can see," she said with a nod at Rhoswen and Rusalka, "they can be a little excitable around newcomers, so it's best to take extra precautions. Over the next few days, you will be taught protocol for interacting with dragons, including kenneling and unkenneling them. Once you can do both, you will be able to pass to the next step: flight preparation. For some of you, graduation to flight preparation will take place sooner than later. Lesson progression here is based on mastery: you move ahead only when you're ready."

"What is there to master?" A knot-faced student—his features all squished up in the center of his head—stepped forward. Practiced defiance radiated from his pinched features as he pointed at Rhoswen and Rusalka. "Looks like these dragons are about as tame as puppies!"

Maven winced. "They do not like being compared to dogs."

"Why not?" the young man persisted. "Can't conscience the idea that they're at our disposal as much as our farm animals are?" As he turned around to laugh with his friends, Rusalka looked up from Rhoswen, her eyes alight. She took in a short breath, and her gut rumbled.

"Rusalka—" Maven admonished, but she was too late.

The tawny let out a short burst of flame across the crown of the knot-faced student's head. He yelped and scurried behind his friends to use them like a shield. When he finally peeked up over their shoulders, he revealed a bald stripe along the top of his head where his hair had been incinerated. Ludicrous tufts of singed red hair stuck out wildly on either side of the gap. A little giggle leapt from Rhoswen's throat before she could stop herself, and the whole group fell into hysterics. Even Rusalka rumbled with what seemed like laughter. Rhoswen patted her nose. The knot-faced boy glowered at them.

"Precisely the implication they seek to avoid," Maven said dryly. She made no move to inspect the student for damages. "If I had my kennelbet," a word Rhoswen recognized as a bet on how long it would take a trainee to unkennel a dragon, "I would give you two-and-a-half weeks."

"Two and a half?!" the trainer from Thane's group called out. "He's already been at it half a year!" The trainees around her hooted, and her red dragon lifted her head to Rusalka conspiratorially. The tawny chortled back.

Maven smiled and waved her colleague off. "So, if there are no more questions or *comments*, let us begin with anatomy."

Rhoswen was more than familiar with the parts of a dragon, so she spent most of the lesson sneaking peaks at the other groups scattered about the arena. Everyone seemed to be at the same point in the lecture until Thane's group escorted their red toward her stall. He waved at Rhoswen in passing.

"Lady Stanburh."

Snapped to attention, Rhoswen cast a sheepish glance around herself.

Between her lack of focus and the use of her title, her cheeks warmed with embarrassment. "Please call me Rhoswen, Darr Maven." A couple trainees whispered among themselves, but most of the group remained silent. She hoped her status, let alone her connection to the royal family, would not create animosity.

"Gladly. And please do not add 'Darr' where it is not yet appropriate, either. I am nearly there, but I do not want the title before I've earned it."

Rhoswen had had no idea their trainers were not all full-fledged Riders. She apologized.

"Not at all," Maven replied warmly. "Now, since you and Rusalka seem to have hit it off, would you mind being my first victim—I mean *helper*?" The group laughed.

"We will begin with kenneling. This is sometimes more difficult than unkenneling but is a far more straightforward process to communicate through gestures, which is all you untethered lot have for now," Maven said. "As you can imagine, dragons are willful creatures, and their size alone gives them an advantage over us. So, if they don't want to be kenneled, you may find yourself in a stalemate, but gesturing correctly to them will circumvent confusing requests."

"But why do dragons even acquiesce to us at all?" one trainee asked.

Maven nodded and leveled a pointed squint at the knot-faced student before she replied. "Keaton provides shelter to the dragons, but they also deserve their freedom, and many Riders allow their beasts to come and go as they please. Still, dragons tend to stay nearby in case of a Descent. Dragons and Riders have a symbiotic relationship. Neither would benefit from being separated from the other at the onset of an attack. They need each other if they wish to defeat the Narxon and have a chance of escaping unharmed.

"So, we do our best to respect each other and communicate our intentions clearly, especially when we cannot nex. When we request that a dragon return to his or her stall, there is no ambiguity about what we're asking. But in offering a dragon to come out, we signal a reason for the request—to hunt, to train, to recreate—and if you signal improperly, you may find yourself with an intransigent beast on your hands. Here, a demonstration.

"Rhoswen, come stand before Rusalka with your arms at your sides," Maven instructed. "Good. Now, to kennel her, you must gain Rusalka's permission to escort her back into her stall. Once you are tethered to a dragon, these kinds of permissions can be readily asked and granted through a mental tie you will share, called nexing. But for dragons you are not tethered to, you must use physical gestures to respectfully convey your wishes. Rusalka is a good-natured beast, and she is clearly fond of you, so she should not be difficult to persuade. But if a dragon were in a more challenging mood, a deeper bow of your head, rather than a slight incline could make all the difference. For you, Rhoswen, a nod should do."

Rhoswen inclined her head toward the dragon, who dipped her own head in response. Then Rusalka passed an amused puff of air through her nose. Rhoswen giggled.

"Good," said Maven. She instructed Rhoswen to maintain eye contact with Rusalka and nod toward the stables. Rusalka dipped her head again, and the pair began walking—*waddling*, in Rhoswen's case—in the direction of her stall. Rhoswen felt silly, playing charades with a dragon; her parents had no need to do this with their beasts and had not taught their children to do it, likely because they were nexing in the background when their children rode them.

Trainees must 'play charades,' as you call it, a voice said in Rhoswen's mind. *Your parents do it with each other's dragons, as well. You just never noticed.*

Rhoswen shot a glance at Maven and then at the rest of the group, none of whom seemed to have spoken or even heard the comment. Finally, Rhoswen's eyes traveled to Rusalka. The dragon winked. Rhoswen gave her head a shake. She could not have heard that.

Of course you heard that. Rusalka nodded encouragingly at her.

But I should not have, Rhoswen replied mentally. She was nexing. Her parents nexed with their own dragons, but they were tethered to them. She should not be nexing with a dragon to whom she was not tethered—let alone one who was tethered to someone else. Somehow more startling, though—nexing felt completely natural, even untethered. *How am I doing this?*

Rusalka blew air through her nose again but did not respond. When they reached her stall, Rhoswen pulled the door wide, and Maven directed her to gesture toward the opening with a sweep of her arm. As Rhoswen stepped back in front of Rusalka, she hesitated, her arm still at her side. *Would you care to enter?* she nexed instead.

Yes, but you had best do as Maven said.

Rhoswen frowned. *But you just said you would be happy to go in....*

But no one else knows that. And this may be a gift you want to keep to yourself for a while.

Rhoswen held out her arm toward the stall. *After you,* she nexed.

Rusalka ambled inside, amusement shining in her eyes. The tawny turned around to face the group and gave a little bow as everyone applauded.

"Excellent," Maven cheered before beginning the process of unkenneling Rusalka for the next student. "Who will be next?"

As hands shot up to volunteer, Rusalka nexed to Rhoswen again. *It looks as though you have not gone completely unnoticed.*

Rhoswen glanced around and felt her heart skip a beat as her eyes met Darr Beval's. His head spun back around toward his group.

Realm it, Rhoswen thought to herself. Rusalka snorted in reply.

XVI

Aethelburh

Rhoswen was too distracted by what had happened during training to fight her waiting-women's efforts to dress her for dinner. When Thane arrived to escort her down, he was still buzzing about his own experiences. "Did you have any trouble kenneling your dragon?" he asked.

"No," Rhoswen replied. She could not say more in front of her waiting-women.

"Nor I," he said. "Pretty much the same procedure Mother and Father taught us."

Rhoswen's head swiveled in his direction, and her hair caught painfully in the brush her waiting-woman was using on her. "Ow! You remember being taught to kennel Cahal and Kuney that way?" she asked Thane.

Kuney was the nickname Magge had given her tawny, Kyne, which had proven useful when Rhoswen and Thane were yet too young to pronounce the dragon's name. Their mother considered Kyne's name, which translated roughly to "royal," comically ironic, as she and her dragon were farther removed from the crown than Allistair and Cahal.

"Do you not remember? You were pretty young when I learned. I suppose our parents nexed them the signals more often than we gestured, but I still don't remember it being quite so *formal* a process…."

Thane went on about the gestures he would use to kennel their parents' dragons, but none felt familiar to Rhoswen, and her mind began to wander. Thane was right: all Rhoswen's memories involved their parents doing the kenneling; she didn't remember seeing Thane do it or using a gesture to do it herself. Nor did she remember nexing with Cahal or Kuney. So, how did she kennel them—if she ever did?

Thane's tone changed, and she realized he was repeating a question. "Are you ready for dinner?" he asked her again.

The waiting-woman—whose name Rhoswen *still* had not managed to discover—had already finished her hair. Rhoswen turned her head this way and that before a mirror. Admittedly, it looked lovely all twisted and swept up into a high pile on her head. She had even managed to tuck away that short piece that drove Rhoswen crazy. "Yes, sorry," she replied and followed him out of her room.

Dinner seemed to stretch on forever. Without a room full of guests, there was no escaping one another, and the dining hall remained quiet but for the clanging of silverware and the crunching of Rhoswen's puffy dress. After the king had arrived and told everyone to be seated, he had not spoken again. Gethin said little more than his father, and the four of them ate most of their six-course meal in awkward silence.

Rhoswen's appetite diminished as her mind whirled, yet she nibbled at whatever appeared in front of her. Gethin commented on how exhausted she must be after a full day of training, which was excuse enough for her. After dinner, she apologized for her lackluster demeanor and hurried to her chamber for "an early night in." No one argued.

She made it back to her room before her waiting-women arrived, so she slipped on her nightgown and collapsed into bed, hoping they'd find her "asleep" and leave her alone. It worked. She could hear Elsie chastising the other woman for their repeated tardiness as their footsteps faded away, and Rhoswen winced at her part in the admonishment. When she could no longer hear them, Rhoswen threw back the covers and jumped out of bed. In no time, she'd redressed in her leathers and padded her way toward the stairs, dimmed oil lamp in hand.

Once again, she met no one on her way to the cellar. She knew from the warning Darr Thorndon had given Thane that they were being watched, and it unnerved her that she was unable to find evidence of their surveillance. Seemingly alone in the overflow library, she tipped up the book beside the empty section of shelving and heard the familiar *click* of the latch. She widened the gap in the shelves and slipped into the darkness of the maps room.

Rhoswen turned up her lamp and retrieved the maps of Castle Aethelburh from the barrel. She spread them out, this time with the ground floor map on the top of the pile, and grabbed up the magnifying glass. The twisting castle corridors had turned her around, and as she thought to pull out her compass, fear ripped through her chest. Had she replaced the compass in her leathers after her transition from roughs earlier in the day? She dropped the magnifying glass as her hand shot to her pocket—and found the familiar metal bulge. She removed the treasure from her leathers with a sigh and lined it up on top of the identical compass rose on the bottom left corner of the map.

The pressure in the room changed. She looked up, her gut cinching at the prospect of being discovered by someone entering the maps room, when her eyes caught on an empty wall.

It was shimmering.

Rhoswen froze and watched the once-solid stone dance until the image of a room took shape before her. It was as if she were looking into the room through a window that reached from the floor to the level of her collarbone. She edged toward the image, willing it not to move or fade away.

The walls in the room beyond were covered in dark wooden shelves, much like the overflow library, and housed books, scrolls, inkwells, and other writing supplies. Atop an ornate rug sat two wooden chairs with claw feet and legs carved to resemble scaled dragon hide. On the wall hung a framed map, only its legend and the edge of a landmass visible from this angle. Finally, at the right-most edge of the image, she saw a desk with carved dragon feet that each held—instead of the traditional ball—a dead, dragon-like creature with its tongue lolling out of its mouth: *Narxon.*

This is the king's study.

Atop Badrick's massive desk lay ornate boxes, quills, an open inkwell, a half-moon-shaped ink blotter with a stubby handle, a magnifying glass that looked very much like the one she was using in the secret maps room, and handwritten sheets of parchment. She stepped backward and felt for the table, her eyes glued to the image of the study on the wall.

In the wall. The image had a slightly unfocused look, as if it were being viewed through old glass.

She groped for the magnifier, hoping it could help her see what might be written on the parchment on the king's desk, but as she lifted it up from the maps, the study began to shimmer and fade away. She gasped and ran to the wall, but by the time she reached it, the stone had solidified. She beat on the wall with her empty fist. Nothing happened.

Rhoswen returned to the table and let her eyes drift across the castle map. Suddenly aware of the heft of the magnifying glass in her hand, she set the instrument over the outlines of the king's study.

The shimmering feeling nudged at her senses again, and she spun around to see the image of the study rematerializing. She yipped and clamped a hand over her mouth. Still, the study looked sunken into the stone, as if it were far away. She crossed to the wall and reached a hand forward, but her fingertips struck an invisible barrier flush with the stone of the maps-room wall. She glanced back at the map on the table and stepped over to pick up the magnifying glass, her eyes still on the wall. As the object left the parchment, the image of the study began to shimmer and fade. She dropped the magnifying glass back onto the table, but the study continued to disappear.

Rhoswen inspected the map. The magnifying glass was splayed across three rooms, only the tip of its handle overlapping the boundaries of the study. She slid the glass more squarely over the study's four walls and looked back up to see the distant image of the study reappearing once more. She practically skipped back to it and tried to reach her hand into the room again but met the same unseen barrier as before. *It's like there's a gap between here and the study that I can't bridge….*

Bridge. I need to connect *them.* She returned to the table, slid the cellar map out from under the pile, and placed it beside the first-floor map. She considered the layouts of each floor and traced the path she would take on foot to reach the king's study from the overflow library. *If the magnifying glass opened a pathway to the study, I may need something to represent each of the rooms in between here and there.*

She surveyed the objects on the table. The inkwell could signify the upstairs library, as could some of the paperweights that more closely resembled bookends… but the sharp, angular instrument was still a complete mystery to her. Figuring it had to have something to do with maps, she placed it on the ellipsis where the secret maps room ought to have been. A change in the shimmering nudged at her senses again, and she looked up in time to see the study disappearing.

"No," she breathed and scrutinized the map. She had bumped her compass from its precise placement over the compass rose. Uncertain whether that could be the problem, she made the adjustment and looked back to the wall. The image of the study reappeared, this time in slightly better focus. *My compass is part of this?*

She returned to the wall and reached out, fingers bracing for impact with invisible stone. Instead, she watched in amazement as they passed beyond the surface of the wall—and hit a similar barrier farther in. She glanced back at the map. That metal thing was, indeed, connected to this hidden room. *What else do I need to connect to the study?*

"Something for the overflow library," she murmured, her eyes vacillating between the bookends and the inkwell. She moved the latter onto the map, but the barrier in the stone wall remained. When she replaced the inkwell with a bookend, still nothing happened. She scanned the room, but nothing struck her as appropriate. Her eyes caught on the gap in the shelving that led to the book-lined walls of the overflow library. *Does the object necessarily have to be found* within *the maps room?* she wondered, slipping through the opening.

She walked across the room to the history section, where the striking blue-and-silver cover of *An Index of Realms: Judged and Unjudged* resided. It was the epitome of research material. Gently, she slid the book from the shelf and carried it back to the maps room.

She placed it on the cellar floorplan and looked up in time to see the image of the study crystalize before her. She glanced around herself, as if to confirm she was still alone, and crept toward the wall. She held her breath and reached through the opening. *Finally*, she met no resistance.

She shifted her weight forward and stepped over the threshold. When the opening didn't collapse on her or begin shimmering again, she took another small step. And another. She was at the edge of the study when she heard a door unlatch and her uncle's voice grow in volume as he entered. "... what you *don't* understand...."

Rhoswen backed away from the opening until her rear end collided with the maps-room table. Her uncle's cape swirled into view at the edge of the opening, and she batted her compass off the twin rose in the map's corner, nearly sending it flying. The study sputtered out of view, replaced with hard stone, and she gasped for air. She had been holding her breath since stepping through the wall. Her heart raced, and blood pounded in her ears. Had she been heard—or *seen*? Or had the...

... portal?

This is a portal.

Had it been noticed?

She couldn't risk finding out here. Rhoswen shoved her compass into her pocket and pushed all the objects on the maps aside with one broad sweep of her arm. The maps rolled themselves up. She threw the parchment tube into its barrel and flew out of the hidden room, closing the shelf-wall behind her with a *click*.

The next morning, Rhoswen's waiting-women arrived together, but Elsie quickly excused herself again, as Rhoswen would not need roughs for training. Finally, Rhoswen learned from their exchange that the other waiting-woman's name was Lorelle. Rhoswen rubbed her eyes and stifled a yawn as Lorelle tied up her vest.

"Did you not sleep well, milady?" the waiting-woman asked, her deft fingers pulling at the strings. Lorelle was friendlier than Elsie and closer to Rhoswen's age, although probably still nearing thirty. Elsie, whose liver-spotted skin and angry wrinkles made her look at least fifteen years older than Rhoswen's mother, would have been tutting over her charge's ever-underwhelming imperfections had she been there to help. It wasn't hard to prefer Lorelle's more impartial demeanor.

"A bit fitfully," Rhoswen replied through another yawn.

Lorelle gave a sympathetic nod and escorted her to the vanity to brush her hair. Rhoswen closed her eyes as the brush raked through the tangles from the previous evening's styling. When the worst of the tugging and pinching was over, she opened her eyes once more and inspected Lorelle in the mirror.

The waiting-woman was pretty, although the stress of her job was beginning to show in the nascent lines around her mouth and eyes. *Perhaps she is already in her thirties,* Rhoswen thought as she stared at her. It was hard to tell. Lorelle's drab gray frock did her no favors, though it couldn't hide her petite and curvy frame completely. She had long eyelashes, brown skin, and thick black hair that, today, was braided to the side. Rhoswen followed the trail of her hair down to a strange metal pendant hanging from her neck. It was like a key with many bits. "What is that?" she asked.

The waiting-woman followed her eyes in the mirror and touched the pendant at her throat. "Oh, this? Family heirloom," she said with the same indifferent tone Rhoswen had used when she'd lied about the quality of her sleep. Not interested in offending the only waiting-woman she cared for, she decided not to inquire further. "Pretty," she said simply and smiled at Lorelle in the mirror.

Rhoswen's sluggishness drew notice at the breakfast table, as well. Gethin's profession that she "merely looked unrested" seemed like a kindness, coming from him. She poured herself an extra cup of vine water, wishing it were her strong, homemade rootwine. *Would Mother send me some if I wrote her for it?* She had already written her parents once to tell them of their safe arrival, but she distrusted the messengers and included little additional information. Her father had even advised against her keeping a diary, lest someone should find it.

"You cannot expect anyone to be an ally—including those who seem most trustworthy. *Even* your own waiting-women," her father had insisted over dinner one night before they'd left home.

"*Especially* your waiting-women," her mother had chimed in. "They do not work for you, helpful as they may be at times."

"Waiting-women?" Rhoswen had repeated in awe. "We will be given our own waiting-women?"

Her mother had laughed. "*You* will."

"Thane will have waitmen." Her father's smile had betrayed his amusement at his daughter's astonishment, but his next words had grown stern. "And you'll both treat them well."

"Of course, Father," Thane had replied through a mouthful of food.

"And do not eat like that with the king, Thane!" Magge had chided, laughing as she'd wiped a smudge from her son's lower lip with her napkin-dressed finger. He had swallowed and smiled back guiltily.

Rhoswen stared into her vine water, overcome with homesickness. She thought of her recent exchange with Lorelle and how mistrustful they obviously were of each other. *Even my own waiting-women....* Grateful as she was for the privilege of training with dragons, she disliked the threatening feeling that seemed to simmer throughout this place. She lifted the mug to her lips, tilting it back just enough to let the brew drain slowly into her mouth as she blinked back tears.

Suddenly, the king's personal waitman burst into the kitchen. He appeared to make a frantic search... especially around the floor.

"Delwyn," Gethin snapped. "What are you doing?"

The waitman was already bent over, but he bowed lower before the prince. "I beg pardon, highness. I have... dropped something, and I did not want anyone stepping on it and... hurting themselves."

Gethin screwed up his face. "What is it?"

Delwyn paused in a transparent attempt at improvisation. "It is... ah... a charm, my prince. From a bracelet. Family heirloom... but somewhat sharp to the tender footed."

"Well," Gethin replied with disinterest, "as we all wear boots here, you shouldn't let it distract you *from your duties*."

Delwyn took the hint and began babbling his apologies as he backed from the room.

Rhoswen glanced at Thane, her eyebrow raised, but he turned his attention to his plate and prodded its contents with his fork.

"Servants," Gethin tutted.

XVII

Keaton

In the sanctuary of Keaton, where her fatigue would no longer be the focus of others' scrutiny, Rhoswen thought she would be able to relax. Instead, however, a thin and fair-haired young man named Aeduuin stood at the head of their group, teaching everyone how to tie knots.

Rhoswen was terrible at knots.

"Once you have mastered this knot with your piece of rope, you will tie it onto actual dragon mounts," he explained. "If your mount comes apart in the air and you fall to the ground, you will know you have not tied it properly." A couple girls gasped, one nearly dropping her rope, but Aeduuin's eyes twinkled as his fingers loosened the knot he had just demonstrated for the third time. "Just kidding."

Clearly Aeduuin was trying to slow down his nimble fingers for his students to watch, but he was too adept, and there was one twist Rhoswen simply couldn't understand. The trainees practiced tying their knots around the horizontal top rails of the fence that skirted the arena. Rhoswen sighed, playing over in her mind what she had just witnessed Aeduuin do—but she always seemed to miss a step.

"You're almost there," Aeduuin said as he approached her. He was wandering along the opposite side of the fence, helping students individually. He squinted at her rope. "All right. Wait—stop. You're missing the final twist. When you move that loop over to put it through there, you have to twist it over itself. That allows you to tighten it down when you pull the end through. Watch." He instructed Rhoswen to restart the knot, and when she got to the point that had frustrated her most, he took her hands in his and turned her right hand over to make the twist. "Like this. Then, pull the end through… yes! Just like that."

Rhoswen pulled on the rope, and the knot tightened down, exactly as he'd said it would. She smiled up at him. "Thank you."

"Do it again," he instructed with a grin.

Rhoswen pulled the end back through the knot and shook the rope loose. Her hands moved almost as deftly as Aeduuin's through the first part—she had practiced it seemingly a hundred times—and then she slowed down a little through the twist she had just learned. As she pulled the end through and tightened the knot, Aeduuin clapped his hands. "There you go!" He began moving along the fence line again. "Who else needs my expertise?"

The students continued to practice until Aeduuin felt most of the group had gotten the hang of it. Then, he took them over to a tall wooden sawhorse with two enormous dragon saddles slung over it and a wide strap of leather laid out on the ground beneath each one. "You cannot pass this lesson until the saddle is secure on the mountblock," Aeduuin explained, referring to the large sawhorse. Rhoswen inspected the familiar saddles.

The horn was replaced with two leather loops, large enough to wrap around each hand a time or two for added grip. Allistair had once likened the loops sticking out of the pommel to the reins used with horses. "Could you imagine trying to get a bit in a dragon's mouth?" he'd joked.

Rather than one foothold for a stirrup, there were several, like the rungs of a ladder, which allowed the Rider to climb up from the ground instead of requiring a step ladder to reach a single stirrup. The top stirrup hung at the edge of the fender, with a hard leather pocket on the forward side of it, which acted as a toe hold during flight.

On either side of the fenders were two metal rigging dees, each the size of Rhoswen's hand. These connected to a wide billet strap that went under the dragon's belly—now on the ground beneath the saddles on the mountblock—and tied in place with the rope the trainees were learning to knot. Time for each to demonstrate their proficiency on a real saddle.

"You will connect the billet strap to the dees in a manner suitable for flight. Once you have cleared this task, you can go over to Darr Beval's station to continue your lesson on general care of dragons." Aeduuin asked for two volunteers.

Rhoswen's hand shot up at the same time as a strong-looking young man with short blond hair. He had been in Thane's group yesterday. Aeduuin pointed first to him, and then to Rhoswen, and they each approached a saddle. The young man glanced up at the looming mount. Then he passed the leather ropes through the dees and grabbed up one end of the billet strap. He wore an intense expression as he tied, and he moved fast; in no time, he scrambled to the other side of the saddle and repeated the procedure. He finally stepped away to let Aeduuin inspect his work.

The trainer tugged on the ropes and mount. "Good work, Haylan. I believe Aelfraed wanted you to go work with him instead of Darr Beval. Untie your knots fully before you go. Rhoswen?"

Rhoswen took a deep breath, forced her hair out of her eye, and slid her ropes through the dees while Haylan worried away at the knots he had expertly fastened. Out of the corner of her eye, she could see him shake out his fingers as he worked, and she praised herself for slipping her leather gloves into her back pocket before leaving her room this morning. Haylan was just walking away from his untied mount as she pulled her second knot tight. She moved to the other side and tied knots at the last two dees as if that final twist had never given her any trouble. She smiled and stepped back from the saddle. Aeduuin nodded as he checked her work and dismissed her to join Darr Beval. She donned her gloves and pulled the knots free with considerably less pain and effort than Haylan had endured before making her way toward the stables.

An assembly of students was forming around Darr Beval. He addressed the group with a friendly and—in Rhoswen's opinion—disarming smile. "Today, you will continue to learn how to care for a dragon. After this lesson, it will be your duty to help with the care of the beasts in these stables, and you will rotate responsibilities with the other students on a weekly basis. Now, everyone is working at a different pace, so some of you may repeat certain tasks on the rotation until others catch up."

He stepped backward toward one of the stalls nearby. "How many of you have met Bassett, our young red?" A few hands shot up, and Darr Beval nodded. "Then let me introduce him to the rest of you."

He opened the door to the stall, and a small dragon with a deep maroon hide crept toward the threshold. Bassett looked around bashfully at the group until his eyes locked on Rhoswen. His golden irises shone brightly, and he took several eager steps in her direction, but Darr Beval placed a hand on his front flank to stop him.

"Hold on there, Bassett. We will work with adolescents like Bassett at the beginning of your training because they are still possessed of small size and youthful temperament." He lowered his voice conspiratorially. "When dragons come into their own, their personalities develop with them, and they can get rather fickle in their more... *established* age."

Students—especially the females—tittered amicably, but Rhoswen was watching Bassett. The red's eyes never left her. Darr Beval did not miss the connection, either. "Rhoswen, I hear you had a successful kenneling with Rusalka the other day. It would seem word has spread among the dragons, too, and Bassett is eager to work with you. Will you assist me first, if only to placate this little beast?"

Rhoswen hesitated to step forward. Sure, even as an adolescent, there was nothing "little" about Bassett. Darr Beval was tall, and his chin fell in line with the red's shoulder. But Rhoswen's hesitation had nothing to do with Bassett's size. Her fear of standing out as a Stanburh was swiftly being replaced with a fear of standing out for her... *mental proficiencies* with the dragons. She trusted Rusalka's suggestion that she keep her nexing abilities quiet for a while. Beginner's luck was one thing, but she didn't want a reputation for showing off, when she had that secret to hide. She swallowed thickly.

The Rider winked at her in an obvious ploy to calm her nerves. Instead, it made her heart race. "Bassett is hungry," he said as if speaking only to her. "I want you to kennel the young red before I teach you how to unkennel for feedings. Bassett is still young enough to hunt with his mother. If I let her out first, she will simply call to him to come out, and I will have no dragon with whom to teach." More giggling ensued.

Rhoswen stood by the stall door and swept out her arm toward the stall. When the young red simply stared at her, she sighed. *Do I dare?* she asked herself. *Hello, Bassett,* she finally nexed to him.

He seemed happy to be communicating with her in this way. *Hi! I'm hungry.*

Rhoswen suppressed a smile. She thought of her mental discussion with Rusalka the day before. *So, it wasn't a fluke....* Bassett shifted around, clearly eager to hunt. How could *anyone* get this "little" beast back into his stall without nexing to him? *If you go inside for a minute, I will ask you to come back out so you can go hunt.*

Bassett's confusion was obvious from the tilt of his head. *Why do I have to go in to come back out?* the red asked, slinking into his stall. *I'm starving!*

Rhoswen chuckled. *I have to prove to the others that I know how to get you back out!*

Bassett began to protest, but a beautiful adult red dipped her head over the wall from the next stall. It was the dragon who had praised Rusalka when she'd widened the part in the knot-faced boy's hair. *Do as she says, Bassett,* she cooed mentally. *Do not be difficult.* The adult red winked at Rhoswen and retracted her neck, once more out of sight. Bassett slinked into his stall and waited.

Rhoswen glanced at her trainer. Darr Beval's eyes were wide. She cleared her throat to get his attention, and he blinked. "Looks like you had a little help from Bassett's mother, Eostre. No fair cheating," he quipped. A few students broke out in whispers.

"Now," Darr Beval began, quieting them, "unkenneling a dragon is much like kenneling one, but it is most polite—and effective—to indicate why the dragon is being brought out of his or her stall. This kind of acknowledgment sets the mood for the encounter. If a dragon is expecting to feed when he is unkenneled and a trainer attempts to practice flying instead, there could be some serious repercussions! To signal that you will be letting Bassett out to hunt, Rhoswen, you will place your open palm near your mouth and sweep your arm down and out to your side. Just use the opposite arm—farthest from the stall—that's right."

Rhoswen did as he asked her, her hand swooping down from her lips and out beside her in the typical "after you" gesture that trainers always used to coax dragons into obliging them.

Now I can come out? Bassett asked, his talons slipping against the hay-strewn floor as he scurried out of his stall. *I was out before you made me come back in!*

Eostre chortled and hung her head over the door of her stall. She blew air through her nose at Darr Beval, and Rhoswen stifled a laugh.

"Yes, Eostre, all right. Rhoswen, that was very good, although I do not believe you had to try very hard with hungry little Bassett." He moved to open the door of Eostre's adjacent stall and gestured for her to go out and hunt with her son. The two dragons took off running and leapt into the air, Eostre with more grace than her frantic, shorter-legged whelp.

"He's fine," Darr Beval said, watching the group tense at the young red's mangled take-off. "He acts as though he has not been fed for an eternity, but I promise you, he has only been kenneled since late yesterday when they last hunted." He smiled as the group relaxed, and he drew Rhoswen aside. His eyes wore red rims, as if from lack of sleep, and his stubble appeared thicker than the day before. Around his neck, she noticed the thin leather straps of a necklace trailing down into his shirt, which hid whatever hung at the end. His voice dropped low and shoulders hunched upward. "Rhoswen, I am about to dismiss you, but before I do, I want to ask you something for your ears alone. Does the royal family have specific plans for dinner tonight, or would you be able to join the Riders here in Keaton for a meal?"

Rhoswen's eyes widened. "Join the Riders? For dinner?" she repeated.

"Yes. Unless there's some frilly banquet you must attend."

Rhoswen was certain her heart had stopped beating. She did not know why he was extending such an honor to her—or whether it truly was an honor. Darr Beval's open disdain for royal airs gave her hope that the invitation could be positive, but with all the attention she had been garnering lately, she couldn't be sure. "There probably is, but I could feign illness," she offered.

He smiled. "Whatever it takes." He turned back to the group, and his voice grew louder again. "Off you go, then, Rhoswen! Head on into lecture; it will begin shortly. The rest of you, come this way. We're going to need another beast. Who's next?"

XVIII

Aethelburh

"She's communicating with them." Gethin stood in his father's shadowy chambers again.

"Nonsense."

The prince could hardly see his father in the scant light of the half-closed oil lamp, but he could *smell* him. Badrick reeked of musky herbs from the bath he had just taken, and water droplets from his sodden hair reignited the smell with each *smack* on the floor around his feet. "She has some kind of connection with them!" Gethin insisted. "She barely has to blink, and the dragons do whatever she wants. It's like they're entranced by her. And Darr Beval is watching her, too. He—"

The whites of Badrick's eyes flashed in the dim light. "What do you mean he's watching her?" he hissed.

"He had his eye on her like a Failsafe on her first flight. He pulled her aside and whispered to her after she unkenneled a young red on her first try—not that it was much of a feat, considering Bassett flew off to hunt with his mother as soon as she got him out. But it looked like she was communicating with the red's mother during the process, too." Gethin's tone sounded bitter, even to him, but his father was not in a coddling mood. *As if he ever were.*

"Communicating with the red's mother," Badrick repeated flatly.

"Eostre. It's not like Rhoswen tethered to her—she's already tethered."

"Already tethered… " Badrick muttered.

Gethin wondered whether his father were going to parrot him all day. He should not have wondered it aloud.

After Badrick explained the remarkably dissimilar lifespans of endearing birds who repeated what they heard and pathetic sons who *repeatedly* disappointed their fathers, he returned to the subject at hand. "Who else saw Beval speak to your cousin?"

"Her whole group, I suppose," Gethin replied, his shoulders lowering from their defensive hunch around his ears. "She was the first student to unkennel. But the others aren't smart enough to recognize what they saw—probably thought it was beginner's luck."

Badrick grumbled something unintelligible to the darkness, then asked, "How did Thane do?"

Gethin shrugged. "The beast was hesitant, but he managed to do it on the first try, too." His tone grew dismissive.

Badrick sneered at his son. "Jealous, are we?"

"Of Thane? I'd be jealous of Rhoswen first, and I would never be jealous of a girl."

"You should be, Gethin, for that *girl* is more of a threat to you than I ever will be."

A confusing, albeit harrowing, thought. Gethin felt the hair rise on the back of his neck, and his eyes widened.

"Indeed," Badrick said, recognizing his son's concern. "What do you think is going on?"

Badrick had never asked for his son's opinion, and Gethin was so taken aback, he began to stammer. "I-I-I, uh, I think she might m-make, uh, good caretaker stock."

The king nodded and ran his fingers over his beard. "Has Aelfraed shown any interest in her?"

"None that I know of," Gethin replied.

Badrick rolled his eyes. "Of course. You'd only know that if you *paid attention!* Perhaps you should start *now*. Your first lesson: barracks gossip is almost impossible to quell once it has taken hold. Your second: beginner's luck loses its shine when it never seems to fade away. It's only a matter of time before the few who have already noticed a pattern will verify it with others. She is a Stanburh *and* your cousin, and if that is not enough to give her status among her peers, the addition of an obvious predilection toward Realm Riding will." His fingers drummed on the closed lid of the ornate, inlaid jewelry box on the table beside him. *Mother's,* Gethin thought. "Watch her. Watch her as much as Beval does—*more*. Getting a hungry whelp out of a stall is of little consequence. When she begins flying, *that* will prove telling."

Once Gethin had left the room, Badrick slumped into his wingback chair and eyed the familiar jewelry box on his late wife's vanity. He sneered at it and then looked up toward the ceiling, which was invisible in the darkness.

"She's *just* like her father," Badrick muttered. "Allistair was always so proficient with dragons, even before he tethered. He had a way with them—

made it look so easy, like he could have tethered to them all. I'm sure *you* remember." He grimaced at the memory as a droplet of cool water slipped down the nape of his neck. He shivered. "It was like he could have *everything* he wanted…." His grimace curved into a devilish smirk. "Well, *almost* everything. I still got the one thing that realmed brother of mine desired most." Badrick closed his eyes, relishing the thought before it morphed from something pleasurable into inevitable agony.

"You always knew what to say to make me understand why the realm is like it is." He spoke softly, addressing the room as if he were not alone. "You always made everything seem fairer—as if your justifications could actually make D'Erenelle as worthy a place as you thought it was."

His eyes popped open. "It isn't worthy anymore," he spat, his conviction mounting, "but that won't stop me from saving it for you, Orla."

Rhoswen walked with Thane to his room after lecture. As he chattered about his experience unkenneling Audrey, a young and exhausted tawny, she realized how engaged and vibrant he seemed—no more of that indifference he had feigned before arriving in Aethelburh. She had paused on her way to lecture to watch him coax the dragon from her stall with graceful gestures that made the lad who had failed before him grumble bitterly. But she could tell that *Thane* had not nexed with Audrey to get her to come out….

After nexing with Rusalka, Rhoswen had privately hoped that their connection had been a fluke—one that would not be replicated with any other dragon but the one to whom she finally tethered. Maybe Rusalka was a relative of Kuney or Cahal…. There had to be a *logical* explanation. But Bassett's refusal to heed Rhoswen without nexing, as if he already knew of her ability and expected her to use it, confirmed that something was different about her—perhaps *wrong* with her.

Rhoswen had never kept secrets from Thane, but her uncertainty about whether she was somehow broken or freakish made her hesitate sharing with him now, when they finally had the privacy to talk. She thought back to Darr Beval's offer. At least she could reveal one thing to her brother.

"… I don't know why she was so tired—"

"We have been invited to eat with the Riders tonight," she blurted out, somewhat inaccurately, before she could reconsider his inclusion.

Thane stopped in the middle of the hallway, his eyes widening. "Pardon?"

Rhoswen nodded.

"Since when?"

They were halfway to Thane's room, and Rhoswen began walking backward through the hall waving him to follow her as he processed this information. She belatedly realized how little she wanted to discuss this in public—regardless of how deserted it appeared. "Since I finished unkenneling Bassett. Darr Beval pulled me aside and asked if we could join them for dinner down in Keaton." Thane was her one ally; she *had* to invite him. Then, he could only be half as mad when he found out what else she was hiding from him.... She just hoped Darr Beval wouldn't object.

"*We*?" Thane asked, following her. They'd almost reached his door. "That's quite an honor, Rose. Why would they invite us?"

Rhoswen hoped he was right. She stepped into his room and closed the door behind them. "That, I do not know. But the invitation seemed serious enough. We need to come up with an excuse to avoid joining our family at dinner."

Coming up with excuses intrigued Thane enough to rouse him from his shock. "Illness would not do for both of us," he said.

"No," she agreed. "Even if we could pull it off, Badrick would probably behead his cook for giving us food poisoning or a servant for not closing a window against a draught. I will not have anyone executed on our behalf."

Thane shot her a look like she was being dramatic. "Training fatigue?" he suggested instead.

"After we both unkenneled on the first try?"

"Uncle Badrick doesn't know that."

"Oh, I am certain he does." She stared at him.

He sighed. "Gethin."

She nodded. "Or any other spy. You know our every move is being reported to the king." *Or, at least, that's what our parents told us to expect.* Thane didn't argue.

They racked their brains—additional training could not be corroborated, disinterest was unacceptable, taking dinner in their rooms could limit their mobility—and they kiboshed every suggestion.

"Touring nearby villages," Thane said.

"To what end?" Rhoswen asked.

"For dinner. Peasant food. Like home," he joked. "Homesickness is always acceptable."

"So homesick that we want to snub Badrick's chef and eat with commoners?" She made a face. "We're probably better fed at home, Thane."

"Maybe, but we live more humbly than *this*," he said, glancing around them. "We'll say we want to go exploring—see how the other half lives—and we'll find something to eat while we're out. When we return, we'll give a vague enough description not to draw any suspicion. Anyway, they probably spend little time in the nearby villages, so why should we worry too much about accuracy?"

Rhoswen shrugged. "It will have to do."

Thane frowned. "Why, thank you for your enthusiastic vote of confidence."

It seemed as good a plan as any, but Rhoswen knew her lackluster reaction would goad her brother into talking, and she had questions about his earlier behavior. "Why were you acting strangely at breakfast this morning—you know, when Delwyn came in?"

He grimaced. "I think I know what he was looking for."

"You found his family heirloom?"

He nodded. "The other night—when we were snooping around in the cellar. It must have broken and fallen off Delwyn's wrist when he and the cook were moving a sack of flour."

"So, why not give it back to him?" she asked. "He looked worried sick."

He shook his head. "Then he'd know I've been roaming the castle. Darr Thorndon said we could be punished for leaving our rooms at night.... I'm not sure we're supposed to explore the castle at *any* time of day. Delwyn is Uncle Badrick's waitman; we can't risk his reporting our movements to the king."

"That would be a pretty ungrateful way of repaying us for returning his family heirloom," Rhoswen replied.

"I don't think it's an heirloom," Thane said. He drew the broken bracelet from his pocket and handed it to his sister. "It doesn't look old or worn with time. It's like nothing I've ever seen before."

"But I have," she replied, turning it over in her hands. It matched the weird sun-key her waiting-woman wore. "Lorelle has something just like this."

"You don't think he stole it from her, do you?" he asked.

She shook her head. "She still has hers. It's a necklace. I inquired, but she didn't want to discuss it. Whatever this is, they both seem to value it. We need to give it back." She looked at her brother, whose expression had turned skeptical. "We *are* going to return it to Delwyn, aren't we?"

He hesitated. "Shouldn't we find out why he places so much value on it first?"

"Thane!" Rhoswen chided. "It's not *ours* to trifle with. Delwyn looked wretched when he couldn't find it."

"I know." Thane grabbed the bracelet and stuffed it back in his pocket. "But now, I also know they're both being secretive about it. No one looks that stricken by the loss of a *charm*." Rhoswen flashed him an intractable look, and he held up his palms in surrender. "Let's just see if Lorelle will give us a clue as to what it is, so we can find a way to return it without incriminating ourselves." He flashed her a devilish grin. "We have more important things to tend to. Let's go report our intended travel for the evening."

"Again? So soon?" Elsie asked in exasperation as she bustled down the hall.

Lorelle chased after her, marveling at how mismatched the woman's name was to her demeanor. "Elsie" seemed so sweet, and its bearer... *wasn't*. The older waiting-woman had a mousey look about her, with her petite frame, fuzzy brown-gray hair, and small features, but none of that made her any more endearing. No one, as far as Lorelle knew, had ever seen Elsie smile, and her brow was permanently creased from her constant frowning.

"Lorelle, that will be the third time this month. And in case you've forgotten, your late return this morning prevented us from helping Lady Rhoswen into her leathers before breakfast." She paused at the corner to fix Lorelle with a perturbed glare. Then, she turned on her heel and continued down the next hall.

"I know," Lorelle said, following her. "I'm sorry, but my mother—she—she is so ill. I moved her to D'Aethely, so she would be close to the castle, and I would have to take off less time to visit her."

"But instead, you are taking off more."

Elsie was not the worst superior Lorelle had ever worked for, but she was in the worst position. As head of the female staff in the castle and former waiting-woman to the queen, she had both all the power her position implied and none of it. With Queen Orla gone, Elsie had to report to the king, and she did not have the kind of rapport with him that she had had with her former mistress. Generally, King Badrick did not much care what Elsie did or how well she coordinated her staff of waiting-women. But if one of them did something wrong, then Elsie heard about it directly from him, and that was never a pleasant ordeal.

"You are putting me in a terrible spot, Lorelle," Elsie continued. "We are understaffed as it is. No one flocks to Aethelburh for a position in the royal household anymore."

Lorelle did not relish putting Elsie in such a bind. She was not the warmest of women, but Lorelle did not envy the amount of pressure Elsie could find herself under at any given moment—nor did she wish to add to it.

Still.... "I have been looking for additional waiting-women to help us...." Lorelle trailed off in dismay. She had had little success.

"Exactly my point," Elsie snapped. She stopped to sigh at Lorelle and offload her armful of linens to her. "Go take care of your mother. But you'll be pulling additional duties when you return—the ones I'm struggling to get the other girls to do. I can give them more tasks to cover you, but only if they're not unsavory. Those I will save for you. Do you understand?"

Delightful, Lorelle thought. She nodded. "Thank you, Elsie. I truly appreciate it." She hauled the linens toward the stairs to take them to the washers on her way out.

"And keep looking for another waiting-woman!" Elsie's small but powerful voice boomed through the hall.

XIX

Keaton

When Thane and Rhoswen asked Gethin to excuse them from dinner, their cousin asked which village they planned to visit.

Thane shrugged. "Whatever one catches our eye, I suppose."

Gethin sneered at them, and a chill ran up Rhoswen's spine. "Certainly any one you choose would be more readily accessible on horseback," he suggested.

Something about his tone made Rhoswen believe they had already erred in their story. After some futile debate, the Stanburhs begrudgingly saddled their horses and rode away from the castle. Once the highest turret of Aethelburh was out of sight behind a hill, they turned into the woods, tied up their mounts, and snuck to the drakiary on foot.

"I don't think he bought it," Rhoswen said to Thane as they crunched through the coarse brush along the forest floor. "Do you think he'll track us?"

Thane snorted. "If you continue to break every twig in our path, he won't have to track us at all. He will simply *follow* us to Keaton."

Rhoswen scowled as another loud *snap* sounded under her right foot. They snuck out of the forest near the bottom of the valley and made their way through the drakiary toward the dining hall.

Rhoswen had not yet told Thane how her training experiences might have contributed to their dinner invitation. She had *intended* to tell him, but not only had she found little opportunity, she also did not know *how* to explain it. Now, she only hoped he wouldn't be angry with her postponement when she finally *did*.

The dining hall felt quite warm. The long tables that spanned the length of the room were lined on both sides with students, and the heat from roaring fires seeped through the open archways leading from the kitchen. Its inhabitants were in a raucous state of feigned starvation. With flatware gripped in each fist, they slammed the tables on either side of their plates in a continuous and rattling beat. Finally, their noisy impatience shifted to celebration as large platters of food emerged from the kitchen. Hands flew faster than the platters could move, and the cheering dulled to the rumble of idle chatter and the clanking of utensils. Across the front of the room, perpendicular to the students, stretched the long Riders' table where the instructors sat. Rhoswen didn't know they ate with the trainees. *Perhaps he simply wanted us to share a meal with the other students,* she thought as she scanned the length of the head table for Darr Beval. Their eyes met, and her heart raced as he crossed toward her.

"You made it!" he called over the din. "You'd think we never feed them!"

Rhoswen surveyed the enormous trays of food passing down the length of each table; it took two or three pairs of hands at a time to keep the platters moving. "Clearly the opposite," she said, adding, "Thank you for having us."

The Rider seemed unperturbed that she had extended the invitation to her brother. "You're always welcome. Join us! I hate to separate you, but the only empty seats are at either end of the main table. Thane, why not sit with Darr Thorndon, there? I know he wants to praise you for your marvelous unkenneling skills this afternoon. Rhoswen, come sit by me, so I may praise you for yours."

Thane and Rhoswen exchanged glances—no other students were seated at the head table. With a shrug, Thane bounded off to sit beside his trainer as Darr Beval guided Rhoswen to the seat beside his.

"So," Darr Beval's eyes sparkled with mischief, "what tale of intrigue—or boredom—did you have to create to escape the royal clutches?"

His impudence toward the royal family surprised her, especially in front of the king's niece and on the king's own grounds. But Keaton had an air of rebellion about it that seemed to permit, if not *encourage,* such behavior, and *she* certainly wouldn't defend her uncle's honor—if she could call it that. "Visiting nearby villages."

"Hm," Darr Beval hedged, "we probably should have worked on that. With D'Aethely ringing the castle grounds, it's not the likeliest of stories."

"Is that why Gethin didn't seem to believe us?" Rhoswen asked, tucking rogue bangs behind her ear. No ring town was denoted on the old map she had used to trace their route from Stanburh, and she and Thane had come to Aethelburh through the uninhabited King's Forest. *Why didn't I think to research our plan with a map from the hidden room behind the layered library?* She grimaced at yet another secret she had kept from Thane.

"Probably," Darr Beval replied. "It's not a nice area and definitely not somewhere you two should be roaming unprotected. Still, I think we can supply you with enough details to impress your cousin and throw him off your scent." He winked.

Gethin's attention wasn't the only scrutiny Rhoswen meant to avoid. She glanced around the room at the engrossed students devouring their meals. "Should we really be sitting at this table, Thane and I?" she asked. Her gaze met that of a trainee she didn't know, and he turned to whisper in his neighbor's ear. Rhoswen moved her bangs back into her face to shield herself from view. She and her brother had come in relatively unnoticed for all the commotion, and it had been her hope to maintain that anonymity.... Sitting at this table seemed at odds with that notion.

"Why not?" Darr Beval asked, leaning closer. "You are so concerned about blending in, Rhoswen, but the arena is not the place to do it. Stand out when you train, or the dragons will not respect you. Although, so far, that has not been an issue, has it?"

Their discussion was interrupted by a platter of food, and Rhoswen eagerly selected a warm roll, a chicken leg, and several scoops of vegetables. She dug in, hopeful that her occupied mouth could help her avoid this conversation. As much as she wanted to talk about her experiences with someone, she could not shake the feeling of danger, given the number of ears nearby. She did not know whom she could trust. Yet, she wanted to trust Darr Beval so badly....

Her host smiled. "Eat away, Rhoswen! But you shan't escape me this evening. We will chat after dinner."

Thane had been right: the food at Keaton was much more like the fare she was accustomed to at home, which instilled in Rhoswen both comfort and homesickness. The combination disarmed her, and as she engaged in pleasant conversation with Darr Beval, she struggled to maintain her guard. She enjoyed his rebellious commentary on the royal family more and more with every well-placed remark.

"You know Aelfraed, our caretaker?" Darr Beval asked between mouthfuls.

Rhoswen swallowed. "Of course."

"He would like to see you, as well. We can meet up with him after dinner if that's all right."

"Ah, the true purpose of my invitation finally comes to light," Rhoswen said. "I am to muck out the stables."

"You had to find out eventually," Darr Beval replied with a grin. "Whether you wish to stand out in training or not, you have not gone unnoticed. Anyone who has paid even the slightest attention as you work your magic with the dragons—"

At the word "magic," Rhoswen's thoughts flashed to her compass, and her heart began to pound. "It—it's *not magic*," she stammered, her eyes widening. *He does not know about my compass,* she reminded herself. But those who worked magic could often develop an unfavorable reputation, and although she had no idea whether magic let her do what she did—with the compass *or* the dragons—she wanted to avoid any negative impressions about her abilities. Her mind raced, and she realized she was babbling something unintelligible when Darr Beval lifted his palms to stop her.

"Easy," he said gently. "Please know that there is nothing wrong with what you do, and you would be a fool not to use your skills, whatever they are. It was not a reproachful statement." His eyes held a kindness that eased Rhoswen's anxiety, but her heartbeat did not slow as he smiled at her.

Darr Beval's gaze grew more serious, and his voice dropped in volume. "I appreciate your caution, Rhoswen. I joke about your uncle and cousin, but they are no laughing matter. If they feel threatened by your… *powers of persuasion* with the dragons, then you had better believe they will make *you* feel threatened in return—and it will not merely be a 'feeling.'"

Rhoswen had not expected such candor from the Rider, but as much as it frightened her, a part of her already knew the truth of it.

"What does your brother think about all this?"

"He doesn't know," she replied, adding hastily, "but he can be trusted, and I meant to tell him…. We just don't get much privacy in Aethelburh, and I didn't know how—or what—to say." Her host seemed to understand, and she did not try to further justify her reticence.

After that, dinner seemed to come all too quickly to a close. Students and Riders began easing themselves from their benches and chairs. Darrs Beval and Thorndon exchanged glances across the long table and stood, each whisking a Stanburh away from the dining hall in different directions. Once outside, Darr Beval increased his speed, leaving Rhoswen to jog in his wake. They traveled from one end of the stalls to the other, stopping outside the door to Darr Beval's quarters. A faint blush crept into Rhoswen's cheeks, and not from the exercise.

Darr Beval groaned as he opened the door. "You beat us."

Rhoswen peered around him to find Darr Thorndon and Thane already seated on a tattered loveseat. Mismatched furniture outlined the Rider's generous sitting room. Other than some sprinklings of warm oranges and browns, the whole room was outfitted in various shades of tan, as if the décor had been inspired by the color of Fleta's hide. A common decorating convention for Riders. Foreign-looking knickknacks and countless books were strewn about the room in a careless way that made them look both frequently used and long forgotten. Even the ceiling beams were home to various hanging objects: gourds, pitchers, light catchers… and countless other things she could not identify. Rhoswen's eyes traveled to a stairwell at the back of the room that presumably led to Darr Beval's sleeping quarters…. His deflated sigh broke her reverie.

"We were racing them?" she asked breathlessly. "Is this how you two spend your free time?"

"Occasionally," Darr Beval replied, closing the door.

Darr Thorndon grinned. "I guess my way is better, eh?" he asked, his eyebrow bouncing with the insinuation of an inside joke.

"I'm sure," Darr Beval replied with a roll of his eyes.

"So, what is this all about, anyway?" Thane asked. "Rose, do you know why we're here?"

Before she could answer, they were interrupted by a knock at the door.

"Aelfraed," Darr Beval said and let the caretaker in.

"Am I late?" the old man asked, gray eyes twinkling. His coarse white hair highlighted the thick stubble along his chin and brushed the shoulder strap of his rough leather crossbody satchel. The fasteners strained at the sides of the heavy bag as he lifted it over his head and lowered it to the floor. Rhoswen noticed light, worn patches in the soft material of his long caretaker's vest, where he had repeatedly wiped hands and instruments, and its pockets sagged tiredly from years of overloading.

"Not at all," Darr Thorndon replied. "We were *running* a little ahead of schedule." He glanced conspiratorially at Thane, who grinned back.

"Does she know why she's here?" Aelfraed asked, eyeing Rhoswen.

"I think she may have pieced it together by now," Darr Beval said with a wink.

"Well I haven't," Thane said, his tone growing more serious. "What's going on?"

"You haven't told him," Aelfraed said with surprise.

Rhoswen swallowed. "I didn't know how—"

"Tell me what?" Thane asked, looking from face to face.

"What she can do," Aelfraed answered, his eyes still on Rhoswen. She couldn't tell whether he was excited or concerned.

Thane's brow furrowed. "What can she do?"

"Easy, son," Darr Thorndon said, placing a hand on the young man's shoulder.

"What do you think my sister can do?" Thane asked again, ignoring his trainer's warning and rising to his feet.

This was getting out of hand. "I nexed with a dragon!" Rhoswen blurted. The room fell suddenly, deafeningly quiet.

Thane stared at his sister and lowered himself back onto the loveseat. He looked shocked, confused… crestfallen. "Well, then you've already tethered?"

Darr Beval took over. "Rhoswen, did you tether to young Bassett today?" he asked gently.

She shook her head.

"I didn't think so," Darr Beval replied, shooting Aelfraed an unreadable look.

"And Bassett wasn't the only one you nexed with, was he?" Darr

Thorndon asked.

She shook her head again.

Thane looked at Darr Thorndon as if he didn't know him. His face scrunched up tight. "I'm sorry, what is going on here?"

Darr Beval held up his palms. "Let's all sit," he suggested.

XX

Aethelburh

"Lorelle!" a man's tenor called after her as she trudged down the path away from Castle Aethelburh. She spun around, her metal-soled shoes scraping loudly in the dirt and gravel.

"Delwyn? What is it?" Lorelle glanced around them; the king's personal waitman chasing after a waiting-woman as she left the castle might draw the wrong sort of attention.

Delwyn, too, scanned for onlookers. *"I've lost my Transitor key,"* he hissed at her.

Lorelle struggled to remain calm, but her eyes grew wide anyway. *"Delwyn,"* she breathed, "that is not good!"

"I know," he replied miserably.

"When?"

"Yesterday. I'm sure of it.... Or maybe the day before."

She rolled her eyes. "Retrace your steps."

"I have," he whined. "I fear someone might have picked it up."

"Realm it!" she cursed. "You have to keep looking. When do you go back?"

"Soon. Are you going now? Again?"

She nodded.

"So, you won't need yours for a while after that...."

"I'm not lending you mine, Delwyn," she said sternly. "It wouldn't open your Transitor anyway. We're on different teams, remember? You'll just have to find yours."

"What if I can't?" he asked with a nervous glance to either side.

"Do you want me to report it missing?" she offered, already knowing the answer.

"No!" he blurted and shrank from his own volume. *"No,"* he breathed, "not yet. I will keep looking and let you know when you get back."

Movement at the castle gates caught Lorelle's eye; it was time to change the guards. "I have to go," she said and turned on her heel without another word or backward glance. This had to remain Delwyn's problem; she had enough of her own.

BY the time the Heir Whelp is conceived, an Heir Rider will have been chosen to tether to the young Beast. The process behind this selection has never been understood in all the years of our existence; it is conjectured to stem from an instinctive and almost prophetic power of the Queen Dragon and is a well-kept Dragon secret.

- an excerpt, *From Those Outlying*

XXI

Keaton

Rhoswen felt breathless after she finished her tale, and it hadn't taken her long to tell. It was hard to verbalize her experiences but even harder to watch Thane's face as she tried. For the first time in her life, she struggled to decipher her brother's emotions, and by the time she punctuated the ending with a ragged exhalation, he was wearing that same inscrutable expression that Aelfraed had worn earlier. The silence that followed her story did nothing to assuage her fears. She watched her hands fidget in her lap, if only to avoid making eye contact with anyone.

"I don't understand," Thane mumbled.

Aelfraed addressed the Riders. "How many students have witnessed her abilities?"

They shrugged. "Quite a few—if they were paying attention," Darr Thorndon said.

"But I don't know how much they would have gleaned about what she can do," Darr Beval added. "She hides it well enough." Rhoswen appreciated his protectiveness, although she didn't understand his motives.

Aelfraed's expression grew serious. "And the prince? Is he aware of her skills?"

No one spoke again. The silence was dreadful. Rhoswen felt as though she had committed treason, and everyone in the room was formulating an elaborate plan to conceal her mistake.

"We cannot know for sure," Darr Beval said.

"Then we must assume so." Aelfraed closed his eyes. "We must assume that Gethin has seen and reported Rhoswen's actions to his father."

"Well, what is she supposed to do, Aelfraed? Deliberately err in training?" Darr Thorndon asked. "Or should we hold her back? Either would do her a disservice."

"I hardly think someone who can communicate with any dragon in

D'Erenelle could suffer such a disservice, but it matters not," the caretaker replied. "What *does* matter is protecting Rhoswen from the consequences of her powers."

"'*Consequences of her powers?*'" Thane repeated, his voice rising in pitch. "What are we talking about here? Is she in some sort of trouble? From what are we protecting her?"

"From *whom*," Darr Beval corrected darkly.

Aelfraed frowned. "Your family." He reached for his bag, and Rhoswen watched the ropy muscles in the back of his hand flex as his long, knobby fingers clamped onto the spine of a thick book. He slipped it from the bag as if it weighed nothing. All that hard work around the stables may have aged him, but she had seen him lugging bales of hay and buckets of water around the drakiary; he was still as strong as a man half his age.

Rhoswen stared at the book: *Between Realms: The Progression of Dragons*. Its blue-and-silver binding resembled their copies of *An Index of Realms: Judged and Unjudged*, which had been announced as required reading earlier that day.

Aelfraed opened the book and began flipping pages with his callused fingers. "I have a theory."

The binding on the text in Aelfraed's lap was worn and cracked with age—clearly a much earlier edition than the companion text assigned to the students. Yet theirs was also considerably thinner than the less-modernized version she had seen on her parents' shelves and in the overflow library. She began to wonder how the publishers had gotten all that information into so much smaller a space without diminishing the typeset… until she realized the conversation around her was already well underway.

"—but Deowynn and Blaxton have never produced any offspring," Aelfraed was saying. "She will be in heat again soon, and Blaxton will fly her, whether Badrick wants him to or not. It is entirely possible that Deowynn is finally readying herself for a *different* Judgment."

Darr Beval's brows creased. "We've all been expecting that for years."

"What does this have to do with Rhoswen's abilities?" Thane asked.

"Where are you in their history lessons?" Aelfraed asked the Riders.

"Just starting," Darr Thorndon replied.

Aelfraed shook his head. "Still beginning with care and feeding before they know *why* they're caring for and feeding them, eh?"

Darr Beval ran a hand through his hair, whether in nervousness or annoyance. "We find they focus better on lecture when they aren't distracted by the idea of interacting with the dragons for the first time," he explained.

Aelfraed dismissed the trainer's notions. "So, they are, as yet, aware of very little. Well, I will attempt to tell these two the rest—*not* so you can sleep through lecture, mind you—but so that you have a better idea of why Rhoswen's power is so dangerous."

"Dangerous?" Thane asked, his pitch increased by worry.

"It isn't in today's books," Aelfraed continued, scanning the page. He found what he was looking for near the top and placed a wrinkled fingertip on the spot. "To *un*-educate the masses, the books used in lecture now are heavily abridged—censored, even. I do not agree with King Badrick's dubious attempt at keeping this realm in the dark. But this older text has what I need."

"How did you get that?" Darr Beval asked. "Badrick had all the copies confiscated when his new versions were published."

Aelfraed simply winked at him. "In particular, the new texts leave out the list of telltale traits that are possessed of an Heir Rider." He stared at Rhoswen, gray eyes sparkling again.

"Heir Rider?" Thane asked.

"Heir Rider," Aelfraed confirmed. "Rhoswen, you fit the description."

No one spoke. They all looked as though they were processing the caretaker's mystifying claim. Rhoswen's heart hammered in her chest, and a rush of blood overwhelmed her senses. She suddenly felt faint—and it had nothing to do with her required reading.

"You think she's the Heir Rider?" Thane asked, paling. His reaction made Rhoswen feel like crawling under her chair.

Aelfraed leaned back, readying himself to lecture. "You already know that our realm is predicated on a system of balance. The king, queen, and their royal dragons must be mated to stabilize the benevolent and malevolent forces in the realm. If imbalance becomes permanent, the queen dragon will forsake the realm, leaving it to the Narxon to cleanse."

This much Rhoswen knew, but she had never heard the Narxon's vulture-like predation described quite so generously. It must have shown on her face.

Aelfraed smiled at her. "Yes, *cleanse,*" he repeated. "Don't forget, Rhoswen, that while the Narxon bring absolute destruction to the realm, they do so to allow it to regenerate and once again sustain dragons, Riders, and the life they protect.

"The royal line had balanced this realm for hundreds of years, but when Queen Orla passed away, King Badrick took advantage of his unchecked power. Our royal dragons have not yet produced the offspring necessary to move to another realm, but if you have already been chosen as the Heir Rider, then it is only a matter of time before Deowynn conceives in preparation to hand the reins of rulership over to her Heir Whelp—and you—in the new realm."

"Rulership?" Thane repeated.

Rhoswen stared at Aelfraed, wide-eyed. "But I can't be the Heir *Rider;* I'm not a Rider yet. I haven't tethered—"

"And if I am right, you won't until your dragon is born," Aelfraed replied.

Again, a blank-faced silence ensued. Rhoswen squirmed in her seat, her mind numbed by racing thoughts. Finally, Thane asked the one question she couldn't even begin to verbalize. "How can we be sure my sister has been chosen as the Heir?"

"Thank you, Thane." Taking his cue, Aelfraed tipped up the book in his lap and cleared his throat. "*The Heir Rider,*" he read, "*is possessed of a long list of proficiencies, the array of which shall be encompassed by no other trainee in entirety. While another trainee may exhibit the occasional, analogous aptitude, the Heir Rider is identifiable by his or her possession of most, if not all, of those listed forthwith. (Note: These traits have been compiled severally from sources of inconsistent merit, and this should be considered in their overall validity and applicableness to the Heir Rider's identification.)*"

Darr Beval rolled his eyes. "This is why we use the new text."

"Translation?" Darr Thorndon asked through a yawn.

Aelfraed glared at them, but a flicker of humor lit behind his narrowed eyes. "Although this list may not be entirely accurate," he explained, "what follows is a tenuous compilation of traits the Heir Rider could possess." He fixed the Riders with a more serious stare. "Jest as you please, but Badrick has outlawed this text for a reason; yours doesn't contain this information—*deliberately.*" The Riders exchanged cowed glances, and Aelfraed returned to the book. "*Can predict the onset of rain.*"

"How far in advance?" Thane asked.

"It says several days." Aelfraed reapplied his finger to mark his spot as he looked up.

Thane turned to his sister. "You can do that."

"Only by three days," Rhoswen replied.

"That's more than most can do!" her brother insisted.

"Why is that important?" Darr Beval asked.

Aelfraed consulted the text. "Apparently, it relates to the ability to guess when the Narxon Rain will fall—it predicts Descents."

"Handy," Darr Thorndon quipped.

"*Aptitude in training and when working with dragons,*" Aelfraed continued reading aloud. "It says dragons will even be eager to work with the Heir."

"I've seen that," Darr Beval said.

"Bassett was just being sweet," she replied.

"And Rusalka?" Darr Beval asked.

Rhoswen felt her cheeks warm.

"There are more," Aelfraed said, scanning down the page. "She may be possessed of strong intuition or special assistance from the dragons in the form of a device or preternatural power. She might be able to read special languages or have '*extraordinary memory skills, either in detail or chronological prematurity,*'" Aelfraed read. He smiled at the confused expressions surrounding him. "That means the Heir can remember some of the earliest happenings in his or her life—events that would have occurred long before most memories are normally formed."

"Well, that's Thane," Rhoswen blurted. "He has memories from before I was born—when he was less than two."

Thane's cheeks colored at her words.

"You may not have all the traits," Aelfraed reminded her. "And it is common for other Riders to possess the occasional Heir-like skill. In Thane's case, an exceptional memory."

"So, how do we know *he* isn't the Heir?" Rhoswen asked.

"Because I'm not nexing with every dragon I meet," Thane replied in a tone Rhoswen could not decipher.

"And that is the most important one: the Heir has the power to nex with any and all dragons. This is a trait that is singular to the Heir—and it would seem Rhoswen possesses it. There can be no greater sign than that," Aelfraed said.

"I've only nexed with three—" Rhoswen began to protest.

"And two were tethered to someone else," Darr Beval interjected.

"Did you nex with Deowynn?" Darr Thorndon asked. Rhoswen shook her head. "But she asked for and quite readily approved of you, from what I heard. That should tell us something, too."

Darr Beval hunched over and pinched the bridge of his nose between his forefingers and thumb. "So, she is in danger because of me."

"Darr Beval," Aelfraed began, "I do not mean to damage your pride, but Rhoswen is not the Heir simply because you introduced her to the queen dragon for a requested audience. Deowynn knew of Rhoswen long before they met. Dragons possess senses that we do not. It was only a matter of time before the two came together—and likely in a far more conspicuous setting, had you not facilitated the meeting privately."

"In other words, you're not *that* special," Darr Thorndon assured his friend, "but you did protect her from making a scene."

"She still made enough of one; Gethin knows the two have met. He has almost certainly told the king of what transpired," Darr Beval said.

"Again, an inevitability," Aelfraed said. "Knowing that has already happened only prepares us that much more. We must decide how to handle Rhoswen's gift. She is your future queen, and we must all protect her with our lives."

The way the word "your" morphed into "our" in that sentence struck Rhoswen even before the implication of her impending royal status. "What do you mean, Aelfraed?" she asked.

The sparkle faded from Aelfraed's gray eyes, but Rhoswen couldn't decide whether he looked sad or tired. "I will protect you as fiercely as the rest while you are in this realm, dear Rhoswen, but you will not be *my* queen. I cannot travel forth to the next realm. I will perish with the rest when the Narxon come, for I am not a Rider and cannot Move like you can. But it will be my pleasure and my honor to make certain that *you do.*"

Tears formed in Rhoswen's eyes. She did not know this man—any of these men, save Thane—and they would protect her as fiercely as her brother. If Aelfraed spoke true, she would be *queen*, and these men were ready to predicate their every move on that notion. She would owe them *everything*, and they owed her *nothing*. She was a young, inexperienced Rider-in-training, and everyone in Keaton—every Rider in the *realm*—would be obliged to lay down his or her life for her. How was she supposed to feel about that?

Aelfraed seemed to read her mind—or perhaps her face. "This is a lot to take in," he said softly. "We must discuss this in doses. It's getting late. Thane, it may be prudent to return your sister to her chambers. I suppose you have a lie in place to justify your absence from the castle?"

Thane nodded and explained their plan. The men wove together a tighter alibi, describing some nearby sites to Thane, who perched on the edge of the couch, nodding at every detail, as if to confirm he had memorized it.

But Rhoswen barely heard a word. She was watching her brother. She recognized the sharp determination behind his eyes and realized, with relief, that he had gone into protection mode. It was a mindset she had grown to love him for, once she was old enough to appreciate that he was trying to shelter her rather than restrain her. Despite his inscrutable, earlier reactions to her supposed identity, he had commited a contrived alibi to memory to safeguard her. And she was grateful for it because—

"She has not heard a word of this," Aelfraed observed to Thane with amusement. "Get her to bed. Try to do all the talking if you run into someone." His voice grew sterner. "And do not mention any of this to a soul outside this room."

They all stood, and Thane ushered his sister toward the door.

"Sleep well, you two," the caretaker added.

XXII

Aethelburh

Rhoswen's head swam as Thane escorted her back to her room. She did not remember saying goodbye to the Riders and Aelfraed, but she had a hazy memory of gathering the horses and her brother repeating their alibi on the way back to the castle. Thankfully, they hadn't needed to use it.

Thane helped her into bed. "Rose, are you all right?"

She shook her head. "I have endangered everyone."

"What?" His eyebrows furrowed, and he sat down beside her. When she did not look at him, he turned her chin in his direction. "This isn't your fault. It isn't *a fault*. This is supposed to be a good thing—a tremendously wonderful thing! And now that we know about it, we can help everyone to safety. This whole realm has been in danger since Aunt Orla passed away. You haven't endangered a soul. You will save us all."

"Not all," she protested, thinking of Aelfraed's kind, gray eyes. "So many will stay behind…."

"That's just the way of things," he muttered.

"It shouldn't be." She gazed up at him. She didn't know how to repair the inequality between those who Moved or stayed, but her first concern was her brother. She couldn't do this without him. "Aren't you mad at me? Mother and Father kept you from training for over a year because of me! You could have tethered by now—been protected by a bond with your dragon—but you're not *because of me.* Instead, you are just another trainee, trying to tether before it's too late—before you can't Move. On top of it, I'm in danger now—and you might be, too, by association." Tears welled up in Rhoswen's eyes again. "You can't even fly away from here at the first sign of trouble. *Aren't you furious with me?!*" she hissed at him. She wished she could yell. Tears streamed down her face.

He shrugged. "Well, you can't fly away yet either, and my horse can outrun yours…."

She stared at him. The corners of his mouth quirked upward, and she swatted at him as her sobs vacillated between anguish and laughter. He cradled her into his arms and rocked her until the raggedness of her breathing smoothed. Finally, she pulled away enough to look into his eyes.

He wiped at her face with his thumbs and smiled. "I could not be mad at you for what Mother and Father did. Had *you* been older, they would have held *you* back. They wanted us to protect each other."

"But it has delayed your tethering."

"It's not about the delay, Rose." He rubbed a hand over his face. "It's… about what I've lost—*after* tethering. I'll admit it is a disappointment to know I I'll not inherit…." His voice broke before he could finish.

A wave of guilt overtook Rhoswen as she realized what her brother was sacrificing. Her voice quavered. "Stanburh—"

"It was to be *mine*, Rose. It… won't be now." He forced his lips into a smile and continued before she could apologize. "Of course, if you're queen in the next realm, you can give me an even bigger territory of my own to lord over!"

They both chuckled, but Rhoswen could not shake the feeling that she had wronged her brother. Her uncertainty must have shown.

"We will get through this together," he assured her. "It's what we Stanburhs do."

We Stanburhs. Her eyes popped wide. "What about our parents?" she blurted.

"They're Realm Riders. They'll come with us when we Move."

"But only if they know to protect themselves," she countered. "I've put them in danger, as well. What if someone goes after them?"

"'Goes after them…?'" Thane put his hands on her shoulders. "Rose, breathe. Badrick has no reason to 'go after' our parents. Still, I already asked the Darrs about getting word to them—if they don't know everything already."

Rhoswen searched her brother's face. "What are you talking about?"

Thane stood and paced the room. "I'm beginning to wonder whether our parents already know that you're the… *you know*. When you and I were talking about Cahal and Kuney the other day, you seemed surprised that I remembered what gestures I used to kennel them. At first, I thought you were just too young to remember what we were taught, but then I realized that you should have still been using them. But you never had to gesture to them, did you?"

Rhoswen shook her head. "I don't think so. They always just did what I wanted them to do."

"Did you nex with them?"

"No. I mean, I guess I must have thought things at them, but they never *responded*. They just… did what I wanted."

Thane continued along his path across the room. "Mother and Father must have realized what you were doing early on and asked their dragons not to nex back."

"Why would they do that?"

"To keep you from thinking you were different."

"But I would not have known I was different if I'd always been able to do that."

"Yes, but you might have mentioned it to someone… possibly even outside the family."

"Well, we're talking about it with others outside the family now."

"Only a select few." He rubbed his eyes, and his shoulders slumped as if exhaustion pulled at his frame.

She watched him as her mind reeled. As much as she wanted him to get some rest…. "There is more, Thane."

"More what?" he asked through his hands.

She swallowed audibly. "I don't know whether this is another special power or if anyone could make it work, but I think the compass Father gave me is… *magical*. Maybe he wanted me to have it—as a way of protecting myself—but—"

"Whoa, whoa, wait." Thane was gaping at her now, his eyebrows a crumpled mess of confusion. "Start from the beginning. It's *magical*?"

She was almost taken aback by the note of disbelief in his voice. They had just been told the unthinkable—that she could be the *Heir Rider*. Was a magical compass really beyond comprehension at this point? "Yes."

"Explain."

"Remember all those old maps our parents told us Uncle Badrick was obsessed with when he was younger? He still has them." She told her brother about the hidden maps room in the cellar library and how she had activated the castle floorplans. "When I placed my compass and the right combination of objects on the maps, one of the stone walls in the room began to shimmer, and it opened a portal through the castle to our uncle's study."

"A portal," he repeated.

"Yes, and I started to go through it, but then Uncle Badrick walked into the study, and he almost caught me. I had to close the portal before he realized I was there." She exhaled, and the weight of her secret finally lifted from her shoulders.

Thane stared at her, his mouth still agape. She wondered if he would begin drooling. "Show me," he said finally.

"Now?" she asked.

"Why not?"

"Aren't you tired?"

"I'll sleep after we Move!" he exclaimed.

The elongated knock of Gethin's personal waitman sounded on the door to his chambers. The prince recognized the long pause between each *thunk*. "Come," he called before the third.

A tall man with a long face and thinning salt-and-pepper hair gradually entered the room. His long-tailed gray waitman's livery was worn with age, and he kept his hands behind his back as he creaked over into a bow. "Siiiiir."

"Yes, Baul?"

"Siiiiir, you had aaaasked about the wheeeereabouts of our visitors this eeeevening."

Gethin rolled his eyes. The man did everything at a snail's pace—knocked, talked, bowed—he probably even breathed slowly. "I had hoped that you might enlighten me *tonight*, Baul."

"Yes, siiiiir. It would seeeeem that your cousins tethered their steeeeeeeds to treeeeees in the forest at the eeeeedge of Aethelburh's groooo-ounds and made their waaaaay on foot into Keeeeeeaton," Baul reported.

Gethin's eyes widened. "Where are they now?" he asked, wishing he didn't have to.

"In Lady Rhoswen's roooooom, siiiiir."

"Indeed, they must be by now, at the rate you've told me this. You have informed no one else?"

"Siiiiir, not a soooooul."

"And you will continue to keep that confidence, Baul?"

"Naturally, siiiiir…."

"Thank you, Baul. That will be—"

Baul interrupted, his eyes half-closed, "Will that be aaaaall, *siiiiir*?"

He even blinks slowly, Gethin thought with impatience. "*That will be all, Baul,*" he said through gritted teeth.

"Thaaaank youuuuu, *siiiiir*." With another overlong bow, Baul shuffled from the room and closed the door behind him.

Despite how much Gethin wanted to scream—as he always did in Baul's protracted wake—his cousins' ruse distracted him. He was wise to have them tracked on their supposed journey to a nearby "village." There wasn't a soul he could conceive of who would willingly spend time in D'Aethely, the filthy assembly of reprobates and unfortunates that ringed the territory of Aethelburh.

If only his father would be as proud of him as he was of himself.

But I will not be telling him any of this, Gethin mused. *At least, not until I can figure out what they are up to. Who's thinking now, Father?*

Gethin moved to his door and peeked out into the hall. It was empty but for his two sentries. With princely purpose, he strode from his chambers and headed for the stairs.

Rhoswen pulled on the book that unlatched the secret door and watched with satisfaction as her brother's eyes widened along with the gap in the shelving.

"How did you figure this out?" he asked.

She rolled her eyes. "How do you think? We're in a library." The only thing Rhoswen loved more than maps was books. Step into a room lined with them, and she would be instantly transported by all the compelling titles—lost in the forest of spines. Her hands would take over, touching interesting covers and picking up hearty tomes to flip through their secrets before she could stop herself.

She slipped in through the gap and moved to the barrel with the maps of Aethelburh. She fished out the parchment rolls and spread them across the table, as her brother took in the space. "Are these all maps?" he asked. "There must be hundreds in here." Rhoswen began weighing down the corners, and Thane peered over her shoulder. "I didn't know there were floorplans in Uncle Badrick's collection," he admitted.

"I didn't know much of anything about Uncle Badrick's collection."

"That makes sense," he said. "I only recall visiting Aethelburh once a few years after the Royal Flight. Were you born yet…? You must have been, but I don't remember Mother being pregnant with you at all. Anyway, I had to have been around two, and I wasn't enjoying the long carriage ride to the castle. Mother tried to excite me with the promise of a peek at Uncle Badrick's huge, colorful maps. But as soon as we got there, a wild argument started up between Uncle Badrick and Father—about what, I didn't understand. The violence of it confused me. We left soon after."

Rhoswen could only nod.

"I don't even know why we went there in the first place," Thane continued. "Oh, but I do remember Mother picking you up and whisking us both out of the castle in the middle of their fight, so you were obviously born. It was a long time ago. You were still in swaddling clothes."

"It's a wonder you remember, Thane," she replied.

He shrugged. "I do, though."

She removed the compass from her pocket and held it in her palm. "Do you remember whether Father had my compass by then?"

Thane's brow furrowed in thought. "I have no idea. I don't know when it came into Father's possession. Weren't you pretty young when he gave it to you?"

Rhoswen nodded. "I remember he put it on a chain, so I could wear it around my neck like a big locket. Maybe he thought I'd be less apt to misplace it that way." Her father never missed an opportunity to remind her not to lose it. "When I got older and started wearing leathers, I turned it back into a pocket piece." It felt to her like she had had it all her life. She was sad to think she could not remember the special moment when her father had given it to her; then again, she might have been too young to appreciate how precious a gift it was anyway. *Could that also have been a deliberate act by my parents?* she wondered. "I honestly can't remember him giving it to me," she admitted.

Thane nodded. "Then you've had it a long time. Mother and Father must have realized what you could do from an early age and given you the compass as a safeguard in case anything ever happened to them."

At Thane's words, Rhoswen felt the knot of worry for her parents' safety tighten in the pit of her stomach. She hoped the Riders would know a secure way of contacting them.

Thane seemed to read her mind and put a hand on her shoulder. "They'll be all right, Rose. The Darrs will help us reach them."

Rhoswen pushed the ominous thoughts from her mind and looked down at her compass. "Do you know where Father got this?" Thane shook his head. "Do you think this is the special device Aelfraed mentioned? The one from the dragons?"

Thane shrugged and studied the maps. "Why don't you show me what these things do?"

"Where do you want to go?" she asked.

"Nowhere," Thane replied. "Can you just show me without leaving this room?"

"Well, sort of." Rhoswen slid out another floorplan and put one finger on each of their rooms. "You have to use something that represents the room to open it. What would you use for a guest room?"

"Maybe it depends on who is staying in it," he offered.

"What if it's empty?" she countered.

"Each room must have something specific in it, then." Thane began to wander the room, running his fingers over the edges of its dusty shelves as he searched for more objects.

Rhoswen closed her eyes, trying to envision the contents of her chambers. She heard a soft scraping sound, and her brother spoke her name.

"What's this?" he asked, pulling a jewelry-sized box from the back of the shelf just above her eye-level. Its lid and base were carved into mirrored cove ogees that came together in a sharp edge of well-polished black wood. Rhoswen ran her fingers along its smooth, swooping surface.

Inside, they found a selection of tiny trinkets and odd bits of broken objects, some more distinguishable than others. She shoved her finger through the pile, and her eyes alighted on a child's magnifying glass no bigger than the length of her finger. She plucked the tiny instrument from the pile and held it up to her eye. The room looked distorted but not larger. "These are for the maps," she half-whispered.

"But you said you used the things on the desk."

"I did because I was trying to weigh the map down, and they happened to fall in the correct places. Why else would he have these trinkets?"

"Doll house?" Thane suggested with a smirk.

She rolled her eyes. "Even *I* didn't play with one of those." She took the box from her brother's hands and set it between them on the table. Then, she sorted the tiny replicas into piles by floor. The little bookend and the magnifying glass sat in one pile for the main floor; the small jam jar, a scrap of roughs leather, and a palm-sized book of poetry sat in another for the cellar. She found objects that could pertain to bedrooms—and a few that didn't correspond to any obvious location.

As Rhoswen fished through the box, the tip of her finger brushed against something soft. She expected to pull out another minature book. Instead, a smooth scrap of worn leather emerged between her fingers. Thane took it from her and held it to his nose.

"What are you doing?" Rhoswen asked.

"Can you not smell it?" he asked, sniffing again.

"I'm not certain I care to," she replied. He held it out to her anyway, and she leaned in toward the scrap. "Is that—dragon?"

He nodded, a triumphant smile on his face. "Saddle leather."

"Are you saying these trinkets can take us *outside* the castle?"

Thane shrugged. "If you think Keaton is that much *outside* of it.... It is still on Aethelburh grounds."

Rhoswen checked the pile of maps she had laid out again. None of them outlined the drakiary. "See if you can find other trinkets for Keaton," she said, moving back to the barrel of floorplans. It held a dozen rolls or better, each with multiple maps curled together. She slid one out and unrolled it between her hands. She did not recognize the place, nor could she read the print, which seemed even more ancient than that used to label the maps of Aethelburh. Several scrolls later, she found one that used a recognizable font, but Rhoswen did not need to read the title to know what she was looking at. "*Thane,*" she breathed.

Thane let the trinket in his hand fall back in the box, and he moved to her side. Out of the corner of her eye, Rhoswen saw his jaw drop in much the same way hers had when she had first seen a solid, stone wall shimmer into transparency.

"It can't be," he whispered, eyeing the parchment.

Rhoswen moved the map over to the table to spread it out, and Thane weighed it down. Laid out before them, there was no denying which floorplan was traced onto the map before them.

Stanburh.

XXIII

The Exchange

"How's she doing?" Lyndon asked with a grin that usually turned women to putty in his hands.

"I can't tell you that," Felicitae snapped. "Are you going to place a bet or not?"

"Well, how am I supposed to place an informed bet without any information?" he asked, stepping closer to her. He could smell her sweet, vaguely floral perfume, which was a feat in this beer-soaked club.

"You're the one who was interested in her," Felicitae reminded him, adjusting her thick-rimmed blue glasses. Her tone was all business, but she did not back away from his advance.

He looked through the lenses at her magnified eyes. *Is it the glasses, or are her pupils dilating?* he wondered, searching her for other signs of desire. "Everyone is interested in her," he replied over the booming Luthean music. He liked hearing the stuff from home in the Exchange—made him feel like he was part of something. But the volume detracted from the smoothness of his voice. He attempted seduction with half-closed eyelids instead. "She's walking into a veritable trap."

"Well, if you haven't continued to research whatever piqued your interest in the first place, that's not my fault. So, if you don't have the information you need, either you have faith in Rhoswen, or you don't." She maintained eye contact with him. "What's it gonna be?"

Can't tear her eyes away, he mused. "Okay, okay. This is running long, right?"

She nodded.

There were a couple ways to lay a bet in the G'Ambit. Those that ran long followed a subject for an extended period, letting the pot ride as the terms of the bet continued to morph with each development. Long runs tended to suit fluid situations that had the potential to change over time, like how a person would fare in a new job—or how long the Heir could hide before detection by a warring faction.

"I remember my first long run," he hollered. "Before your time, naturally. I followed a nightmarish affair in Keaton between an obsessive student and her sadistic trainer. The Rider used her terribly. Still, no request was off limits, even when he asked her to do something truly unsettling to the queen dragon…." He shuddered. "I bankrolled two weeks' vacation and spent the whole time wondering if she deserved what had happened to her." He came away from that trip not with an answer but with some incredible memories.

"This one runs long with termination rights," Felicitae called back.

Lyndon groaned and rolled his eyes. Termination rights allowed whoever ran the bet to end it at any time. Handy in situations where a bet seemed to be going one way when it was placed but took a turn and stood to lose whoever ran it some serious money as a result.

"Oh, nice. So, if this goes sideways, we all get cut off," he yelled. The shoddy clause frustrated Lyndon to no end, even if he often collected cash despite a termination. He had a great instinct for gambling—and the subjects he gambled on.

"You could just place side bets," Felicitae reminded him. She glanced at her watch as a Minister came within spitting distance of their conversation.

Side bets were inconsequential one-offs that anyone could initiate, like whether someone would get a promotion or commit a crime. All you needed was a bookie and one other Exchanger to bet against you. Side bets concluded quickly—so much so that they often paid out by the gambler's next visit to the Exchange. Only if the situation turned complex and gained any real traction in the G'Ambit would an Arbiter or Datist buy out the gambler and turn the side bet into a long run. But that was rare.

The Minister paid them no mind.

Lyndon watched Felicitae's steadying exhalation in the wake of the black jacket. "Fine," he yelled. "For your information, *Felicitae*, I haven't had a chance to get back with my source yet, but I'll let it ride for now. And add this to it." He palmed her the bet with a kiss on the back of her hand. She jerked out of his grasp and pocketed the cash. It was a pittance by Lyndon's standards, but it was early in the game yet—and he was betting blind.

"You don't usually bet on the long runs. It's good to see you divert your interests to someone else in D'Erenelle. Your regular guy boring you?"

"Never," Lyndon snorted. "The diversion is only temporary. And it's not *my* idea to run long on Rhoswen."

Lyndon often broke up his bets on his "regular guy." Broken, or series, bets followed a subject with a sequence of wagers, each determined by a projected outcome that paid out when that outcome came to pass—or didn't. Series bets were good for events that followed a prescribed set of steps, like what transpired in a realm as it reached the end of its lifecycle.

Admittedly, Rhoswen's identification made more sense as a long run, but Lyndon didn't have to like it. Series bets were safer and easier to get out of.

"Pity," Felicitae replied. "I thought you were making progress."

"Progress?" Lyndon repeated. "You know I've been betting on him since he was a trainee? I followed him start to finish in Keaton. From how quickly he would master each phase of his training to whether he would put in for freedom of transfer when he tethered. I watched it all." *And came out a much wealthier man.*

A feisty grin overtook Felicitae's face. "If only your ladies knew where your interests really lie."

"Hold on, now," he began. "That's not—"

"Pleasure doing business with you," she hollered, turning away from him.

He grabbed her by the arm before she could step away. *Last chance.* "How much of a pleasure?" he breathed in her ear.

"Not enough to become one of your overflowing—and *misguided*—chair bunnies," Felicitae replied. She flashed him a condescending grimace and tore free of his grasp.

"Yet!" Lyndon called after her.

XXIV

Keaton

Beval stared at his Riding partner through half-closed, bloodshot eyes. Thorndon had stayed behind long after the Stanburhs and Aelfraed had taken their leave.

"Hey," Thorndon barked to recapture his friend's waning attention, "Beval, what do we do about this? Neither of us would be allowed to make the journey to Stanburh, and I cannot conscience the idea of endangering one of our older trainees on untethered dragonback to send such a message."

Beval waved his hand in helpless acknowledgment. He straddled his chair, slumping over its back, his chin resting on one of his arms and the other arm dangling beside his knee. "What about one of the other Riders?" he asked. *Did I already ask that?* His head drooped a little, and he shook it clear.

"Whom do you suppose we can trust with this? Are you aware of another Rider who yearns to commit treason? I don't remember that coming up at the last Rider meeting. 'This year, rather than a Quaerfest party, let us commit treason against our insane ruler! All in favor?'"

Beval grunted. "Moving is not treason. What of Carnell or Wynnie?"

"Carnell? He's a staunch royalist. Haven't you noticed his sickening behavior around Gethin? And Wynflaeth—the Rider most likely to bed every man in Keaton before Judgment? She knows a lot and says twice as much."

"How do you know her to be a gossip?"

Thorndon scoffed. "Who do you think told me about Carnell?"

"Of course," Beval replied with a grin. "We could go. Feign illness or something."

"We'd have to feign *death* before being allowed to leave," Thorndon insisted. "Aelfraed has messengers...."

"Whose lives he would not want to risk."

Thorndon looked around the room as if someone unwanted could have snuck in without their noticing. "You know, this isn't simply a message to notify Allistair of his daughter's new responsibilities. Moving might not be treason, but reestablishing the Triars is."

Beval's heavy eyelids shot open. *"What?"*

"If you think Badrick won't assemble a counter-faction, you're mad. Someone has to protect Rhoswen."

"I'm not arguing that, but there isn't *any* method of communication secure enough to send *that* kind of message. If such a thing were intercepted, Allistair and Magge would become prime targets."

Thorndon snorted. "Those two have been Badrick's targets for years." He paused, and a smirk curled his lips."If it's treason we're going for, why not aim a little *higher*?"

Beval's head swam in the spiral of his friend's logic. "Thorndon, reestablishing the Triars already *is* high treason. It's a plot against the king."

"Then we have nothing to lose," Thorndon replied.

XXV

Aethelburh

The prince made his way around the balcony from Thane's silent room to press his ear to Rhoswen's door. Either the chamber beyond lay vacant, or the wood and stone muffled any noise within. Gethin's eyes darted around the hall before he reached for the handle. He turned it soundlessly and pushed the door inward, bracing himself for the slightest creak of the hinge—although he was certain his heart was beating more loudly than a hinge could complain. When no light showed through the crack, he continued forward until one of his cousin's bedposts came into view in the moonlight. He squinted at the covers but could not make out a form underneath them. By the time the door was halfway open, all concern for being caught slid off him like an untied cape. He crossed to the bed and laid a hand on the cool covers. He checked the water closet: empty.

"Where could they have gone?" he wondered aloud, crossing to the windows. His eyes settled on Keaton, where a few lights still shone in the Riders' apartments. *Could they be in the drakiary?*

In a swirl of fabric, Gethin stormed from the room, giving the door one good pull behind him as he went. He headed down the hall toward the stairwell, cape flying out behind him and feet pounding so raucously that he did not even hear the slam of the wood against the frame.

Thane looked up at his sister, his eyes wide. "This changes everything."

"Why is there a map of Stanburh down here?" Rhoswen asked.

He shook his head. "I don't know, but if these maps can do what you say they can, we may have found a way to contact our parents."

Rhoswen stared at her brother. "We haven't tried going to Keaton yet—if that's even possible. How do we know we can jump from town to town?

There has to be an object on practically every room along the path between where you are and where you want to go. What could fill the gap *between* castles—between *towns*?"

He shrugged. "What did you use between floors?"

Rhoswen's brow crinkled as she considered the answer. She hadn't used anything; she had simply overlapped the maps at the edges.

Thane let the map of Stanburh roll up to one side of the table. He fished out several trinkets from the box and held them out to her in his cupped hand. "Think any of these could work for our bedrooms?" he asked, extending his hand toward her.

Rhoswen surveyed the miniatures her brother had selected: a straight razor, a hairbrush, a hand mirror, and one specific thing Rhoswen recognized immediately: a tiny replica of the jewelry box that housed the fuchsia bauble she had worn to her first dinner party at Aethelburh. The real box was still in her chambers on the corner of her vanity. "This one is for my room," she said, picking up the tiny box between her finger and thumb.

She traced the most direct route across the three maps and placed the magnifying glass, the history of realms, and a bookend on the map accordingly. Then, she held up the angular, two-armed object. "And this thing is for *this* room."

"A compass," Thane said with a nod. "Makes sense."

Rhoswen scrunched up her nose at her brother. "This pointy thing? It's not a compass." She pointed at the round metal case on the table. "*That* is a compass."

"It's a drawing tool. It measures distances," Thane explained, amusement plain in his voice, "for making maps."

"Oh." Rhoswen looked down at the sharp object in her hand. She had no idea such a device existed. Her enthusiasm for maps had never extended beyond their beauty and function to their creation. "For making parchment *and* portal maps, it would seem." She placed it on the three dots on the map and slid her own compass into place.

The wall across the room shimmered to life. Despite a gasp from her brother, she could not take her eyes off the image of the upstairs library. Rhoswen realized she was squeezing the tiny jewelry box in her right hand as it cut painfully into her palm. She relaxed her grip and stepped toward the portal to look inside.

"Wait— " Thane whispered, but Rhoswen ignored him. She could only see a portion of the library from inside the maps room. "I thought we were going to your room," he hissed.

"Don't you want to see the library?" she asked, edging forward. "We barely had the chance on our tour with Gethin."

A wooden groan sounded from the far end of the library, and Rhoswen realized a door had opened. Heavy, agitated footsteps grew louder as someone hurried across the room. Dark leathers came into view at the edge of the portal as Rhoswen rushed back to the table and slammed the tiny replica of the jewelry box onto the map. Their cousin was turning toward the portal opening as the image in the wall changed to that of her dark, abandoned bedroom.

XXVI

The Exchange

"How did your first double go?" Vonn asked, clinking his gin and tonic against Emmelyn's gin and soda. Tonight, they were trying Otends, a gin from Welsamar. A stark improvement over the Tallulahdurian gin from her previous visit to the Exchange. They had tried it at Randy's insistence, but Vonn confided to Emmelyn that the Tallulahdurian way of making alcohol tended to produce booze that was a little on the harsher side. "A technique better suited to whiskey than herbal liquors," he'd told her. She had to agree.

"The Atrium was amazing," she yelled. "But I thought I was only supposed to deliver Lorelle's message to Emile. I wasn't aware I would have to take another one from Emile back to Janelle."

"You what?" Vonn called back over the music. She could tell from his expression that he was not asking her to repeat herself. He had most certainly heard her in spite of the old-timey Dellatees jazz blaring around them. "That's not good...."

"What's not good?" Kyle asked, suddenly interested. She was starting to understand that Kyle's standoffishness crumbled in the presence of two things: drama and gossip. Vonn repeated Emmelyn's experience. "Really? Emile?" Kyle asked. Emmelyn couldn't tell if Kyle was surprised or vindicated.

Odore, another Transfer Emmelyn had just met, wore a transparent expression of dismay. Emmelyn originally thought he had truncated his name from Theodore. He seemed like the extremist type, who'd reinvent himself so completely that he would annihilate his past but for a single element that would forever remind him of his roots. But he swore Odore had always been his full name, and something about the emphatic way he rolled the R at the end made her believe him. He came from a realm called Assalya, and his accent was unlike anything she had ever heard. If you could marry the musical aspects of Spanish with the harsh edges of German and the lingering vowels of Arabic, you might get something close to the way Odore spoke. Maybe. "I couldn't Transfer for a bad Arbiter. I would quit the Exchange," he declared.

"You can't quit the Exchange," Kyle called back snottily.

"I'd sabotage myself and get exiled, then!" Odore insisted. "I couldn't help a bad Arbiter corrupt a realm for his own financial gain."

Emmelyn appreciated Odore's passion, but she found it hard to discern when he was speaking in facts or opinions.

"Do we even know for sure whether Emile participates in the G'Ambit?" Kyle asked, ever the contrarian. "It could have been legit."

Odore rolled his eyes. "Come on."

"I don't understand," Emmelyn interjected. "What did Emile do that was so bad?"

"We don't know if it was bad exactly," Vonn replied. "But what you Transferred was a *triple*—not a double. Those aren't really protocol, and while they can occasionally occur for legitimate reasons, they are more often… sinister."

He leaned in to explain. "Information from a Runner is supposed to be processed by Arbiters, Datists, and Ivers before the Arbiters hand down an order via Transfer-delivered Transitor. It's a gross violation of protocol for an Arbiter to cut out this processing and decide on the resultant action himself. Unless certain circumstances permit it—and those are rare."

"Then why did Janelle take my Transitor?" Emmelyn asked.

"Like I said: some are legitimate. And Janelle doesn't ask questions," Vonn replied. "We all have our functions here at the Exchange. Questioning things is not one of hers. She just processes what is brought to her."

Odore asked a couple more questions about Emmelyn's experience and shrugged. "It's possible that the Ivers were fast-tracking a move, and all Emile had to do was put the appropriate Iver-sanctioned response in the Transitor, based on the information Lorelle had supplied."

"On her *first* double?" Kyle yelled, his nose scrunching. "Seems to set a dubious precedent, if you ask me."

Emmelyn appreciated Odore's kindness, but Kyle's skepticism was infectious. "But Lorelle had already gone back. How would that 'fast-track' anything if she won't get the message until she returns to the Exchange?"

"It could be delivered to her through another Runner in her area," Vonn explained. "It happens on occasion."

"Either way, Lorelle is good," Emmelyn insisted. "I know she is."

"Runners just do what they're told," Odore hollered in as kindly a tone as one could manage while yelling over loud music. Verbal emotion didn't translate well in the club. That's why lip reading was a must—you often needed facial expressions to augment discussion. "They have to, or they could be exiled."

"You didn't seem to think that was such a bad fate a second ago," Emmelyn countered.

Odore shook his head. "It's not the same for Transfers. Exile a Transfer, and he goes back to his home realm. Exile a *Runner*, and she gets trapped in the realm she is Running in, never to return to her home realm again."

"Wait," Emmelyn hollered, shaking her head as if to clear it. "Runners don't work in their own realms?"

"Sometimes," Vonn yelled. "I do, for example."

Odore rolled his eyes. "That's because you're a Welsamodel."

"Welsamarian," Vonn replied, protesting the at-once flattering and derogatory term.

But Odore rolled right over him. Emmelyn hadn't imagined he could yell any louder. "Welsamodels can't just go anywhere—"

"We can, too!" Vonn hollered back.

"Well, you wouldn't accept a *non*-Welsamodel in your realm," Odore countered. "Anyone not as gorgeous as all of you would stick out like a dragon in the Exchange."

Vonn waved his words away and shifted the conversation to gossip about another recent triple he'd heard of. Struggling to make out the conversation, Emmelyn took the opportunity to check for Lorelle and noticed her waving from across the room. Emmelyn excused herself from her friends and wove through the crowd toward her Runner.

The waiting-woman looked particularly uneasy, and Emmelyn couldn't help but think of the Crew's theories about Emile's behavior. She handed the Transitor to Lorelle, who opened it instantly and read the parchment in front of Emmelyn—just like last time.

Is she just comfortable with me, or is she that *distracted by whatever is going on here…?* Emmelyn wondered.

The parchment strip was too small to hold much script, but Lorelle stood there, reading it for quite some time. Finally, she tucked a reply into the Transitor, locked it, and handed the white block back to Emmelyn. Her face was devoid of emotion except for a slight crease between her eyebrows. Suddenly, she grabbed Emmelyn's hand and gave it a squeeze. "Thanks, Emmelyn," she called sadly, and turned toward the portal doors at the back of the bar.

Emmelyn stood there, dumbstruck by the unusually affectionate gesture. Lorelle's swift departure signalled an unwillingness to answer questions, and Emmelyn made no effort to follow. She watched her Runner disappear and was left staring at the portal doors until someone bumped into her in passing. Reverie broken, she returned to the Crew. Kyle had gone, but Vonn and Odore hadn't moved. "Lorelle was upset," she announced to them, reclaiming her seat. She glanced at her wrist. *One stamp left.*

Emmelyn would be Transferring doubles from now on. A new Transfer was phased in with one-way jobs as an old Transfer was phased out. She had completed her first double—*triple,* actually—so she was a full-on Transfer now. Only, her last few moments with Lorelle told her something had changed yet again.

Odore shook his head. "Maybe her job in D'Erenelle was altered. It's the only thing that makes sense after Emile's triple."

"*Or* she's being reassigned," Vonn yelled.

"Or *she* is," Odore suggested with a nod at Emmelyn.

The idea of her own reassignment put Emmelyn in two minds: if she were being assigned to another Arbiter, that might be okay… but if she were being assigned a new Runner under Emile, that had the potential to be less than ideal. "You're a Runner," she yelled to Vonn, "and you know Lorelle. Can you talk to her? Ask her what's going on?"

Vonn shook his head. "There are some things Runners don't discuss with each other… even Runners within the same realm or on the same team…. Although, I think some chat more than they should." He looked despondent. "I'm sorry, but I can't help you in that way. Transfers aren't supposed to get too connected to their Runners. It's technically meant to be an impermanent relationship." He smiled at her. "I will, however, keep my ears open on this one."

"Perhaps you'll get lucky and be assigned to another *good* Runner," Odore offered. But something about his and Vonn's expressions told Emmelyn that her luck was changing—and not necessarily for the better.

XXVII

Keaton

Beval was still shaking his head, as if by perpetuating the motion, he could somehow change his partner's mind. "We cannot do this."

"Why not?" Thorndon countered. "Is our king not endangering us all? He is doing something to keep us from Moving. *That* is real treason—treason against the Realm Cycle. It supersedes all else."

"You can't prove that."

"No? Deowynn should have long ago produced a whelp with Blaxton, but she has not. Why do you think that is?"

"She might have been waiting for Rhoswen," Beval suggested, his words stretched by a yawn.

"Well, with that logic, one could assume Deowynn knew when Rhoswen would come to Keaton, too. Blaxton flew her shortly before Rhoswen's arrival, and *still*, our queen is not with whelp. Badrick must be doing something to prevent her."

"Perhaps she wants Rhoswen to learn how to Ride before the Move. She cannot expect the girl to fly a whelp through a portal without some basic skills."

"Then you deny that the king is plotting against the natural order of things? Perhaps you think Rhoswen is *safe* in that maniac's castle."

"Of course not!" Beval could feel exhaustion tugging at the backs of his eyes, but a sudden rush of anxiety at his partner's words kept him from passing out in the middle of his sitting room. "Doubtless, Badrick will try something, if he has not already, but this is all too hasty. Rhoswen must be trained before she can Move, or she will not be capable of guiding the whelp to the next realm. If Deowynn has been waiting this long for Rhoswen, she can wait a little longer." He sighed through his nose. He could not believe he had to say the words that followed. "But *killing the king* may not restore this realm to balance—not with Gethin set to inherit the throne."

"He hasn't tethered yet—he can't inherit."

"So, we kill Badrick and prevent Gethin from tethering, too? Why? So Rhoswen can take over D'Erenelle, or so she can Move without threat of war?" Beval shook his head. "Both scenarios are dubious, and there's a third you're not considering: upsetting the Realm Cycle could endanger all of us, Riders and dragons included. If you'll remember, something like this was suggested twenty years ago and look where we are now."

"That's because it wasn't executed twenty years ago." Thorndon glared at his friend. The two had grown used to being at odds with each other, but these odds were fairly substantial. "Just tell me you'll consider it. If everything else falls apart, we may have no other option."

A pregnant silence ensued as Beval considered the request. "As an absolute *last* resort," he relented. "But not sooner."

Thorndon nodded and stood, his eyes lingering on his Riding partner's face. Finally, he left the room without another word. Beval ran a hand through his hair and rubbed his eyes. Somehow, he did not feel as though they had truly reached an accord.

XXVIII

Aethelburh

"Was that Gethin?" Thane asked, his voice breathy with terror. "Did he see you?"

"I don't know," Rhoswen replied, deafened by her own heartbeat. "We have to get out of here."

"What if he goes back to your room? You have to be in there now, or he'll know he saw you in the library. If he knows about the portal system, he'll tell Uncle Badrick we figured it out."

"Well, what do you want me to do?" Rhoswen asked. "It's not like I can have an open portal in my wall if he barges into my room to confront me."

"No, but you can walk through this portal, and I can close it behind you. I'll sneak back to my room on foot. He couldn't have seen me from that angle."

"Thane, no, I don't want you to get caught roaming around at this hour because of my carelessness."

"I won't get caught."

"Tell that to Darr Thorndon. He won't be around to rescue you this time." Rhoswen stared at her frowning brother. They were out of options. She trudged through the opening and turned to face him on the other side.

Thane stepped hesitantly after her, his pace slowing even more as he crossed the threshold of what should have been a solid stone wall. He came out in Rhoswen's bedroom, gasping for breath.

She chuckled. "I held my breath the first time, too," she admitted. "But here we are," she said as she turned up the oil lamp and replaced it at her bedside. She glanced at her brother, who stood, staring at her chamber door. "What is it, Thane?"

"Someone has been in your room. The door is open. Look." Indeed, there was a gap between the wood and the jamb. "I have to go," Thane blurted. He sped through the portal and into the maps room. Rhoswen turned to race after him, but he held up his palms. "Don't follow me! Just stay there. If anyone noticed you weren't in your room before, you can't afford not to be in there now, especially not after what just happened."

"But my compass—"

"I'll get it!" Thane insisted. "Now let me close this realmed thing!" He lifted her compass from the map and disappeared behind solid stone.

Alone, she glanced around her chambers. The room seemed tainted now, and she felt naked without her compass in her pocket. She padded toward the door to push it shut and heard footsteps speeding down the hall in her direction. She scrambled for her nightgown, threw it over her clothes, and jumped into bed. Moments later, her door flew open and banged against the wall.

She started with a gasp. "Gethin?" She hadn't had time to douse the lamp at her bedside. *Realm it!*

"Cousin!" Gethin yelped in surprise. "Forgive me, I—"

Rhoswen's heart thumped. She had to stall him to give her brother a chance to get back upstairs. "What are you doing here, my prince? Is something wrong? Is it Thane? Or my parents?"

The prince flushed, either from running to her room or seeing her so indisposed. She glanced down at her disheveled nightgown. It was backwards. She pulled her covers up around herself.

Gethin held up a palm. "Neither, no. It's not Thane or your parents. Nothing is wrong," he babbled, looking at his feet as she adjusted her duvet.

"Then, it is rather late for a social call, my prince.... Did you want something?" Admittedly, she had not phrased the question with any delicacy, but only once Gethin began sputtering a reply did she realize how much he had misconstrued her meaning.

"No—Cousin—I—no—" Gethin replied, paling.

She struggled to suppress a smirk. When she spoke again, she did so haltingly, as if she were trying to spare his feelings. "My prince... I do appreciate your... *ardor*, but I fear I cannot—"

"No!" Gethin blurted, holding up both hands, as if to fend off the notion. "It's nothing like that, Cousin Rhoswen. I am not... *enamored* with you." He almost choked on the word. "I thought Thane might be in here—" He stopped, his face contorting in terror at the new implication of his words.

"Oh." Rhoswen turned away as if in embarrassment, but she was biting her lip to keep from laughing. "But Thane does not sleep with *me*—"

"Of course he doesn't!" Gethin agreed, his voice rising in pitch. "Why would he? He's your *brother*." He spoke the word as if it were distasteful.

Rhoswen ran her hand over the fabric of her bed linens, making a show of avoiding eye contact with him. "Oh... my prince, I—I had no idea. Well, if it makes you feel any better, we never—well, let's just say you needn't worry about his being entangled with *me* if *you're* interested in him...."

She was not aware that Gethin could look more horrified than he already did. He began protesting nonsensically. "No—I—Thane—no—not—I wouldn't—no—"

"Wouldn't what?" Thane asked from the doorway, a maroon satin robe hanging loosely over his black pajamas and a pewter mug in his hand. Rhoswen thought she could see the hem of his leather pants peeking out from under the black satin cuff at his ankle.

My, he is quick, she mused.

Gethin jumped, startled by Thane's entrance. Rhoswen grinned at Thane over their cousin's shoulder. "Nothing!" Gethin insisted. "I was just checking to make certain you were both all right."

"In *my* room," Rhoswen added cheekily.

"Why would I be in my sister's room?" Thane asked.

Gethin looked back and forth between the two of them, his mouth moving silently.

Thane looked his cousin up and down. "I couldn't sleep, so I went to get some milk and heard the commotion from across the hall when I returned. I guess I'm not the only one awake. You're still fully dressed, my prince. What were your intentions in searching us out?"

"Yes, I—my what? *No.* I—I just thought—*NO.*" Gethin took a deep breath and let it out between pursed lips. "I was just going to bed. I won't keep you—*from sleeping*. Sorry for the intrusion, Cousins. Do try to get some rest—*wherever.*" And with a flourish of his overlong black cape, he tore past Thane with as wide a birth as he could manage and disappeared from the bedroom. Thane leaned out to watch Gethin retreat down the hall before closing the door behind him.

"What in the realm was that?" Thane hissed, taking a seat on Rhoswen's bed. Indeed, his pajamas hiked up to reveal his leathers underneath.

She grinned. "Our cousin is twisted."

He shot her a knowing smirk. "Runs in the family." A gentle tug at his pocket freed Rhoswen's compass from his pajamas, and he placed it in her hand.

"So does speed, apparently," she said.

UPON the passing of the Royal Riders, the mantle of power is taken up by the couple's eldest, tethered child (or, lacking children, the next Rider along the familial hierarchy). To find a suitable mate for this newly crowned Rider and his or her Dragon, a Royal Flight commences at the Royal Drakiary.

All Dragons of opposing gender will assemble from throughout the Realm for the Royal Flight, as if called by instinct. While their Riders accompany them as escorts, they do not fly their beasts during this ritual. Dragons of like gender must stay at their posts to protect against Narxon attack (unless their Riders have been invited to the resultant ceremonies).

When the Royal Dragon is ready, he or she will soar into the sky, trailed by all the eligible Dragons in attendance. A suitor's worthiness appears to be based on complementary temperaments of both Dragons' Riders, seemingly to induce and prolong balance among the rulers. This fitness seems to extend to the beasts' aptitude in the flight: Dragons of similar disposition to the Royal Dragon will often fall behind, eliminating themselves by default. However, as suitors are weeded out, a few borderline courters may outfly their welcome, and the Royal Dragon will fend them off in swift displays of violence.

After a dazzling array of aerial acrobatics and dismissals, the chase will single out the mate who is best suited to the Royal Dragon and his or her Rider. The chosen mate will advance upon the Royal Dragon until the flight is consummated; this is called "winning" the Royal Flight.

The Riders of these paired Dragons are then joined in a royal wedding, often on the same day as the Royal Flight.

- an excerpt, *From Those Outlying*

XXIX

Keaton

Gethin had spent the last week dodging Rhoswen and Thane as if they were diseased. Rhoswen giggled every time their cousin darted around corners and behind doors after spotting them. While their near discovery had resulted in this serendipitous hilarity, she and Thane decided not to return to the maps room until Gethin's suspicions died down. But Rhoswen felt drawn to the portal, and her denial of it made her antsier by the day. They would need to return—and soon.

After an extra cup of vine water to combat the enervating gray skies, the Stanburhs trudged through the rain and down the hill to the drakiary below.

"Why didn't you tell me it was going to rain today?" Thane asked as his feet *slished* through the sodden grass.

She shrugged. "I had been up half the night, thinking about the portal, when I felt the ache the next morning. I wasn't certain whether it was from the coming rain or just sleeping poorly. Anyway, it seemed unimportant, compared with everything else going on at the time." She widened her eyes to insinuate the wealth of things they could not talk about. Thane nodded.

The weather forced the trainees inside for lecture, with only bleak hope of outdoor lessons later in the day. Thane and Rhoswen followed a stream of students ambling into a huge lecture hall—*if that's what you call it,* Rhoswen mused. Rather than rows of desks or tables, she was surprised to walk into a sea of tattered armchairs and loveseats. Only the direction of the furniture lent the appearance of a classroom: every piece was angled to face a table that stood before a drawing board.

Riders stationed themselves around the edges of the room, watching as the last of the students filed in. Rhoswen leaned close to her brother. "This is not what I pictured from our parents' description of this place," she whispered. Thane shook his head and led her toward the front to find two seats together.

As Rhoswen lowered herself into a plush armchair, she noticed Darr Beval leaning against the front edge of the table, his arms folded over his chest and his ankles crossed out in front of him. She couldn't tell if he looked relaxed or exhausted. Darr Thorndon was nowhere to be seen. Behind the table, Aelfraed sat in a simple wooden chair. He nodded to Rhoswen before shifting his attention elsewhere.

Darr Beval put up a hand to get everyone's attention, and the room fell silent. "Welcome, all of you. You may be wondering why all the mastery levels have converged in a single hall. This is the first in a new lecture series on realm history. Yes, some of this may be review for you," he said in response to the stray groans that filtered through the room, "but we want to be certain everyone begins this part of their training on the same talon—I mean, foot."

A weak guffaw rumbled from the few students who weren't complaining. "Don't you want to know *why* you're working with the dragons the way you are?" Darr Beval asked, echoing Aelfraed's words from their secret meeting a week ago.

"We already know why we're working with dragons—to become Realm Riders!" a voice called from the back. It was the knot-faced student from Rhoswen's first day of training. Thickening fuzz had sprouted in his newly widened part, which made him look even more ridiculous than when Rusalka had razed his hair to the scalp. *Rusalka must thrill whenever she sees him.*

"Aye, Rowley," Darr Beval said, "but why are Realm Riders needed?"

At first, no one offered an explanation, but finally, a couple voices mumbled "Narxon."

The Rider smiled. "Precisely! And that is our topic for discussion today. Our caretaker, Aelfraed, has graciously offered to help me with lecture. Open your histories to chapter one. I will work from your text, and Aelfraed will lecture from his vast stores of knowledge...."

So, they're going to teach what is no longer in the books, Rhoswen thought. She cast Thane a sideways glance.

"To start," Darr Beval said, "you must first understand that D'Erenelle and all other realms must be in a state of balance to retain dragon life. Especially in the realm tales of our youth, this balance is oversimplified as a battle of good versus evil, but in reality, it's about utilizing a realm's resources without depleting or abusing them. This includes maintaining the peace and safety of a realm's inhabitants."

One student raised her hand; Rhoswen didn't know her name but recalled that she was also new to Keaton. "But aren't those realm tales reductive for a reason? Isn't one dragon-Rider pair in the royal family usually... *kinder* than the other?"

Darr Beval nodded. "Certainly. Now, we seem to be living out the realm tale rather literally, Laila. But Queen Orla's parents contrasted less starkly when they ruled D'Erenelle. King Edmundus and Queen Norma had more in common than King Badrick and Queen Orla, but they balanced each other's weaker tendencies just as well. Like Orla, Norma was generous to a fault, and Badrick and Edmundus shared a shrewd and protective nature. Each prevented the other from giving too much or too little to the realm."

Laila nodded, and he continued. "But that equilibrium is precarious, and with the loss of one partner, a royal imbalance can readily occur. Unlike Edmundus, Badrick is not a man of conscience, and without Orla to act as one for him, he has lost any hope of balancing this realm—" his eyes cast around searchingly, "—*and* he may have lost Prince Gethin the chance of inheriting it. With every royal mating flight, a queen dragon gauges the balance of the realm's rulers. This is called Judgment. Should she decide that the Royal Riders cannot reestablish their equilibrium, she will become pregnant in preparation for Movement.

"After the Heir Whelp is born, the queen dragon uses a portal device that has been handed down through generations to Move all the dragons and their Riders—save the king and queen Riders—to another realm. Then, the Narxon come in to cleanse the realm they leave behind."

"More like suck it dry, you mean," Rowley jeered. His cronies chuckled, and several students murmured their agreement. Clearly, the Stanburhs were not the only family to believe that the Narxon were ruthless, mindless, realm-destroying scavengers.

Darr Beval raised his hand again for quiet. "I understand your protests. Let me assure you that there are two sides to every story. Many of your parents are Riders, or you have Riders in your families, and these Darrs have been charged for generations with protecting D'Erenelle from the Narxon that slip into our realm and wreak havoc.

"But remember: Narxon, as far as we understand them, are simply parasites. They don't think, so they act without discrimination. If they find a tear with life on the other side, they attempt to devour its lifeforce because that is their instinct. When Riders leave a realm because it is, in effect, broken, these reviled creatures *cleanse* it in our wake, so it may start anew. The Narxon are part of the Realm System, just as we are. Make sense?"

Many students nodded, but their squinting eyes and hunching postures betrayed residual reluctance toward such a charitable view of their long-villainized foes. Rowley, however, was not so easily swayed. "What kind of lesson is this?" he asked. "Are we supposed to be Narxon-lovers now?"

Darr Beval's brow furrowed. "Considering your lineage, Rowley, I would expect you've heard something akin to this lecture before. So, I will appeal to your parents' teachings. Do you know what happens when the Narxon have finished cleansing a realm?"

Rowley looked about as happy to be called out as Darr Beval did to be heckled. When the young man replied, his voice thinned. "The Quaerlithe come," he mumbled.

"What's that, Rowley? I can barely hear you," Darr Beval pressed.

"Quaerlithe," he repeated with more volume than confidence.

"Right," Darr Beval agreed, returning his attention to the room at large. "A Quaerlith is the life force of a fallen dragon. You might liken it to a dragon's ghost or soul. When a dragon dies, its Quaerlith escapes its corporeal shell and becomes one with the realm. The Quaerlithe lie dormant and inaccessible until the realm must be regenerated. After the Narxon leave, the Quaerlithe emerge to imbue the realm with their preserved lifeforce to replace what the Narxon 'sucked dry.'" Darr Beval shot a final, challenging glance at Rowley. "This allows life to once again flourish in the realm, so the cycle can begin anew."

"But what happens to a realm before it's home to dragons and Riders? How can it protect itself against Narxon?" asked another student, whom Rhoswen also didn't know. She was sitting between Laila and Haylan, the young man who had tied expert knots on the mountblock before Rhoswen.

Darr Beval glanced back at Aelfraed. "Perhaps I should pass that on to someone who remembers those days," he joked.

The class giggled, and Aelfraed inclined his head to the Rider. "Thank you, Darr Beval. May you live as long as I have, so you, too, can see how the next realm fares."

Darr Beval patted Aelfraed's shoulder as he moved toward the seat the caretaker had vacated.

"A good question, Golda," Aelfraed answered with a smile. "Indeed, it would seem there are still a *few* things that took place before my time. Many theories exist, but I do not know how realms protect themselves before dragons and Riders inhabit them. Perhaps they cannot.

"What we do know is the threat to our realm has increased. D'Erenelle is no longer balanced with Queen Orla gone. A dragon cannot retether after his or her Rider is lost. So, the king cannot remarry to find a new Rider for the queen dragon, nor can he depose Deowynn by marrying another tethered Rider." Aelfraed's tone darkened. "This increases the chance that Deowynn could pass Judgment on this realm that will result in Movement. If so, she will become pregnant with the Heir Whelp. Then, someone—likely one of *you*—will become the Heir Rider to tether to the young beast and rule the next realm."

Aelfraed's words hung in the air like the dense, choking smoke of a Descent. He scrutinized the students as they gaped at him, speechless—but Rhoswen was watching the Riders around the room. Most adopted blank expressions, and some were unable to hide their shock, but a few did nothing to mask their hostility toward the caretaker's lecture. Rhoswen's heart began to race. *Would Aelfraed reveal me already?*

Finally, Aelfraed's face broke into a smile. "You'd think I'd just told you all the Narxon were coming tomorrow, and none of you would have time to tether!" He chuckled, and the sound chipped away at the tension in the room.

"I am glad to see that you all understand the gravity of the situation," he said. "This is not merely conjecture; there are signs that portend the coming of Judgment and the Heir, and rather inconveniently, your histories no longer detail them. Another imbalance in our resources, if you ask me." Aelfraed stole a glance over his shoulder at Darr Beval before continuing. Rhoswen's heart thumped in anticipation.

"The reason this missing information is still important—contrary to the beliefs of your histories publishers—," Aelfraed added, grabbing a text from a student in the front row and brandishing it before the class, "is because you may one day see these signs in your fellow trainees, and you must be able to recognize them for what they are. Once identified, the Heir Rider must be fiercely protected, or all of our Riders and dragons could be lost to the Narxon if Movement is impeded." Rhoswen expected muttering from the class. No one said a word.

Finally, a student sitting beside Aeduuin raised his hand. "You speak as if you are certain D'Erenelle is doomed to imbalanced Judgment."

Aelfraed stared at the young man, waiting for a question to accompany his statement. When none was forthcoming, he returned the book he had borrowed and said out of the corner of his mouth, "Do you foresee another outcome, Sterling?"

Sterling gave an almost imperceptible shake of his head. Aeduuin smiled at him and nudged him with a shoulder.

"I appreciate your reticence, but it is not treason for us to make conjectures about the impending Judgment," Aelfraed insisted. "This is what you and countless generations of your predecessors have been training for! All the Riders before you received these same lectures in preparation for a fate many of them never saw—a fate that *you* may finally witness. Remember: Judgment is passed every time Queen Deowynn and King Blaxton mate. She can just as easily choose to stay, as she has all the times before. Regardless of what she decides, as Riders-in-training, you are here to learn how to handle her decision. Understand?" Sterling and a few other students nodded.

Aelfraed began detailing the list of traits they had discussed in their private meeting the night before. Students scribbled furiously onto sheets of parchment, desperate to keep up. Occasionally, Rhoswen noticed little pockets of whispering and students glancing at each other as they pointed to their parchment. She and Thane took sparse notes to appear engaged, but the details were already burned into Rhoswen's mind. She was more preoccupied with sneaking peeks at her classmates. So far, none of them had gestured toward her, for which she was both grateful... and concerned.

"And finally," Aelfraed said, his eyes scanning the sea of faces, "the Heir Rider will have the ability to nex with *all* dragons long before he or she is tethered to the Heir Whelp. This being a mental connection, it may not be a trait that is easy to spot, but it will often present as a natural proficiency during training."

Rhoswen's blood pounded through her veins, and she shoved her hands under her thighs to keep them from shaking. She thought of the times her groupmates had whispered and Darr Beval had stared at her unusual exchanges with dragons during training. Aelfraed might as well have just pointed at her and screamed, "She's the Heir! She's the Heir!"

Nausea flared up in her gut as she glanced around, expecting to see every eye in the room trained on her. But no one was looking at her at all. She couldn't decide if she were relieved or offended. *Don't be conceited,* she chided herself. Others had shown considerable aptitude, as well, and if no one knew who she was, she wouldn't need to be protected from anyone.

Aelfraed continued his lecture. "Now, some trainees will just finesse dragons better than others, and everyone has the chance to possess one or two gifts that might make them look like candidates for the Heir Rider. This lesson is not meant to spur a hunt for the Heir, nor is it meant to create jealousy. Being chosen as the Heir does not make you any more worthy of your dragon or your Rider status once you have tethered. That you can all exhibit some of the traits should remind us that we are all valuable and should always protect one another. Any one of you may be key to *safeguarding* the Heir, and that is equally important to *being* the Heir. In a way, Riders are all Heirs of the realms, whether they rule them or guard them. They are what keep the Realm Cycle alive."

Again, the room fell quiet but for the sound of a few scratching quills. Laila raised her hand again. "What about the portal to the new realm? How does that work?"

"That will have to wait until our next lecture," a familiar voice boomed from the back of the room. All heads turned toward Darr Thorndon, who stood in the doorway, his leathers darkened with water spots. "The rain has let up some, and it's warm," he announced. "It's bathing day."

XXX

The Exchange

"So, you're saying Vonn was right?" Kyle asked in disbelief. "*You*, Randy?"

"I don't like it any more 'an y'all do!" Randy insisted.

"What's going on?" Emmelyn called to them, sitting down with a water. She had been at work in her realm when she'd portaled to the Exchange. Suddenly returning with beer—or another of Vonn's gin selections—on her breath would raise questions.

"Randy is starting to see the truth behind Vonn's latest rumor," a blonde girl about Emmelyn's age hollered in her ear. She had a high-pitched but not unpleasant voice. Her light hair was straight and long, and she seemed to have donned a skein of multicolored yarn from baret to boot. She was very girl-next-door meets my-grandmother-knitted-all-my-clothes. "You must be Emmelyn," she said with a smile.

It turned out her name was Inzay, she was a Transfer, and she had knitted her clothes herself. While not Emmelyn's style, she was highly impressed. Every time Emmelyn had tried to knit, her inconsistent tension had resulted in creations only duplicated in the illustrations of wacky, rhyming children's books.

"Where is Vonn?" Emmelyn asked.

"He just left," Inzay replied. She was drinking something pink.

Why can she drink pink, and I have to learn about gin? Emmelyn mused. In truth, she appreciated the juniper berry more with every glass Vonn forced into her hand. "So, which rumor is this, then?" Emmelyn asked and took a sip of water.

"The one about the two factions," Kyle said, as if that should have cleared it up.

Emmelyn remembered Randy and Vonn arguing about this last time, but much of it had been too far over her head to make any sense. She flashed a confused expression at the group, and Kyle heaved a dramatic sigh. He opened his mouth to explain, but Inzay took over, her words rushing together with excitement. Behind her, Kyle's perturbation increased. Emmelyn hid a smirk behind her glass.

"Vonn believes the Arbiters running the G'Ambit are not just trying to line their pockets anymore," Inzay yelled. "The Datists are fed up with their inability to understand the Narxon. They've been studying them... *forever* or something, and they haven't discovered how to stop them. A group of them theorize that the only way to defeat the Narxon is to let all the realms die, so they have nothing to feed on! Some Arbiters seem to have picked up the idea, and there are more triples occurring now than, well, ever."

"WHAT?!" Emmelyn roared. She tried to put her eyeballs back in her head. She had been Transferring triples since her first trip to the Atrium. What if she had been *helping* these maniacs all this time? "But how do they know the realms will come back if they are allowed to disappear?"

"They don't," Randy yelled to her, his hand raised in a gesture of calm. "It's just a theory—one that's crazier 'an a soup sandwich." He shot Inzay a cool glance. "And we don't know if the increase in triples is even related to it." Emmelyn relaxed a bit at this amendment. "But if Vonn is right—" He stopped short, his eyes fixed on something over Emmelyn's shoulder.

She turned to see a young man standing behind her. His looks rivaled Vonn's but with a grungier edge: his symmetrical face boasted thicker eyebrows, a jaw shadowed with dark stubble, and wavy black hair that brushed his shoulders but retained enough volume to avoid looking stringy. He had broad shoulders and pecks so well defined, they would probably still be visible under a closed suit jacket; the muscles in his arms bulged out of the sleeves of his tight olive-green T-shirt. Emmelyn's eyes traveled down to his acid-washed jeans. Usually a dealbreaker for her, this pair hugged his well-defined thighs, making their faded hue almost forgivable.

"You Emmelyn?" he hollered. He looked to be around her age, but the flashing lights made it hard to be certain.

Her mouth had gone dry—either from Vonn's ridiculous theory or this newcomer's distracting good looks—and she swallowed with difficulty. "I am," she finally replied. "Who are you?"

"Denver." Something about him—maybe the way he spoke—felt borderline threatening.

Inzay leaned close to Emmelyn's ear. "I bet he's from Welsamar. Welsamarians are notoriously gorgeous."

"So I've heard," Emmelyn replied, not taking her eyes off the young man.

"You have my Transitor?" he asked her.

Maybe his demeanor was putting her off. Emmelyn was never comfortable with people who were all business. "I transfer for Lorelle," she replied.

He shook his head. "Not anymore." A pause ensued as he waited for this news to sink in. "Do you have my Transitor?" he asked again when she made no move to give it to him. His toneless voice betrayed nothing, not even impatience.

Emmelyn hesitated. "Janelle didn't tell me I had changed Runners."

Denver shrugged.

This is not going well. Emmelyn flashed a helpless glance at the group.

Kyle stepped up to Denver. "There's been a lot of weird stuff going on around here lately," he yelled to the Runner, "and she's new. Not eager to mess up. You have documentation for her?"

Kyle was the last person Emmelyn expected to come to her rescue, but as a fellow Transfer, he was one of the only Crew members who *could* help her out. Runners rarely meddled in one another's Exchange business. She beamed at him appreciatively.

Denver pulled a folded slip of parchment from his back pocket and held it up between his first two fingers. *Do they only use old-timey paper around here?* Emmelyn wondered. Kyle read it over and looked to Emmelyn, his expression grim. He simply nodded. Denver removed the parchment from Kyle's grasp and, without offering it to Emmelyn, refolded it and placed it back in his jeans.

Emmelyn pulled out the Transitor from her purse and handed it to her new Runner. Denver unlocked the white block, exchanged one piece of parchment for another, and handed the locked Transitor back to her. Then, he gave her a chilly pleasure-doing-business-with-you nod and walked toward the portal doors at the back of the bar. Perhaps "pleasure" was a bit strong. *Indifferent*-doing-business-with-you seemed more like it.

The Crew stared at one another, stymied as Welsamarian techno blared around them. Finally, Emmelyn looked at her wrist. She was down to a single stamp. "He didn't tell me the name of his Arbiter," she realized.

"It's Emile," Kyle replied. "Said it on the slip." He looked sympathetic. It was a strange emotion to witness through coal-lined eyes that normally betrayed only sarcasm.

Emmelyn nodded and stood. Desperate as she was to finish their previous conversation, she was already down to half a stamp. *That's disappearing faster than before,* she thought, the hair on her neck prickling with suspicion. With a feeble farewell, she headed out of the club and down the long staircase.

Emmelyn didn't pause for a waiter's escort. She walked up the four wide steps and into the Atrium, scanning for Emile. He sat at the same table with the same woman as before. *Does this place have assigned seating?* She made her way to him—still somewhat gingerly for all those stairs—on as direct a route as possible.

"Emile," she said with a curt nod of greeting. "Why am I transferring for a new Runner?"

Beneath another large hat, Olivia appeared scandalized, and Emmelyn realized it was not her place to ask such things—at least, not of Arbiters.

Emile was unflappable. "What is your name, dear?" he asked kindly.

"Emmelyn," she replied. *Shouldn't he know who I am?*

Emile nodded slowly, searching his mental roster. "Emmelyn… Darrow. Yes. Things change, Emmelyn. Relationships between Transfers and Runners are meant to be impermanent."

Did Janelle forget to give me a handbook? Vonn had used the same words when they'd discussed Emmelyn's possible separation from Lorelle. Hearing them again did not make her feel better.

"I'm sure you and Denver will get along fine…. If not, well, you'll barely see each other." Emile opened the Transitor as Emmelyn watched. Olivia cleared her throat, and Emile looked up from the parchment slip in his hand. He lifted a domed silver lid the size of a saucer from the middle of the table, fed the empty Transitor into a square hole beneath it, closed the lid, and smiled. "Thank you, Emmelyn. You may go now," he said.

Emmelyn walked away without another word. *He knew exactly who I was,* she realized. *He was making it clear that my identity was of little consequence to him—just like any of my other concerns.* She wove through the platforms toward the four stairs that would dump her out into the lobby, but she was unable to loosen her white-knuckling fists before she stepped out of the Exchange—

—and back behind the counter at WE Dress, where she had been interning for the last four years.

WE Dress (the "WE" stood for Women Executives) was a local shop that helped women of insubstantial means dress for interviews and jobs, so they could improve their positions in life. It gave women the tools to take back their power in this world—*realm.* When Emmelyn learned about it, she knew she had to help.

"Emmelyn? Emmelyn, are you okay?" her boss, Lydia, asked as she came out of the dressing room area. She slid a pair of scissors out of a wide-mouthed mason jar on the back counter.

Emmelyn uncurled her fists and flexed her fingers. "Oh, sorry, yeah. Uh, computer froze. It's fine now."

"Darn thing has been doing a lot of that lately." Lydia glanced out through the large shop windows. "Looks like someone new is coming in. I'm with a client. You've got this, right?" she asked as she disappeared around the corner again.

"Absolutely," Emmelyn replied, smiling at the back of Lydia's head.

Her internship had begun with sorting stock, but as she stayed with the shop, she eventually began doing intake, which put her in front of the women WE Dress helped. They would chat as they completed their paperwork, often sharing stories of inequality and damning social stigmas. Single mothers navigated unrealistic schedules that disregarded their children's needs. Young professionals mired in debt were viewed as too inexperienced to showcase their pricey educations. Widows who had to return to the workforce were considered too old for the jobs they were once overqualified to hold. It was gut-wrenching to learn of the close scrapes these women had had with success and how far many of them had fallen as a result of missing the mark.

Emmelyn thought of the bewildering system at the Exchange and how insignificant Emile had just made her feel for being an involuntary part of it. A furious heat radiated through her, and she had to force her hands to unclench themselves again.

The bells on the door jingled as a woman with a Peter Pan haircut and an orange velour sweatsuit walked through the door.

"Hi. How can I help you?" Emmelyn asked through the smile she had plastered on her face.

"I have an interview on Friday, and you guys were recommended to me," the woman said, her voice husky. She looked down at her bright outfit. "Lord knows I can't wear this ugly thing."

Emmelyn's smile turned genuine, and she grabbed a clipboard. "Let's get you set up." She rounded the counter and escorted the woman to the empty lobby area. "I'm Emmelyn."

"Nancy," the woman replied, tucking a ratty purse into the chair beside her.

"It's nice to meet you," Emmelyn said as she took the next seat over.

Nancy's eyes raked over her face. "Maybe now, but you weren't happy when I walked in. Bad day?"

This woman is asking if I *am having a bad day?* "Sorry," Emmelyn blurted, feeling unprofessional. "It has nothing to do with you—or WE Dress."

Nancy held up a hand. "You don't have to cover for this place. I know it does good work."

Emmelyn smiled. "Can I ask you a few questions about what brings you here today?"

"Sure thing."

"Are you experiencing financial hardship?"

Nancy tilted her head in Emmelyn's direction and looked at her over the top of her black-rimmed cat-eye glasses.

Emmelyn grimaced. "I'm required to ask."

Nancy sighed and nodded. "Yeah, you could definitely say that. Did it to myself, though, so I can't complain. Blackjack is an expensive habit."

"I can only imagine," Emmelyn said as she checked a box on the sheet.

She couldn't help but like this woman's straightforward attitude. Nancy was the kind of person who could spill red wine on her white sneakers and be totally unfazed by it. Emmelyn admired that.

Nancy shrugged. "Gamblers Anonymous is cheaper."

Emmelyn looked up at her. "Does it help?"

"I go every Thursday," Nancy said with a nod.

"That's awesome," Emmelyn replied.

"Ever play blackjack?"

"Can't say I have."

Nancy smirked. "It's fun. I'd offer to teach you, but I think GA frowns on such things."

Emmelyn chuckled. "I'd love to hear what you learned at the meetings to overcome it instead."

"It's hard to beat the house," Nancy replied flatly. She flashed Emmelyn a mischievous grin. "Not impossible, though."

Emmelyn thought back to her first triple in the Exchange and the Crew's explanation that most triples contributed to G'Ambit bets. *Now, they might also contribute to total annihilation.* She passed Nancy the pen and clipboard so she could complete her intake form. "Do tell."

XXXI

Keaton

Rhoswen scrambled out of her chair after Darr Thorndon and disappeared among the rest of the class. Aelfraed's lecture had put enough of a spotlight on the Heir, and it was a wonder she had gotten out with her anonymity intact; she did not want to be seen lingering behind like some Rider's pet. Thane would catch up with her. She only hoped it would be some time yet before her endless supply of "beginner's luck" did the same.

"This will be one of the wettest lessons you experience here in Keaton," Darr Thorndon announced to the fidgety group of students. "Normally, dragons can bathe themselves, and we recommend they do! But we are not teaching you about an ordinary bath. Today's lesson will focus on how to use rainwater to help clean out your dragon's wounds, in case of Narxon injury. Now, many of you are too inexperienced to practice this yet, but this will give you an idea of the kind of maneuvering you will be expected to learn. Without its mastery, you will not be capable of saving your dragon or gaining the title of Darr." He gestured to a dragon in a nearby stall to join him.

Thane edged in beside Rhoswen and leaned close to her ear. "Why did you run off like that?" he whispered, taking advantage of the break in lecture.

"Why do you think?" she whispered back.

"Darr Beval wanted to speak to you—"

"What could he possibly have to say to me after that revealing lecture?" she hissed, brows furrowed. "Did Aelfraed leave something out?"

Before Thane could reply, a large green dragon ambled up beside Darr Thorndon and trumpeted a greeting. "Say hello to my dragon, Merry," the Rider prompted. The group murmured their greetings to the beast, but she lost interest in them as the rain beat down on her tail, which stuck out beyond the shelter of the awning. She closed her eyes as the warm droplets massaged her scales.

"Who knows about the phenomenon we like to call 'Narxon Rain?'" A few hands shot up into the air, and Darr Thorndon nodded at them. "It tends to rain when the Narxon enter the realm. This is incredibly helpful because Narxon Rain is not normal water. Rather, it is some similar-looking substance that heals burnt hide and flesh upon contact. We don't know why this rain falls in tandem with Descents, but when it doesn't—a rarity, but still a possibility—our dragons and Riders are much the worse for it. To combat this situation, we collect Narxon Rainwater and create a salve that helps ease the discomfort. It cannot stop the burning like the real thing, but it can slow it."

"Why not just use the water?" Sterling asked.

Darr Thorndon's eyebrows lifted in approval of the question. "Because it grows stagnant over time, essentially becoming normal water. If preserved as a salve, the healing properties are better maintained." He shrugged. "Just another peculiarity of the stuff."

A long handle extended from a tall bucket near the Rider's feet. He lifted it up to reveal a brush head, dripping with something red. "This warming paint will represent injuries to Merry's hide from a Narxon attack." He fell silent, and the crowd watched as Merry let him mark various parts of her body with the paint. Rhoswen listened to the green's nexed replies as he requested she turn this way and that, but the students heard none of it, filling the space with their own muttering instead.

"The Narxon may not be able to soar upward," he said between brush strokes, "but they still have exceptional maneuverability… and can attack some pretty… obscure places. It may take an equivalent bit of… maneuvering on the Rider's part… to clean out the burns in the rain." He dropped the long-handled brush back into the bucket, and a thin spray of paint spattered his hand; he held it out past the cover of the awning to let the rain wash it off.

Thane raised his hand. "If you're flying through the air, how will you know if your dragon is clean?"

Darr Thorndon nodded. "She will tell me what needs to be done. This paint feels warm on her hide, but a Narxon burn is excruciating. A Rider must communicate with his injured beast, midair, to figure out where and how to clean her. Under normal circumstances, you will generally instruct your dragon where to take you. But when she is injured in a Narxon battle, she'll most certainly tell *you* where to go." He smirked.

"Maven and Aeduuin will be flying out first today," he announced, handing the bucket of paint to Darr Beval. "Have them ready their dragons. This won't take me long." Rhoswen sensed a coolness to Darr Thorndon's tone that she interpreted as bored familiarity with this routine lesson. But as she watched Darr Beval's tight-lipped reaction, she discerned something more behind the exchange. The second Rider nodded, his face hard, and moved toward the stables with the bucket.

Darr Thorndon climbed up the stirrups and hoisted himself into the saddle on Merry's back. "Here we go," he said, and they took off into the air without further preamble.

Merry careened through the rain, turning and twisting her massive body as if possessed. She rose and fell through the air, and her contortions washed away the faux gashes from her body. Thorndon clung low to the saddle, his body shifting with Merry's as she soared through the sky. In an instant, all thoughts of lecture slipped from Rhoswen's mind, and she was once again able to enjoy the idea of working with the beasts that had sparked passion in her at a young age.

After a long bout of midair flailing, the green finally descended and slowed to land in front of the students. Jaws were still closing as the class broke into fevered applause. Darr Thorndon waved it all away as his feet hit the sodden gravel. His soaked leathers had darkened, matching the loose tendrils of dark hair that clung to his face and neck, but he couldn't keep the grin from his face.

He patted Merry's flank. "As you can see from our gorgeous model here," Merry turned and twisted to display her now-unmarked hide, "not a spot of paint on her. She told me how she needed to maneuver to clean herself off, and I just hung on for the ride."

"Why don't you just let them wash themselves, then?" one of Rowley's cronies called out.

"Because, Brentley, sometimes wounds must be cleaned out *during* a Descent. So, it's my job to look out for more Narxon that could attack us as she bathes."

"You mean you have to dodge Narxon while she's flying erratically like that?" Sterling asked, wide-eyed.

"Sometimes while I've been injured, too. Dragons aren't the only ones who can get burned." Darr Thorndon smiled at him. "*That* is why it takes a lot of training and a deep internal connection to become a Rider."

Darr Beval came over and wrapped a thick blanket around his partner's shoulders. "A thrilling display, Darr Thorndon. And you have two more to adjudicate before you can change out of those wet leathers. Maven is waiting for you. I can take it from here."

"Failsafes?" Darr Thorndon asked him.

"Darrs Wynflaeth and Elmina," Darr Beval replied. The two named Riders sat poised on their dragons' backs on opposite sides of the arena. Rhoswen recognized Eostre—Darr Wynflaeth's red—as Bassett's mother and Darr Elmina's frisky tawny to be Rusalka.

Darr Thorndon nodded, caught up both ends of the blanket in one fist, and moved to a nearby chair. His demeanor toward his Riding partner was softening, but it still lacked its usual warmth.

Darr Beval stood before the group and announced that they would resume their lecture inside. An outcry of mutinous protests exploded from the students, and he laughed, his palms raised in surrender. "Allow me to narrate, then," he offered.

"Now, this is not Maven's first bath," he explained. At the entrance to the arena, the blonde trainee sat astride a black dragon named Brenna. The beast sported red slashes all over her onyx hide, and the pair watched Darr Thorndon for the signal to proceed. "For the first bath or two, the trainee will put on the marks herself, giving her some idea of what to expect during her flight. But after she has mastered that, someone else applies the paint, as I have for Maven, so she will have a more authentic experience as Brenna instructs her on what needs to be done. It's called blind-marking."

Laila's hand shot up over her head. "How could Brenna instruct her if they can't nex?"

Darr Beval beamed at her. "As an untethered pair, they will have to rely on each others' body language to know what to expect as they go. This exercise strengthens their physical understanding of each other and should help the pair develop a permanent connection, if they're meant to share one."

With a wave of Darr Thorndon's still-damp hand, Brenna took off into the air. The pair soared upward, Rider and dragon moving as one. Between Maven's black leathers and Brenna's black hide, they were almost indistinguishable from each other. Maven's light hair blew out behind her like a squat flame flashing against the gray sky. Both Rider and dragon Failsafes followed the pair's every move, their heads bobbing in unison with each dip and turn.

High in the air, Brenna twirled and ducked; she flew in circles and upside down, twisted and spun, and never once did Maven seem disconnected from her. Finally, the pair descended to the arena, and Brenna touched down on the muddy ground without a splash. Maven beamed. She hopped down from the saddle and patted the dragon's neck as Brenna nudged her shoulder with her snout.

Darr Thorndon slipped out from under the blanket and inspected the beast's hide for traces of paint. Finally, he extended his hand to Maven—Brenna was spotless. Maven took his arm in hers and moved in closer to whisper something in his ear. He pulled away and stared at her, glancing at Brenna before wrapping Maven in a huge hug. His booming laughter filled the arena.

"Oh, you're kidding." Darr Beval gestured for his students to stay put and ran out to his wet colleagues in the arena. He, too, threw his arms around Maven as Darr Thorndon turned to the expectant crowd. "They've tethered!" he yelled.

The crowd exploded, hooting and clapping, some even jumping up and down. Brenna let out a cheerful bellow that was echoed by the dragons in their stalls. The deafening noise caused a few students to clamp their hands over their ears. Maven jumped back up in her saddle, and the pair took off into the air again to fly a victory circle over the arena.

Back on the ground, Darr Thorndon held out his hand to his friend. When Darr Beval took him by the elbow, Darr Thorndon pulled him into a fierce hug, and Rhoswen could just make out their laughter over the dying cacophony from the stables. The tension in her shoulders loosened.

Finally, Darr Beval jogged back to his dry students under the awning. Dark water spots seeped over his shoulders and across his vest, and his damp hair clung to the edges of his face. *He's even gorgeous wet,* Rhoswen thought, forcing herself to pay attention as he spoke.

"Apparently, Brenna nexed her congratulations to Maven as the last of the paint washed from her hide," he told them. "Darr Maven is now a full-fledged Rider and will be formally inducted on Aetheldaeg, our new-Rider ceremony. When you next see her, congratulate her, and don't forget to use her new title!"

So that's how it happens, Rhoswen mused as the class continued their raucous celebrations. Her memory flashed on Rusalka's first, startling nex to her, and she realized that was as close as she would come to experiencing Maven's joyous surprise. Rhoswen's first nex had not meant she'd tethered to her own beast, but she had the privilege of nexing with any and every dragon in the realm. It was a bittersweet compromise.

When Darr Maven and Brenna left the arena, Aeduuin and a green named Corliss took their place. Darr Beval announced that this would be Aeduuin's first blind-marked bath. Keaton grew quiet once more, and Darr Thorndon waved to the trainee to begin.

Corliss took a few quick steps forward and threw herself into the air with somewhat less finesse than Brenna. As she found her stride and swooped around more effortlessly, Aeduuin moving easily with her, she turned to expose her underbelly to the rain. Upside-down and halfway through her circle, her body contorted in a strange twist as she rushed to right herself, but it was too late: Aeduuin lost his grip and slipped from her back.

Rusalka and Eostre shot up into the sky. They flew close together, overlapping their wings between them to create a net below the trainee's downward path. Aeduuin landed on target with a *thud,* and the two dragons beat at the air with their free wings to direct themselves to the ground.

Several Riders ran toward their landing site, including Darrs Thorndon and Beval. The worried din grew with the chatter of students; even the dragons in the stables fidgeted with unease. As the group reached Aeduuin, Corliss landed nearby. Her neck hung low, but her eyes never left her fallen trainee.

Maven and another Rider helped Aeduuin to his feet, and the group escorted him back to the stables, a stricken Corliss bringing up the rear. Aeduuin lifted a hand to the onlookers, and the arena resounded with applause. Maven spoke to Aeduuin as they passed. Rhoswen wondered whether the new Rider's presence was a comfort or a torture to the trainee in the wake of his less-successful bath.

Corliss slumped into her stall and pulled the door shut with her tail. Rhoswen could hear Rusalka and Eostre trying to soothe her, but their gentle nexing provoked no response from the green.

Darr Beval jogged back to his class. "Aeduuin is fine. He and Corliss suffered a misunderstanding in the air. This is common when a trainee and dragon are untethered because they cannot nex directions to each other. Up there, body language is an easy thing to misconstrue. It's why we have Failsafes watch for signs of trouble during flight practice." The group muttered its uncertainty, but their protests were drowned out by a thunderclap and the heavy pounding of rain. Darr Beval squinted at the darkening sky. "I expect we are all a little too high-strung to return to lecture. Class dismissed."

He caught Rhoswen's eye and motioned for her to wait. The students around them dispersed, and Thane held onto his sister's arm, as if to keep her from bolting.

"Rhoswen," Darr Beval murmured as the last of the trainees moved away, "I need to ask you a favor."

Gethin skipped breakfast to avoid his idiot cousins after their awkward encounter. He still had no desire to try to clear things up with them, fearing they would only twist his explanations further. Instead, he stayed in his room, replaying the situation over and over in his mind.

His inability to curb the embarrassing, familial exchange spelled his inescapable exhaustion. It also explained his hallucination in the main floor library. He had gone there to get a better view of Keaton. Now, he didn't know what he thought he'd seen. *A hole in the wall? A shadow? His own reflection?*

Gethin took a leisurely brunch and ambled down to the drakiary in time to witness Aeduuin's colossal failure on his practice bath. As the crowd dispersed from the arena, Gethin decided to head back to the castle to remind his father how much more adept he was than the current lot of trainees. It was time the king made him a trainer—perhaps even replacing Aeduuin—since the Riders had failed to recognize Gethin's potential.

His confidence mounting, he lengthened his stride, only to be stopped short by a group of students, who were gossiping as they trudged their way around the congested arena. Unable to pass the group amid the throng, he forced himself to exert princely patience as he watched for the first opportunity to slip by them.

"You could see the difference in the way they were flying," one student said. "Maven and Brenna moved together as one. Their communication was flawless from the start."

Another student nodded in agreement. "Yeah, but it wasn't their first blind-marked bath. Did you see the way Corliss juddered during takeoff? I don't know who was more uncertain about the flight, she or Aeduuin."

A third leaned in closer and dropped his voice. "Maven made it look easy—like the Heir Rider would."

Gethin blinked. He ceased his search for an escape route and crept closer to the group.

"But that's only because they tethered," the first student said. "The Heir *wouldn't* be tethered to a dragon and would still make it look easy."

"Have you noticed anyone like that?" the second student asked.

A fourth student spoke for the first time. He was older than the others, and Gethin recognized him from his own training level, though he hadn't bothered to learn his name. "There are a few who have made lessons look easy," he said, "but the real trick is whether it was easy because they were nexing with the dragons or because they were adept at the lesson."

"And you can tell the difference, eh?" the third student asked wryly.

The fourth student shrugged. "I have my eye on one or two who seem particularly skilled."

Gethin rolled his eyes.

"You'd be more likely to see it than we would," the second student fawned. "You've been here longer."

Gethin struggled not to groan. He had no patience for these bookworms' misguided hero worship. *Where in the realm had they learned so much about the Heir Rider?*

The group continued to prattle on as they turned off toward the dormitories. The prince could not justifiably follow them inside. He cursed their ill-timed departure and lengthened his stride, the path before him free from obstructions once more. *Perhaps it's time I do a little research of my own....*

XXXII

Salton

It wasn't often Ravinger could say he hadn't been in a tavern before. Actually, he failed to remember the last time he *could* say that. But Salton was a long way from home, and being stationed down in Dallin all these years, he rarely had cause to come this far north.

He could *not* say, however, that he had never been in a tavern this *early* in the day before. As he stepped over the dark threshold into the windowless and nearly deserted shack of the Two Fords Tavern, he eyed the man behind the bar, who was wiping out a cup with a dirt-smudged rag. Perhaps he wouldn't be having anything to drink after all.

When did I become such a snob? he wondered. He crossed to the rear of the tavern, as instructed, the sole patron amid the dim glow and a dozen tables. He cozied up to an empty one and waited, waving away the bartender's offerings. He had been in places much filthier than this and happily eaten dried-out food from inexplicably greasy plates without a moment's hesitation. But much of that had happened in his previous life—before he had allied himself with the Stanburhs.

In the war, he had vacillated between the two sides, trying to stay alive by not committing himself to either. In the end, however, he had gotten into some trouble that he couldn't squirm his way out of, and the Stanburhs had shown him mercy in exchange for his loyalty. Given that Ravinger had never possessed much of that trait, he figured it would be easy to give away. Over time, though, the Stanburhs had taught him what true loyalty meant, instilling him with it while demanding it from him. It proved a difficult lesson to learn. Now, here he was again, testing that hard-won understanding between them. He was on an errand for someone else, whom the Stanburhs knew nothing about—but almost certainly should.

It occurred to Ravinger that he could simply tell Allistair everything, but the Runner who had approached him had made it very clear that her next task in D'Erenelle would be to assassinate Ravinger if he shared anything with the Stanburhs. The only scrap of loyalty Ravinger had *always* possessed was to himself. So, naturally, he was keeping quiet about this.

Ravinger hadn't bothered to arrive at the tavern early, as demanded. Training the foreigner would be enough of a burden; Ravinger's schedule shouldn't suffer, as well. Now, though, he was beginning to wonder if he had missed the guy altogether. He was eyeing a bottle of brown liquid and a tower of dirty cups when the bartender caught his attention.

"Waiting for someone?"

Ravinger shrugged. "In a manner of speaking."

The bartender nodded. "If you're here for that door, it appears in the back—*outside*," he called. His voice rasped, as though he'd drunk as much as he'd served over the years.

"*Out*side?" Ravinger was surprised the man was so knowledgeable, and yet, how could he not be? A door regularly materializes in the back wall of your tavern, and you somehow miss that phenomenon every time? *Likely not.* "Thank you," he replied, wondering just how many D'Erenelleans knew about the door. He crossed to the bar, dropped a small coin on it as he passed, and headed outside to the back of the shack.

As he came around the corner, he saw a massive portal opening in the back wall of the tavern. A young green dragon edged his way through it and out into the yard. On the dragon's back sat a young man with leathers of a dark olive color that Ravinger had never seen on a Rider. The man appraised the area before spotting Ravinger and made his way down the stirrups as the portal entrance faded once more out of existence.

The young man's wavy black hair swished around his face, ending just above his shoulders. "You Ravinger?" he asked, scraping the hair back around his ears. His accent was strange and unlike anything in D'Erenelle.

"I am," Ravinger replied. He stepped forward to offer the new Rider his arm. "You're Denver?"

The young man nodded and grasped Ravinger's elbow. *At least that custom isn't realm specific,* Ravinger mused, grateful to cross one item off his list of things to teach the newcomer. Denver's foreign speech would present a much greater issue.... The thought made Ravinger reconsider those dirty glasses. "Want a drink?" he asked, gesturing toward the shack.

Denver shook his head.

"You're a man of few words," Ravinger noted. "Probably for the best with that accent. How did you get the dragon through?"

Riders, let alone dragons, couldn't travel through the Exchange's portals; it was one of those rules Runners were always spouting, as if they had memorized some handbook. Ravinger understood little of what Runners said, but he did know what he had just witnessed should not supposedly have happened. Even though he had been told to expect it, he honestly didn't think it would work. *But that's the thing about rules, isn't it? They're meant to be broken.*

Denver just stared at him.

Ravinger nodded. "Probably best you don't talk about that either, I suppose."

Out of the corner of his vision, Ravinger saw his tawny, Norvin, approaching from where he had landed in front of the tavern. He seemed eager to understand where this green had suddenly come from. "Shall we let them get acquainted?" Ravinger suggested. "Are you hungry?"

"You have much to teach me," Denver replied.

"I do," Ravinger agreed, putting his arm around the man's shoulders to steer him toward the front of the tavern. "And the first thing you need to learn is to accept when someone offers you food or drink—*drink,* at least. I'm not sure we should bother with the fare here, but after what you just did, a sturdy tankard of ale couldn't hurt either of us."

XXXIII

Keaton

"These things happen," Darr Beval explained on the way to Corliss' stall. "But Corliss is a sensitive dragon, and we're afraid she is more than a little upset by the bad bath. If you could nex with her… remind her that it was just one miscommunication…."

Rhoswen agreed without hesitation to nex this message to Corliss, given that she was the only one who could. What she couldn't so readily agree with, however, was Darr Beval's plan for her to act as intermediary between Corliss *and Aeduuin.* How many people could they trust with her secret? Darr Beval assured her that both he and Darr Thorndon believed they could confide in Aeduuin, but before she could express her discomfort, Thane expressed his.

"No," her brother said for the third or fourth time.

"They are both inconsolable," Darr Beval argued. "This could help them."

"At what cost?" Thane asked. "I don't care how trustworthy you think Aeduuin is. If he botches his next flight or doesn't become a Rider or finds some other fault with Rose, he could turn on her! I will not subject my sister to that kind of liability. We already have enemies too close to home; we can't even trust half our family, and we are forced to *live* with them."

"There has to be a way around this," Darr Beval insisted. "We would try this through our own dragons, but Corliss doesn't want to talk to her peers right now." He ran a hand through his hair. "We were almost certain the two would tether someday. They have similar, sensitive personalities. It seemed like a good fit…."

"Who's to say it isn't?" Darr Thorndon asked, approaching from behind Darr Beval. "Just give them some time to sort it out. They'll be fine."

Darr Beval shook his head. "Normally, I would agree with you, but you don't know them as well as I do. They're both so eager… this blow could set them both back, whether they're meant to tether to each other or not." He locked eyes with his fellow Rider. "We need as many Riders on our side as we can get."

Darr Thorndon considered this for a moment. "Rhoswen, you go inside and try nexing with Corliss. Thane, unkennel Fleta and bring her over to Corliss' stall; then, stay nearby but out of sight. We'll get Aeduuin." When Thane began to protest, Darr Thorndon held up a hand. "So far, you have entrusted me with your secret; I hope you won't discontinue that trust now." He turned to Rhoswen. "Just see if you can get her to come out of the corner," he said.

Corliss was curled up at the far side of her stall, her back to the door. Melancholy radiated from her like a cool, steady wind. By the time Darr Beval returned, Rhoswen had had no luck in coaxing her into communicating—nexing or otherwise.

The Rider entered in a rush. He grabbed Rhoswen by the shoulders and pulled her to threshold of the stall. "Aeduuin is almost here. Just do as I say and keep your voice low."

Rhoswen nodded, her heart racing at his touch. He spun her around to face Corliss, positioning her in the narrow opening at the door. Then, he stood behind her, facing out toward the arena, his back pressed up against hers. Her skin warmed where their bodies made contact, and a flush crept into her cheeks.

"This will keep me out of Corliss' sight, so as not to stress her further, and it will keep you out of Aeduuin's. Now, you will nex with Corliss and translate to me. Understand?" Darr Beval asked.

The muscles in his back hummed against hers as he spoke, and she struggled to suppress a shiver. "Got it," she choked out. A low rumble of a nex entered her mind, and she turned her head to look up over her shoulder: Fleta was chortling outside the stall.

"Hush, girl," Darr Beval chided aloud for Rhoswen's benefit. His tone sounded about as strangled as hers had a moment ago.

She had never nexed with a dragon whose Rider was present, and it felt strange knowing someone else could hear everything she could. A few more beasts nexed their amusement from the stalls nearby. *Well, he couldn't hear that,* she thought gratefully.

Two pairs of feet shuffled toward the stall, and Darr Thorndon could be heard explaining his plan to Aeduuin. "Since Corliss is willing to speak to Fleta," the Rider lied, "Darr Beval has offered to translate whatever she tells Fleta to you. Then, I want you to respond loudly enough for Corliss to hear your voice, so she knows your words belong to you. Understand?"

"I do," Aeduuin began, "but I *don't* understand why Corliss would only speak to Fl—"

"Dragons are fickle creatures. Just go with it," Darr Thorndon told him. "Go ahead!" he called to Darr Beval with more volume than would have been necessary if he weren't trying to make himself heard inside the stall.

Rhoswen pushed through the overwhelming sensation of having Darr Beval's back pressed against hers and focused her attention on the green in front of her. *Aeduuin is here to see you,* she nexed gently.

He must hate me, Corliss finally replied. She sounded miserable, but at least she was responding.

I am certain he does not. You should see him; he is beside himself with grief, just like you are.

It's my fault.

I don't believe it was, and neither does he. The dragon did not respond. "She thinks he blames her for the outcome of their flight," she whispered to Darr Beval, who reported this to Aeduuin as if he had heard it from his tawny.

Did he say Fleta is here? Corliss asked, lifting her head to gaze at the tawny.

Rhoswen smiled. Of course, this back-to-back ruse was sparing the green nothing. Still, Rhoswen did not move away from Darr Beval. *We are trying to preserve my anonymity. Take a look.*

Corliss peeked through the gap over Darr Beval's shoulder. She let out a bemused puff of air and met Rhoswen's gaze. *Why all the fuss? Is that why you're blushing?*

Rhoswen ignored the dragon's second question—*and* Fleta's muffled giggle. You *may know that I can nex to dragons,* she explained, *but no one else does—aside from my brother and the two Darrs here.*

"Tell her that's nonsense," Aeduuin said outside the stall.

"*You* tell her," Darr Thorndon reminded him.

We can't tell Aeduuin we're nexing? Corliss asked her.

Not yet, Rhoswen nexed back.

"Don't be silly, Corliss!" Aeduuin called to her. "This wasn't your fault. It just... happens sometimes."

Is he hurt? Corliss asked.

No, Rhoswen nexed. Corliss stared at her. She sighed. "She wants to know if he's hurt," she whispered to Darr Beval. Warm vibrations pulsed through her back as he spoke again.

"No, I'm not hurt," came the delayed reply. "But I wish I could see you."

Corliss appealed to Rhoswen, who shook her head. *He can't know I'm here, and he would have to pass me to come inside.*

Can I look over the door then? Corliss asked.

Rhoswen nodded.

The green stood and dipped her head low over her stall door. Rhoswen heard the shuffling of Aeduuin's feet again as he stepped forward to stroke the dragon's snout. Corliss rumbled her affection.

See? He really doesn't blame you, Rhoswen told her.

Tell him I'm sorry anyway, Corliss nexed. *He wants this so much.*

Rhoswen turned her head to whisper in Darr Beval's ear. Aeduuin was so close now that she barely breathed the dragon's message. Darr Beval's posture stiffened before he relayed the message.

"I'm sorry, too," Aeduuin finally replied. "We'll get it."

Corliss nexed to Rhoswen again.

"She's happy you're here," Darr Beval translated.

"I know." Aeduuin's voice sounded confident.

"You do?" Darr Beval asked, his feet shifting slightly. Rhoswen had to scramble to match his stance so her legs wouldn't show.

"How?" Darr Thorndon breathed.

"We didn't tether, if that's what you're asking," Aeduuin replied graciously. "But she flexed her muscles under my hand, and I got the idea. Can I go in?"

Rhoswen's and Darr Beval's bodies tensed from head to toe. They should have anticipated this. There was a brief pause as no one spoke.

"I'm not sure Corliss is ready for visitors," Darr Thorndon suggested.

Yes, I am, Corliss insisted with a snort that Aeduuin interpreted easily.

"See? She's fine," he said.

Rhoswen's heart raced. *Corliss, we can't let him in! He can't see me!*

Aeduuin is trustworthy, Corliss protested.

I know, but–

"Merry? Thane?" Darr Thorndon asked outside.

"I retrieved Merry for you, Darr Thorndon," Thane announced as he approached the stall. "I know you two are eager to head out once more before you change your wet leathers."

Fleta's voice sounded inside Rhoswen's—and presumably Darr Beval's—head. *Rhoswen, Aeduuin is distracted. Slip behind me while he is talking to Thane.*

Without a word, the pressure from Darr Beval's back shifted more firmly to the right, and Rhoswen escaped the stall behind him. She scampered around the tawny and emerged near her opposite flank, just as Aeduuin turned back around.

"Hello, Rhoswen, " Aeduuin said. He glanced over at Darr Thorndon, his eyebrows knitting together. "You're going out again?"

The Rider winked at him. "Just a little extra practice, so I can stay sharp enough to teach. Now, go in and see Corliss. We'll let you be."

"Thank you," Aeduuin said before disappearing inside the stall.

The Riders and trainees exchanged glances before finally expelling a relieved sigh. Fleta and Merry rumbled with laughter.

XXXIV

Detroit

"I probably already know the answer to this, but do you want to go?" Josie asked from the driver's seat, a position that had only, in recent years, ceased to scare Emmelyn half to death. She usually drove instead.

Their conversation derailed as they placed an order at the drive-thru for some supposedly healthy smoothies. As they pulled forward, Emmelyn began second-guessing her order. She was simply hoping for something tasty, but Josie was trying another new health craze.

"Yeah, why not?" Emmelyn replied, pulling a few dollars from her wallet. She couldn't remember the total, but she was pretty sure it was overpriced.

"*'Yeah, why not?'* Who are you, and what have you done with my best homebody—I mean, friend?"

"Maybe it's time I got out a bit more. I've heard so much about the place, and we're legal to drink now—"

"We've been legal to drink for over a year," Josie pointed out.

"—so, maybe it's time to live a little."

Josie stared at her friend for far too long, her eyes wide. "Are we dead?"

"Shut up," Emmelyn replied, rolling her eyes.

"No, really, because I'm pretty sure you once said that you would go to a nightclub 'over your dead body,' which, *logistically*...."

"Just shut up," Emmelyn repeated with a laugh. "Do you want to go or not? Cuz we don't have to...."

"Yes! Yes, I do," Josie insisted.

The woman at the drive-thru window slid the glass aside and asked for payment. Emmelyn's eyes bulged the way Josie's had a moment ago. She grabbed more singles from her wallet and handed them over as if at gun point. In turn, Josie passed her a plastic cup of fuchsia slush.

"When is it again?" Emmelyn asked and took a sip. She doubted it would add twenty years to her life, but it was decent.

"Friday. Everyone is meeting at Jere's and carpooling to Dissonance from there."

Emmelyn withheld the real reason she wanted to go to the nightclub. She had to know what it was like apart from the Exchange. Did everyone see that lobby? Were the Ministers there? Would the Crew be there? If so, how would she explain knowing them? They definitely didn't resemble a college study group. *Maybe a local theatre troupe....*

Dissonance was probably just a standard nightclub when outside the Exchange... but she had to risk it. She *had* to know for sure.

"You know Jere has a crush on you, right?" Josie asked, making a wild turn as the light shifted from yellow to red. Emmelyn flashed back to their teenage years as frightfully bad drivers and grabbed for the emergency handle overhead. "Sorry," Josie said. They'd come a long way, really—no apologies back then. Just maniacal giggling.

"I thought he was into Dierdre," Emmelyn replied.

Dierdre was the oddly sexy, girl-next-door, study-abroad student from Ireland—so, her next door was more like "next continent." But it didn't make her any less appealing to every guy Emmelyn knew. She couldn't dislike Dierdre, though; she was by far the nicest person Emmelyn had ever met. That almost made it worse—but in a good way.

Josie shook her head and came to an impressively smooth stop at the next red light, which they had not been able to avoid. "Not anymore. He asked her out early last semester, and she said no. Didn't I tell you?"

"You most certainly did not," Emmelyn said in mock outrage. "You were clearly withholding this from me."

"If I were withholding things from you," Josie said, easing her foot onto the gas as the light changed, "would I have even bothered to invite you to Dissonance?"

"Of course you would," Emmelyn replied, "because you wouldn't want to face my wrath when I got wind of your *betrayal of our friendship*!" She emphasized the last words with such flair that Josie actually took her hands off the wheel to applaud her performance.

"Good point," Josie said and turned into a gas station.

On Friday, Josie and Emmelyn began their beautification process well in advance of their departure time. They raided each other's closets, trying to assemble nightclub-worthy outfits. This proved far more difficult for Emmelyn. Thankfully, as roommates, they had a full array of options between them.

After high school, both girls had wanted to stay home and go to the local university to save money, but Emmelyn's folks decided to move to a warmer climate, and it looked like she and Josie would be separated for the first time in their fifteen years of friendship. That was when Josie decided they should room together at school so Emmelyn could stay local and they could stay together.

"What about these?" Josie asked, holding up Emmelyn's second-tightest pair of pants. Her tightest pair were actual tights.

"Those are probably the most unforgiving pants I own," Emmelyn said, sliding several uninteresting shirts along the bar in her closet.

"What's to forgive?" Josie asked. "Oh, and this." She brandished a sparkling black top with suspiciously placed cutouts from her own collection.

"No," Emmelyn said definitively.

Minutes later, she was wearing Josie's prescribed outfit.

"Yes," Josie declared.

Emmelyn squinted at the cutouts in the mirror, head cocked to one side. "I don't know.... Is it good?"

"Would I have put you in it if it weren't?" Josie asked. "Anyway, what else would you wear?"

Emmelyn had no idea; she didn't own "clubbing" apparel. "I just don't want to look too...." Her words trailed off as she searched for an adjective that Josie wouldn't interpret as an affront.

"Slutty?" Josie suggested without offense. She rolled her eyes. "That's how you're supposed to look. It's a *club*, remember? Honestly, Em, how do you do your job when you can barely dress yourself?"

Emmelyn scoffed. "We don't dress women in miniskirts and bralettes! Anyway, I do paperwork all day!"

"Good thing," Josie joked.

Emmelyn gave her friend a gentle shove. Her internship had been the only thing that had made staying with Josie possible.

Emmelyn's freshman year had marked the launch of the new Charitable Internship Program at the university. The college partnered with local nonprofits to provide them with reliable help a few months at a time. Students could switch charities every semester, but Emmelyn never left WE Dress.

Though unpaid, CIP reduced tuition costs. Emmelyn suspected the school received some sort of tax break for their "donation," but she couldn't protest. Together, CIP and her academic scholarships cut the cost of her bachelor's degree by more than half, and a small (but appreciated) stipend from her parents covered living expenses.

Emmelyn nodded at herself in the mirror as she had seen so many women do at the shop. She loved watching the ladies' hopeful faces as they saw themselves transformed into business professionals amid three-way mirrors and racks of suits and separates. Emmelyn did not feel the same bright sense of transformation, but this was a far cry from a new start in life.

With a shrug, she relented and moved on to makeup.

Josie was still trying to narrow down her shoe selection by alternating feet in the mirror like a flamingo. "This pair… or this pair?" she asked. Emmelyn pointed to her favorites. "You always say those."

"I always like those."

Josie sighed. "Can't you try something new? Go outside your box, Em."

Emmelyn looked down at a cutout in her skin-tight top and thought of the grommeted pleather pants on the musical composer at the Exchange. She held her tongue.

After an almost unendurably long car ride—during which Josie continued to harp on the idea that Jeremy had a crush on Emmelyn—they made it to their host's house. Jeremy had decided to complete the first half of his degree at a local community college, so he still lived with his parents. Their home could have easily housed two families, it was so large. A few familiar cars lined the street out front.

"Are we late?" Emmelyn asked as she stepped out of the car.

"No," Josie replied. She was texting someone as she came around to the sidewalk. "The guys had some sports thing today, so they're already together."

"Oh, so they'll be primed with all kinds of annoying inside jokes," Emmelyn said, rolling her eyes. "Delightful."

Josie rang the doorbell and reached for the handle, not waiting to be invited in. That was standard practice among this group. Locked doors signaled that someone was truly angry… or truly forgetful. The latter was forgivable.

Emmelyn heard whispering and the quick shuffling of feet as she stepped inside behind her friend.

"Well, let's see you!" Josie called out from the rug in the foyer, hands on her hips. Jeremy had been warned that the guys would have to be presentable to participate in this outing. Josie stood there like a den mother—in club attire—waiting to approve them.

After some more whispering and shuffling around the corner, the guys strutted across the foyer, one by one, like fashion models, jutting their hips and placing one foot deliberately in front of the other. Over-pursed lips made their faces skinny and angular. They looked like a school of disjointed, upright fish.

Emmelyn and Josie cat-called through their laughter until Jeremy began narrating the men's outfits like a pageant announcer. Tears threatened to stream down the girls' cheeks, and they tilted their heads back, desperate to preserve their mascara.

"… and here, we have Nate in skinny black jeans—a *daring* choice… " Jeremy continued in a ridiculous, schmoozy voice.

More friends entered through the open door behind them and added to the cacophony. Once the last model had paraded across the overlarge foyer, they all returned to line up for a grand bow. Naturally, their audience applauded and whistled as though they had never witnessed a better performance in their lives.

Jeremy approached Josie. "So, can we tag along?" he asked her.

"I suppose," she replied. She watched as he moved to hug Emmelyn and flashed her an I-told-you-so look over his shoulder. Emmelyn returned a threatening squint before he let her go.

"Glad you could make it out tonight," he told Emmelyn with obvious surprise.

Emmelyn looked skyward. "Okay! I get it! I never go out. Can't an old dog learn a new trick on occasion?"

"Don't goooo changing… " Neal droned musically over Jeremy's shoulder. His girlfriend, Andrea, slapped his arm and flashed Emmelyn an apologetic look that seemed to ask, "Boys: what can you do?"

The final couple—Claire and Leo—waltzed through the door with a bottle of flavored vodka held high in the air like a trophy. Everyone cheered and raced to the kitchen for the pregame. Clearly, Emmelyn would be driving.

Jeremy also offered. "If we take our two cars, we'll only need one more."

Claire raised a hand and surrendered her shot glass to Leo. "I'll take one for the team."

"Oh, even better," Jeremy replied. "If we take your SUV, we won't need my car." He looked at Emmelyn and smiled. "I can ride with you!"

Josie shot Emmelyn another pointed glance.

Emmelyn's stomach flipped as she pulled the car up to the curb and stared at the familiar black awning above the door to the nightclub. She'd be hyperventilating by now if the sky were bright gray instead of black.

Josie sat in the passenger seat, playing on her phone and half-listening to Jeremy, Nate, and Darryn recap their day. Emmelyn had heard everything up to the impulsive Silly String purchase, but the rest had been drowned out by the pounding of her heart and the idle chatter from the line of people standing outside the club. She rolled up her car windows and killed the ignition.

Jeremy launched himself out of the backseat to open her door for her—a gesture that Josie found extremely romantic, if her puppy-dog eyes offered any indication. Emmelyn just smiled and nodded in appreciation of his chivalry. He *had* spared her the exertion of pulling the handle on her own.

She glanced at the club's entrance. It was far from deserted. The street was studded with cars on both sides, and people stood around in a bunchy line that began under the awning and snaked down the sidewalk. They met up with their friends at the back of the line, and everyone dug out IDs as they neared the door. Emmelyn glanced at the bouncer. He was not one of the ones she recognized from the Exchange club. *So far, so good.*

The man held up the group to check all their IDs at once. The delay set Emmelyn's heart racing. Jeremy and Josie frowned at her in concern.

"Are you okay?" Jeremy asked.

"I'm fine," Emmelyn replied and flashed him an unconvincing smile.

Jeremy put an arm around her shoulder. "Don't worry. I won't let anything happen to you."

He thinks I'm nervous about being at a club, Emmelyn mused. She thought of all the times she had magically appeared here—in the middle of everyday life—and sat around with the Crew, drinking beer or gin and receiving an education on the new life that none of her friends knew she lived. *What if I walk through these doors with my friends and come out alone in the marble lobby on the other side?*

The bouncer gave them a nod and unclasped the thick red rope barrier from its stanchion in front of the door. Jeremy gave Emmelyn a squeeze, his arm still around her shoulders, and steered her through the doors into Dissonance.

MY QUEEN,

War is still fresh in the minds of the realm. Rewriting the histories will do little to heal the wounds suffered during this heinous time. It is folly to think we will so readily forget what has transpired!

Of course, it is a trifle if it brings us a truce. But it proves my brother to be genuinely unstable if he believes it an effective course. I fear for your safety. Badrick must not know what you conveyed to me in your last letter. You must do whatever you can to hide the truth from him. It is a blow from which he might never recover, and you would bear the brunt of it.

I will do everything in my power to protect you.

Yours in this realm,
Allistair

XXXV

Aethelburh

Gethin did not really know what he should be looking for in the main floor library. He had already flipped through his histories from lecture to see what he could find on the Heir Rider, but much of what the students in Keaton had been discussing had not been in the pages. *Where could they have gotten this information?* Clearly, if it were being discussed in lecture, it had to be printed somewhere for the Riders to have read about it.

A memory of an overheard discussion from many years ago tugged at Gethin's mind. Still a youngster, Gethin had not understood much of it, but from what he remembered, the king had ordered the local printer to abridge the histories. The printer had argued against it, but his father had simply reminded the man how easily he could be replaced, and the conversation had ended.

If the histories had been altered, perhaps the information Gethin was looking for came from an older version of the books. He searched the shelves for familiar titles, but the only editions he could locate were current.

I don't just need another book, he realized. *I need another library.* The overflow library in the cellar held more obscure titles—mostly translations of old-language texts paired with their original counterparts.

Gethin's classes on the dying language had always been his favorite. They made him feel like he was learning the secrets that others had condemned to obscurity, and he fancied the idea of one day being sought out—*the last of the script readers*—to decode them. For years, those texts offered his primary method of escape; he would spend all day reading the archaic scrollwork and avoiding his father. But he had not ventured there since beginning his training in Keaton.

Lately, his favorite things—his exploration of an ancient language or the feeling of Aethelia petals perishing on his tongue—could not bring him any lasting joy. Mortality was no longer a sufficient reminder of his vitality; it only reminded him of his helplessness. Even flying on dragonback failed to distract him. He wanted—*needed* something *more*. And now, he finally knew what that something was. He simply had to implement his plan to get it.

As he reached for the door handle, he heard footsteps outside. His father threw open the door of the library, and Gethin had to stumble backward to avoid being slammed in face. The king strode into the room, unaware of his son's brush with injury. *And very probably unconsciousness.*

Badrick turned on his heel to face his son. He was only a head taller than Gethin, but his imposing figure made the prince feel half his own height. Badrick surveyed Gethin's empty hands. "You did not find what you were looking for," he observed.

Gethin forced his shoulders down and his back straight to make him look—and feel—more confident. "I am headed to the cellar library."

"Since when have you become so studious?" Badrick grimaced. "It's not to read those worthless old texts again, is it?"

Gethin had never perceived his academic childhood pleasure as "worthless." He did not appreciate the notion. "Oh? And can *you* read those ancient books you haven't yet bothered to discard, Father?" he asked before he could stop himself.

Badrick's expression shifted to disinterest. "Why would I waste my time when they have all been translated? Students aren't even taught anything about the old language anymore. Your tutors just capitalized on your interest as a way of teaching you something."

Gethin seemed unable to stop his mouth. "Well, *I* will know how to read them if ever we need something translated. Pity that you, the king, wouldn't be of any service in that regard."

His father's eyes flashed with amusement or anger—Gethin couldn't decide between the two, which was frightening. "Kings don't trouble themselves with *service*," Badrick spat. "That's why they have idiot sons with a fetish for putrefaction and all things archaic." He turned away and moved to the desk near the windows. Gethin was about to leave when the king called him back. "What are you looking for, then?" He began flipping through a book on the desk.

"An old version of the histories we use in class."

"*They* use in class."

Gethin ground his teeth together. "*I* attend, too, Father."

"Not often enough to care about the texts. Or is this one written in the old language?"

"Either way, I will be able to read it, so I will find what I'm looking for." He turned on his heel and took one emboldened step toward the door, his back to the king.

"Which is?" his father asked with deliberate slowness, as if his son were trying him past the limit of his patience—that was, if he'd had any.

"Information on the Heir," Gethin said, turning back to his father.

Badrick chuckled. "You are not the Heir."

"So you tell me."

Badrick rolled his eyes. "There will be no Heir," he declared.

Gethin didn't believe it the first time his father said it, and it still didn't resonate with him now. "There is always an Heir when the king has failed a realm," he said, his voice tinged with venom.

Badrick ignored his son's impertinence. "Have you listened to nothing I've said since your cousins arrived? There will be *no Heir*. By keeping the portal object from Deowynn, she will not be able to Move and, therefore, will have no reason to conceive; she will have no use for an Heir. Therefore, I cannot understand what interest you could possibly have in such information when it would be made obsolete by my brilliant plan."

'Would be' made obsolete? "Why are you speaking in hypotheticals? You are withholding the Realm Portal object from the queen dragon. The histories should *already be* obsolete if your plan is so brilliant. Or are you as skeptical as I am?"

Badrick's resultant expression was not a pleasant one. Yet, despite his father's fury, Gethin could tell that Badrick really did doubt his plan's validity, and his father disliked being questioned.

"There is more to it than you could possibly understand," Badrick replied.

"Enlighten me," Gethin pressed. "Save me the trip to the cellar."

Badrick gestured for his son to close the door. "Perhaps you will recognize that my plan is only as foolproof as the hiding place of the Realm Portal object." Gethin nodded. "And were that hiding place compromised in any way and the object to fall back into Deowynn's possession, it would prove nearly impossible to recover."

Gethin's brow furrowed. "Why not destroy it then?"

"And how do you propose I do that?" Badrick sneered.

Pride flooded Gethin's chest. Could he have proposed an idea his father had not yet considered? *It seemed so obvious....* "There must be a way."

"Oh, how *clever*, Gethin." Badrick rolled his eyes. "Well, *I* haven't found one. And yes, I've tried. The object is made of dragon metal forged in the blood of the most ancient king and queen dragons in history. The fiery breath of today's beasts could not even scorch the ring—if they would acquiesce. This is why it must be hidden—and exceptionally well—until I can figure out how to destroy it."

"You must keep it on you then," Gethin suggested, neglecting to name the object. Twice now, his father had let slip the Realm Portal's shape, but the prince had no interest in revealing his notice of it. *Let him think I'm not paying attention.*

"As if I would tell you where it is hidden," Badrick replied.

Regardless of his futile attempt to gain his father's confidence—something he never truly expected anyway—Gethin felt his own convictions strengthening in the wake of the king's doubt. "It seems there is only one way to prevent Deowynn from Moving, then." *Kill the queen dragon,* he finished in his head, not daring to speak the words aloud.

"Blaxton would never allow it," Badrick replied, seeming to intuit his son's suggestion. "Dragons have an eighth sense about such danger; all of Keaton's beasts would converge upon me before I could get near either of the royal dragons if they thought me a threat."

Gethin considered this for a moment. *But the queen dragon is only half of the equation....* "Well, if ever the... *object* does slip through your grasp, perhaps my errand to the library won't be entirely for naught. It would appear the Riders don't think the information in the older versions of our histories is obsolete, regardless of what you—or the printers you threaten—would have them believe."

"What are you talking about?"

"I heard some students in the halls of Keaton. They were discussing the Heir and how to recognize him. They seemed to know a lot about the subject. I can only surmise they learned about it in lecture."

Badrick closed his eyes. When they opened again, they flared with unmistakable rage. "Not that you would know for certain because *you never attend!* DELWYN!" the king bellowed. The royal pair waited in tense silence, only Badrick's uneven breathing breaching the quiet. Finally, Baul entered, long-faced and agonizingly sluggish. When he began to explain why he was there instead of Delwyn, Badrick cut him off. "Have someone who knows how to use his feet bring Aelfraed to me. *Now.*"

"Maybe that's what we should be working on today," Thane suggested through a mouthful of apple.

They had been discussing their tenuous grasp of the portal over the meagerest of snacks. Thane wanted to continue their research during their waking hours, but Rhoswen felt the risk was high enough at night when Badrick's staff was, at least, *supposed* to be sleeping. They had nearly exposed her identity to Aeduuin, trustworthy as he might be; how many more chances should they take?

She looked down at the half-eaten carrot in her hand and saw in it a metaphor for how much they understood about the portal system; they weren't even certain whether they could close it behind them. Her bangs fell into her eye, and she gently tucked the lock behind her ear, focusing instead on her growling stomach. If nothing else, they could venture down to the cellar on the pretense of finding a better snack. Before she could suggest it,

Delwyn entered the kitchen.

"Have either of you seen a peculiar-looking key?" the waitman asked.

Rhoswen and Thane exchanged glances. They had agreed to hand the pendant over to Delwyn only after Rhoswen had talked to Lorelle about it, but she had not yet found the opportunity. They shook their heads, and he slumped unhappily, still scanning the floor.

"Well, if you do, please let me know?" he begged. Before they could promise to do so, he was gone again.

"We have to give it back to him," Rhoswen muttered.

"I know," Thane replied. "As soon as Lorelle returns."

Rhoswen nodded. "Can we grab some cheese while we're down there? I'm starving."

"Sure," Thane said. He screwed up his face in distaste. "Just not the purple kind."

Prospective Riders may submit themselves from all different locations to train and tether, earning the right to defend the part of the Realm whence they hail.

After tethering in the Royal Drakiary, Riders with a more adventurous spirit may opt for Freedom of Transfer, allowing the King Rider to place them wherever he needs the most assistance, rather than returning home. Because Narxon Descents can take place anywhere and at any time, distributing Riders across the Realm is of exceptional importance.

- an excerpt, *Wanderer the Realm*

XXXVI

Dallin

The gray skies above the outskirts of Dallin were shot through with streaks of brilliant white flame and inky black smoke. Dragons swooped through the air, fire blazing from their jaws in large, roiling gusts. Streams of smoke poured in through a gash in the sky and collected into the forms of young, decrepit smoke-beasts. The Narxon plummeted downward like lead-weighted kites in a dying wind, yet their wings maneuvered them away from the flame of their pursuers with surprising agility. They careened hungrily toward the green grass, coming together like a stampeding herd as they made landfall, a trail of blinding ash pluming in their wake.

Dragons split off into groups, some chasing after Narxon that had already made it to the ground, while others tended to the parasites still falling from the sky. Yet another assembly swarmed the river, guarding the swift flow of water heading downstream. No Narxon could touch the river: they would spread through the water like dissipating ink and seep onto the land, ravaging both with speed that rivaled flight.

Magge and Allistair drew nearer on dragonback. Their eyes followed the dark clumps of Narxon up to the gaping tear from which they were issuing.

It was as if someone had taken a sword and sliced through the air, transforming the sky from something endless and intangible into a bounded, flat object, like a tapestry.

With only the slightest urging from their Riders, Cahal and Kuney sped toward the tear, their guts churning up a blaze in preparation for their task.

As they neared the rift, Allistair heard Cahal nex a dismissal to the beasts nearby, and the dragons fell back to assist other groups below. Kuney, the smaller and more agile of the pair, approached the front of the slash as Narxon seeped from it. One clump of smoke paused at the opening, allowing itself to half form into a beast before thrusting itself outward at her.

Magge pulled hard on her pommel loops and thrust her feet downward in the toeholds to brace herself as Kuney circled upward, out of harm's way.

Allistair tensed until the pair resumed their position, as Cahal hovered behind the tear. From the back, the gash looked like nothing more than a faint, horizontal shimmer in the sky, and that was before his dragon began shooting flame at it—the heat from the fire would distort the image nearly to invisibility.

For this very reason, cauterizing a tear required extraordinary precision—one misstep from either side, and a blast of flame would hit the other dragon. Only the most skilled Rider-dragon pairs took on the challenge.

Narxon continued to pour from the rift, eliciting more shouts from the Riders below, who tried to torch what Kuney was allowing to pass by her. Finally, with both beasts in place on opposite sides of the tear, their guts churning furiously, the dragons counted off.

Kuney and Cahal opened their jaws and blasted out streams of fire that met each other at the top of the tear. Riders all around them took up a traditional chant to help the beasts keep time as they moved along the opening. The olden words had dulled into unintelligible sounds through the ages, but the rhythmic pulse of the song did its job. The dragons moved down along the gash in time with each other, cauterizing the sky where their jets of flame met. The stream of Narxon thinned as the gap narrowed, and the singing grew louder. At the bottom, both dragons pushed out one final ball of flame to seal the rift shut. As the blasts met, pluming together in a roiling mass, Cahal and Kuney thrashed the air with their wings, soaring out and away from the explosion. The final, guttural beat of the chant faded as dragons burned the remaining parasites from the land and sky.

Allistair was heading toward the ground when Riders began shouting and pointing upward. He looked back at the tear, his eyes wide. *It isn't closed,* he nexed to his dragon. A chill rose up his spine.

Cahal passed the message on to Kuney, and Magge turned to look skyward, her mouth agape. Thin streams of Narxon smoke trickled through gaps in the tear and merged into tiny, leaden beasts. Cahal and Kuney flew close together so their Riders could hear each other.

"What do we do?" Magge yelled to her husband over a crack of thunder.

"Try to seal it again?" Allistair suggested.

Kuney and Cahal balked.

We can't be that *precise in our streams,* Cahal protested. *Those gaps are too thin; we'll burn each other.* Kuney relayed the concerns to her Rider.

Magge shrugged. "What about fireballs? The ones we use at the end to complete the cauterization. We could blast one at every gap." Kuney bellowed her agreement, which seemed to convince Cahal and Allistair, as well.

The dragons surged upward, resuming their positions on either side of the tear. Hesitant chanting started up again from a few Riders below, but the normal routine had been broken. Cahal and Kuney counted themselves off; they timed their blasts and darted away from the burgeoning flame, over and over, until they'd resealed every break in the seam.

Before they were through, they had cauterized nearly a half-dozen holes, one requiring the treatment twice. Finally, the pair surveyed the scar. No more trails of smoke penetrated the sky. It was holding.

Only the screech of injured dragons remained of the Descent.

Where is the rain? Cahal asked his Rider.

Below them, dragons deposited their Riders on the ground and hurled themselves in the river. Screaming beasts splashed about, desperate for something to soothe their burning hides. Even a few Riders who had been singed by the parasites thrust their marred, ashy limbs into the water. It was a poor substitute for the healing rain, and it did not stop the crawling spread of deterioration.

Cahal and Kuney flew back down to the riverbank and dropped off their Riders before flinging themselves into the water. Although unharmed, they had been forced to create an excess of fire to complete the cauterization, and Allistair appreciated their desperation to cool down.

High overhead, clouds darkened around the silver scar hanging in the sky and finally let forth a cleansing Narxon Rain that drenched everyone in an instant. The ash marring the torched landscape turned to thin mud, and the agonizing wails subsided as the rainwater rinsed the wounds of the dragons and Riders. Injured beasts who were still able to fly shot up out of the river, glittering streams of water falling in sheets from their gemstone hides as they vaulted into the air.

"Good Ride," Allistair said, hugging Magge tightly. She caught up his sweaty, rain-drenched leathers in her fists.

Riders shuffled around nearby, their voices hushed as if they feared that vocalizing their observations might reopen the tear or dispel the rain.

"What happened?" Ordway, a Rider from Radbourne, finally asked. "You two never miss."

"They didn't miss," his Riding partner, Nickson, said as he descended from the saddle. Nickson was gifted with extraordinary sight. He was always put to the task of checking the area for straggling Narxon they might have missed. He had been the first to alert the others to the failed cauterization and the last to land after the tear was finally closed. "That tear opened back up! After they blasted what should have been the final fireball, the seam split."

"It *reopened*?" Ravinger repeated in disbelief from his place at the edge of the group. "That doesn't happen." More voices echoed his denial.

"Is that why the rain was late?" a strange voice asked from beside Ravinger. Allistair and Magge stared at the newcomer. He sported an unusual set of olive-green leathers and an unrecognizable accent.

This question seemed to break the dam, unleashing all manner of other inquiries from the assembled Riders. Finally, Allistair called for silence. "It isn't clear what happened here. Magge and I have never seen anything like it," he said, glancing to his wife for verification. She shook her head. "We will look into it. I'm sure there's a logical explanation." He singled out a few Riders and instructed them to find out if other towns had had similar experiences.

Allistair gazed back up at the ghostly silver slash hanging in the sky and was reminded of a similar scar on his forearm from all those years ago. "For now, we've done what we can. Ravinger, as head Rider in Dallin, I want you to monitor that tear in case it breaks open again. Keep me informed." He addressed the group. "Thank you, everyone, for your help. Go home; rest up. Our battle is changing, and I fear we must prepare for unpredictable Descents ahead. Ravinger—you and your new friend—stay a moment."

Everyone ambled away, still muttering as they sought out their dragons. Ravinger and Denver approached the Stanburhs.

"Whom do we have here?" Allistair asked.

"My Lord and Lady of Stanburh, this is Denver, Rider of Kipling." Ravinger pointed to the small green still splashing in the river.

"Don't throw around our titles simply because you're in trouble," Magge snapped. "Why haven't we met this new recruit before?"

Ravinger dipped his head in apology. "He is new to Dallin and only just arrived. I was getting him acclimated—"

"To Dallin?" Magge asked with a distasteful curl of her lip.

Allistair glanced at her. She was obviously furious at this breach, and that *Ravinger* had been the one to break protocol was not improving matters. "Depending on whence he hails, Dallin could take some getting used to, Magge. No offense," he added for Ravinger's benefit. "But my wife is right. We should have known about him sooner, Rav—"

"Like when you asked us to requisition you another Rider," Magge suggested venomously. Indeed, he had done nothing of the kind; how he had come by a new Rider remained a mystery. Ravinger ducked his head, but Magge continued her interrogation before Allistair could stop her or Ravinger could explain himself. "Whence *do* you hail, Denver?"

"A little village in the south by the name of Hazlitt," Denver replied.

Magge and Allistair exchanged glances. That was no southern accent.

"He's newly tethered," Ravinger offered.

Magge rolled her eyes. "I figured as much, given his youthful appearance, Ravinger." She turned to the new Rider and flashed him a weak smile. "Welcome, Denver—and Kipling. Good Ride today. It was noble of you to request freedom of transfer. I hope you find yourself at home in Dallin." It was clear from her expression that she found the prospect dubious at best.

Denver bowed. "Very much so, Lady Stanburh, thank you. It is a pleasure to meet you both." He took Allistair's outstretched arm before he and Ravinger were dismissed to retrieve their dragons.

Once the pair walked out of earshot, Magge leaned in close to her husband. "I don't remember hearing about Dallin needing a new Rider."

Allistair sighed. "Ravinger never asked for one. He's not the type to avoid asking for what he wants," he agreed. "Just one more thing to look into, I suppose."

Magge snaked her arm around his waist. She looked exhausted. "Let's take a little break first."

"Oh, that's not good," Ravinger mumbled as they came up beside the river where Kipling and some of the other dragons still splashed around. When Denver didn't ask him what he was talking about, he volunteered the information. "The Stanburhs were not happy."

"They're probably exhausted," Denver replied.

"You don't know him—*or her,*" Ravinger said. "She has never liked me, and he is married to her, so you can figure the rest."

"What does it matter?" Denver asked. He beamed at his beast.

"He'll look into you now," Ravinger said. "That realmed accent didn't help either...."

"Well, if he does, won't it be telling when he discovers that the town I supposedly come from doesn't exist?" Denver asked.

"I told you, that was intentional."

The pair had received the call to the Descent on their return from the Two Fords Tavern. Ravinger had barely begun coaching his new protégé and had been forced to induct him on their way, nexing their cover story through Norvin to Kipling to Denver. All things considered, Denver had done pretty well. *Except for that accent!*

Ravinger scanned for Norvin, squinting through the rain as he looked skyward, but the tawny was nowhere to be seen. "The south is pretty volatile—names change constantly down there. He would almost expect the name you gave him to be out of date by now, as towns try to establish some sort of standing for themselves."

"Well, then, how could he look into me?" Denver asked, nonplussed.

"He'll inquire with the king. Your uncle couldn't forge some sort of royal decree that would justify your allocation to Dallin's Rider force. And I had no time to make a formal petition. That's why the Stanburhs, who hold lordship over this entire territory, were so surprised by your sudden presence here—you showed up unrequested and unannounced to them. I don't know what we'll do if he gets anywhere with that inquiry."

Denver's eyebrow rose, but he did not ask for details. "Well, that explains a lot... including why I have to go back for another Run."

"Already? You just got here."

Denver nodded. "My uncle told me to return after I'd met the Stanburhs. From what you just told me, he probably wants to know if we got away with my unexpected assignment here." He frowned. "I have several return trips to make in short order. Sounds like he left a lot to chance and wants to see if he beat the odds."

Ravinger stared at Denver for a moment. "What's it like?" he asked finally.

"What?"

"Walking through those portals."

Denver stared back.

"It's got to be spectacular, right? Like walking into another realm?" Ravinger prompted.

"It *is* walking into another realm," Denver replied.

"Yeah, right, but what's it like to actually *walk through that door* from one realm into another?" Ravinger asked before waving to his dragon, who had emerged above the tree line and was gliding down toward them.

"Like walking through a door," Denver replied without inflection.

XXXVII

Detroit

Dissonance was exactly like the club in the Exchange: dark but for towers of multicolored lights, swarming with people, and filled with deafening music. It was also attended by oddly dressed clubgoers with big, frizzy hair; off-the-shoulder, baggy sweatshirts; neon tops and acid-washed jeans....

Exchangers.

Emmelyn felt her stomach drop—how could this be the Exchange with no fracture in time? No gray, abandoned street? No grand lobby or preposterous staircase? She glanced around for signs of stamped wrists and Transitors—

"Aww, I didn't know it was '80s night!" Claire whined. "I *so* have the perfect outfit for this!"

Emmelyn's shoulders dropped. These weren't Runners and Transfers from a realm with seriously questionable fashion sense. These were *costumes*. She exhaled the last of the tension from her body, and Jeremy glanced over at her.

"You all right?" he asked in her ear.

She nodded and flashed him a smile that wiped the concern from his face. As they moved farther into the club, she reached instinctively into the tiny pocket in her purse where she stored her orange earplugs. She compressed them between her fingers and fed them into her ears, delighting, as she always did, as the music faded to a comfortable volume.

Jeremy asked her if she wanted a drink, and she nodded, tucking her hair behind her ear. His eyes caught on her bright-orange earplugs, and he smiled, obviously impressed with her preparedness. *What a boy scout,* she thought fondly. He guided her toward the bar, his arm still around her, and she was hit with a memory of Vonn doing the same thing during her first Exchange visit. She shook the thought from her head and shifted her focus to the bartender. The woman had not ratted out her blonde hair or donned a head-to-toe jean ensemble; she had opted instead for a push-up bra, black tank top, and a high ponytail at the back of her head. *Definitely not Trevor,* Emmelyn mused.

"What'll it be?" the bartender asked.

Jeremy gestured for Emmelyn to order first.

"Otends and soda," she yelled, instantly wishing she hadn't. *Don't order gin from another realm!* The bartender gave her an appropriately confused look. Emmelyn's eyes darted across the wall of booze behind the woman and picked out a rose-and-cucumber gin that Vonn had promised would be their next selection. She would have to try it without him—this was an emergency. The bartender nodded and took Jeremy's order.

He raised an eyebrow at Emmelyn. "I didn't know you drink gin," he hollered.

"It's a new thing," she yelled back.

"You're trying all kinds of new things." He pulled out his wallet.

Oh, right, she thought, resisting the urge to face-palm herself. *We pay in this realm.* "I can get mine," she offered and opened her purse.

"No," Jeremy insisted, pulling down the flap on her bag. "My treat."

The bartender set down the drinks and stepped away with Jeremy's cash. As he dropped a couple singles into a fishbowl, Emmelyn suddenly wondered if she should have been tipping Trevor all this time. She had never noticed a tip jar on *his* bar....

Clearly believing these foreign surroundings to be a source of anxiety for Emmelyn, Jeremy slipped his arm back around her as they stepped away from the bar. She appreciated his attempt at comforting her, even if he had no idea how benign this scene had become for her.

Even the circles of mismatched chairs and couches were the same. They passed the spot the Crew normally occupied to find Josie, Nate, Selma, and Andrea in the next circle over. At first, Emmelyn felt like she was trespassing on someone else's turf, but she figured it was probably better to avoid her usual spot with people who weren't part of the Crew. *Keep your realms separate.*

She spotted an oversize armchair open to Jeremy's left. In the Exchange, it frequently held a lean but muscular, dark-blond Luthean and two fawning Welsamodels—perhaps one more person than that chair could comfortably hold... not that the trio ever seemed bothered. Kyle had once told Emmelyn the Luthean's name; she could only remember that it started with an L. She shook her head to dislodge the thought. Jeremy gestured to the chair, and Emmelyn nodded. Indeed, it was a cozy squeeze for the two of them; she had no idea how the three Exchangers did it.

"So, what do you think?" Jeremy asked in her ear.

Emmelyn shrugged. People around them were dancing or standing around, yelling at one another, sipping drinks, and gesticulating exaggeratedly to communicate over the music. "It's loud and dark," she hollered back.

Jeremy laughed. He had a nice smile. His thick, dark eyebrows and well-defined jaw made his age hard for others to pin down, and he was carded less often than his friends if he forgot to shave. He sported a fresh haircut; the sides were newly trimmed, but the top was still rather long and gelled in place. An emerald stud in his left ear caught the light—his birthstone. He had told her a while back that he had been considering gauges in both ears, but she had expressed her distaste for them, and he never followed through with the idea. *Perhaps that should have been my first clue,* she mused.

The music shifted into an all-too-familiar '80s power ballad. "Do you want to dance?" he asked her.

She did not dance.

"Come on," he wheedled, his breath tickling her ear. "Who will be able to see you in this light—or lack thereof?"

"You?" Emmelyn suggested.

Jeremy drew an X over his heart with his finger. "I won't judge," he promised.

With a sigh, Emmelyn entrusted her drink to Josie and joined Jeremy on the dance floor. People danced at the Exchange's version of Dissonance, but relatively few members of the Crew participated unless a random admirer invited them out for a song. Bernadette was pulled away the most often; of course, she danced for a living, so it worked for her.

Jeremy snaked a hand around Emmelyn's waist, pulling her close as they swayed back and forth. Someone bumped into her in passing, and she clung to Jeremy to steady herself. They had been friends for almost a decade and had gone to the same school for years, but she didn't remember the slim curve of muscle under his shirt from when they were younger. He'd been working out.

"What happened with Dierdre?" she found herself asking in his ear. *The gin must be working already.* She would have to stop now if she wanted to be ready to drive at a moment's notice. Many things had remained constant about her group of friends over the years, and a short attention span was one of them.

"Dierdre who?" Jeremy joked. Emmelyn flashed him a look that made him grimace, and he lifted her hand over her head to turn her around like they were waltzing. "Wasn't the right fit," he yelled. He spun her around for another half turn and pulled her back against his front in what she could only describe as an upright spooning position. "Not like this," he added. He wrapped his arms around her and swayed back and forth again. A smile turned up the corners of her mouth.

The music changed again, and she pulled away from him a little, grateful for the opportunity to create some space between them. "I need a drink," she said in his ear, and he escorted her back to the group.

Thankfully, everyone was either too preoccupied or considerate to comment on their dance together. Claire and Leo had occupied a standard-sized armchair—with much the same effect as the trio of Exchangers in the oversize chair—and were making out enthusiastically. Josie made a here-they-go-again face at Emmelyn as she handed her back her gin and soda. Emmelyn laughed.

Jeremy wanted to go back out to the dance floor, but Emmelyn wasn't ready to indulge him. She signaled for Josie to join her in the restroom, and they downed their drinks before abandoning their glasses on the metal coffee table in the middle of their circle.

"I told you," Josie hollered as soon as they were out of sight.

"I know," Emmelyn replied with a groan.

In some ways, this seemed like the perfect chick-flick-romance scenario. She and Jeremy had known each other for years; he was a good, trustworthy, sweet guy—and cute to boot—but she had just been plunged into this double-life as a Transfer. It wasn't something she had learned to reconcile with her single life, let alone a relationship. And she couldn't confide in him about it. It would be that one misunderstanding that came between the two main characters and created tension for the length of the movie, except she didn't know how she could ever break it to him for the happy ending. "How could this have happened?"

Josie laughed. "You ask that like you're staring at the wreck of the Titanic. What's so wrong with it?"

Emmelyn hesitated, uncertain of how to answer. "What if it ruins the friendship?" She led Josie into the restroom and pulled the orange plugs from her ears. The closed door muted the music a fraction.

"Oh, the friendship is toast," Josie declared as she inspected a stall. It must have passed muster because she walked into it and closed the door behind her. Emmelyn peered into the next one and was relieved to see it, too, was in decent shape. "After that dance, there is no turning back. You either break his heart or give it a go."

Emmelyn groaned.

"What are you going to do?" Josie asked.

I have no idea, Emmelyn thought.

"I'd go for it," Josie said, punctuating her statement with the flush of her toilet.

Emmelyn groped for a way to deflect the situation and joined her friend at the sink a moment later. "*You'd* go for it? Is that your way of telling me *you* like Jere? Because if you have a thing for him, I'll step aside—"

"I do *not* have a thing for Jere," Josie replied. "I just think you two could be good together." She handed Emmelyn some paper towel and made her way toward the door. She paused mid-step and turned back to her friend.

"Hey, how did you know where the bathroom was in this place?"

Emmelyn's heart thudded in her chest. She remembered asking Bernadette where the bathrooms were once. "In the back, just befoah the portal doahs tuh the othuh realms," she had told her. *Explain that one, Em.* "Asked the bartender," she replied while fishing her earplugs back out of her pocket.

XXXVIII

Aethelburh

Despite a strong desire to flee, Gethin's feet felt stuck to the floor as he watched his father question the caretaker in the main floor library. Badrick's interrogations always made the prince's skin crawl.

"My son tells me the students are discussing the prospect of an Heir to this realm," the king said with eerie evenness. Light from the window behind him silhouetted his features, but nothing could conceal his displeasure.

"Last I knew, that was not a crime, your majesty," Aelfraed replied just as evenly. "It's in the histories."

Gethin was surprised by the old man's boldness. If he were in the caretaker's position, he would not be as collected as Aelfraed appeared to be.

"But not in the current editions," Badrick countered. "Gethin says he has scoured them for the information he overheard today, but he could find no trace of it. So, Aelfraed, I submit that *none* of it is in the histories. Where could the trainees be acquiring this knowledge?"

"In lecture," Aelfraed answered simply. "A lecture, might I add, that the prince did not attend, which means he could not know it was a lecture *I* gave. So, your highness, how did you know to approach me, rather than the head Riders, with your concerns?"

Aelfraed's boldness had turned to outright impertinence. But rather than call the old man out for it—which Gethin believed a good king would do—Badrick *smiled* at the jibe leveled at his son.

"Because *you* are the only one sly enough to preserve copies of those old texts." Badrick stared at the caretaker in silence. When the man offered no comment, the king's expression turned impatient. "What are you teaching them?" he asked, his voice bordering on a bark.

If the king's outburst unsettled Aelfraed in any way, he didn't show it. "Queen Orla is dead, your majesty, and given how little effort you have made in keeping her memory alive, our realm is doomed to Movement—

likely sooner than later. I am simply preparing them."

Gethin's mouth fell open.

"And what makes you think sooner?" Badrick asked. "Orla has been dead for years."

If Gethin's jaw could have dropped onto the floor and rolled across it, it would have. Twice now, Aelfraed's brazen insolence had been met not with admonishment but with *interest*. His father was *entertaining*—even *soliciting*—the man's impudent opinions. The prince forced his mouth shut, but his eyes remained wide.

"You still fail to temper your imbalanced rule, leading some to argue that Movement is inevitable. Isn't that growing timespan not proof enough that Movement is looming?" Aelfraed asked.

"To the contrary," Badrick replied. "Given that logic, the Riders should have Moved long ago. So, why the sudden hurry, Aelfraed?"

Now, Gethin was certain he had cause to worry. His father's tone was entirely novel: it seemed to imply not only genuine interest but *concern*. Badrick had not sent Aelfraed to the dungeon for his comments because he needed answers. The king's behavior was so transparent that Gethin couldn't imagine the truth was lost on the caretaker.

"I grow old, majesty," Aelfraed replied with a casual shrug. "If the trainers are not aware of their resources before I die, whom will they entreat in my stead?"

Badrick turned away and moved toward the window. "They need not entreat anyone, now or in the future. They have their resources. If there were need of these teachings, they would be in the histories. Concision is not a bad thing, Aelfraed. It speeds up the learning process."

"Certainly you did not call me here to give me a treatise on your support of concision in the classroom, your highness," Aelfraed replied. "So, why don't you tell me exactly what worries you about our Riders and trainees having this knowledge?"

Badrick grew very still.

Gethin felt like he might need to sit down. He suddenly understood the caretaker's powerful position. Locking Aelfraed away would lend weight to his suspicions about the imminent Judgment. And if Aelfraed's hunch was correct, Badrick's omissions from the histories could be construed as treason to the Realm Cycle. Such an accusation could accelerate the hunt for the Heir—and the king's demise.

"Gethin!" Badrick snapped as he whirled around to face his son. "You were headed to the overflow library. Aelfraed will accompany you. Help him pick out a few morsels to take back to Keaton. He is to be rewarded for his good sense in this matter of academia." He locked eyes with the old man. "Always a pleasure, Master Aelfraed."

The caretaker bowed. "Likewise, your majesty."

Thane unlocked the hidden maps room as Rhoswen peeled back the cornflower blue cheesecloth from a small hunk of cheese she had found in the larder.

He grimaced at the smell. "I know we need to learn how to close the portal behind us, but we might as well focus on the part of the process we do understand. Let's try to access Keaton," he suggested.

She swallowed a creamy mouthful of fragrant cheese. "In the middle of the day, with Riders and trainees all over the drakiary? And where will we come out? We don't even know which trinkets correspond to Keaton."

"Well, that is what we need to figure out," Thane replied, spreading out the map of Keaton and weighing down the corners.

Rhoswen stuffed the last bite of cheese into her mouth, surprised that she had already devoured the whole piece. She grabbed up the trinket box and poked through it with a finger.

"Shhh!" Thane placed a hand over hers to stop the jangling of odds and ends and met her gaze, his eyes wide. Footsteps sounded from the long hall to the overflow library. The pair sprang into quiet, harried motion, fleeing the maps room as if it were collapsing behind them. Rhoswen rushed to browse the shelves on the opposite side of the room as she willed her breathing to steady. Thane shoved the shelf-wall back into place, and it made a soft *click* just as Gethin and Aelfraed entered the library.

"Cousins," Gethin said in surprise.

Rhoswen looked over her shoulder at him. "Prince Gethin! A pleasure. We regretted not seeing you at breakfast this morning. Hello, Aelfraed," she said with a smile at the caretaker. Thane gave a little bow.

Gethin looked back and forth from the faces of his cousins. "What are you doing down here?" he asked.

"Probably reading, my prince," Aelfraed suggested. "That is the purpose of these rooms filled with books."

Gethin did not appear to appreciate the lesson in sarcasm. "Reading *what*?" he asked through gritted teeth.

"Just browsing, actually," Thane volunteered. "Rhoswen has a fondness for books, especially old ones."

Gethin's eyes narrowed. "Runs in the family."

"Oh?" Rhoswen inquired. "Are you looking for something in particular? Perhaps we can help—"

"No, thank you," Gethin interrupted. "We're here for Aelfraed. I'm certain he can find his own tomes without your assistance."

He stared at his cousins a moment too long, and Rhoswen recognized their cue to depart. "Very well. I think I will read my histories from lecture, then." She gestured to her brother to follow her out, and they gave their cousin a small bow.

Gethin sneered at them. "I'm not certain how accurate your histories shall prove to be in the coming days, Cousins. But enjoy your reading while you can."

Back in her room, Rhoswen paced at the foot of her bed. Not only was she uneasy about abandoning the maps room in a state other than how they had found it, but their cousin's dismissal had also struck her as odd and foreboding. "What did Gethin mean by that? 'While you can?'" she asked. "And what could suddenly make the histories *inaccurate*?"

Thane shrugged. He was sitting on the edge of her bed, a leg dangling off the side. "I don't put much stock in anything our cousin says," he replied.

She couldn't stop moving. Nervous energy tingled through her with every step. "I wish I could have grabbed the box of trinkets. We can't get anything done now." She scowled. "How are we supposed to master the portal if we never get a moment's peace down there?"

Thane hopped off the bed and crossed to his sister. He placed his hands on her shoulders and stooped a little to look into her eyes. "We'll go at night again, as is your preference anyway. But in the meantime, maybe Keaton is too close a goal…."

"Too close?"

He grinned. "The map of Stanburh. It's been too long since we've seen Mother and Father, don't you think?"

XXXIX

Keaton

Thorndon was stretched across the couch in Beval's sitting room, a mug of ale dangling precariously from the tips of his fingers. Beval had grown used to his companion's deft ability to hold onto things with more balance than force—a metaphor for how he lived his life. Watching Thorndon cavalierly handling full mugs and sharp knives used to make Beval nervous. Now, it amused him to secretly wait for his partner to drop something when he least expected to. It rarely happened.

They had been celebrating Maven's success with an unacknowledged nod to their personal mending of ways. It was an unspoken tradition for them to drink at the end of their spats… *and* to exchange any new gossip—even if they had to invent it for the good of the truce.

"I haven't had the chance to tell you a rumor I heard," Thorndon said. "Lord Twyford is said to be trading something on the black market."

Beval grinned. "Good one," he replied.

"No, no," Thorndon said, holding up a hand. "This one is real."

"Trading what, then?"

Thorndon shrugged. "That's what I can't figure out. Most reports point to some sort of secretive dealings with dragons—"

"He can't deal in dragons," Beval interjected.

Thorndon tipped his head in acknowledgment. "Others suggest things that make no sense."

"Like what?" Beval scooted forward a little.

"Doors."

"Come again?"

"He trades in *doors,*" Thorndon repeated. "I told you it made no sense."

"Perhaps you heard wro—," Beval began before cutting himself off and quirking an ear toward the door. "Did you hear that?"

Thorndon shook his head.

There was another faint knock on the door before Aelfraed bustled inside, his arms laden with books of various colors and sizes. "I have been to see the king," he said by way of greeting.

"And he's giving you his entire library?" Thorndon suggested. "Awfully friendly of him."

"What's going on, Aelfraed?" Beval asked, helping to unburden the man.

"Gethin has overheard talk of our most recent lecture—"

"As he could not be bothered to hear it in person," Thorndon interjected.

"—and he reported it, most dutifully, to his father," Aelfraed continued. "I was summoned to explain how the trainees had learned about the Heir's qualities. And then, in the spirit of royal fortitude, he sent me with the prince to the cellar library to retrieve additional materials for our teachings."

"Good to know that if we're going to assemble an uprising against the king, he wants us to get it right," Thorndon quipped.

Beval was not feeling half as saucy. He was also one mug of ale behind his friend. "What does this mean?"

"The king is aware that harming me will validate our teachings and add urgency to their implications.... But I doubt he will tolerate my position of advantage forever."

Beval scrutinized the composed face of the old man. "What is he up to?"

Aelfraed shook his head. "I'm not entirely certain. He could have simply sent me away, but he chose to arm me with books instead. It is not as though I am too young to remember the teachings from before he struck them from the histories. Perhaps he figured, since I didn't need the books, sending me to retrieve them was nothing more than a display of his power."

"I had forgotten much of that information," Thorndon admitted.

"And it was new to me," Beval agreed. "I was the first generation to use the new texts. But why encourage us to disseminate that knowledge now?"

Aelfraed looked at the Riders, his face drawn. "Perhaps he doesn't believe we'll be able to use it against him."

DEAR ALLISTAIR,

Your news is most serendipitous—and convenient! It is the best possible scenario and the greatest honor this family could have hoped for! You should be proud, my boy. Your mother and I certainly are.

Still, this will not be easy for any of you. It is not understood how such a selection is made—or whether it can be unmade.

If what you say is true, then our girl must not lose the qualities that have made her eligible for this honor. She must not be told by anyone of her selection or be made to think she is special. She must grow into the humble and kind woman who would be worthy of such a position.

We should also consider that your prejudices might taint her realmview. You must be careful, Allistair, not to imbue her with knowledge or opinions that could subvert her birthright. If she can be unselected, this would be the most expeditious path—and a grave error. You must walk the line between education and naivety. I do not envy you this hairline task.

Congratulations, my boy, and good luck.

Until the next Ride, your loving
Father

XL

Stanburh

Magge pushed her empty plate away. She and Allistair had just wolfed down a post-Ride meal, and exhaustion was beginning to nag at her. "Maybe Badrick simply sent one of his newest crop to Dallin... " she suggested, but she knew neither of them believed it.

"I'm not sure my brother even remembers that Dallin exists. And if Ravinger needed another Rider, he'd have *asked* us for one. He knows how things work," he told her.

"Oh, really?" she asked. "So, what is your explanation for his not bringing Denver to us for introductions?"

"Perhaps he really had just arrived, and the Descent brought us together before Rav had the chance."

"Rav," she echoed derisively. "I know you two have history, Allistair, but—"

He sighed. "But you 'don't trust him.' I know, Magge. You've reminded me of your position on that matter for years. I believed you then, and I believe you now."

"But *you* trust him?" she pressed. "You *must* if you handed him the reins to Dallin." It was an appointment she had never agreed with.

"Not entirely," he admitted. "But he has been doing what is expected of him for a long time, and we need all the allies we can get, even submissive ones. He made mistakes, Magge, but men can change."

"Not men like him," she grumbled loudly enough that her husband could not have misheard her.

"Well, whatever Rav is capable of, he cannot fake a Rider," he insisted. "Denver is tethered to a young green and came out of today's Descent unscathed."

Magge sighed through her nose. "But those off-colored leathers and that *accent*.... I don't know where any of that comes from. What if he's some outlaw Rider, who landed in Dallin—*the consummate place for an outlaw*—and found Ravinger—*the consummate host for an outlaw*—and is now *our* problem?"

"Who better to keep an eye on a rebel than us?" Allistair asked with a sideways grin.

Magge smiled. "He did Ride well," she admitted, softening.

"He did," Allistair agreed. "If he isn't a *villain,* he may actually turn out to be an asset."

She ignored his gibe. "We'll need all the assets we can manage if those Descents continue to change."

"It *was* strange."

Magge nodded. Her gaze grew unfocused as she replayed the unending cauterization in her mind. "We should write to Rhoswen and Thane," she said finally.

"What exactly do you think we should tell them?" he asked, eyebrows askew. "We can't explain what we know—it could change things. Plus, they're probably being watched. If the Descents are changing because we are headed for Judgment, Aethelburh must be in a state of mounting chaos. Badrick should have told us about Denver's coming, so he's clearly too preoccupied to bother with his *duties*. Who knows what's going on in that castle?"

It was not a comforting thought. "We need an ally in Keaton—a Rider. And our children need to figure out whom they can trust, but they won't be discerning if they don't know they need to be."

Allistair shifted a little. "I'm sure you're right, but I don't know how to tell them without… telling them *everything*."

"If we're this close to Judgment, does it matter anymore?" They had been having this argument for years. She was deathly sick of it.

"My father said—"

"Yes, all right," she interrupted. "Then we'll just have to figure it out."

"Or wait for them to," he mumbled.

XLI

The Exchange

"But he didn't try nothin' when ya got back tuh his place?" Bernadette asked through her smacking bubblegum. She and Inzay were perched on the edges of their seats, lipreading Emmelyn's tale of her first clubbing experience. They could barely hear one another over the twangy country music that only Randy could have appreciated. Ironically, he was missing it.

Emmelyn shook her head. "Josie and I didn't even go in. We just dropped the boys off, and that was that." She shrugged. "How do you two do it?"

"What? Live a normal life outside of your Exchange life?" Inzay asked. "Has anything really changed for you?"

"Everything!" Emmelyn blurted. Inzay and Bernadette laughed.

"Has it really, though, hun?" Bernadette asked. "So, ya space out for a moment while time stops, and ya make a quick visit tuh the Exchange. Nobody knows any different in yuh realm, so what does it mattah?"

"But it's like living some strange double-life," Emmelyn yelled. "I mean, now I know even more about our world—*realm*—than my friends do, and there's no sharing it with them. There's no explaining *any* of this to them."

"Well, no," Inzay replied, "but having a secret can be fun. It doesn't change how you live in your other life."

Emmelyn kept no secrets in her other life—until now.

Bernadette agreed with Inzay. "Transfuhs and Runnahs don't tend tuh date othuh Transfuhs and Runnahs. They'd nevah see each othuh. Look how hit-'n'-miss our seein' each othuh can be."

"Yeah," Inzay added, "it's not like you should expect to find someone to share this experience with on that intimate kind of level. That's not what the Exchange is about. It's fragmented for a reason. What we learn here—the realities of our realms—that's our best-kept secret."

"What about Kyle?" Emmelyn countered. "He was seeing a Datist."

"Datists live heah," Bernadette replied. "We come and go, but they're always heah. Sure, it's still like a long-distance thing, but it's more reliable than what ya'd get with anothuh Transfuh or Runnah."

Emmelyn sighed. "So, what do I do?" she asked them.

"Do ya like 'im?" Bernadette asked.

"I never really thought about it before. He's been my friend for… ever," Emmelyn replied.

Bernadette and Inzay shared an unreadable glance, but their reply was quashed by the appearance of Denver over Emmelyn's shoulder. He loomed behind her, wearing his normally unimpressed expression and close-fitting clothes. She pulled the Transitor out of her purse and handed it to him. He unlocked it, stuffed the parchment into his pocket without reading it, put a replacement roll inside, snapped it shut, and gave it back to her without a word.

Emmelyn stared at her friends in bewilderment as her Runner walked away. "What am I going to do about him?" she asked them.

Bernadette looked surprised by the question, as if it were a scandalous one, which was saying something for a scantily clad burlesque dancer. "Do yuh job," she replied simply.

Not interested in ruffling any feathers, Emmelyn nodded and stood up. Her visits seemed shorter since she'd been reassigned to Denver, which provided no help in getting her questions answered. "Thanks for your advice. Until next time," she yelled with a wave and a smile.

"Dance like nobody's watching!" Inzay called after her, like an audible, clichéd, home-store wall hanging.

XLII

Aethelburh

"Does he have his books?" Badrick's voice asked from somewhere in the darkness of his chambers.

The door had only just closed behind Gethin before the question had emanated from the gloom. His father's haste made the prince uneasy. "He has them," he replied.

"Did you happen to pay attention to which texts he took?"

Gethin produced a piece of parchment from the vest of his leathers. "I tore the list from the registry." He thought he saw the glimmer of something—maybe the whites of his father's eyes—dance in the shadows.

"For once, you were thinking," the king said, stepping into the light of a lamp on a nearby table. "Fetch the old-language duplicates to each of those texts and figure out what the next lecture is going to entail before it is given." Gethin inhaled to reply, but Badrick cut him off. "And if you say *one realm-forsaken word* about how this quaint little hobby of yours has suddenly proven useful, I will personally throw you down the cellar stairs to *accelerate* your research."

Gethin turned on his heel, his vindicated grin hidden from view, and slipped from his father's chambers.

As the door shut once more, Badrick could only imagine the smirk on his son's face. "He thinks he has finally proven his value," he scoffed in the darkness. He slumped into a nearby wingback chair, its plush upholstery of no comfort, even as it cocooned around him.

He looked upward, his eyes pleading. "But he should not even *be.* Neither of us should be in this position. If you had survived, Arietta...." His voice trailed off, lost in the darkness.

"Just ask them: I wasn't *supposed* to be king," he croaked through his rapidly constricting throat. He gripped the ends of the armrests, his knuckles whitening, and drew a ragged breath. "And *he* wasn't supposed to exist to plague me as he does." With one swift motion, he stood, grabbed up the oil lamp, and hurled it against the wall. Glass shattered, and the brass base clanked as it rolled along the cold stone.

Badrick stared in the direction of the damage, his eyes blind in the resultant darkness. "DELWYN!" he bellowed. Metallic footsteps clacked hurriedly through the hall, and the door to the king's chambers creaked open. Light filtered in over the threshold in a long, narrow line, broken only by Delwyn's silhouette.

Badrick spared him none of his disgruntlement. "What kept you? Are you still looking for that realmed trinket?" he barked.

"Forgive me, sire," Delwyn begged of the floor as he bent over in a deep bow. "I haven't found it quite yet."

"Do I need to put my entire force of Riders on this task, so you can *get back to work?*" the king growled through gritted teeth.

"Of course not, sire," Delwyn yipped and looked up from his bow. "How may I assist you?"

"Come in and close the door. Do you have any connection with the staff down in Keaton?"

Delwyn hesitated before pulling the door shut behind him. The room was thrown once more into total darkness. "The Riders, sire? Or the servants?"

"Whomever!" Badrick snapped.

Delwyn jumped a little, as evidenced by the slight clack of his shoes against the stone floor. "Oh, yes, I suppose I do, sire. What shall I ask of them?"

"I need someone to keep an eye on Aelfraed," Badrick said, "and any of the Riders who might be colluding with him. Do you know of a *discreet* servant who can do this for us?"

"Yes, sire, of course. I will contact him at once," Delwyn replied.

"Report to me whenever you hear anything," Badrick said with a dismissive wave his servant could not see, "and don't keep me waiting."

Lorelle and Elsie came in to ready Rhoswen for bed. As usual, Elsie turned down the bedclothes, while Lorelle brushed the tangles from Rhoswen's hair.

"Welcome back," Rhoswen said with a smile to Lorelle in the mirror. The waiting-woman seemed to take regular leave of the castle and her duties. Rhoswen only hoped it wasn't for any unfortunate reason. She winced as the brush caught in a tangle.

Lorelle held tightly above the knot and worked the bristles through the snarl until they passed smoothly through her locks. "Thank you," she said in her thick accent Rhoswen had never heard elsewhere. The odd pendant gleamed silver against her brown skin. It practically begged Rhoswen to ask about it.

Lorelle was almost done brushing when Elsie excused herself to retrieve some hot water. Rhoswen turned around to face Lorelle and lowered her voice. "My brother found a pendant like yours in the castle," she said. The waiting-woman looked uncomfortable, but Rhoswen pressed on. "Delwyn has been searching for it, but... I wanted to make certain it wasn't yours before we gave it to him," she improvised.

"He will be most pleased to have it back," Lorelle replied. "I can give it to him if you have it."

"I don't. Why does he have the same family heirloom as you, Lorelle?" Rhoswen ventured. She knew she shouldn't risk offending the only waiting-woman she liked, but this felt greater than a matter of missing jewelry. Delwyn had been tearing the castle apart, searching for this pendant, and Rhoswen wanted to know why.

Lorelle hesitated. "We... we are... cousins," she said finally. "By marriage."

"But why—" Rhoswen heard Elsie tromping back to the room with a heavy cauldron to install over the fire. *Realm it.* "That's nice," she replied instead.

Lorelle flashed her a weak smile and put away the hairbrush.

"We've been at this forever," Rhoswen grumbled, her exhaustion gnawing at her. It had taken much encouragement to convince her waiting-women to stop fussing over her so she could retire for the evening. Now, she almost wished she had gone to bed instead of sneaking down to the cellar.

"To be fair, some of that time was spent sorting trinkets," Thane countered with an eye roll. Rhoswen had found some small muslin bags for teas and herbs in the pantry. Perfect for separating their trinkets by location.

"We've done more than that," she said, glowering at him. "Speaking of trinkets, I asked Lorelle about Delwyn's bracelet. Supposedly, they are cousins, which explains why they would have the same family heirloom."

"Cousins?" Thane's face scrunched up in disbelief.

She shrugged. "By marriage, I guess. But I'm not sure I believe it either."

"Did she tell you what it symbolizes?"

"I didn't have a chance to ask."

"But she knows we have it now?" Thane asked, a look of contemplation stealing over his face.

"Yes," Rhoswen replied with a nod, "so we have to give it back to him."

"Do you think Lorelle will tell him we have it?"

"Absolutely."

"Then let him come get it. We could use this to our advantage."

"Thane," she chided, "that's not exactly fair."

"Rose," he parroted, "so little in this castle *is*. We have to play the game, too."

She stared at him for a moment and sighed. "So be it," she said, too tired to argue. "But *give* it to him when he comes for it, all right?" She approached the wall where the portal would appear and placed her hand against the uneven stone. Her fingers traced the grooves in its mottled surface as if she might find answers there. They had spent most of the day whispering about how to manipulate the maps and trinkets to portal home. But since they had been in the maps room, they had already exhausted all their well-thought-out ideas and even a few shoddily improvised ones.

Stymied, Thane began rifling through the maps on the table. He rolled up Stanburh and laid the map of Keaton on top of the pile. "Maybe we should go back to a closer target before we try to portal to another town."

Rhoswen doubted they would have more luck portaling to Keaton—they still couldn't decide where to come out. Thane reopened the debate by suggesting Darr Beval's chambers, but Rhoswen rejected the idea (as she willed away the blush in her cheeks). She extended her refusal to Darr Thorndon's and Aelfraed's rooms, as well. The men had been made privy to Rhoswen's greatest secret already, and she wanted to keep this one to themselves in case they ever needed to use it as a means of escape. The dining hall and the arena were far too exposed and could easily harbor insomniacs and partyers; the lecture halls were too close to the dormitories.

"Well, you've rejected every idea we've had," Thane pointed out with a sigh.

"They weren't good ideas," Rhoswen insisted, waving them away with her hand. "But there is one place we haven't considered." She began rummaging in the trinkets box again, her fingers combing through the tiny replicas. Finally, she made a small, exclamatory noise and withdrew her hand to display a small crown around the tip of her pinky finger.

"I thought we decided that was for the royal bedchambers," he said, puzzled.

"Who's to say they can't be used more than once? There aren't enough trinkets here for every map to have its own set."

"Then we wasted time sorting them out."

She narrowed her eyes at her brother. "We can deal with that later." She surveyed the map and traced her finger along its surface.

"Well, I still don't see what the crown has to do with Kea—*no*." He shook his head as her hand stopped moving. "Absolutely not."

Rhoswen's finger had landed on Deowynn's stall. "Why not? She likes me. She may have even *chosen* me. No one would be in there, either."

"*She* will be! And you saw how much bowing and scraping we had to do just to walk in through the *door.* I can't *imagine* what we would have to do after bursting through a hole in her *wall.*"

Rhoswen grinned at her brother. "Bow lower?"

The quill in Gethin's hand scratched fiercely against the parchment before him. Per his father's request, he was taking notes on the histories Aelfraed had selected from the cellar library. An untranslated copy was propped up against a modest stack of books to his left, and a key he had created for a few hard-to-remember symbols lay to his right. He glanced at the old-language reference and dipped his quill in the inkwell once more.

Usually, Gethin loved the way the old language read. It was like poetry. Sentences unfolded in strange orders, and words were like vaguely familiar ancestors to those in use today. But as he pored over the minute details that could define the Heir, he found the untranslated text more cumbersome than cathartic.

Obscure tricks, like knowing dragons' names before being told, were tempered with peculiar quirks, like an ability to predict rain well in advance of its coming. He wondered whom the caretaker suspected to possess all these traits—or if he even suspected anyone at all. Gethin would have to watch the proceedings in the arena more closely from now on. His mind flashed on the newest group of recruits, who struggled to tie knots and unkennel beasts—or, in Aeduuin's case, stay on dragonback. *How could any of them be the Heir to the next realm?*

Gethin figured he would tether any day now... although, he was not certain to which beast. There were a couple he enjoyed working with, but training with any of them was preferable to attending class. He had a hard time believing that lectures about history and the Realm Cycle could be as important as working with dragons. And not simply because he was so much more accomplished at flying than most of his fellow students—although he was. *Sitting in a classroom can't tether you to a dragon, and knowing the details of the Realm System won't save you from falling off its back,* he'd decided.

Gethin looked again to the parchment to find an expanding black blot, its edges fraying outward with the haphazard fibers of the paper. He lifted the quill away, cursed, and returned his attention to the open book. *Still, they teach this... or they used to.* Gethin reconsidered his impatience with lecture. *Would the knowledge I am gaining here allow me to tether, even if I didn't learn it in the drakiary?* Trainees learned everything in Keaton—that was the way of things.

He shook the question from his head and squinted at the text. His room had grown quite dark. He widened the lamp on his desk and forced open his drooping eyelids. Still, the words began to swim before him, and he relinquished his quill to rub his eyes with both hands. *A walk would dispel these ridiculous thoughts and wake me up,* he decided. Perhaps he would stroll down to Keaton and back. Surrounding himself with halfwit trainees would agitate him to wakefulness.

Maps of Aethelburh and Keaton lay spread over the table, trinkets dotting the royal castle's floorplans along their path to Deowynn's stall. Rhoswen and Thane stared at Keaton's empty map. Their destination was on the far side of the drakiary—as the dragon flies—and separated from them by numerous stalls.... But its location on an outside wall might preclude the need to represent the places in between.

"I still don't know how we're going to activate maps of both castles with one compass," Thane said for the third time. He had given up figuring out the trinkets for this greater concern. "There doesn't appear to an object to represent the space between places."

"Can we just overlap the edges of the maps?" Rhoswen asked, growing weary of puzzling over something she didn't truly understand. She fished through the trinket box, looking for objects of use other than the tiny bucket they'd placed on the supply room near the royal stalls. "That's what we do with floorplans of the same castle."

Her brother didn't immediately respond. "That's odd," he mumbled as he realigned the map of Keaton. "I didn't think these maps had two compass roses."

"What?" she asked, peering over his shoulder. Indeed, both bottom corners of all three maps held an identical compass rose. "Have they always had that?" she asked.

"Well, they must have, right? How could they change?" he asked.

Rhoswen had no answer to that, but she was certain she did not remember seeing two before. "You don't think someone could have tampered with the maps, do you?"

"Who?" Thane asked, his brows knitting together. "No one else accesses this room—the dust never moves unless we move it."

She shook her head as she peered at the parchment. Her bangs dislodged with the motion, and she forced them back behind her ear. "But how could a map develop a second compass rose?"

Thane unrolled the map with their bed chambers. "This one has it, too."

He continued searching through the maps in the barrel. "They… *all* do. We must have missed it until now."

"Then why would we always place the compass on the left? If we'd had options, we wouldn't have bothered to do it the same way every time. No, something is going on here. These maps are changing."

Thane snorted.

Rhoswen ignored her brother's protest, contemplating what could happen if they were in a portal when a map changed. She pushed the unsettling idea from her mind. "Let's just try to get to the supply room—as a test run."

He nodded, although he looked more apprehensive than he had a moment ago. He slid her compass onto its image on the left corner of the cellar map. The stone wall before them shimmered. It flashed an image of the overflow library and then the study, which was directly above them and overlooked Keaton.

And then, it stopped.

They stared down at the tiny bucket on the supply room in Keaton.

"It didn't work," Thane whispered, cocking an ear toward the open portal. "But that trinket fits its placement…."

"I don't think it's the trinket," Rhoswen replied. She studied the maps. "Maybe it's the extra compass rose. What if these maps knew we would begin venturing outside the palace walls, and they added the extra compass to help us do it?"

Thane's mouth began to open when the clacking of footsteps could be heard nearing the open door of the study. He scrambled to lift the compass off the map, and the wall returned to solid stone.

"I guess those metal-soled shoes *do* provide some privacy," Rhoswen mused.

Thane stared at her. "Do you hear yourself?"

"It was just a joke—"

"Not that," he said. "You think the maps just added a compass rose to themselves?"

Her eyebrows knitted, and she stamped her foot. "We are walking through walls into other parts of the castle from a hidden room behind the shelves of a layered library, and a changing map is the part that seems unbelievable to you?!"

He crossed his arms in front of him and stamped a foot. "Yes."

She shoved him lightly and refocused her attention on the maps. "This could be the dragon's device, Thane. Father always said those beasts have their own kind of magic. Maybe he meant it more literally than we imagined—" She inhaled suddenly. "Thane, you genius," she breathed, moving things around on the table.

"Come again?"

"The second compass. The maps need to overlap on the compass roses.

That's why there's one in both corners now—to connect them to one another!" She slid the maps together until their compass roses overlapped. Then, she grabbed her metal compass and held it over the stack. "May the Realm Ride on," she breathed and set it down.

Images flashed on the wall as the portal transitioned through the rooms again, but this time, the study faded from view as quickly as it appeared, and the stable supply room became visible, bales of hay and coiled ropes piled all over its floor.

"We did it!" Rhoswen squealed, hugging her brother. Thane grabbed her shoulders and put a finger to his lips in warning.

Rhoswen took a deep breath and set the tiny crown onto the queen dragon's stall. The image on the wall changed once again: a floor strewn with fresh hay, the dark-gray stone of the walls, and the tip of a thumping golden-white tail.

Rhoswen didn't even glance at her brother. She bowed low in a show of respect for the beast on the other side and crept through the portal. With every step, more and more of the queen dragon came into view—she was curled up to one side of the spacious stall, her eyes closed and head resting on her front feet. She was beautiful. Rhoswen's breath hitched in her throat.

Deowynn's left eye opened slowly to meet her gaze. Rhoswen froze. She knew she should avert her eyes, but she could not look away. She could sense Thane edging closer through the portal behind her, but even that could not dislodge her focus from the white dragon.

It is terribly late for visitors, Deowynn nexed.

It startled her to hear the queen dragon's voice in her head, but Rhoswen thought she could discern a hint of amusement behind her regal tone. *Please forgive my intrusion, especially at this late hour, your highness. I do not mean to disturb you.*

Of course you do, the queen dragon replied simply. *Or you would not be here.*

Good point, Rhoswen thought to herself. *I do not prefer it then, majesty,* she nexed.

Deowynn chuckled in Rhoswen's mind and lifted her head. *Stand freely—both of you. What do you need?*

Rhoswen straightened from her bow and gestured for Thane to come forward. *Guidance,* she replied. *I know not whom to trust, my queen.*

But you trust me?

Rhoswen chose her words with caution. *You have the least reason in this realm to be untrustworthy, your highness. And your preference at our last audience did not go unnoticed,* she added, remembering Deowynn's snarl at her cousin's intrusion.

The queen dragon gave a single, slow nod. *And your reason for needing an audience tonight?*

Rhoswen gestured to the hole in the stone wall. *We are trying to master a portal system. As we are not yet tethered, we have no other means of efficient travel.*

Deowynn nodded. *A wise choice, Rhoswen of Stanburh. Portals are indeed efficient – even more so than flying.*

The queen dragon's use of her name was disarming. *Indeed, highness,* Rhoswen continued. *They are also far more mysterious, and we do not understand them.*

You have come from the castle?

We have. There is a hidden maps room in the cellar. My compass opens the portals connected to each map. But we have not yet discovered how to close the portal behind us and reopen it remotely. We had hoped you might have some idea.

Again, Deowynn nodded. *Your compass is the first and final key,* she said.

Rhoswen's brow furrowed. *I fear I do not understand, highness.*

You will, she replied. *Your compass activates the maps. There are keys for each portal that will assist you in controlling them. Find those keys, and the rest will fall into place.*

Can you tell me where to look, majesty?

The maps have already changed for you. The keys will also present themselves if only you pay attention. Deowynn placed her head back on her forefeet but held her guest's gaze.

Rhoswen reminded herself to gloat to Thane about the changing maps. She knew her audience was waning, but she was desperate for answers. *Is that something we should be concerned about when we're using the portal – the maps changing?*

The queen dragon shook her head without lifting it from where it lay on her forefeet. Her eyes drooped.

Rhoswen exhaled in relief and bowed deeply. *Thank you, your majesty. Please pardon the intrusion.* She took several steps back toward the portal, her hand flapping behind her for Thane to do the same.

Naturally. Deowynn closed her eyes. *Until the next Ride, Rhoswen.*

Rhoswen's steps faltered: only Riders said that phrase to each other. Deowynn technically should not have used it to bid an untethered trainee farewell… *unless that trainee was only waiting on her dragon to be born….*

The queen dragon chuckled but did not open her eyes.

Rhoswen wasn't ready for any more confirmation than that. She turned toward the opening of the portal, and a thin, shimmering segment of stone in the wall of the shallow tunnel caught her eye. Her fingers brushed its surface, and it hummed at her touch, its vibration quickening. She eased her fingertips around the edge of the stone and pulled it free from the portal wall. The shimmering dimmed out as the two-finger-width stone lay across the length of her palm. She stepped over the threshold into the maps room. Thane slid the compass from its place on the map, and the portal snapped shut. They exchanged glances.

"What did she say?" Thane asked.

"She bid me until the next Ride," Rhoswen murmured, her eyes locked on the stone in her hand.

"Whoa," Thane breathed.

It was too much to take in. She told him about the maps instead, forgetting to gloat as she had planned. "It's a key," she explained. "It has markings all over it."

"Can you make them out?"

She could not. The curving lines and broad strokes created flowing characters she had never seen before. The text felt ancient.

"So, Deowynn said we should be able to use this to control the portals?" he asked.

She nodded. "Although, she didn't say *how*.... Lay out the map to our rooms. Let's try it within the castle."

Thane removed the Keaton map and added the floorplan with their rooms to the spread. The portal to Rhoswen's room opened easily, and they tested every combination they could think of: swapping the compass for the key, placing both the key and the compass on the map, holding the key on their way through—but nothing gave them control of the portal on the other end.

"What haven't we tried?" Rhoswen asked, frowning at the sliver of stone.

Thane shook his head. "I wish we understood what the markings mean. Like directions for use or something." Thane's eyes brightened with inspiration. "Or *location*."

"I'm sorry?"

Thane stepped toward the portal. "What if this key is only for Keaton? You told me Deowynn said *keys*, plural. What if there is a key for each of the places we need to travel? One for Keaton, one for Aethelburh, one for Stanburh, one for... *wherever!*" He slipped past her and began inspecting the portal walls. "You found this in the wall just inside the portal—"

"On the other end," Rhoswen reminded him.

Thane took a step toward her chambers. He scanned the walls, his fingers brushing over the stone. "Ha!" He extracted another sliver identical in shape and size to the one in Rhoswen's hand.

"Looks like you might have been right about that one," she admitted, wishing she had remembered to tell Thane about the changing maps.

He held his stone key beside hers. "The markings are different." He looked at his sister. "How will we find out what they say without arousing suspicion about the portals?"

"Should we ask Aelfraed...? Do you think he already knows about the portal system? Deowynn certainly did." She wondered if the caretaker might know of a book that could translate it for them, but she was not sure about divulging anything to him yet.

Thane shrugged and walked over to a nearby shelf. He snagged up a small piece of blank parchment, dipped a quill from the table into the inkwell, and transcribed the symbols from the keys onto the parchment twice—once at the top and again at the bottom. At the top, beneath each transcription, he wrote the name of the place where the sliver was found. Then, he ripped the paper in half. He handed the bottom half to Rhoswen and secreted the labeled top half in the trinket box. "Now we know where each key represents if we get them mixed up. Meanwhile, you take that slip to Aelfraed and ask him where we can find translations of unfamiliar symbols. If you have to show him an example, you'll have the parchment with you—not the keys." He popped them into the trinket box, too.

Rhoswen smiled at him as she folded the parchment slip and shoved it into one of her vest pockets. She couldn't help but feel impressed. "When?"

"Why wait?" He grinned.

"This late at night?"

"Who sleeps here?"

XLIII

Keaton

Beval did not want to consider the direction their conversation was taking. "Are you saying there are traitors among us?"

"It isn't that surprising, Beval," Thorndon said.

Since Aelfraed's entrance to Beval's apartments, the caretaker had suggested that the king could be engendering a counter-initiative to keep Deowynn from Moving, that others might be interested in supporting such a scheme, and that the actual execution of it was… *plausible.*

Not the most cheerful of visits.

Beval wouldn't put it past the king, but the idea that other Riders might consider joining such an uprising was unconscionable. "I understand that Badrick has always had sympathizers, but we are talking about Riders working against *the Heir*—against the *Realm Cycle*—to protect the man who has doomed our realm to *Movement!* Why in the name of D'Erenelle would anyone turn his back on our future to save a broken past? That's not what we're meant to do!"

"That is precisely what we need to discover," Aelfraed replied. "Sympathizers can become staunch proponents if adequately tempted."

"What could he possibly offer?" Beval asked. "Death by Narxon is no enticement!"

Thorndon held up a palm. "Easy, Beval."

Aelfraed shrugged, unruffled by the outburst. "Some Riders with status and land may have concerns about losing both in the new realm…. Others of a more sentimental nature may simply be disinclined to lose their untethered family members."

Beval looked down at his lap, embarrassed that Aelfraed, himself untethered and ineligible to Move, had had to remind him of that. Beval didn't have many untethered acquaintances left, and he often tried to forget the more heart-wrenching aspects of a Move. Moreover, he wouldn't have to think about such infuriating things if the king didn't cavalierly disregard his subjects' lives through his own lopsided governance.

Aelfraed pressed on. "He is up to something. While I am fairly certain he does not know the identity of the Heir at present, he must know he cannot sequester her from the protection of the dragons and their Riders."

"Then how could he achieve this?" Thorndon asked.

"I am sad to report that it may not be an inordinate task." Without the queen dragon's Realm Portal object, Aelfraed explained, a Move would be impossible, regardless of a Judgment against D'Erenelle. Worse yet, as far as he knew, Deowynn could already be bereft of it. "I've never seen it," he admitted. "The Realm Portal object changes shape with every realm, and its identity is a closely guarded secret of the kings and queens. But how Badrick or his henchmen could have stolen it from Deowynn is more mysterious than the form of the object itself. I can't imagine the queen dragon letting it go without a fight, and I remember no such altercation."

Thorndon cast a dubious glance at his Riding partner but said nothing.

"So, how do we find out what the Realm Portal object looks like?" Beval asked.

Aelfraed stood and gathered his stack of books. "Therein lies our dilemma, gentlemen." Without another word, the caretaker moved to the door, opened it easily despite his laden arms, and closed it behind him as if he had never broken their revelry in the first place.

Thorndon cast an exhausted glance at Beval. "Realm it," he cursed.

"Rhoswen!" Aelfraed exclaimed, juggling his armload.

In the process of looking over her shoulder to check her surroundings, Rhoswen had very nearly run into the caretaker as he was exiting Darr Beval's apartments. She helped him steady his books. "I'm sorry, Aelfraed, I—"

"How long have you been out here?" he asked.

"I was only just passing by—to come see you, actually," Rhoswen said, catching her breath. "May I help you with those?"

Aelfraed conceded a small portion of his stack to Rhoswen, who followed him into his apartments at the other end of Keaton. "It's rather late for visiting," he told her, as he ushered her inside.

I'm hearing that a lot lately, Rhoswen mused, not bothering to mention that the caretaker had just been visiting Darr Beval. Aelfraed's chambers were the mirror image of Darr Beval's in layout, but his seemed to have become the overflow closet for the stables' supply rooms.

"I apologize for the lateness of the hour, but I was having trouble sleeping, and I thought I'd see if you could put an issue to rest for me. You see,

I'm trying to decipher some unfamiliar characters I found while perusing the cellar library. Do you know any books that might help with translations of rare scripts?"

"Most of the cellar library has accompanying manuscripts in recent translations," Aelfraed replied.

"This doesn't have such a companion."

Aelfraed peered at Rhoswen. "You are unable to sleep because you cannot decipher some old script you stumbled upon in the overflow library?"

Rhoswen sighed and handed the caretaker the bit of parchment her brother had given her. Thane was back in the maps room, occasionally opening the portal into the supply room near Aelfraed's chambers to check for her return. She hoped he wouldn't have to abandon his post and leave her to walk back to the castle in the dark. "I didn't really want to trouble you with it, if you could just point me to a resource that could help me."

"Where did you get this?" Aelfraed interrupted, staring at the parchment.

"I copied it," Rhoswen replied cagily. She wondered if he would let her get away with such an unsatisfactory answer.

He studied her again and, seeming to think better of calling her bluff, took the parchment to his desk. He dipped a quill in ink and scrawled something across the page before handing it back to her. "These are the translations. I doubt you will find a book in any library that will help with this. The script is based on poetic descriptions rather than specific words, and it is written in another language altogether from that used in books." He smiled at her, his narrowed eyes unmasking his skepticism. "I hope that provides you with the tonic you need for sweet dreams."

Rhoswen read the new additions to the page, thanked Aelfraed sincerely, and scurried back to the supply closet.

Gethin retreated into the shadows as his cousin emerged from Aelfraed's apartments and slipped into the night. He took a step to follow her but slid back into hiding as Aelfraed, too, emerged from his apartments and headed in the same direction. As he peeked back out to watch them, Gethin realized Rhoswen had completely disappeared. Aelfraed, on the other hand, circled the arena to Darr Beval's room, knocked on the Rider's door, and let himself in.

The prince stayed in the shadows, scanning for any further movement, but the stables remained quiet. He walked to the edge of Aelfraed's tower and gazed toward the castle. He expected to see his cousin running up the side of the hill, but the sliver of moon that hung in the sky illuminated the land poorly, and he could not make her out. Aelfraed was not leaving Darr

Beval's apartments either. Gethin thought back to the conversation his father and Aelfraed had had earlier that day and wondered whether his cousin could be playing a role in the treasonous teachings in Keaton. Seeing her fraternizing with the old man at such a late hour was veritable proof of her collaboration, as far as the prince was concerned.

Keeping to the shadows, Gethin moved back toward the castle to continue his work on the translations. But he had one stop to make first. *We'll see what you're up to, Cousin.*

XLIV

Aethelburh

"I think she can lead us to the Heir," Gethin said, his chest puffing with confidence.

"If slinking around Keaton in the dead of night constitutes proof of a connection to the Heir, we will be forced to begin a formal investigation of all our staff, Riders, and trainees, beginning with my insomniac son." Badrick's eyes moved skyward. "Does no one sleep in this realm?"

Gethin fought the urge to glare at his father. "She is colluding with Aelfraed, whom we already know to be working with the Riders against you. They all know something, or their lectures would not have changed. She is part of this. And I bet Thane is, too."

"Aren't we the *amateur* sleuth?" Badrick replied. "If you'll do your best to think back to just a few days ago, you might remember that I warned you about your cousins. They hail from my brother, and his kind *always* means trouble. But you have no proof of *anything*. Your mother always told me, 'Conjecture is no substitute for certainty,.' I will not base our actions on guesses. How are your translations coming? Do you have an idea of Aelfraed's next lesson plan?"

The prince swallowed an acerbic commentary on his father's ignorance of his mother's lessons, but it went down like bile. He cleared his throat to answer. "I have made some progress, but there is much to—"

"I want information, not excuses."

Gethin scowled. "I cannot read Aelfraed's mind, Father. But the trainees I'd overheard said nothing about how the Heir should align with the queen dragon's disposition. If we know Deowynn's Heir will be of a more... benevolent persuasion, we can devise a list of candidates from the trainees here at Keaton."

Badrick glared at his son. "And who would be the judge of those individuals?"

Gethin ground his teeth together. "*In spite of* all you have taught me, I am a decent judge of character."

"In spite of *all* I have taught you, you have only progressed to a *middling* judge of character," Badrick corrected. "Fine. Continue your work with the texts and put together a list of potential Heirs for my perusal. As you learn about the Heir's qualities, slim down the list. Bring me updated copies as you go. *Daily*."

Gethin nodded stiffly and turned to leave the king's apartments.

"And Gethin?" Badrick crooned with mock sweetness. The prince turned back to face his father. "You will leave *only* when I am through with you."

Enough, Gethin thought. "You are through," he snapped and turned on his heel to exit his father's chamber before the king could reply.

Badrick bit back on a growl, lest his son should hear how effectively he had frustrated him. *That boy will be the death of me….*

"No," he corrected himself aloud. "No, the *Heir* will be the death of me. You—*you* did this to me, Orla." He began pacing the room. "Perhaps if this were still a matter of lineage, this realm could be saved. Of course, I would have to be out of the way…. And wouldn't my brother just *love* to see that! I won't give him the satisfaction. I'd let him portal to another realm before I'd step aside for someone who *shouldn't exist*," he added gruffly, addressing the ceiling. "Another curse you've saddled me with!"

A knock at the door stopped Badrick cold.

"Majesty?" It was Delwyn. "The messenger you requested is here."

Exhaling slowly, Badrick moved to the door and yanked it open. "Get in," he barked at the lanky young man, who cowered beside the waitman. Badrick left the messenger little room to sidle past him and slammed the door in Delwyn's face. The young man jumped and landed in a low bow.

"Over there." Badrick motioned to a desk with a dim oil lamp on it.

The messenger reached for the knob on the lamp and turned up the flame as he began setting up his materials. Realizing he had not asked permission to increase the light, he turned to the king, terrified eyes pleading forgiveness.

As enjoyable as the young man's horror would normally be to Badrick, he was too annoyed by the interruption to his previous line of thought to relish it. "Write down these names. I want these men located but not engaged. Do you understand?"

The messenger nodded, scrambling to uncork his ink and nearly spilling it over his parchment. He held the inkwell still for a moment and took a deep breath before letting it go. *This may take the rest of my lifetime,* Badrick thought, massaging the bridge of his nose.

XLV

Keaton

Aelfraed blew into Beval's apartments and shut the door behind him. "There has been a turn of events," he announced. The Riders had just decided to surrender themselves to their exhaustion and call it a night. Instead, Aelfraed's abrupt reentrance lowered them back into their seats. They stared at the old man in bewilderment.

"Rhoswen was just here. She had me translate something of singular importance," Aelfraed explained with mounting excitement. "It has begun."

Beval's brow furrowed. "Slow down, Aelfraed. You're not making sense." He nudged the leg of a nearby chair with his foot, inviting the man to sit. "What did she have you translate?"

Aelfraed took a deep breath. "There is a language known only to dragons and their caretakers. Even Riders cannot read its written form. It is the visible translation of nexing."

"I can write down anything Merry tells me," Thorndon said.

"But not in 'Agonex, you can't," Aelfraed replied.

"'Agonex?" Beval repeated.

"It's short for Daragonosinagonex. It is the direct translation of nexing conversations into written word."

"But Thorndon is right. We can just write out conversations in today's script," Beval said.

Aelfraed shook his head. "Dragons can't read that."

Silence ensued as the idea that dragons could read settled in around them like a dense fog. "Rhoswen just brought you something written in… 'Agonex?" Thorndon finally asked, avoiding the full name for the script.

"She did," Aelfraed replied. "And we must hope she *only* came to me because I'm the sole D'Erenellean on these grounds who could read it, but I'm not the sole D'Erenellean who could recognize it."

Beval did not like the sound of that. "What did she need translated?"

"I'm not exactly sure.... I don't know what it was from. But if she found it, she has been busier at the castle than we could have ever imagined. 'Agonex is not used for menial messages. Dragons only bother reading or inscribing things that are of dire importance. They have incredible memories—they don't need to write things down. 'Agonex is used to educate *you,* their Riders."

"But Riders can't read it," Thorndon protested.

"It ensures that Riders who have a good relationship with their caretakers can." Aelfraed gave a casual wave of his hand. "Dragons have a special fondness for their caretakers and tend to have a low opinion of Riders who do not share it. 'Agonex helps to hide information, not divulge it, because if you are not accompanied by a dragon or caretaker, you will not be able to decipher it."

"So, what did it say?" Thorndon asked.

"There were two lines of text scribbled on the parchment she handed me. The first read, 'harbinger of duplicitous creation'; the second, 'extension toward otherness.'" Aelfraed continued before the obvious questions could arise. "Without knowing whence these phrases hailed, I couldn't possibly attempt to decipher their meaning. 'Agonex is poetic, and it deliberately obscures meanings to hide truths from the uninitiated. Whatever Rhoswen is up to, it's important, or she would not have been given access to such information."

"What if she just stumbled upon it?" Beval asked.

The caretaker smiled. "You don't just stumble upon 'Agonex. You are granted access to it. It finds *you.*"

XLVI

Aethelburh

Thane slipped the compass off the map to close the wall behind his sister. "Did he tell you where to look?"

Rhoswen shook her head and handed Thane the slip of parchment. "He made it clear that no book would translate this text. But *he* could. What are we supposed to do if we need more of these translated?"

"Did he give you any trouble about it?" Thane asked.

"Not exactly, but how much do we want to share with him?"

Thane was busy reading what Aelfraed had written under each set of symbols. "'Harbinger of duplicitous creation?' 'Extension toward otherness?' Well, we don't appear to be sharing *much* with him—what do these even mean?"

Rhoswen wondered that herself. She picked up the Aethelburh key. "Harbinger of duplicitous creation.... Does Aethelburh create anything?"

"Who knows if these transcriptions are even meant to reference their locations? I'm not sure anymore," Thane grumbled.

Rhoswen yawned. "Nor am I. But I *am* sure that we have lecture in the morning, and I'm exhausted."

It was late when Lorelle finally dragged herself toward her quarters. She had been hard at work, completing all those unsavory tasks Elsie had promised her as penance for her last absence. She probably should have paced herself better, but at least she was almost caught up. Now, she just needed to catch up on her sleep—before she had to leave again.

"Lorelle," someone hissed to her in a loud whisper. Or, at least, it seemed loud after bouncing off the stone walls.

Uncertain where to turn, she waited for the whisperer to reveal himself.

"Lorelle," the voice whispered again. Out of the dark came a familiar face stricken with worry: Delwyn. "You're back," he added. "I'm sorry if I frightened you. How did it go?"

"Fine. You're the one who looks frightened," Lorelle whispered back.

"You didn't report my lost key, did you?" he asked.

She sighed. "I told you I wouldn't. Delwyn—"

"I know. Thank you, thank you! I know you should have reported it…."

"Those rules are far too strict," Lorelle replied through a yawn.

"Still—what am I going to do? Things are progressing quickly around here. I have to Run soon! In all the time you were gone, I've been searching the castle high and low, drawing far too much attention to myself—"

The admission woke Lorelle up considerably. "What?!" she asked in full voice.

Delwyn ducked as if she had thrown something at him. "I used the heirloom story—"

"This is not something you can be careless about, Delwyn!" Lorelle hissed. *I should not have to tell him this,* she thought. *He's been Running longer than I have.*

"I know…!"

"What changed?"

Delwyn detailed the forbidden lecture in Keaton, Badrick's assignment for Gethin to discover the Heir's identity, and the king's own plans for thwarting the Movement. He might not have loved the espionage associated with his job, but Delwyn was undeniably good at eavesdropping. "And he wants me to find someone to spy on Aelfraed for him," he added.

Lorelle knew she should be scandalized by this admission, and she was—to a point. But she expected unscrupulous behavior from King Badrick, and even though she liked Aelfraed, he was technically as expendable as every other non-Rider in this realm.

More to the point, however, Delwyn's report signaled that the timeline in this realm was, indeed, accelerating. This would surely necessitate she take off more time. She wondered how she was going to ask for it and keep her job, even if they were understaffed. "Do you know of anyone who would spy for you?"

"There's a Rider who might be of use," Delwyn replied cagily before resuming his usual tirade about the stresses of the job. He was getting all worked up again when Lorelle held up her hand to stop him.

"I know where your Transitor key is," she whispered.

Delwyn's eyes bulged. "You do?" He clamped a hand over his mouth in response to his own volume.

She nodded. "Thane has it." Delwyn began grumbling about how he had asked Thane and Rhoswen about it, but she stopped him again. "Rhoswen saw that I had the same necklace and wanted to make sure you hadn't stolen it from me before they gave it back to you. They're learning not to trust anyone in this castle. Get it from him in the morning." A yawn stretched her jaw and made her shiver. "Oh, and we're cousins now, by the way."

XLVII

Detroit

The group had plans a week later to head down to Dissonance once again. Josie was convinced that Jeremy had put this reprisal together as a way of getting closer to Emmelyn.

"So?" Josie asked. "You said yourself you didn't mind the place."

Emmelyn was putting the finishing touches on her mascara and replied between brush strokes. "That doesn't mean... I want to... live there... every... weekend." She surveyed her work in the mirror and twisted the tube closed.

Josie had the contents of her purse spread out over the bed as she re-packed the essentials into a sequined clutch. "What are you going to do about Jere?"

It was a topic they hadn't discussed much since the last time they saw him, thanks solely to Emmelyn's evasive tactics. She was still at a loss for how to reconcile her two lives—even with her own best friend, let alone a *boyfriend*, or whatever Jeremy would be to her. Bernadette and Inzay had made it seem so simple. *Do ya like 'im?* she could hear Bernadette yelling over the Tallulahdurian music, as if that were all that mattered. "I'll just see how it goes, I guess."

"Good," Josie said. "That's what I was hoping you'd say. Allow yourself to be happy, Em. You've been really off lately—even before the whole Jere thing. Just let go a bit. You can't control the world."

Tell that to the Exchange, Emmelyn mused. It was the greatest of all tradeoffs: live a normal life, possibly with a normal boyfriend, doing normal college things... or help save countless lives in a web of interconnected realms.

In reality, the two were not mutually exclusive. Emmelyn simply had to learn to live with the secrecy and separation that her dual life required. *Had to.* Because something was not right about the Exchange system, and there was too much at stake for her to be blithe about her part. In a non-realm supposedly built on data acquisition, everyone's understanding of how the Exchange worked seemed based on rumor and hearsay. And her sudden switch from Lorelle to Denver reeked of mischief. If Emile were up to something, she wanted—no, *needed*—to know what it was.

She just had to figure out how to keep that need from interfering with her life in her own realm.

Jeremy was antsier than he'd been the last time they were at the club. He escorted Emmelyn straight to the bar. Tonight, she just wanted a beer.

"No fancy gin?" he asked in her ear, as if gin had been her drink all her life and this departure were tantamount to renouncing her religion.

"Not tonight," she replied with a shrug.

"Draft or bottle?" a redheaded bartender asked in passing.

Jeremy yelled "draft," as Emmelyn asked for a bottle. He stared at her as if she were an alien. She laughed. "Easier for dancing," she told him.

He perked up at her answer, and she felt like slapping her own forehead. *Let go,* she reminded herself. *What happens, happens.*

Drinks in hand—which Jeremy paid for once again—they made their way over to the rest of the group, who had taken up residence in the Crew's circle. Her heartbeat quickened. *So much for keeping my realms separate.*

"Isn't this where we sat last time?" Leo asked as he came up behind Jeremy and Emmelyn.

"No," Emmelyn yelled back automatically. She caught herself and added, "I think we were in the next circle over.... Different coffee table."

Leo nodded and took Claire's hand to escort her into the circle ahead of him. They had been together since high school, and everyone was fairly certain they were marriage material.... Some just doubted they were marriage material *for each other.* Emmelyn glanced over at Nate, who was watching Claire with far too much interest. She sighed and took a swig of her beer. *Was everything this complicated in other realms?*

She almost choked. *Do not speak of realms,* she reminded herself.

"So, you have your portable beer," Jeremy yelled to Emmelyn. "Want to take it onto the dance floor?"

Josie lifted the bottle from Emmelyn's grasp. "No need," she hollered. "Dancing takes two hands. Go have fun!"

Jeremy grinned. He set down his own beer on the ring-splotched coffee table and took Emmelyn's hand. Tonight, with no quirky theme, the club had returned to a more typical mode of techno mixes of current radio hits. It wouldn't normally be her choice of music, but it gave Jeremy the opportunity to pull her in close as they bounced back and forth to the beat. He hollered something to her that she couldn't hear or lipread. She popped out an earplug and tried not to wince.

"Sorry?" she asked in his ear.

"You dance well," he repeated. Emmelyn shot him a confused glance as she replaced the earplug, and he laughed. "You let me lead," he explained. The tip of his nose brushed her ear. "Strong women tend to struggle with that."

Emmelyn had never been called a strong woman before. She stared at Jeremy. His expression reminded her of Vonn's when she had declined to read the message that Lorelle had forgotten to lock away in her Transitor. *Don't think of Vonn now,* she chided. *Or Lorelle.*

She shrugged, and he twirled her around to bring her in close to him again. "You're easy to follow," she replied honestly.

"I think I'd follow you anywhere," he replied in her ear.

There are some places you can't go, Emmelyn thought. Then, she reconsidered his words and took a step back to flash him a you-did-not-just-say-that look.

"Too corny?" he yelled, an embarrassed grin spreading across his face.

"Way too corny!" she said through a laugh.

They enjoyed several songs together before the music became undanceable, and they were forced to return to the group. Leo and Claire had claimed the oversize chair in their circle, lips locked in their typical fashion. Jeremy gestured toward an armchair Emmelyn had occupied on numerous occasions within the Exchange, and he perched on the padded arm beside her. She closed her eyes and took a swig of beer.

"You okay?" Jeremy leaned down to ask, his breath in her hair and his nose brushing her ear.

She nodded, savoring the coolness of the shandy as it slid down her throat. The club was so packed that the whole place was growing humid and sticky. Although her white sateen blouse was sleeveless and tied just above her navel, the fabric clung mercilessly to her. She tugged at the front of it, pulling it away from her sweaty skin to try to cool down. Her eyes closed as her mind wandered back to Jeremy's "strong woman" comment and Vonn's expression.... She forced the memories to a halt and considered undoing one more button on her blouse. As she set down the bottle, her hand brushed the coffee table, and she opened her eyes—

—to find Vonn, Randy, and Inzay staring back at her.

They sat, blinking, their jaws slack like they had just had their wisdom teeth out and couldn't feel their faces.

"I'm pretty sure you weren't here a moment ago," Vonn yelled to her.

"And you didn't come through the door like usual," Inzay added.

"How am I here?" Emmelyn asked, glancing around. The club was just as full, but her friends from her home realm were nowhere to be seen. She turned to look at the bar: Trevor—not the redhead—was doling out drinks.

"Do y'all take some small comfort in the fact that she doesn't know how she got here either?" Randy asked the Crew.

"What just happened?" Vonn asked her.

Emmelyn shook her head, her eyes wide with panic. "I don't know."

A Minister neared their circle, her gaze fixated on Emmelyn. Inzay smiled at the woman, and she eventually passed them after being distracted by a pair of wild dancers that wandered into her path. Emmelyn's breathing grew shallow and ragged.

Vonn stood up from his chair and sat on the arm of hers—exactly where Jeremy had been before she'd closed her eyes. "Easy," he yelled into her ear. He reached for her wrists to check them for stamps and ran his thumbs lightly over her unblemished skin. "Don't make a scene. Tell us exactly what you were just doing, so we can figure out how you got here."

Emmelyn explained that she had been drinking a beer in this chair in the nightclub in her own realm… when she wound up *here*.

"That doesn't make sense," Inzay yelled.

Vonn agreed. "You had to have done *something*."

"Were you thinking of the Exchange while you were there?" Inzay asked.

Emmelyn nodded. "How could I not? It's practically the same place."

Vonn looked around at the Crew. "Have you ever seen anything like this?"

"I ain't even *heard* uh anythin' like this," Randy drawled.

"Do you think that's it?" Emmelyn asked Vonn. "Do you think I… *thought* myself here?"

"I don't know," Vonn replied.

"Try thinking yourself back," Inzay suggested simply.

"But how?" Emmelyn asked. "I don't even know how I thought myself here in the first place!"

Everyone shrugged.

Vonn leaned down toward her ear again. "What were you thinking of before? Try… reversing it," he suggested. She could feel his breath against her hair as he spoke. She shivered and closed her eyes, unwilling to tell him that *he* had been on her mind before she wound up in the Exchange. This couldn't be more confusing. She swigged her beer—a larger gulp this time.

The tip of Vonn's nose brushed her ear—as Jeremy's had moments ago—and she opened her eyes—

—to find herself surrounded by her friends from her own realm again. She could still feel Vonn's breath against her hair, and she turned to see Jeremy was still bent over near her ear. Time had stopped as it did when she was portaled into the Exchange. She clenched her jaw to keep it from falling open and lifted her hand away from where it rested, curled around her beer, against the coffee table.

"You wanna head back out there?" Jeremy asked, oblivious.

She forced thoughts of the Exchange from her mind, lest she should so much as blink and wind up back there. When she didn't immediately answer, Jeremy's brow furrowed. "You sure you're okay?" he hollered.

"Yeah, sorry," she yelled back. "Headache."

"Oh." His face was full of concern. "Do you want to leave?"

"No," she replied, standing. "Let's go dance it away."

Jeremy really did have a nice smile.

XLVIII

Aethelburh

Almost a week later, Rhoswen overslept, and her waiting-women scrambled to dress her for training. She found her brother alone in the breakfast room, his plate nearly empty.

"I was just about to come up and make certain you hadn't portaled to another realm without the rest of us," he joked.

Rhoswen shushed him and threw some food on a plate. She would have to eat fast, but she was unusually famished, and her joints ached again as if she had slept wrong. "It's going to rain," she said. "I thought I'd tell you this time."

"When?" Thane asked with a knowing smile.

She bit into a piece of toast piled high with eggs and a creamy greenish sauce she had come to adore since living at the castle. She couldn't have described the taste if she tried—especially today—but she hoped she could one day learn how to make it. *Perhaps I could ask the kitchen staff about it sometime.* "Mmm, in about two days, I think. Maybe three."

"Three then," he said. "You always oversleep *three* days before rain, not two."

Rhoswen blinked at her brother. "I do?" She shook her head. "I didn't last time."

"I woke you, remember? Otherwise, you would have," Thane replied. "That's why I didn't know it was going to rain when it did—you couldn't oversleep. How do *you* know it's going to rain?"

"My joints hurt," Rhoswen said.

"Everyone's joints hurt before rain," Thane countered. "Maybe not three whole days before, but still. No, how do you really know?"

Rhoswen thought about it as she chewed a weird, tangy fruit. It was sort of star shaped and bright red, with deep-purple seeds. She was pretty sure she liked it, but she would have to taste it again—preferably after the rain passed. "I suppose it's the taste."

"What?"

"It makes everything taste a little *off*. I wake up—apparently *late*—with that ache in my bones, and whatever I eat tastes, I don't know, like the way the land smells after a rain."

"Wet?"

She chuckled, rolling her eyes at her brother's oversimplification. "Yes, wet."

Thane smiled and took a bite of something that resembled ham but tasted to her a bit sweeter and oakier. She had pushed her own serving of it aside. "Sounds disgusting," he said with his mouth full. Rhoswen smacked his shoulder playfully.

A waitman appeared at the entrance to the room. He bowed and extended a tray with a letter on it to Thane. Thane picked up the folded parchment and thanked the man, who immediately retreated.

"It's from Mother and Father," Thane said, breaking the dark-green wax impressed with a tiny likeness of Castle Stanburh.

"What do they say?" she asked as he read it to himself.

His face screwed up in confusion. "Apparently, a new Rider was posted in Dallin… but they didn't request him. They want us to ask someone trustworthy in Keaton about it," he said, handing her the letter.

"Trustworthy?" she asked, alarmed by her parents' choice of words. "What do they think is going on?"

He shook his head. "I have no idea, but they emphasized—again—that we should be careful."

Rhoswen stopped reading to look up at him over the top of the parchment. "They're not telling us something," she intuited.

"Right," Thane agreed simply and took another sip of vine water.

XLIX

Keaton

Once again, students of all ages were being directed into a lecture hall. Rhoswen's stomach knotted at the memory of the last lecture given in this room. Students around them chatted about why they were sitting in class on a training day.

Darr Beval stepped forward and motioned for everyone to settle down. "Thank you," he said, pacing back and forth across the front of the room. "To avoid large gaps between lessons, we've decided to reorganize your schedules to include daily morning lectures. Hands-on training will take place afterward from now on." Groans issued from around the room. "I know you wish to train, but these lectures are equally important. Hopefully, this streak of sun will continue a while longer."

"It won't," Rhoswen muttered.

Darr Beval's pacing had brought him in front of her at that very moment. "Pardon?"

Rhoswen's eyes grew large; she hadn't realized she had spoken loudly enough to be heard. She apologized for interrupting.

"That's all right. I just didn't hear you," the Rider said. "What did you say?"

She hadn't wanted to be heard. In fact, now, more than ever, she wanted to be ignored. Her cheeks warmed, and she looked down at her lap, hoping he would take her cue to drop his questions.

He didn't. "Go ahead."

"Just—it's going to rain soon," she mumbled.

"What's going on?" Darr Thorndon asked, drawing nearer to the conversation.

Rhoswen shrugged. She wished she'd kept her mouth shut. "I just tend to know when it will rain."

"It's a talent of sorts," Thane added, trying to downplay the situation.

"She's eerily good at it; always has been."

Darr Beval's expression shifted as if he were suddenly in pain, and he waved off his partner, who left the room through the door near the head of the classroom. "Will it rain today?" he asked her, his voice low.

She shook her head. "In a few days."

Darr Beval barely nodded in return. The class waited and watched as a few students murmured around the room. "Right," Darr Beval said cheerfully. He straightened back up to address the class as if the exchange had never taken place. "Well, then, let us proceed. Aelfraed has consented to continue his lecture."

Darr Thorndon reentered with the caretaker, who strode to the head of the classroom and gazed out at the group of despondent trainees. "Excited, are we?" he asked drily. A couple students gave him a weak laugh. "All right. Let's jump right in, then. Last time we spoke of some of the possible traits of the Heir—most importantly: a distinct ability to work with and even nex with all dragons, an affinity for training and flying, a tendency toward premonitions or psychic ability, and a firm grasp of the weather."

"What do you mean 'a firm grasp of the weather?'" Rowley blurted out. He had cropped the remainder of his hair, so it more closely matched the shadow of new growth along the crown of his head. Rhoswen wasn't sure what tool he had used to accomplish this, but he had done such a poor job that tufts stuck out at all angles along his scalp. He looked positively mangy.

Rowley eyed her suspiciously as Gethin came up to join him, and her amusement at his hair waned.

Aelfraed squinted at the class. "Heirs tend to know when it will rain long before others do. This helps them identify and prepare for Narxon attacks because Narxon Rain accompanies most every Descent. Did I forget to mention that last time?" he asked.

But Rowley wasn't listening; none of the class was anymore. All eyes had turned to Rhoswen, and several heads were ducked together in fevered discussion. Rowley whispered in Gethin's ear, and the prince peered at Rhoswen with a deep interest that made her squirm. She glanced back at Aelfraed, who appealed to the Riders behind him. The pair looked stricken.

Darr Thorndon recovered first. "Funny you should mention it, Aelfraed, but Rhoswen was just telling us of her prediction for rain—"

"A *few days* from now," Rowley interjected.

Rhoswen's heart dropped into her stomach; her body felt ice cold but for the fire in her cheeks. She hadn't just spoken out of turn a moment ago—she had given herself away. Now, her cousin knew her secret and would go tell his father. Finally, the blood drained from her head, and she thought she might faint.

Thane put a hand on her shoulder. "Aelfraed, didn't you say the Heir would have a 'firm grasp' on the weather? Rhoswen's just guessing because her joints hurt." His voice was impressively casual for all the lying he was doing.

Aelfraed cleared his throat. "Thane is right," he said smoothly. "Given the long list of traits associated with the Heir, it's almost impossible for established Riders and gifted trainees not to possess a similar trait or two. Even the Heir might not exhibit them *all*." He winked at her. "Forgive me, Rhoswen, but until you start nexing with dragons, I fear we won't be able to crown you the Heir—much as Rowley might want that for you."

Thane chuckled a little and nudged his sister in the ribs. As laughter slowly mounted around them, Rhoswen glanced over her shoulder at Rowley scowling at the back of the classroom. Next to him, Gethin's eyes remained locked on Rhoswen. She spun back around to watch Aelfraed at the front.

The caretaker resumed his lecture, but Rhoswen couldn't focus. Her eyes wandered to the Riders standing behind him: Darr Thorndon had reassembled his features to appear pensive, but Darr Beval's pained expression was only visible for a moment before he whispered something to his partner and left the room altogether.

"Last time, one of you… " Aelfraed was saying as he scanned the room, his eyes finally alighting on his target, "*Laila*, asked about how the portal to the new realm works." Laila nodded. "So, that is what I will explain today."

That recaptured Rhoswen's attention.

"The Realm Portal allows all the dragons and their Riders to Move from this realm into the next. The queen dragon safeguards the object that opens the portal until she entrusts it to the Heir Whelp in the subsequent realm. Peculiarly enough, the Realm Portal object is rumored to take on a different form in every realm. We believe it does this as a way of protecting itself from falling into the wrong hands. It is far more difficult to look for something if you do not know what you are looking for."

Rhoswen stole a glance at Thane. *We need to know if Deowynn has it,* she tried to convey to him with her eyes. He nodded, his raised eyebrow seeming to suggest another nighttime visit to the stables.

"What shape is it in D'Erenelle?" Golda asked from beside Laila.

"I am not privy to that information, Golda, but I'm certain our Deowynn has it under control," Aelfraed reassured her. His gaze flitted past Rhoswen as he scanned the room again. "When the queen dragon is ready to Move to the next realm, she activates the portal, beckons her dragons and Riders through, and helps the Heirs—both Whelp and Rider—travel safely to the other side."

Laila raised her hand. "What happens to the queen dragon then?" she asked, her hesitant tone suggesting she already knew—and didn't like the answer.

"Should the queen dragon survive, she would raise the Whelp into adulthood." Aelfraed's face took on a sorrowful expression. "But it depends on when the Realm Portal is activated after the birth of the Heir Whelp. It can take some dragons quite a while to recover after giving birth, and the queen dragon may not deem a realm stable enough to wait. Activating a portal is draining as it is, but then holding it open for a whole passel of Riders and guiding the Heir Whelp through it—all while weak from childbirth and pursued by a flood of Narxon... that's a lot. Not all queen dragons survive the stress. It then falls to the Heir Rider and the rest of the dragons to raise the Heir Whelp."

Rhoswen thought of Deowynn, and her heart sank at the possibility of her demise. The more she learned about Movement, the less she liked the concept.

Behind Aelfraed, a composed Darr Beval slipped back in through the door at the front of the classroom to stand beside his partner. Darr Thorndon leaned over and whispered something in his ear. Rhoswen began to ponder what the pair could be discussing, and she lost track of Aelfraed's words. By the time Darr Thorndon had dismissed the class, she had missed the end of lecture and the Rider's instructions. Students streamed out of the room, and she waited for the tide to recede before she finally approached Darr Beval.

"We need to talk," she said in a low voice. Thane came up behind her.

Darr Beval looked at them both. "Tonight, after dinner. My chambers. I'll tell the others."

Rhoswen nodded and turned away to find her cousin hadn't left with the rest. He was staring at her from the back of the room. She felt lightheaded and leaned in close to her brother, her hand tightening on his arm. "What are we supposed to be doing now?" she whispered as they walked toward the door.

Thane made a show of grinning at her for their cousin's benefit. "Training. It's going to rain soon, you know."

Apparently, it had been announced that the arena would be used for peer training. Rather than the trainers teaching, students who had passed their lessons were expected to help their fellow classmates get up to speed. Riders strolled around, lending a hand as needed and watching the students tutor one another.

At Rhoswen's urging, Thane stepped away to help Sterling and another student at the unkennelling station. Her brother was skilled in manual dexterity, and she smiled to see him working at an open stable door instead, his arm cast out in polite offering to the beast in the stall. That was the station she most excelled at—for obvious reasons—but she couldn't tutor someone there now, especially after that lecture.

She scanned the arena, hoping to find Laila and Golda, but they were busy tutoring others. *Of course they don't need help,* she thought to herself. Aelfraed recruited Haylan to help him with something, and the pair took their leave of the girls with a wave. Rhoswen stepped in their direction, but she noticed Gethin strutting out of the lecture hall, his head swiveling in an obvious search for someone. She turned away in time to watch Thane coaxing the dragon out of the stall. Her chest constricted with a mix of jealousy and concern.

Working with dragons is out of the question, she reminded herself. She surveyed the other available stations, desperate to busy herself so Gethin might not approach her. A student she recognized as a friend of Rowley's was struggling with knots over at the mountblocks. With all the Riders otherwise occupied and most students less than fond of Rowley's cronies, no one helped him.

She paused. A friend of Rowley's might also be a friend of her cousin's, which made helping him almost as risky as working with the dragons. She sighed. In homage to Aeduuin's patient tutelage when she had been struggling, she would risk it. *If Thane can unkennel, I can tie.*

"Hello," she ventured. "I'm Rhoswen."

"Brentley," the student grunted, his fingers tangling in the rope at the same step that had given her so much trouble.

"I hate that part," Rhoswen commiserated. "Aeduuin had to review it with me over and over before I got the hang of it."

"Yeah, well, where is he now?" Brentley asked. He loosened the knot and gave the rope a fierce shake.

Rhoswen watched until he approached the final loop. When he paused and glanced up at her, she guided his hands with her own. "You have to twist it over as you push it through the loop, so you can fish the end through and pull it tight. See? You've got it!"

As Brentley finally completed his first knot, he smiled at her with unexpected gratitude. "Try again," she urged him, risking a glance over her shoulder and meeting Gethin's gaze. Her head snapped back around as Brentley made the twist and pulled the knot tight again. He hollered triumphantly, and Rhoswen applauded his effort. "Good work," she said.

Brentley noticed the prince glaring at him over Rhoswen's shoulder. "You should go," he said with a little less gruffness. Rhoswen nodded. She walked toward Thane, forcing her feet to maintain a leisurely pace as her heartrate quickened with every step.

Around lunchtime, the Riders announced a transition from peer tutoring to flying practice for the older students. The younger trainees were released.

Thane and Rhoswen made their way up the hill to the castle and had barely stepped through the front entrance when their cousin strode out before them. Rhoswen had not seen him leave Keaton. *Why isn't he at practice?*

Gethin's cape was all a-flourish, and he wore an officious expression that made Rhoswen's muscles tense. "The king is holding a dinner tonight with many of the upper echelon from the nearby estates. As part of the royal family and guests in his castle, you are invited to attend."

That was not what Rhoswen had expected him to say, but it was nonetheless inconvenient. How could they go to Keaton tonight if they had to attend some ridiculous dinner party? She couldn't bear to think of flouncing around in puffy layers of gauche fabric again. And the *shoes*...! "How unfailingly kind," Rhoswen dissembled, "but I am feeling a bit under the weather. I fear I should be poor company for your guests."

Gethin's look of importance withered to one of annoyance. "I can only imagine you are exhausted by your *prophetic* morning.... But by 'invited,' I really meant 'expected,'" he said.

"Oh." Rhoswen looked to her brother for help.

Thane cleared his throat. "We are honored, my prince, but I fear for my sister's health. She has looked somewhat peaked these past few days. I would feel better knowing she were getting adequate rest instead of tiring herself with such excitements. Would it be possible for me to attend—alone—while she retires for the evening?"

Rhoswen shot her brother a desperate glance, but he was not looking at her. His eyes, which had narrowed in challenge, were locked on Gethin's. The men appeared fixed in some unspoken battle of wills.

Before Gethin could reply, however, another voice echoed through the foyer. "Of course, Thane. We can't have Rhoswen exhausting herself for the sake of appearances." The king slinked out of the shadows in his pitch-black riding apparel and liquid-like gold-and-purple cape.

Rhoswen had not heard him approach, and she wondered how long he had been listening. "Thank you, my king," she said with a curtsey. "It is kind and generous of you to be so conscientious of my wellbeing."

"Rhoswen, you are my niece," Badrick said smoothly. "Nothing could be more important than *your wellbeing*." There was something ironically threatening about those last two words. "As a matter of fact, I think it would be best if you went up to your chambers now and began resting immediately. I will put two of my best guards at your door, so you won't be disturbed before or during the party."

Rhoswen's mouth went dry, and she swallowed with difficulty. "How thoughtful, my king. Are you certain you can spare such extravagance on my behalf?"

"It would be my *pleasure*." Badrick grinned, his teeth gleaming through his inky black mustache and beard.

So, Gethin had spoken to his father, and he decided to keep an eye on Rhoswen, whether she could attend the party or not. She felt panic begin to seize her when a messenger arrived at the king's elbow.

"Correspondence from Stanburh," he announced.

Rhoswen exchanged glances with Thane. This was doing nothing to ease her anxiety.

Badrick grabbed up the letter, broke the seal, and scanned its contents.

"Will our parents be coming for a visit?" Thane asked.

Their uncle did not look up from the parchment. "It would appear they are *far* too busy for that," he said with a sneer.

"Of course," Thane said. He took the opportunity to redirect their plan. "Rose, I know it can be difficult for you to fall asleep without something to read. Perhaps his highness would permit me to escort you to the overflow library to pick out a short tale to lull you to sleep before I ready myself for the evening?"

The king's expression had grown dark, but at Thane's suggestion, a devilish smile crept over his face. "An excellent idea, Nephew. Gethin, why don't you go with them?"

"It's my fault—they almost figured it out," Beval said through gritted teeth. He couldn't stop pacing.

"All the better," Thorndon replied from the couch. "Aelfraed told them to *protect* the Heir once they found her, not roast her on a spit."

"How do we know we can trust them all? *Gethin* was there; we can't trust *him,*" Beval replied as the door to his apartments opened behind him.

"We can't trust any of them until we know which side they're on," Aelfraed interjected upon entering. "The sooner they recognize the Heir, the sooner Badrick will, too—if he hasn't already. Both her defenses and the danger to her will increase simultaneously. It is the peril of her position."

"We have to protect her somehow," Beval insisted. He ran a hand through his dark-gold hair.

"We are," Aelfraed replied. "Right now, there are already three of us—four, counting Thane—safeguarding her. Not to mention the dragons. When the Riders and trainers identify her, there will be that many more of us to protect her—"

"And countless more on Badrick's side against her," Beval interrupted.

"In the end, I expect the good will outnumber the bad," Thorndon said. "Aelfraed is right. We don't know Badrick's plan, but I still can't believe the majority of the Riders and trainees will side with him. We have all been ingrained with the inevitability of a Move. The power of greed aside, those instincts should win out for most of us."

Beval looked from his partner to the caretaker, his eyes wide with disbelief. "Have you two forgotten where she *sleeps*? She's in the realm-forsaken castle with that monster! He is *steps* away from her at all times. How can we protect her from a castle away?"

Aelfraed took a seat and motioned to Beval to take another. Thorndon sat up from where he was reclining on the couch, mug hanging from his fingertips. Aelfraed exhaled evenly. "Rhoswen is up to something, and I expect it is because the dragons are giving her access to tools only Heirs can use to protect themselves. Whatever she is doing, it will somehow make this whole 'castle away' idea moot. She is connecting with the dragons, and their script will lead her on a path to safety. Our job is to make certain she is educated and practiced enough to navigate that path with swiftness and sureness by the time everyone figures out who she is."

"You speak as though you have an inkling of what she has discovered," Thorndon said.

"I haven't a clue." Aelfraed shrugged. "The dragons have powers to do things we cannot even fathom. They must have a defensive system of some kind in place, and she is learning it, whatever it is. Perhaps we can try to coax that from her at our next meeting."

"Well, that'll be tonight," Beval said. "She asked to speak to us all, so I told her we would meet here after dinner."

Aelfraed opened his mouth to speak, but he was stopped by a deafening racket outside Beval's apartments: beating wings, bellows, grunts, and thumps—the dragons were a-flurry with panic. All three men rushed out into the stables. Awestruck trainees were backing away from the stalls as Riders rushed into them, trying in vain to soothe their beasts.

"What's going on?!" Thorndon called out. When no one answered, he bolted down the hall in Merry's direction.

Beval stepped into his tawny's stall, Aelfraed hot on his heels. *What is it, Fleta?* he nexed.

The reply in his head rang anxious and strong. *Interference at the castle.*

What kind of interference? He knew better than to try to convince her to calm down. As long as she was coherent in her fit of clairvoyance, he would have to be satisfied.

Rhoswen and Thane. Badrick is trying to keep them from coming to Keaton. He is trying to discover their plan.

What plan?

The plan they were going to come to you with tonight. They are close. They must not divulge it to him, nor must they be kept from it.

This was not making complete sense to Beval, but in light of what Aelfraed had just told them, he figured it must have something to do with a system the dragons had put in place for Rhoswen's safety. *What can we do?*

Assist them! Fleta curled up and rested her chin on her forelegs. Her eyes remained wide and intent upon Beval, and her breathing continued to race with distress. Her tail thudded against the hay-strewn floor like an anxious cat's.

Thorndon peeked in around the stall door, panting from his run to the other end of the stables and back. "Merry says Thane and Rhoswen need our help."

Beval nodded. "Fleta said the same. What do we do?"

"I'll go," Aelfraed volunteered. "The sudden arrival of either of you at the castle would be quite conspicuous. Remain in contact with your dragons. If something goes astray, they will make you aware of it."

"And then what will we do?" Beval asked.

"Whatever they instruct you to," Aelfraed replied with a nod toward Fleta, and he was gone.

L

The Exchange

The Crew was staring at her once again—well, her and Vonn. "So, y'all are sayin' yer realm's Dissonance looks like the Exchange's Dissonance?" Randy asked.

Both Emmelyn and Vonn nodded. "Exactly the same," Emmelyn verbalized for them both. "Doesn't it in your realms?"

Randy shook his head. "Mine's a saloon," he drawled. "I felt loopier 'an a cross-eyed rodeo clown when I walked into that pearly marble lobby the first time."

Emmelyn's face scrunched.

"Runners enter the lobby on their very first Run," Vonn explained. "Then they're sent upstairs to be offered the job. If they accept, they enter through the back of the club after that."

Emmelyn scowled. *They get a* choice*?*

"Mine's the burlesque," Bernadette yelled.

"The burlesque you work in?" Emmelyn asked in surprise.

She nodded.

Emmelyn's eyebrows lifted. "Your first time must have been a shock, too."

"Yuh not kiddin'!" she replied. "I thought I was goin' tuh woik."

"So, why does it look the same in our realms?" Emmelyn asked Vonn.

He shook his head. "Couldn't tell you, really. It fits into our realms—just like a saloon fits into Randy's—but this would fit in yours, too, wouldn't it, Bernadette?"

"It's a bit too high-tech fuh my realm," Bernadette replied with a shrug.

"It's probably a bit low-tech for mine," Vonn admitted. "They're talking about renovating the club in Welsamar."

"Would that hurt the connection?" Emmelyn asked.

Vonn shrugged. "Can't imagine it would, but who knows how portals work?"

"Datists," Kyle answered, as he returned with his drink.

It didn't happen often, but it was nice having the original group back together. "Where are these Datists, anyway?" Emmelyn asked. "If they're not hidden away in the basement anymore, why don't we ever see them?"

Randy squinted in confusion. "They're all around us, Emmelyn," he yelled with a wide gesture toward the club at large.

Bernadette nodded. "They're practically everywheah. They love getting' dressed up and blendin' in with the Runnahs and Transfuhs."

So, Emmelyn *had* seen Datists before. She realized with embarrassment that she had been envisioning them as nerdy desk jockeys in short-sleeved, button-down dress shirts, ill-fitting khakis, and thick-rimmed glasses.

"Why else would this place be swarmin' with Ministuhs?" Bernadette continued.

Emmelyn looked around at all the black-jacketed stoics mingling in the club. The darkness camouflaged them so well, she hadn't noticed them before. She stared at her friends. "Wait. Are you saying *I'm in the G'Ambit?"* The Crew didn't seem remotely scandalized by this notion.

Kyle rolled his eyes. "The G'Ambit isn't exactly a location. A lot of transactions take place in this club—bets are sent back and forth through Transitor exchanges and money often changes palms in here—but the Datists crunch the numbers elsewhere. The G'Ambit is more of an institution than a gambling hall."

Emmelyn's head was beginning to swim again. "So, every level is in on the G'Ambit?"

"All but the Transfers and Ivers," Randy hollered with a nod. "Most uh the time, Transfers don't even know they're movin' a bet, and Universals put the laws in place against gamblin'. So, the system don't include the highest and lowest rungs of the Exchange—no offense."

"None taken," Emmelyn replied before she had even given his words any thought. "But if I'm the lowest rung in the Exchange, how did I pop in here the way I did? Wouldn't that be some kind of special power reserved for Arbiters or better? Or am I flattering myself? Because you all looked at me like what I had done was miraculous."

"It was," Vonn replied, glancing up from his wrist after counting the remaining stamps. The rest of the Crew nodded in agreement—even Kyle. "We don't know how you were able to do what you did."

"Well there has to be some explanation," Emmelyn insisted. "How are any of us chosen for the Exchange anyway?"

"It's not entirely cleah...." Bernadette shrugged.

Kyle got a theatrical twinkle in his eye. "There is Orphan Theory—"

"I'm not an orphan," Emmelyn countered.

"Neither am I," Vonn replied, taking over for Kyle before he could make a one-act of the tale. "But your folks moved away, and you're an only child, right?" Emmelyn nodded, and he continued. "A lot of us are distanced from our families in similar ways. Mine lives on the other side of Welsamar."

"But some of us actually are orphans," Randy offered. "My folks died when I was eighteen, but Inzay was given up fer adoption at birth."

"Ya asked last time about how tuh reconcile yuh realm life with yuh Exchange life," Bernadette reminded her. "And we told ya: ya don't really have tuh. That's what seems tuh make ya—tuh make all of us—good candidates fuh our positions."

"But it's just a theory," Kyle yelled to her. "There are others who think it has to do with temperament or open-mindedness. You have to *want* to do this job, don't you? You have to be interested enough in the reality of the realms to accept your higher purpose. Not everyone is suited to look behind the curtain."

Randy jumped in before Kyle could expand his metaphor. "Fact is, ain't no one really knows how we're selected or why we're given a specific job in the Exchange. It just... happens."

Emmelyn could barely hear over the strange confluence of Bollywood and alternative rock drowning out their discussion, but she got the gist—and she wasn't sure she bought it. *Perhaps* they *don't know, but someone must.* Still, there was truth to Kyle's words. Working for the Exchange required a certain sort of person, and she couldn't help but realize she was that sort. She might not understand the Exchange, but now that she knew about it, she couldn't turn her back on the realms it protected.

"Whatevuh the reason ya are what ya are, yuh... *appearance* the othuh night was somethin' ya probably don't want any uh the highuh-ups knowin' about," Bernadette suggested.

"I got no idea when such a power'd come in handy as a Transfer," Randy mused. "Now, as a Runner...."

Vonn nodded. "That would shave off all kinds of time and hassle! No more escaping from daily life to go to the portal location, only to return from the Exchange, not knowing how long you'd been gone...."

"There's no time differential for me," Emmelyn yelled to them, "whether I pop in or portal in legitimately."

"That's because you're a Transfer," Kyle explained. "Runners use Realm Portals to return to the Exchange. When a rule change generates sufficient energy to create a Realm Portal, those keys Runners wear harness that power and open the portal to the Exchange. A small, residual amount of energy from that Realm Portal then triggers the Exchange Portal that brings their Transfer here. Exchange Portals cannot exist without a Realm Portal being used first."

"So, why is there no drag in time?" Emmelyn asked.

Kyle looked pleased to be afforded such an opening. "Because Exchange

Portals are basically manmade. They're powered by this naturally occurring, residual energy, but they're engineered by the Exchange—and in such a way that they don't create a drag in time for us."

"How do you know all this?" Emmelyn asked.

"His Datist goilfriend," Bernadette yelled.

Kyle ignored her. "You familiar with String Theory? Quantum Mechanics?"

Vonn glanced around again and spotted his Transfer. He excused himself and flashed Emmelyn an apologetic look as she waved goodbye. It appeared Kyle would get his time on the stage after all. She hid a smile behind a sip of her gin (which she had decided not to tell Vonn she had recently tried on her own).

"Oh, Kyle," Bernadette sighed, "don't get too technical...."

Kyle made a face like someone had spat in his drink. He scooted forward on the couch and leaned across the coffee table toward Emmelyn. "Fine. You ever heard of planes of existence? This theory that there are multiple versions of you out there, all experiencing various outcomes of a moment's existence, and all you have to do to change your circumstances is channel the one you prefer?"

Emmelyn felt as though she had watched some mind-bending documentary about something like this once. *Or was it a self-help book?* Either way, it sounded familiar. She nodded.

"The realms operate on much the same principle," Kyle continued, "but rather than existing in the same time, they all exist in the same *space*."

"Except fer the Exchange," Randy interjected.

"Exactly," Kyle yelled. "You can't just move directly from one realm to another. Realms are impenetrable unless you enter them by way of the Exchange. It's like a stopover, a go-between."

Emmelyn squinted at him. "So... the Exchange occupies a different space?"

Kyle and Randy nodded.

"It's why ya have to go through the Exchange to move from realm to realm," Randy repeated. "Ya have to leave one realm space to switch to another realm within that same space."

"How do we know any of this?" Emmelyn asked.

"How do we know String Theory?" Kyle asked back.

Before Emmelyn could respond, Vonn rushed back to the circle. "Almost forgot," he yelled to them, "we lost a Rider in a bad Descent in Welsamar. It was reported earlier today. They're finishing up the shrine for the vigil now." His expression was grim as he pointed to the far side of the club and then disappeared once more toward the realm doors.

"That's too bad," Randy hollered to the group. "Shall we go extend our sympathies?"

The Crew wove their way through the dance floor in the direction Vonn had pointed. A crowd had already begun to form around the shrine—*if you could call it that*. A mirror framed in flowers leaned against the wall, palm-size white candles scattered at its base. Exchangers were pulling slim white candles from baskets near the mirror, lighting them, and standing them up in tiered racks on either side of the glass as tribute. In the middle of the mirror was a name: Jerold Illisan of Welsamar.

"That's odd," Bernadette mused, leaning in toward Emmelyn. "Usually, there's a pictuh tuh go with it, not a mirruh. Especially a Welsamodel. I think the entire population has new glamuh shots taken annually."

Emmelyn smiled at the joke, but it also struck her as odd that a picture should be missing from the shrine of a fallen warrior. Usually, the idea was not simply to honor the person but also to protect them from an anonymous death in appreciation for their service. A mirror failed to make the death real, to make the war on Narxon real. This shrine was entirely for the mourners—almost at the expense of the mourned.

"Maybe he didn't bother with all that vanity stuff," Kyle yelled.

Bernadette rolled her eyes, and Emmelyn had to suppress a smile.

Kyle pressed on, "Or maybe he wanted us to *reflect* on the tragedy."

Bernadette flashed Kyle a sideways glance for his dubious pun and shrugged. "I just nevuh seen one without a pictuh befoah."

LI

Aethelburh

Rhoswen, Thane, and Gethin stood in the overflow library, scanning the shelves. Rhoswen tried to focus on the spines before her as her mind raced. Should she make a genuine selection or pick something that Gethin would have no reason to report back to his father?

"What about this?" Thane offered, bringing her a book. He leaned in close, displaying the cover, and whispered, "We have to get the maps to your room."

"What if the portal can't be triggered from there?" she whispered back.

"Find something?" Gethin asked with an impatient sigh from across the room.

"I think I'd prefer a different genre. This one is too exciting for slumber," Rhoswen called over her brother's shoulder. "How do you expect me to do that while our cousin is skulking at the opening of the maps room?" she whispered.

Thane winked at her and replaced the book on its shelf. "Shall we get you a snack before you retire, Rose?" he asked, glancing at his cousin. He obviously hoped he could coax Gethin away while one of them moved the maps into her chambers through the portal.

"That might be nice," Rhoswen said, eager for a late lunch. She would have lots of time to kill before the secret meeting, and it looked like she would be skipping dinner.

Gethin had his back turned to them as he thumbed through a book on the other side of the room. "Whatever you want can be sent up to your chambers," he muttered. He set the book on the table behind him and continued moving along the shelves as he scanned the spines. He was edging dangerously close to the book that triggered the maps room to open. Rhoswen began to wonder how he had not stumbled upon it before.

Thane cursed under his breath and took another book to her. "What about this one?" he asked. "We should have stayed up and figured out how to work the realmed thing," he whispered to her.

She shrugged. All they could do now was get their cousin out of this library. "Perhaps you and Prince Gethin could go ask for some warm milk and porridge to be sent up to me. You need not wait for me to find a book. I'll meet you in my room."

"You two can stop by the kitchen on your way up. Select your book so we can get out of here. We have other things to tend to before the party," Gethin barked.

An idea struck Rhoswen. "Forgive me, my prince. I had no idea you wanted to pick up where we left off the other night. I figured you would want to wait until after the party—until after I had rested—to be alone with us."

Gethin's brows knitted in confusion. Then, his eyes widened in horrified understanding. He took a step backward.

"Our cousin is right, Thane," Rhoswen continued. "We put him off the other night, but we cannot continue to deny the prince his wishes. Not after he so generously opened his home to us. If he wants to spend time with us—*alone*—we should just forget the book and head straight up to my room. Unless you'd prefer we go to yours, my prince?"

It took Thane a moment to catch on, but his hesitation went unnoticed by Gethin, who was turning red and babbling.

"I—no—I don't—that is not—*no*—" the prince stammered as he continued to back away from them.

"Of course," Thane added. "We should have enough time before the party—"

In a final bid to piece together a coherent sentence, Gethin burst out, "I do not wish to sleep with you!"

And that was the moment Aelfraed walked into the overflow library.

Everyone turned toward the caretaker.

"I've come at a bad time," the old man said.

"Aelfraed?" Thane breathed in surprise. "What are you doing here?"

"It's not what you're thinking," Gethin sputtered, his face crimson.

"I am certain I'm not thinking, my prince," Aelfraed said with a little bow that obscured his expression. "The dragons are in a state, and I'm looking for a text that might provide some sort of explanation. I was told I could find you here to clear a withdrawal with you."

"Take whatever you please, Aelfraed!" Gethin blurted. He closed his eyes in a flustered attempt not to make eye contact with anyone. "Just sign it out and be on your way. Same for you two. I'm going to get changed for the party." He stomped from the room, his hastened footsteps echoing down the hall.

Thane, Rhoswen, and Aelfraed exchanged glances and stifled their laughter behind their hands. Aelfraed wiped at his eyes. "You two are awful," he said gleefully.

"That was all Rose," Thane insisted, palms lifted in innocence.

"I'm sure we'll regret that later, but at least we are rid of him," Rhoswen said.

"What are you doing here, Aelfraed? Did you really come for a book?" Thane asked.

"I did not," Aelfraed admitted. "But the Keaton dragons *are* in a state. They said you were in trouble with the king and your safety was threatened. I came here to help. Yet it would appear you do not require my assistance."

Rhoswen stared at Aelfraed in disbelief. *The dragons know what's going on here and believe we are in danger.* She grabbed up two books from the history section and scribbled their information into the log. She handed one to Aelfraed and motioned for Thane to open the bookcase to the maps room. "Quite the contrary," Rhoswen said, watching the caretaker's eyes widen in tandem with the expanding gap in the wall. "We most certainly *do* require your assistance."

Gethin stormed across the Great Hall, desperate to shake off another gruesome misunderstanding with his cousins. He could go back and see what they had borrowed from the library later. For now, he would enjoy the sanctuary of his translations until it was time to ready himself for the evening. *But how can I avoid Thane during the gathering…?*

His father stepped in front of him from behind a massive stone pillar. Gethin stopped short, scrambling for his footing before he ran into the king.

"Is she in her room?" Badrick asked.

Gethin took a steadying breath. "She will be shortly."

His father's eyes flashed with anger. "What in the realm does that mean?"

Gethin was not keen to describe what had happened downstairs. "When I left them, she was selecting a book, and Thane was heading up to the kitchen to order hot milk and porridge for her. I suspect they are on their way to their separate errands now—"

"What book did she select?"

"I don't know. Aelfraed came down to the library to borrow another text. I asked them to write their books in the log before they left."

"Before they left? And what is your excuse for abandoning them?"

"I am not their babysitter," Gethin replied.

Badrick glared at his son, his eyebrows falling flat with disgust. "Certainly not. No one would entrust their children to your *attentive* care. Did you not think them capable of falsifying records in that log?"

Gethin swallowed. The horror he had felt at the misunderstanding with his cousins was compounded by this unexpected revelation. His voice sounded small when he spoke again. "Why should they? You just gave Aelfraed free rein over the library."

Badrick sighed through his nose and gazed upward as though searching for patience in the balcony. "Because they are not half-wits like you. Aelfraed already knows you are scrutinizing which books he removes from the library, and now that you have left them alone together down there, he has the opportunity to warn Rhoswen that her own borrowings could be similarly treated. If they are indeed working together as you proposed, then why shouldn't they endeavor to hide their dealings within that room?"

Gethin felt his stomach drop. "This is why you sent me with them," he realized.

Badrick nodded, pulling his lips into his mouth to hold them closed between his teeth. It looked as though his facial hair had swallowed the entire bottom half of his face.

Gethin cast his eyes downward to avoid his father's gaze and found he had been unconsciously wringing his hands; he forced them back down to his sides in fists. "There was a miscommunication downstairs," he heard himself say, "and it was taking Rhoswen forever to select a book. I figured it was better that I spend my time working on translations rather than—"

Badrick freed his lips from his teeth. "What kind of miscommunication?"

"Just an awkward moment," the prince replied breezily. His father's eyes flared. Gethin did not know which was more frightening: his father unleashing his anger or trying to restrain it. "She thought… I was… trying… to… *court them.*" He said the last two words much more quietly than the rest, hoping his father's impatience would preclude him from asking Gethin to repeat himself.

"To *court them,*" The king repeated slowly. "Explain."

Gethin squirmed. "Rhoswen originally thought I was trying to court *her,* but when I tried to correct her, she thought my intentions were toward Thane. My further denial was then misconstrued as interest in the *pair* of them…." He could say no more. Every word made his flesh crawl. He had never intended to share any of these misinterpretations with his father. His self-defense had morphed into self-recrimination.

Badrick stared at him a moment longer before making a sucking sound behind his teeth. "And you *believed* her."

This was not the reply Gethin had been expecting. He froze as his father stared at him.

Badrick massaged the bridge of his nose. "They were toying with you. A rather sordid joke, I'll warrant, but you played right into it. *Not another word,*" he added when Gethin tried to protest. "Just go back down and try to intercept them, you idiot!"

"What's wrong?" Lorelle asked Delwyn as they passed each other in the hall. She shifted the armload of new linens for Rhoswen's chambers against her hip.

"The dragons are in a state," Delwyn blustered. "Can't you hear them?"

In the silence that followed the question, Lorelle strained to make out some sort of racket from Keaton, but there was nothing to be heard. She shook her head.

"They must have stopped," he said.

"Why? What was going on?"

He shrugged. "No one knows."

"Not even the Riders?" she asked.

He stared at her. "Something must have changed."

A chill ran up Lorelle's spine. Sometimes, their unrealmly knowledge of the rule changes that affected D'Erenelle unsettled her greatly. While everyone around them tried to find rational reasons for the odd things taking place in the realm, the Runners saw a much broader justification behind the goings-on around them. She looked down at Delwyn's unadorned wrist. "I see you still haven't gotten your key back, either." *No wonder he's in such a state.*

"I wanted to give Thane the chance to give it back to me without my asking him for it," he explained, his fingers fidgeting together. "But after a few days, I realized he wouldn't. I've been trying to track him down, but with their busy training schedule and all this preparation for tonight's dinner party, every time I think I've found him, he's moved again." He glanced around as if he might spot Thane nearby. "He came back to the castle around the time the din started up, but I lost him."

"Well, he's not going anywhere," Lorelle replied. "Let me know if you figure out why the dragons were panicking, will you?"

Delwyn nodded and pranced nervously away. Lorelle shook her head, smiled, and headed up the stairs to Rhoswen's room.

As Gethin sped back toward the cellar stairs, his waitman, Baul, shuffled toward him.

"What is it, Baul?" the prince asked, annoyed at the delay.

"Siiiiir, there has been an eveeeeent down in Keeeeeeaton," Baul announced.

Gethin perked up a little. "What kind of event?"

"The draaaaaaagons are in a state of paaaaaaanic, siiiiir. No one is certain whyyyyy or hooooow to calm them." The servant's eyes half closed and then reopened.

Hadn't Aelfraed mentioned something like that in the library...? Gethin took advantage of the break in conversation to listen for the din but heard only silence. "I don't hear anything."

"They must have stoooopped, siiiiir...."

"Thank you, Baul. I will tend to it myself. Have my cousins come up from the library?"

"I haven't seeeeeeen them, siiiiir."

Gethin nodded. "That will—"

"Will that be aaaaaaall, siiiiir?" Baul interrupted.

"*Yes,*" Gethin snapped and resumed his trek to the cellar. His father had said nothing about a ruckus down in Keaton just now, which meant either he was unaware of it, or he didn't want Gethin to know. The former seemed unlikely. *He's hiding this from me for a reason,* he realized and changed course toward the drakiary.

When Rhoswen and Thane had finished explaining the portal system to Aelfraed, a tense silence descended around them. *He thinks we've lost our minds,* Rhoswen feared.

Aelfraed scrutinized the maps spread out on the table. His gaze shifted back and forth from the metal compass to the compass roses on the maps. Finally, his eyes settled on the stone slivers he had unwittingly translated for them. He picked one up and ran his thumb over the engraving. A small smile formed on his lips, and he looked up at them, his gaze intent. "We have to figure out how to use these."

Thane grinned. Rhoswen threw her arms around the caretaker in relief. "I thought you didn't believe us," she said as she released him.

"You are the Heir," Aelfraed said, as if that explained away any uncertainty. "Tell me again what you've tried."

Rhoswen put the compass on the map and activated the portal to Aelfraed's chambers. Out of habit, she listened for a second to make certain no one was in his room before explaining their failed attempts at using the keys.

"Could we be missing a key?" Aelfraed asked.

"I'm not certain whether there are more," Rhoswen said.

"Perhaps it doesn't matter how many you have. There may be an infinite number of them if each came out of a portal to a specific place." Aelfraed moved toward the opening of the portal with the Keaton key in hand. Without any of the hesitation Rhoswen and Thane had exhibited upon first entering the shallow tunnel, he stepped across the threshold and inspected the opening. He reached out his fingers and began probing the shallow walls as they had done to find the keys in the first place.

Rhoswen stepped forward. "We found it right here," she said, guiding him to the point from which they'd taken the key. Aelfraed winked at her and pushed the key back into the wall. It sank, recessing itself in the stone, and lit up—brightly at first—before dimming to a dull, pulsing glow.

"Hey," Thane called to them from the far side of the table. "What does this mean?" Rhoswen ran back to him, Aelfraed one step behind her. On the table, her compass was glowing like the key in the wall. "It shimmered like when a portal is being opened," Thane explained. "Then, it flared brightly, and now this."

Something in Rhoswen told her to pick up the compass. Her fingers slid around its cool, metal surface, and she lifted it off the map. All three of them turned their attention to the portal. It remained open.

"Aelfraed," she breathed. "You did it!"

At that same moment, the door to Aelfraed's apartments swung open, and Gethin strode into the room. When his eyes landed on the portal—and the three of them standing on the other side of it—his mouth fell open.

LII

Detroit

Emmelyn couldn't believe she was doing this—a sentiment she had repeated to Josie maybe three-dozen times before Jeremy came to pick her up for their first date. Now, she was sitting across from him in a "MexicAsian" fusion restaurant called *Ohayo Sí,* which specialized in things like sashimi salsa and tamago burritos. Until now, she had successfully avoided the place.

"Remind me why we chose this restaurant," Emmelyn said when the server walked out of earshot.

"We had heard good things," Jeremy replied, eyeing his napkin, which had been folded into a pocket to hold standard silverware and chopsticks. "Plus, it puts us on an even playing field."

"We can both get food poisoning?" Emmelyn suggested.

Jeremy laughed. "Neither of us has been here before." He smiled at her. "I'm really glad you came out tonight.... I wasn't sure you would."

It was hard not to smile when he was grinning at her like that, but Emmelyn tried her best to look taken aback. "Geez, you go to all that trouble to set down your drink so you can dance unencumbered, and *still* he can't take a hint...."

"Okay, okay! I get it," Jeremy said, adding quietly, "I just don't want to mess this up."

Before she knew what she was doing, Emmelyn put a hand over his where it was lying on the table and met his gaze. His thick black hair had been gelled into a gravity-defying swoop over his forehead, and his dark-blue eyes shone like cobalt-colored glass under his knitted brows. *He even looks fantastic when he's nervous.* Her heart skipped a beat. "I don't either. I'm sorry that I've been weird lately. I've just had some... stress crop up. I'm trying to figure out how to deal with it."

Jeremy's face scrunched up in confusion. "Are you taking an extra summer class or something?"

The server cut off any opportunity for explanation. *Thank the realm*, she thought and grimaced inwardly at the phrase.

"We're all out of the yellowtail fajitas. Can I offer you tuna or salmon fajitas instead?" he asked, holding up a menu. "Or perhaps you'd like to select something else?"

Jeremy held up his palms in surrender. "Please! Not the menu again," he joked. It had taken them well over twenty minutes to figure out what they wanted to eat, and even their final decisions hadn't been convincingly made. "Tuna is fine with me. How about you, Em?"

She threw up her hands. "Tuna's great."

"Excellent," the server said. As he was leaving to adjust their order, Emmelyn caught a glimpse of this name tag: Trevor.

Her stomach flipped. Had he introduced himself? She would have recognized the name of the bartender in the club. *Don't think of the Exchange!* "Which of our idiot friends said this place was good?" she asked, leaning forward, her voice low.

"Nate and Neal," Jeremy leaned in to reply.

"*No*," Emmelyn breathed. "Tell me we did not take a restaurant recommendation from *Nate and Neal!* Their favorite food is corn dogs dipped in cheesy refried beans—a combination I don't know how they discovered, by the way!" They were still laughing when their second round of beers arrived. At least the drinks were good.

"So, are you interested in another trip to Dissonance?" he asked. "I was shocked you joined us at all, and then you came twice!"

For nearly two years, she had never given the nightclub a second thought, and suddenly, she couldn't get away from the place. "Yeah, I could go back," she said, the irony ringing in her head. "And Leo and Claire can make out anywhere, so I'm sure they'd be game." She rolled her eyes playfully.

Jeremy laughed. "They have it figured out," he said.

"Do they?"

He nodded. "They've been together how many years now? Almost a decade?"

She did a quick count on her fingers. "Eight years."

"See?" He leaned back in his chair. "They've always known."

"Nate doesn't seem to share your enthusiasm."

Jeremy's face fell. "Oh, Nate," he muttered. "He's loved Claire from the moment Leo introduced them."

"But why?" Emmelyn asked. "She's off-limits."

"I know." Jeremy sighed. "We've tried setting him up with countless girls. None of them are *Claire*. He doesn't even know Claire all that well; he just thinks he does. He has this… *image* of her, and he's convinced she's the girl for him."

"You seem *un*convinced," she replied.

"I'm not sure he would even make a move if she were single again," he said. "It's gotten to the point where he has idealized her so much that having the real thing might actually ruin the dream."

Trevor approached with their food held high on a large tray. They had decided to split a few appetizers—more to try to find something palatable than for any romantic reasons.

Trevor began setting things on the table. "Tuna fajitas with pickled cucumber salsa, chef's selection sushi with mole sauce, and the nigiramole—fried nigiri with our house-made guac. Anything else I can get you?"

"Can you do some tamago sashimi on the side?" Emmelyn asked. "*Just* tamago. No fusion. Please?"

Trevor made a face like she had requested he swing by Mars to bring back her order. "No problem. I'll bring that right out," he replied in a singsong voice.

"Thank you," she called after him and flashed Jeremy a wide-mouthed grimace.

"I don't think they want you un-fusing anything here," he replied with a laugh.

The food wasn't *that* bad—if a little strange—but the company was infinitely better. Emmelyn really hadn't spent much time alone with Jeremy over the years; their friends tended to hang out in groups of six or more. She had always enjoyed the dynamic he brought to the group, but she realized she had never given him much thought in an individual kind of way. She liked this version of Jeremy. *A lot.*

She looked up at him as he slid a piece of the sauce-covered sushi into his mouth. His chewing slowed a bit as he met her gaze. His brow furrowed. "Why would anyone put mole on sushi?" he asked her, unable to keep the horror from his voice—and his eyes.

Emmelyn started laughing and had to clamp a hand over her mouth as Trevor reappeared with her side-plate of "plain" yellow egg squares. He flashed them a forced smile, as if his opinion of them had deteriorated greatly, and asked how everything was. Still hyperventilating with laughter, Emmelyn couldn't answer, so Jeremy complimented the food to get him to go away.

"I'm beginning to think Nate and Neal pranked us," Emmelyn whispered when she was able to speak again.

"I don't understand how they stay in business," Jeremy said as they walked back to his car.

Emmelyn laughed. She felt giddy for the first time in a long time. "Maybe we ordered the wrong things...."

"Maybe we went to the wrong restaurant," he suggested, opening her door.

She smiled at him and sat in the passenger seat. Perhaps chivalry wasn't such a bad thing. Jeremy piled in behind the wheel and looked over at her. "Where to?" he asked.

"I could go for a chocolate malt," she said, the suggestion leaving her mouth before she had even given it any thought. "God, I haven't had one of those in—*years*, maybe? I don't even know why I thought of it."

Jeremy flashed her a mysterious and intriguing smile. "I know just the place," he said, turning the key in the ignition.

LIII

Aethelburh

Gethin appeared to be frozen in place as he stared at his cousins and caretaker through the portal.

Thane, however, was not.

As if by reflex, he bolted around the table and through the portal toward the prince. Before Rhoswen could call out to him, Thane balled his hand into a fist, drew back his right arm, and punched their cousin hard in the face. Rhoswen gasped, and she and Aelfraed rushed forward as Thane guided Gethin to the floor in a heap.

"Thane, what were you thinking?!" Rhoswen asked. A red gash blossomed over Gethin's left eye.

Thane massaged his knuckles, his eyes darting around the room. "Aelfraed, is there water in that metal basin over there?" he asked. The caretaker nodded. At Thane's instruction, the two of them upended the wide, heavy basin, splashing its contents across the stone floor. Then they flipped the bowl and laid it on the floor beside Gethin's shoulder.

Rhoswen leaned over Gethin, inspecting his face. His left eyebrow was bleeding steadily now, and a thin stream of blood made a red path across his temple to pool in his hairline. She checked to see if he were breathing, but her relief quickly turned to disgust as she got a whiff of his putrid Aethelia-laced breath. *Does he just keep a bunch of blossoms in his leathers to snack on throughout the day?* she wondered.

Thane surveyed the scene. "Perfect," he said, turning to Aelfraed. "Can you take this from here?"

Aelfraed nodded. He waved them toward the portal. Thane grabbed Rhoswen's upper arm, practically lifting her from the floor, and guided her toward the maps room.

"But what about Aelfraed?" Rhoswen protested.

"I'll be fine," the caretaker insisted. "Go!"

Thane ushered his sister ahead of him through the shallow tunnel. "Put the compass on the maps," he instructed her, grabbing the book logged out in Aelfraed's name and tossing it to him. He turned to the portal wall and pushed at the recessed stone sliver. The key began to resurface. Once he could get his fingers around it, he slid it out and ran back into the maps room. Rhoswen pulled the compass from the map again, and the stone wall rematerialized behind her brother, hiding Aelfraed and their unconscious cousin from view.

"What do we do now?" Rhoswen asked, her face ashen and heart beating frantically.

"We go get you some milk and porridge," Thane replied with a grin as he massaged his purpling knuckles.

Beval and Thorndon were the first Riders to respond to Aelfraed's calls for assistance. The dragons had already calmed down, but many Riders were now soothing the trainees who had been most upset by the inexplicable chaos.

When Beval and Thorndon reached Aelfraed's door, with several other Riders in close pursuit, the caretaker was kneeling over the unconscious body of the prince of D'Erenelle. "Aelfraed? When did you get back?" Beval asked, stunned. "What happened?"

"He barged into my quarters, slipped on some water, and banged his head on this basin," Aelfraed explained, dabbing at the prince's bleeding eyebrow with a cloth.

"Why did he barge into your chambers?" Thorndon asked, eyeing the shallow metal wash tub.

"I didn't have the opportunity to ask," Aelfraed replied.

Beval motioned to Thorndon to help him move the prince. They each grabbed one of his arms and slung them around their necks. His feet dragged behind them as they squeezed through the doorway and parted the growing crowd of onlookers.

"Aelfraed," Beval called over his shoulder. "You may want to accompany us to the castle. I'm certain you'll be sent for if you don't."

The caretaker nodded and followed the group, locking the door to his room behind them.

Rhoswen tried to inspect Thane's knuckles as he moved some objects around on the map and slid her compass into place, but he shook her off. They had left quite a mess for Aelfraed to clean up. "Will he be all right?"

Rhoswen asked. She didn't really know whether she was asking about Gethin or Aelfraed.

"He will be," Thane answered, not clarifying which one he was referring to either.

"But Gethin *saw* us," she said, her voice hushed with fear, "and you *hit* him. Not only will the king know about the portal, but he will probably execute you for treason."

"None of that will happen," Thane assured her, "if we get up to the kitchen for that milk you said you wanted. Having it will make Gethin sound delusional when he starts talking about seeing us at Aelfraed's." Her room materialized where the stone wall should have been. "Help me," he said, moving inside.

She followed him, watching him closely as he surveyed her chambers. A tall wingback chair covered in rich maroon fabric sat near the portal. He motioned for them to move it in front of the opening and then ushered Rhoswen back into the maps room ahead of him so he could pull the chair in tight. He slipped a stone key into the wall of the portal, locking it open to her chambers.

"We're just going to leave it like this?" Rhoswen asked. She glanced at the back of the chair obscuring the open portal to her room and shuddered.

"Yes," he replied. "We have no idea how to close it behind us, and we don't have time to figure it out, but now we'll have access to it when we return." He nodded at the portal and stepped toward the gap in the overflow library shelving. "Grab your compass and that book you wrote in the log, and let's go."

In the kitchen, Thane and Rhoswen heard a commotion echoing through the Great Hall. Thane cursed as he peered into the milk warming over the hearth. He dipped a finger in and shook his head at his sister. "This isn't nearly hot enough to provide our alibi," he whispered to her as he grabbed a pewter mug from the shelf overhead. The din grew, and he ladled tepid milk into the mug, nearly sloshing it over the side.

"Careful," Rhoswen hissed. "A harried mess won't help our alibi either."

They stepped from the kitchen and approached a group of people gathered around something in the middle of the Great Hall. *A body.*

"If you killed him, Thane Stanburh—" Rhoswen growled under her breath, but he shushed her and slid his bruised hand into the pocket of his leathers. He motioned for her to follow him with his other hand.

But Rhoswen lingered behind. She had the book tucked under her arm and the pewter mug cradled between her hands. She only hoped no one would notice the lack of steam. She wanted to return to her room, where the portal remained open and unguarded, but she did as she was bidden, placing a hand over the mouth of the mug, as if to trap its warmth.

A few onlookers parted to let the royal guests closer. In the middle of the circle, Darrs Beval and Thorndon were holding up an unconscious Prince Gethin while the surrounding servants fussed and argued about what to do with him.

"What happened here?" Thane asked, eyes wide. Rhoswen almost believed he didn't already know.

Darr Beval answered. "The prince slipped in Aelfraed's chambers and hit his head on a wash basin."

"Where's Aelfraed?" Thane asked.

Shouldn't he be asking about the prince's health? Rhoswen wondered, uncertain of how to play the part of worried—and *innocent*—onlooker.

"Alerting the king," Darr Thorndon replied, shifting Gethin's weight a little.

Rhoswen glanced up at Thane, but he did not look at her. She swallowed hard. *What would Badrick do to Aelfraed for this?*

Gethin uttered a faint groan, and Darr Beval instructed everyone to stand back, so he and Darr Thorndon could lay the prince on the floor.

"No!" Lorelle shrieked from the edge of the circle. The Riders gaped at her. She suggested, in a clipped and heavily accented whisper, that they move the prince into the withdrawing room instead, where he might be more comfortable. The Darrs exchanged glances and nodded at Thane to grab Gethin's feet. Darr Beval's gaze fell on Thane's shadowed knuckles as they shifted the prince's weight between them. Rhoswen followed them into the withdrawing room.

As the Riders were settling the prince onto the sofa, Badrick appeared in the doorway with Aelfraed a few steps behind. Everyone bowed. "I hear my son has injured himself," the king said with unmasked disinterest. He half-leaned over the prostrate prince, his lip hitching slightly. The caretaker stood in the doorway, giving orders to Lorelle, who nodded and sped away. Aelfraed gazed blankly at Rhoswen but did not move into the room. Behind him, she saw no trace of the crowd that had gathered in the Great Hall.

Gethin whimpered. Badrick rolled his eyes and stepped away from his son to glare at the Riders. Lorelle returned with a cloth and a bowl of water. Rhoswen set down her book and mug on a nearby table and relieved the waiting-woman of the items. She had no idea why she felt compelled to tend to her cousin, but she knelt at the prince's side and dipped the cloth in the lukewarm water, wringing it out into the bowl before dabbing gently at the cut. He groaned again, and his eyes fluttered open.

"Cousin?" he murmured.

"Yes," Rhoswen cooed. "It's all right now."

The king moved beside his niece and sneered down at his son. "What happened, Gethin?" he snapped. He sounded inconvenienced.

Gethin struggled to keep his eyes open, but his intermittent gaze alternated between Rhoswen and his father. "I saw you," he rasped.

Rhoswen glanced at Thane over her shoulder. He returned her gaze with an almost imperceptible shake of his head. She continued daubing the blood from Gethin's face and hair. "Yes, I'm here," she replied, trying to direct the prince's narrative to the present.

"No, I *saw* you," he repeated, more strength entering his voice. "You were in a… room. In Aelfraed's room… but *not*." He closed his eyes and turned his head back and forth a little as if he were trying to shake it clear.

Thane shrugged and pointed to the steam-less mug on the table. "We were in the kitchen, getting Rhoswen some warm milk."

King Badrick looked at his nephew, then back at his son. "He's out of sorts." He turned to the caretaker. "Why was he in your room?"

"I'm not certain, majesty. He fell before he could explain," Aelfraed replied with a shrug.

"Do you not lock your door?" the king asked.

"The dragons had gotten themselves into such a state—"

"I know about the dragons," Badrick snapped.

This seemed to surprise Aelfraed, but he composed himself swiftly. "I had rushed out at the first sign of commotion, your highness. I didn't think to bother with it," he explained. "I had only just returned to my room when the prince barged—*rushed*—in."

Rhoswen wrung out the cloth again, her mind racing. Unsure where to look, she kept her eyes on her cousin's face. The bright-red cut had stopped bleeding, and she shifted her attention to wiping the last of the blood from his hairline.

"And you two?" Badrick asked the Riders.

"Just delivering the prince, sire," Darr Beval answered as they bowed.

"Did the dragons explain themselves?" the king asked.

Aelfraed and the Riders shook their heads.

Badrick's expression grew strange.

"Rhoswen… " Gethin mumbled as his eyes fluttered open again. "I saw you… and Thane. Why… why were you in Aelfraed's room? You weren't there…. How were you there…?"

"He does not seem well," Rhoswen insisted, her eyebrows contracting with worry.

"Here." The king's eyes landed on Rhoswen's pewter mug, and he moved toward it in a single stride. As his fingers curled around it, a shadow of realization swept over his face and disappeared again. The transition was so quick that Rhoswen wasn't sure she'd even seen it. Her stomach flipped as he handed it to her. "Something to soothe your nerves," he said with a sneer.

Rhoswen sipped obligingly at the milk as the harried clacking of a servant's metal-soled shoes turned every head in the withdrawing room toward the door. Delwyn raced in past Aelfraed, excusing himself as he scurried. "Lord Thane," he said, eyes fixed on his target, "I must speak to you! I—" Finally, he glanced around, his horror growing as he took in the scene. When his gaze landed on the king, his eyes bulged, and he doubled over in a deep, apologetic bow. Rhoswen wouldn't have been surprised if he had thrown himself at her uncle's feet. "My king—forgive me, sire!" he begged of the floor.

Badrick's eyebrows scrunched together in confusion. "What is it, Delwyn? Why do you need to speak to Thane?"

Thane glanced at Rhoswen; they both knew exactly what Delwyn wanted.

"It's my fault, your majesty," Rhoswen blurted before she had formulated the rest of her excuse. She scrambled for an explanation as her uncle turned toward her. "I—uh—I spilled vine water on Thane's formal jacket the last time he wore it, and it wasn't laundered since. I asked for a waitman to help him find a fitting replacement for tonight. It would appear Delwyn has taken charge of the task."

Badrick squinted at her, but disinterest swiftly replaced his uncertainty. "I'm sure the prince has something Thane can borrow, as Gethin will no longer be attending this evening."

The king hadn't told Delwyn to stand up, so the waitman, still bowed, turned his head toward the sofa and nodded. "I will see to it, sire. Is the prince all right?"

"Does he look all right, Delwyn?" Badrick snapped.

"No—no, of course not, sire; I merely—"

"Stand up, Delwyn," the king barked. He gave Lorelle orders for his son's care and turned back to his niece, eyes narrow. "Rhoswen, no amount of *warm* milk will substitute for the rest we have kept you from. With the prince unable to attend the dinner this evening, Thane's presence will be of even greater importance. Do get her settled in before taking a few moments to ready yourself, won't you, Thane? You'll want to be in top form tonight. Delwyn—take care of my nephew before you see to me." With that, he spun around and stalked from the room, his cape furling slightly around his ankles.

"If you'll come this way," Delwyn said to Thane and Rhoswen as waitmen slipped in to move Gethin to his apartments. Delwyn led the way upstairs. As he instructed the guards posted outside Rhoswen's room, Thane ushered Rhoswen inside and closed the door behind him before the waitman could enter.

"That was close," Thane whispered.

"Close?" Rhoswen asked, eyes wide. "He knew that milk was cold, Thane. The only thing that saved me was Delwyn barging in. What was he thinking?"

"The bracelet is definitely more than just a family heirloom," Thane said, pulling it from his pocket. "If the king discovers what really happened to Gethin, I'll need all the help I can get. This is going to buy us a serious ally."

"Thane! Bribery does not make for true friends," she said with a scowl.

"It does in Aethelburh," he countered and called out to Delwyn to join them before his sister could protest further. Delwyn poked his head around the door, and Thane waved him in. "Close the door, will you please?"

Delwyn obliged and edged forward. "How can I be of service, Lord Thane?" Thane held out his palm to display the bracelet, and Delwyn's eyes widened. "You *do* have it," he breathed.

"Lorelle told you," Rhoswen suggested.

Delwyn nodded. "May I have it back please, Lord Thane?"

"You may, Delwyn," Thane said, stepping closer to the waitman, "if you can tell us why it is so important to you."

Delwyn looked as though he had been struck across the face. "That is… rather a complicated answer, Lord Thane."

"We'll do our best to understand," Thane assured him. Rhoswen had never seen her brother like this. She wasn't sure she liked it.

"I really can't explain, milord," Delwyn said. "It is a key that has been handed down for generations. To lose it is to dishonor my family."

"We can appreciate an object like that," Rhoswen said. She glared at her brother. "Can't we, Thane?"

Thane looked thoughtful. "Perhaps if you're not comfortable explaining more, Delwyn, you can make us a promise instead."

Delwyn looked equally uncertain about the deal. "What can I promise you, milord?"

"We don't have many friends in the castle. Will you be our friend, Delwyn?" Thane asked.

Delwyn's discomfort bloomed across his face. Thane was putting the waitman in a terrible position. No one worked more closely with the king, and the relationship could easily turn ugly under the right circumstances. Rhoswen's skin crawled.

"I will do my best, Lord Thane," came Delwyn's meek reply.

Thane considered the man before handing over the trinket. "Please do, Delwyn."

Rhoswen watched as Delwyn's tremendous relief supplanted his discomfort. "Delwyn," she said, "one of the links on that chain is broken. You might want to have it repaired."

"Thank you, Lady Rhoswen," Delwyn said, his appreciation genuine. "I will find something sturdier. I hope you feel better soon." He turned to Thane. "Shall we, sir?"

"Right behind you, Delwyn. I'll meet you in my room."

"Of course, sir," the waitman replied. He excused himself and closed the door behind him.

"Will you be all right?" Thane asked, turning back to Rhoswen. "What is it?"

She hesitated. "He said that key had been handed down for generations."

"And?"

"And Lorelle called hers a family heirloom. She also said she and Delwyn were cousins by marriage." She looked up at Thane. "Could two families possess the same family heirloom—and then be brought together through marriage?"

Thane considered this a moment. "Maybe it's something given to everyone who becomes a part of that family."

The suggestion felt dubious at best, but Rhoswen didn't want to give her brother any more reason to pester Delwyn for information. "Speaking of family—"

Thane nodded. "The letter from Stanburh."

"What do you think it said?"

He shrugged. "If it were something we needed to know about, our parents would have found a way to reach us."

She nodded but remained unconvinced. "You can go. I'll take care of things here. Good luck tonight."

"I'll need it," Thane replied.

When he had gone, Rhoswen changed into a nightgown, lest she should be visited before she escaped to Keaton. Badrick was clearly not interested in letting her wander, and it would be just like him to make an impromptu visit to her room to prove that he had the power to keep her in it.

She slid the wingback chair aside and slipped in through the open portal behind it. Perhaps she shouldn't wait for Thane's help to find a way to get to her parents....

Rhoswen heard a click as the door to her room unlatched. "Milady?" Lorelle called softly. "Are you awake?"

As quietly as she could, Rhoswen slipped back out into her room, pushed the chair in front of the opening with a foot, and threw herself into her bed. She was drawing the covers up over her legs when Lorelle walked in. Rhoswen tried to make her voice sound sleepy. "Somewhat. May I help you, Lorelle?"

The waiting-woman ducked her head in apology. "The prince is stirring and has requested your presence."

Rhoswen's breath hitched a little. "Lorelle, the king put sentries outside my door to ensure I rest until morning—"

"The king insists you see the prince, milady. He says you can sleep for the rest of the evening afterward, and you won't be disturbed further."

Rhoswen sat up. *This is not good.* "Will you give me a moment to dress? I am not attired to roam the halls."

"The king asked that you not tarry," Lorelle replied. Her hands fidgeted in an obvious—*and odd*—display of discomfort. Badrick clearly wanted Rhoswen to feel as vulnerable as possible in this meeting with Gethin… and Lorelle knew enough about it to feel ill-at-ease.

"Of course," Rhoswen said, "but at least permit me to relieve myself before I go."

Lorelle hesitated but was ultimately unable to deny Rhoswen this request. She excused herself to wait outside and shut the door behind her. Rhoswen lunged for her leather trousers and shimmied into them, cuffing the legs above the hem of her nightgown. At least she wouldn't *feel* as vulnerable as Badrick wanted her to, even if she still looked it.

LIV

Detroit

"Have you been hiding this place from me?" Emmelyn asked between sips of malt. The setting sun cast yellow-orange light across the tiny malt shop's parking lot.

"Yes," Jeremy replied. He had opted for a banana split shake rather than a malt. "I have obscured this place with a mirage for years, just so I could surprise you with it on our first date."

Emmelyn glanced at him sideways. *"Years?"* she repeated.

His cheeks flushed. "I've had a thing for you forever," Jeremy replied, guiding her to an empty bench near the children's play area.

"You have not," she replied in disbelief.

"I have," he insisted. "I was just young and dumb and easily distracted by other… things."

"And by 'things,' you mean girls."

He rubbed the back of his neck. "I'm an idiot."

Emmelyn put a hand on his knee. "You're not. I'm glad we did this. Really glad, actually."

"Don't sound so surprised," he joked. He leaned in and gave her a kiss on her cheek, but he didn't pull away from her when his lips left her skin.

When Emmelyn turned to look up at him through bashful eyelashes—

—she found herself outside the Exchange in the deserted road under the bright-gray light of an early spring day.

"Realm it!" she yelled into the empty road around her. "Perfect timing! You know, when I told him I'd go back to the club, I didn't mean *now!*" Her fists clenched, and she exhaled roughly as she stomped across the street and into the Exchange.

Janelle, ignorant of Emmelyn's frustrations, stamped her wrist, handed her a Transitor, and sent her away with barely a word.

Emmelyn stormed up the stairs and through the club door to the Crew's usual circle. People she had never met before sat in their seats, and her attention was caught by someone waving to her from the next circle over.

"They beat us to it," Inzay called as Emmelyn came to take a seat with the Crew. This was the circle she and her realm friends had sat in when they went to the club the first time—the circle the Luthean and the Welsamodels tended to occupy. But this was not an accidental blink into the Exchange; she had been summoned here legitimately this time. *Could I think myself back to Jere even though he's not in the club in our realm?*

Odore and Randy were present, as well. She hadn't even looked around for Denver—or counted the number of stamps she had been allotted for this visit. She couldn't stop scowling. "Can you get promoted in this realmed place?" she barked at the Crew, automatically dropping into the lingo of the Exchange. She hadn't even bothered to find her earplugs yet and began tearing through her purse.

"Uh-oh," Inzay replied with concern, "what happened?"

"I want to be a Runner," Emmelyn declared, squishing the orange foam between her fingers. "They get to plan their trips back here, right? They're not just whisked away in the middle of important life moments?"

"You do look nice." Odore looked her up and down and then gasped. "Oh! You were on a date, weren't you?"

Inzay looked mortified for her. "Oh, Emmelyn, were you out with Jeremy?"

Emmelyn nodded. "I don't even know why I'm back already. I was just here! What do I have to do to regain a little control over my life?"

The three exchanged glances.

"Sometimes new Runners make extra trips as they acclimate to their new rea—" Odore began, stopping short when Emmelyn's scowl deepened.

"Generally speakin', ya can't change ranks," Randy drawled. "That ain't how it works here." He squinted a little as he said it.

"You don't seem entirely convinced of that, Randy," Emmelyn noticed.

"Well...." Randy stole a glance at the other two. "I'm gonna go getcha a drink," he offered and hurried toward the bar.

"Explain," Emmelyn ordered and added a begrudging "*please.*"

"Randy is right," Inzay yelled. "You don't really change jobs here. It's not a matter of promotion or demotion... but... we think an exception has been made in at least one case."

Odore nodded. "Vonn."

"Vonn was a Transfer?" Emmelyn asked.

"He won't admit it," Inzay replied, "but we believe he found a way to get promoted to Runner. He knows way too much about the life of the Transfer not to have been one."

"Vonn started Running before we were recruited," Odore explained. "He helped all of us, just like he helped you."

Emmelyn remembered Bernadette's comment when Vonn walked up to their group that first time: *A new one foah ya, Vonn.* "How did he do it?" she asked.

"By sleeping with an Arbiter," Odore yelled.

Randy returned with a rocks glass in each hand. His shoulders hunched as if to brace himself against Odore's tactlessness. "We think Vonn is *datin'* an Arbiter," he said with a caustic glance at Odore.

Emmelyn accepted the whiskey from Randy. It was his drink of choice, not hers, but the sweet man probably didn't know what she drank after all those trials with Vonn, so he got her something he thought was good—and *strong*. She had to clear her throat to get past the first, stinging sip.

"He won't admit that either," Inzay said. "It's technically not allowed."

Emmelyn nodded. "Why else do you suspect this?" If Vonn had been Running for years, he'd had plenty of time to become educated in the various jobs here. There had to be more evidence.

"Vonn's access to privileged gossip is unparalleled. He must get it from a source higher up in the Exchange. And since Runners don't have prolonged communication with anyone of a rank higher than theirs in this club...." Odore trailed off suggestively.

Emmelyn nodded; she could finally fill in the blanks. "You don't know who the Arbiter is, though, do you?" she asked.

The Crew shook their heads.

"She's probably from Welsamar," Odore conjectured. "Welsamodels tend to date other Welsamodels. People from other realms aren't usually beautiful enough."

"Sorry, Emmelyn," Inzay yelled in her ear. At first, Emmelyn thought Inzay was apologizing because Emmelyn wasn't pretty enough to date Vonn (which was probably true), but she soon realized that Inzay was expressing regret for her slim chance of advancement. She patted the girl's arm appreciatively.

"Speakin' uh Welsamar and Vonn's gossip," Randy began, "last time I saw him, Vonn had more information about that fallen Rider."

"Jerold Illisan?" Odore asked. "Did Vonn happen to say why there's no picture—of him or his dragon—on his shrine?"

Randy nodded. "He thinks his dragon survived the Descent."

"I suppose that would explain half of it," Inzay replied, "but why isn't there a picture of Jerold?"

"That may have somethin' to do with his connection to the Exchange," Randy yelled back. "Vonn thinks Jerold is Emile's nephew."

"No way," Inzay gasped.

"How would he have found that out?" Emmelyn asked.

The Crew stared at her.

"Exactly," Odore yelled with an I-told-you-so expression.

Emmelyn looked down at her wrist. She was already down to a single stamp. *Thank the realm,* she thought.

She didn't have long to wait before Denver arrived to swap out Transitor messages in his usual *droll* fashion. Once he had gone, she downed the last of her whiskey and set the glass on the metal coffee table with more force than intended. She bid her cringing friends goodbye and headed down to the Atrium.

Emmelyn snaked around busy waiters and made her way directly to Emile's table. Without a word, she extended the Transitor to him. She could feel her features assembling into a mirror of Janelle's impatience and suddenly understood the receptionist all too well.

Unfazed by her coolness, Emile took the Transitor, swapped out the parchment, and handed it back to her. *A triple.* "Bad timing, Emmelyn?" he asked. He was alone today; Emmelyn was glad that Olivia wasn't there to chide her for her salty demeanor.

"Is it ever good timing?" Emmelyn spat. "You know, since Transfers don't get much say as to when they visit."

"There isn't much in this life you get a whole lot of say about," Emile replied.

Emmelyn's frostiness thawed a little. Arbiter of questionable morals or not, this man had just lost a nephew; he must be heartbroken. "I'm sorry for your loss," she said.

Emile looked surprised, and he stole a glance at the woman at the table next to him. Emmelyn followed his gaze, catching a glimpse of the woman's face as she turned hastily away. Her skin was pale, and her lips were a deep red; her rich, coppery hair fell in waves around her face and collarbone, and even at the angle she had turned to, the tips of her long eyelashes could be seen around the edge of her satiny locks.

Emile looked back to Emmelyn, his mouth a taught line of annoyance, and gave her a nod. Emmelyn nodded back and turned away from him to make her final delivery so she could get back to Jeremy. She felt for Emile, but she also felt a small surge of pleasure at causing him discomfort in front of this mystery woman—anyone who toyed with the realms for financial gain deserved as much, if not more.

After being relieved of her Transitor, Emmelyn moved from the front desk to the doors of the Exchange. She took a deep breath to steady herself. It was impossible for her to forget what had been taking place in her realm when she'd left it, but it was just as difficult to get back into the moment after time had fractured in the middle of it.

She decided to try reimagining her last few moments with Jeremy. There she was, across from an extremely good-looking friend, who had shown her a wonderful evening, and things had just started getting interesting—

—when she was whisked away to the *Exchange*. There, she learned a man she thought she respected was having an affair with a woman who could be just as devious as Emile. And now, Emmelyn was somehow supposed to drop back into this intimate situation with Jeremy, as if she hadn't just been yanked out of it to play errand girl.

She sighed. *That didn't work.*

She didn't know if she could *exchange* bitterness for excitement at their first kiss. *Maybe that's the real reason for the name of this place,* she mused. Resigned to wing it, she walked through the doors—

—and was back on the bench in front of Jeremy, less than an inch away from his face.

"Jere," she murmured as children screamed on the playground nearby, "maybe not in front of the kids, huh?" She flashed him an apologetic smile. The break in the Exchange was just too jarring for her to move forward like nothing had happened.

"Ah, right," he replied. A nearby mother glared at them in disapproval. "Let's go watch the sun set," he suggested, standing. He held out his hand to her. "I know the perfect place."

"Another place!" she echoed, intrigued. "Great idea." She stood and took his hand, giving it a gentle squeeze.

LV

Aethelburh

Rhoswen slipped into her cousin's chambers without a sound, hoping to find him asleep and unable to hold the audience her uncle demanded. The prince lay in bed, eyes closed, and Rhoswen's breath hitched hopefully. At her gasp, Gethin's head turned slowly toward her, and his eyes fluttered open to meet her gaze. Her heart sank.

Gethin beckoned her to his side and patted the bed with two feeble fingers, as if he could not muster the strength to move his whole hand. Rhoswen took a seat just out of reach of his fingertips. He looked drained, and she began to wonder just how hard her brother had hit him when her thoughts were interrupted by Gethin's heavy whisper.

"Thank you for coming to see me. My father told me you were supposed to be resting. It would seem... neither of us is in the best of health. I hope this will not... tire you too much." Gethin's words came out in awkward and halting spurts, as if he were too exhausted to complete a full sentence.... *Or he's reciting from an unfamiliar script,* Rhoswen thought. Her uncle had probably coached Gethin on what to say. *But what had Gethin told Badrick?*

"I'll be fine, my prince," Rhoswen said. "I hope the same for you. How are you feeling?"

He reached toward the cut on his brow and grimaced. "Somewhat less than myself...." A slow knock sounded outside the door, and Gethin reacted by sitting up, somehow instantly stronger and more alert. *A signal,* Rhoswen realized. Her heart began to race. "I wanted to talk to you," he continued, his lines flowing more easily now—likely because they were no longer *lines.* "You lied to my father today."

Surprised, Rhoswen fumbled for an answer, but her cousin held up a hand.

"When my father came in to check on me, I didn't deny your story, but only because I wanted to know why you invented it."

Rhoswen raised an eyebrow. "What do you mean?" she asked, forgetting to add sycophantic titles of supposed respect.

Gethin glared at her, his eyes open and his charade of weakness falling away. "I'm supposed to be lying here, pathetic and ill, feeding you some story about 'staring death in the face'"—the prince rolled his eyes—"and 'coming to a new conclusion about you—about *us*.'"

"Us?" Rhoswen repeated in horror. Now, she stopped breathing altogether.

Gethin nodded. "As a way of making you squirm. Thanks to your fussing over me in front of my father, he has come up with an idea that you and I should be... *romantically inclined* toward each other." The words stuck a bit as Gethin said them, his lip snarling in disgust.

Rhoswen had not expected this in the least. She might have been able to handle the script his father had given him, but this? This uncharacteristic honesty that flew in the face of Badrick's bidding? No, that was something she did not know how to deal with at all. "Why are you telling me this instead of following his orders?" she asked.

"I am not my father's pawn!" Gethin snapped. "And I do not want to become... *entangled* with *you*. Something tells me this idea was not his own." His expression grew unreadable as he awaited her explanation.

"Who would put such an idea into his head?" she asked.

He glared at her. "You did insinuate that I might be interested in you." He left out the part where she had insinuated his interest in Thane, too.

Rhoswen sat back in surprise. "You cannot believe *I* would suggest—"

Gethin snorted. "No, truthfully, I don't think so. And given your reaction, I no longer think you or Thane believed I might...." He glowered at her rather than finish the thought. "No, this is going too far, even for you. But you and your brother are up to something. That was quick work with the basin, and my father thinks little enough of me to believe it. But this is about more than Thane's punch. You were in Aelfraed's apartments, in an alcove that looked like a storage room, where there is normally *a wall*. Aelfraed lives in a tower; there is no space for some secret alcove in his rooms. Not to mention, you couldn't have gotten to his chambers before I did. So, how do you intend to explain that, Cousin?"

Rhoswen suddenly wanted to hit him herself, and she might have, too, if she'd thought she'd induce amnesia better than her brother had. Her greater concern, though, was not Gethin's memory but his sudden refusal to take orders from his father. That made him unpredictable. *Think, Rhoswen,* she urged herself. *Think!* "You know what people are saying, don't you?" she asked.

The question caught Gethin off guard. "About what?"

"The Heir." She paused for dramatic effect; Gethin was riveted. "They say the Heir will be emerging soon—possibly even within this group of trainees."

Gethin scoffed. "Just because you can predict the weather, Cousin, I wouldn't begin rallying the troops to your cause just yet. Most of your successes have been dumb luck."

His words rankled her, and for a moment, Rhoswen fought the urge to tell him who the dumb one was. Instead, she shook her head. "We have been researching—for lecture—"

"I know what Aelfraed has been reading," he snapped.

"—and we have been storing the books he's borrowed in his chambers…." Rhoswen assumed an air of distress, which wasn't hard, given her situation. She took a deep breath. "I didn't want to tell you this, my prince… and I certainly didn't want to tell your father…."

"What?" he asked eagerly.

She ducked her head a little. "You didn't hit your head on the basin. We left the cellar library shortly after you did and headed down to Keaton because Aelfraed said he had the book I wanted. We arrived just in time to see you get knocked out by a young dragon. The beast was being kenneled, and you didn't see his tail whipping through the air—"

"No," he interrupted, shaking his head. "No, I *saw* you…."

"You did—and the shelf of books in Aelfraed's chambers," she replied. "We gathered you up and took you into his rooms to have a look at you before the Riders arrived to take you up to the castle."

He closed his eyes in frustration. "No! I burst into Aelfraed's chambers—"

Rhoswen shook her head again. "You were slung between Thane and me, and *we* burst into his chambers."

"Thane punched me—"

"You got to your feet when we were over by the bookcase, and Thane tried to catch you as you started to lose consciousness again…. He guided you to the ground." At least that part was true.

Gethin's eyebrows crumpled together. "*Don't* try to convince me I am losing my mind or that you did me some sort of *kindness!* I *know* what happened." He took a deep breath before he continued. "*I* may be smart enough to see through your lies, but my father won't listen to me. He would, however, be interested in why you are stockpiling texts from the library."

"It may just be a rumor… " Rhoswen began with a shrug.

"What?"

This was an even bigger gamble than her previous one. If Gethin were in favor of his father's continued rule over this realm, he could try to twist her story into something resembling treason. *But he has defied his father this much….* She had to risk it. If it diverted his attention at all from the punch Thane had landed, it might be worth it. "Dragons cannot read our texts—"

"That's not a rumor," Gethin interjected. "Dragons can't read."

Rhoswen held up a finger. "Unless the Heir Rider is holding the book," she said. Her pulse quickened as she awaited his response.

Gethin pondered this for a moment. "Then why do you need so many different texts from the library?"

"Because... " she spoke slowly, searching for a decent answer, "we don't know... *which* text would do the trick. We're not sure what... the queen dragon would be able to read," she improvised.

Gethin shook his head again, as if to clear it. "What?" His eyes widened. "Then you must know who the Heir is."

Rhoswen shook her head.

"But you have your suspicions," Gethin insisted.

"Don't you?" she countered. When he didn't answer, she pressed on. "We're trying different combinations of books and trainees. And now Maven is out...."

"It was never *Maven,*" Gethin scoffed. "Next you'll tell me you considered *Aeduuin....*" When Rhoswen did not answer, his fingers fidgeted in the bedclothes. "It has to be Deowynn who reads the text?" he asked finally, his tone deflating.

She nodded, congratulating herself. She knew selecting Deowynn as the only beast to have such powers would frustrate her cousin. "You said it yourself: ordinary dragons can't read."

"Realm me," Gethin cursed. He sat up and threw back the covers, unseating Rhoswen in the process. He stood and took a firm hold of her upper arm. "Let's go."

"Where?" she asked, grimacing at his touch. She tried to tug her arm away, but he held fast.

"To hear a bedtime story," he replied and led her out of his room.

LVI

Ahndalar

Vonn rolled onto his back, and Rehlia scooted away from his side to prop herself up on a pillow. She ran her fingers through his hair, watching it separate into pieces before it feathered back into place. He smiled at her touch, his eyes still closed.

"I saw Emile's new Transfer in the Atrium today. Her name is Emmelyn. Do you know her?" Rehlia asked, adding a sultry affectation to her voice.

"Sure," he replied, eyes opening partway. "She hangs out with our group at the Exchange. Didn't you meet her before? She Transferred for Lorelle first."

She shook her head. "I got Lorelle after the merger of Arbiter groups. Emmelyn didn't come with her; they're not a set. She has always been on Emile's team."

Vonn's eyes widened. "Are mergers commonplace?"

No. Rehlia shrugged and smiled down at him. "That Emmelyn is quite the spitfire, isn't she?"

"Oh, dear. What did she say?" he asked.

She stared at him; he had to know this Emmelyn quite well to have a reaction like that. "She didn't appear happy to be in the Exchange. Her portal must have come at an inopportune moment in her realm."

"She's new," Vonn said, unable to keep the charitable defensiveness from his voice. "She's not used to the inconvenience of suddenly being portaled to the Exchange in the middle of daily life. I can't really imagine *ever* getting used to that...."

"Yes; lucky for you, you didn't have to," she replied, her fingers still working gently through his hair.

He relaxed, closing his eyes again. "She'll settle down. She's a good girl—morally grounded and driven to do the right thing. It's good to see they still make 'em like that." He grinned, his pride in this young woman unmistakable. Rehlia had only witnessed such a reaction when he spoke of one other person, and that was so many years ago, she had not expected she would ever hear that fondness in his voice again. Yet, here it was, plain and—regrettably—unabashed.

"You speak highly of her," Rehlia said, grateful that he could not see the facial expression her smooth voice hid.

"That spunk is charming," Vonn admitted. "You can't help but feel drawn to it. She really… tries to think through things." He opened his mouth, as if to say more, but closed it again instead.

Rehlia scowled. Considering she had entrusted him with the very secret that Emmelyn had *somehow* known when she expressed her condolences to Emile that afternoon, Rehlia didn't appreciate his reticence. "That spunk is dangerous," she argued, her voice growing sterner, "and capable of fostering less-than-ideal qualities in you, it would seem."

Vonn's eyes snapped open. His brow furrowed as he looked up at her.

Rehlia sighed. He was still beautiful—almost innocent-looking. Although, she knew better. That was the problem with Welsamarian men; they were disarming, and biology had a way of inhibiting rational thought in the presence of such a quality. "She extended her sympathies to Emile *for the loss of his nephew.*"

At that, Vonn sat up. He rubbed a hand over the back of his neck. "I'm sorry, Rehlia. That's obviously my fault."

"Obviously," she snapped. "Perhaps, in the future, you wouldn't mind letting me know if we're going to allow another person into our private conversations. Or can I be just as certain that your whole *group* is aware of this tender gossip?" Vonn ducked his head in apology but said nothing. She exhaled her frustration, watching his face. "So, she's a bit impetuous but generally well-meaning. You've told her *my* secrets. What are *hers*?"

It aggrieved Rehlia to see the anguish stealing across Vonn's face. She considered that it could be a response to having wronged her, but he was not that protective of her. Of the two of them, Rehlia held the position of greater power; if anyone could provide protection, it was she. No, his allegiances were shifting. He liked Emmelyn. And if Rehlia's entire existence weren't about protecting realms, she might have afforded herself the luxury of being jealous, hurt, or, at least, disappointed by his transfer of affection—*no pun intended*. Frankly, she didn't have the time.

Vonn sighed. "Emmelyn popped into the Exchange the other day." Rehlia stared at him. "She didn't show up outside; she didn't stop by Janelle in the lobby; she just *appeared* in her chair in the club, a beer to her lips and a look of surprise on her face." The corner of his mouth tugged upward at the memory, his gaze unfocused. When Rehlia didn't reply, he cleared his throat. "Have you ever heard of such a thing?"

Never, Rehlia thought, *because what you're describing is not possible.* She shrugged again. "Depends. How did she get back out?" She'd lied to him before but never by choice. All the other Exchange secrets she had kept from him were *beyond* confidential and couldn't be entrusted to a soul outside her clearance, but *this one*.... She didn't know what this one was.

Vonn shook his head. "The same way she came in—whatever that was. I don't know what she had to think about—"

"She managed this with a mere *thought*?"

Vonn nodded. "We think so."

"We?"

"There were a few of us, sitting together in the Exchange."

"Hopefully, this *few* is more discreet than you are."

Vonn said nothing, his expression remorseful.

Rehlia contemplated this for a moment. *How do I make this less tantalizing gossip?* "It's rare," she said, her tone casual, "but not unheard of. It's not something she should flaunt, but I wouldn't be too worried about it if I were her."

"Well, that's a relief," Vonn replied. He slid out of bed and got dressed.

And it clearly *was* a relief to him. Rehlia felt a tinge of discontent creep into her consciousness, but she pushed it away. She hadn't entered into this arrangement with Vonn blindly; it had been complicated from the start. But she hadn't expected *a Transfer* to come between them.... "Going so soon?" she asked, although she was suddenly eager to be alone.

He nodded. "I have to get to the Exchange." He leaned across the bed to give her a kiss. "See you soon," he said and headed out the door.

"Naturally," she muttered to the empty room.

LVII

Keaton

Gethin still had a firm grasp on Rhoswen's arm when he grabbed the handle to Aelfraed's door. He pushed inward but was surprised to find that, unlike earlier, Aelfraed's door was *not* unlocked. His full weight slammed against the door, crumpling his wrist between him and the wood. He stepped back, cradling his arm and then shaking out his hand, cursing. *Well, now you won't need to knock,* Rhoswen mused, biting her lip to hide a smile.

The muffled sound of harried footsteps could be heard just beyond the caretaker's door, which opened with fierce speed. "What's going on here?" Aelfraed demanded. His eyes focused on Gethin, and he added, "my prince."

Gethin was more furious now than when they'd left his room. "We are going to finish what you started. Grab the books you've been hoarding and meet us at the queen dragon's stall."

Aelfraed's confusion was unmistakable, and Rhoswen feared he'd ask very telling questions. "Allow me to help you gather the books, Aelfraed," Rhoswen offered quickly. She turned to Gethin and added, "There are too many for him to carry alone."

Rhoswen watched as fear crept into her cousin's eyes. "Well I can't go to her alone," Gethin said. "That's why I have you. We'll each take a handful. How many could there be?"

Realm it. "Of course, my prince." Rhoswen looked around for a stack of books and found one on a nearby table. She needed to get Gethin out the door so she could explain this to Aelfraed. "This stack is ready, my prince. We'll grab the rest." She glanced over at Aelfraed, who had rendered his expression blank. She inwardly praised him.

Gethin approached the stack with distaste. "How many books are there? We'll be here all night if we each bring this many," he protested.

"We're bringing what we have. Surely we'll find the right one before we get through all of them," Rhoswen said, adding a final book to the stack in her cousin's arms.

Gethin craned his neck to see around the pile. He grumbled about relieving himself of its weight as he headed out the door. "Hurry up," he barked.

After instructing Aelfraed to gather as many books as he could, Rhoswen explained her plan. The caretaker listened without interruption; he only smirked at the part about Gethin and Deowynn being in the same stall.

Rhoswen adjusted the stack of books in her arms and flashed the man a pleading look. "Aelfraed, I'm sorry to have gotten you into another mess. I didn't mean—"

Aelfraed held up a hand, balancing his own stack in just one arm. "You did right, and I am happy to help. Besides, I have gotten myself out of worse scrapes than this one," he said with a wink.

Gethin stood outside Deowynn's stall, foot tapping as he flipped through one of the books from the stack now at his feet. "These are just histories and other unimportant texts. Shouldn't we be looking for something less ordinary?" he asked as they approached.

"We don't know what we're looking for, my prince," Aelfraed said honestly. "Perhaps Deowynn will guide us on the matter, now that you're here."

Gethin began to grumble something about Deowynn but stopped, seeming to think better of it, given their proximity to her stall.

Rhoswen set down her stack of books, grabbed one from the top, and held it out to her cousin. "Do you wish to request the audience?" she asked.

His eyes fixed on the outstretched book, but he didn't take it from her. "You seem to have a good rapport with her. Why don't you do it?"

She nodded and moved to the stall door. With a backward glance at the other two, she held a finger to her lips for quiet, knocked, and edged her way inside.

Deowynn was pretending to be asleep again. It occurred to Rhoswen that she could tell the difference now. The queen dragon chuckled at the thought and opened her gold eyes.

Rhoswen bent at the middle in a low bow. *I'm sorry to bother you again, your majesty,* she nexed.

Deowynn's reply seemed more amused than irritated. *You have good reason?*

Rhoswen nexed the story she had concocted for her cousin.

Deowynn raised her snout and expelled a forceful burst of air. The impatient noise caught Rhoswen off guard. She heard Gethin gasp outside the stall.

We could be here all night, Deowynn nexed in annoyance. *Obviously, the prince is not bright enough to recognize stall muck when he hears it. I must expedite this matter. Give me that book and get ready to run.*

Run? Rhoswen held out the leather-bound book to the dragon, who grasped it between her teeth and, in one swift motion, hurled it over the stall door and bellowed into the air.

Rhoswen took this as her cue and fled from the stall. Gethin was already sprinting through the Keaton arena, past the confused onlookers heading to the dining hall, and up toward the castle. The prince never looked back.

Aelfraed tried to hustle Rhoswen away from the stall, but she pulled herself free and signaled to him to follow her inside. *Thank you, your highness,* she nexed, trying to stifle her laughter.

Did he run fast? Deowynn asked mischievously.

Rhoswen nodded and translated for Aelfraed. He laughed and winked at the queen dragon.

He may come back, Rhoswen nexed.

Doubtful. If he thinks I've lost patience for you, *he won't dare visit on his own.* Rhoswen sensed the queen dragon's sudden wistfulness. *He could have been a good boy, if….* She stopped as if she hadn't meant to share the thought. She composed herself and locked eyes with Rhoswen. *None of this is as it seems.*

Majesty?

You'll understand in time.

Rhoswen nodded. *Forgive me, your majesty, if I am too forward in asking, but Aelfraed lectured on the Realm Portal today, and he said that the queen dragon safeguards the object until Movement…. Do you have it?*

Deowynn's toes fidgeted beneath her. *I do not.*

A small gasp escaped Rhoswen's throat before she could stop herself. It was the queen dragon's responsibility to guard it. If she didn't have it….

I was bereft of it after… my Rider's passing. If Deowynn had considered saying more, she thought better of it.

Waves of pain radiated from the queen dragon, rendering Rhoswen mute, despite her many questions. None of them seemed appropriate now. At a loss for how to respond, Rhoswen apologized. She thanked Deowynn once more and excused herself and Aelfraed from the audience. As they backed out of the stall, bent low in their requisite bows, the queen dragon nexed one final instruction to her:

Rhoswen, find it.

LVIII

Aethelburh

Gethin was panting by the time he neared the great castle doors. He paused some distance away, desperate to regain his composure before walking inside. His sudden appearance downstairs—when he was supposed to be resting upstairs—would garner enough attention without his conspicuous, breathless gasping. And he had no desire to recall for anyone his narrow escape from death.

Gethin had known for years that his chances of being the Heir were slim, but he couldn't avoid testing his cousin's rumor—if only for the opportunity to prove his father wrong. At least now he knew for sure that Rhoswen and Aelfraed were engaging in acts traitorous to the king. He might not be the Heir, but he had the proof his father had demanded of him.

He had also learned that Rhoswen's first pleasant visit with Deowynn had been a fluke. *Realm her!* Such was his usual response to thoughts of the crotchety queen dragon. *It's like she is realm-bent on keeping me here. She probably instructed the other dragons not to tether with me! As if my disinheritance weren't enough of a blow….*

As his condemnation shifted to his father, Gethin suddenly remembered that Badrick planned to send Thane to the party alone tonight, and Gethin would not be able to watch his half-wit, meddlesome cousin make a fool of himself in front of their esteemed guests—*one* of them in particular….

The prince snuck inside and crept toward the nearest spiral staircase when he was surprised by the sight of his father. The king stood on the second stair up, black cape wrapped around his body like a shadow in the darkness. Gethin hoped the dim light had hidden his startled, backwards jump.

"What are you doing?" the king growled.

Gethin cursed, his breathing ragged and his heart struggling to slow once again. "Heading upstairs—if you'll let me," he snapped.

"And why were you down here in the first place? You had a task—"

"Which I completed."

"And you are now doing *what* exactly?" Badrick snarled.

Gethin had not yet devised a story to tell his father, nor was he certain how much he wanted to share. If the king found it prudent to keep secrets, then perhaps he should take similar care. "Getting something for this cut," he improvised. "It pained me."

Badrick was less than sympathetic. "From where, the forest? You were given a draught earlier."

"I thought Aelfraed might have something stronger."

"Aelfraed cares for *dragons*, not pathetic little princes."

"He owes me," Gethin insisted, utilizing the lie. "It was his fault this happened to me, and it still hurts."

A derisive snort leapt from the back of the king's throat. "I think not. You have until morning to get your story straight." Gethin tried to interject, but his father pressed on. "At that time, you will also tell me how things went with Rhoswen—if you really did complete your task, as you claim. As she is not in her room, and you are not in yours, I suspect the real tale of what transpired is much more interesting than the worthless drivel you just tried to sell me." He eyed his son. "Or if not, do at least try to make the *telling* of your story more entertaining tomorrow. I will attempt to bear my anticipation until then." With that, the king slithered down the steps and into the Great Hall, running his fingertip over the marble of a nearby pillar and inspecting for dust as he went.

Gethin sneered after him. Then, he rushed up the staircase, two steps at a time, toward the only rooms in his father's castle where he felt safe.

Rhoswen crept back through the castle to her chambers, careful to remain unseen as she slipped past the frantic servants preparing the Great Hall for visitors. Gethin had essentially bought her the freedom she needed by taking her from her room, but there was still ample opportunity for her uncle to check up on her before the party. Worse yet, the portal was still open in her chambers. The thought of it gave her gooseflesh.

The sentries did not acknowledge her as she slipped past them and closed the door behind her. For any chance of regaining her freedom to move about the castle, she would need to be in her room if her uncle looked in on her. Still, after everything that had happened, she had one more important errand to run before she could sequester herself—even if it meant risking an empty bedroom.

She stared at the wingback chair, worrying at her lower lip with her teeth. Now that she had told Thane about the portal, she felt more comfortable exploring it with him than without him. She wondered how his own party preparation was coming. Was he lying on his bed, bored and waiting for the festivities to begin, or was a waitman scurrying around, outfitting him in a suit for the evening? She smiled, grateful to avoid all that fussing.

She slid the wingback chair out of the way, slipped into the maps room, and scooted the chair back in place behind her. As she rearranged the maps and trinkets, she imagined her parents' faces when she'd walk through the wall of their family kitchen. Her chest constricted. She missed her mother's smile and her father's warmth as if she hadn't seen them in years. She surveyed her work and took a deep, steadying breath. *Let's try something new,* she thought and placed her compass on the maps.

The wall before her shimmered once more, revealing a split picture: beside the chair-obscured opening to her room now appeared the kitchen of her family home—and her parents, who looked wide-eyed at the image of their daughter in what was formerly a solid, stone wall.

"Mother? Father?" Rhoswen asked, edging toward them through the portal.

Magge stood at the wash basin, her sleeves rolled up and a wet, half-scrubbed potato in her hand. Her knuckles whitened around the spud. "Rhoswen? Is that you? What's happening? Allistair!"

"What in the realm…?" Allistair breathed. He was setting the table, and his hand automatically shifted a knife into a defensive position. As he registered his daughter's presence, he dropped the utensil and smiled. "Rhoswen?"

"It's me," Rhoswen confirmed. She could smell the dark meat that would accompany her mother's herbed potatoes roasting over the fire. She missed eating such dishes. "We found a portal system in the castle. I need to talk to you."

"You did it," Allistair breathed. "Magge? Are you seeing this?"

"A portal system?" Magge repeated in bewilderment. "Allistair, what do you mean 'she did it?'"

"She activated the compass—didn't you?" Allistair asked, turning to his daughter. "So, you know? You know what you are?"

Rhoswen's eyes widened, her comfort at being home replaced by the sudden coolness of revelation. "*You* knew?"

Allistair nodded. "Your grandfather told me what the compass could do. I never expected that someday I would give it to you."

"I don't understand—" Rhoswen began.

Magge dropped the potato and swept up her daughter in an embrace. "Of course you don't," she cooed. She looked to her husband, and her voice grew sterner. "Because *you* have a lot of explaining to do, if you understand what in the realm is going on here, and *I* don't."

Allistair ushered everyone to their seats around the table. "My father gave me that compass after Badrick won Orla," he explained. "He said it was a tool of the Heir Rider and would need to be delivered to the Heir when he or she came to light. I had no idea it was you, Rose, until you started nexing with our dragons...."

"You knew I was nexing with them?" Rhoswen asked, a hundred emotions flooding through her.

"It was hard to miss, honey," Magge said. "Plus, they told us."

"You *both* knew? But you said nothing," Rhoswen said. "You never told me what I was doing was... extraordinary." She screwed up her face in consternation. "You knew I was the—"

"Heir," Allistair and Magge said together.

"How could you not tell me?" Rhoswen asked, hurt finally penetrating her shock.

"Apparently, much went unsaid." Magge shot a perturbed glance at her husband.

Allistair ducked his head. "Your grandfather told us not to tell anyone. To tell you that you were special could preclude you from developing the very traits you would need as the Heir. You had to remain humble, compassionate, and kind—like Deowynn.... Like Orla," he added, his tone strange. Magge flashed him an unreadable look.

Rhoswen doubted those would have been the first words she'd use to describe the queen dragon, but she didn't argue.

"The same went for the compass," he continued. "Your grandfather said telling you what it does could change who you were—who you would become."

"What if I had never learned how to use it?" Rhoswen asked.

"The dragons would not have let that happen," Allistair assured her.

The kitchen fell silent, and she remembered to listen for movement in her chambers. She was on borrowed time. "Let's discuss all of that later," she choked out. Delaying this conversation felt like holding her breath, but she had no choice. "I don't have long. I'm already in enough danger as it is." Magge's expression pinched with worry.

"Indeed, you are," Allistair agreed. If he were at all concerned, he didn't show it. "How can we help?"

Rhoswen summarized all the happenings of the day, ending with Badrick's romantic scheme for her and Gethin.

"He can't do that!" Magge blurted. Allistair shot her a stifling glance, and she composed herself. "What I mean is, you can't marry your cousin. But Badrick is the king. He could order the marriage against our wishes." Magge faltered at her daughter's look of terrified disgust. "Not that we would ever let that happen," she insisted. "We would... find a way to stop it."

Allistair shook his head. "He's toying with you. My brother doesn't want my child any more closely related to his ruling than she already is as his niece and guest. Don't fixate on that. What's more important right now is mastering this portal, because it may one day be your only means of escape. Who knows you can do this?"

When Rhoswen explained her plans to meet with the Riders and Aelfraed that evening, her father's expression hardened. "No," he growled.

Magge looked at him, brows furrowed. "Allistair—"

"*Not Beval.* He probably knows too much already. And if he and this Darr Thorndon are Riding partners, you should probably steer clear of him, too. What is Aelfraed doing, getting mixed up with Beval? I didn't even think he still taught...."

"Still taught...?" Rhoswen echoed him in confusion.

"Maybe Aelfraed is trying to protect her," Magge suggested.

Allistair looked sternly at his daughter. "Don't trust *anyone* with these secrets. They'll say they are trying to train everyone to protect you, but I don't believe it. I do, however, know that Beval cannot be trusted, no matter what he tells you. Stay away from him."

Rhoswen was struck dumb by his words. *Darr Beval, untrustworthy?* She felt like her father had driven a pike through her heart.

When Allistair fell silent, Magge turned to her daughter. "Honey, did you get our message about the new Rider in Dallin?"

Rhoswen was not ready to abandon this discussion either, but it was evident her father would not elaborate on it. She had to clear her throat to speak. "Denver? Yeah, I was going to ask the Riders tonight, but—"

"Find someone else to ask, Rose," Allistair warned.

"What do you suspect?" Rhoswen asked, unable to stop herself. She had to know what made her father mistrust Darr Beval.

"We'll know when you get an answer—from a *reliable* source," her father replied, clearly referring to his suspicions about Denver instead of Darr Beval.

Realm it. "Is that why you sent a message to Uncle Badrick?" Rhoswen asked, growing annoyed with her father's reticence. "Is *he* trustworthy enough to share your secrets with?"

Allistair's eyebrows knitted, and his mouth opened to reply, but Magge cut him off. "That letter was about a strange Descent here. It was our duty to report it to the king."

Rhoswen's eyes darted to her father's arm where a thick gray scar had marred his flesh since before her birth. "Are you both all right?"

Magge nodded, and Allistair grumbled something under his breath, his expression dark. Aware that she would receive no further answer to her inquiries, Rhoswen stood and hugged her parents goodbye.

"Rose," her father called after her as she stepped through the portal, "whatever you do, don't lose your compass." It was the same warning he'd given her for years, but this time, something about it sent a chill up her spine.

As she closed the portal behind her, Rhoswen felt the sting of homesickness mingle with the daunting prospect of her need for independence. For the first time in her life, she experienced relief at being separated from her parents. Their secrecy had tarnished her blind faith in their wisdom, but the possibility of their diminishing guidance made her knees buckle.

She couldn't help but question their mistrust of her alliance with Darr Beval. It shook her to think she could have so misjudged the Rider.... Worse, she wasn't entirely certain that she had. Although she had never before doubted her parents' judgment, she couldn't believe Darr Beval to be anything other than an honest, well-intentioned man. Warmth spread through her chest at the thought of him, but she was jarred back to reality by a knock on her door. Her fingers tightened around the newest stone-key she had pulled from the Stanburh portal on her way back through. She slid the wingback chair in front of the opening to the maps room and threw herself into a seated position on the edge of the bed as Lorelle came in.

"You are still up, milady," the waiting-woman said in surprise.

"I just left Gethin a bit ago," Rhoswen replied, adjusting her grip around the stone-key to keep it out of sight.

"Was your conversation so upsetting that you cannot sleep?" Lorelle asked.

Now Rhoswen was almost certain of her earlier sense that the waiting-woman knew exactly why the prince had called Rhoswen to his chambers. Magge's warning not to trust her own servants echoed in her head. Rhoswen faked a yawn. "On the contrary, I think I am finally ready to rest."

Lorelle smiled and nodded, moving forward to help Rhoswen under the covers. Fearing the waiting-woman would notice she still had her leathers on, Rhoswen lifted the covers up high to obscure her legs as she swung them underneath them and pulled the bedding down fast.

"Can I bring you anything?" Lorelle asked, moving toward the window to close it.

"Please leave the window open," Rhoswen requested. "I like the breeze."

Lorelle inclined her head. "Of course, milady. Pleasant dreams," she said and left the room without another word.

Rhoswen listened for the waiting-woman's footsteps to fade away before jumping back out of bed. It was almost time for the meeting in Keaton. She wished she could ask Thane whether she should even attend.

Regardless, she hated the idea of leaving the portal open to her room or any part of the castle, even if she would be nearby on the other side. If

Badrick wanted her confined to her quarters and she weren't there when he looked in, he might search the castle for her. She simply couldn't risk him discovering the portal system *anywhere*. If she were going to Keaton, she would have to go down on foot.

And she *had* to go to Keaton.

She just had to. She had to *know*.

She exchanged her nightgown for the rest of her leathers and shoved the newest key into her pocket. Back in the maps room, she closed off the portal to her chambers and put all the maps and paraphernalia back where they belonged. The gap in the shelving was still open to the overflow library. She slipped through it, closed the wall behind her with a *click*, and padded down the hall.

A peek into the cellar foyer proved it was devoid of servants. She had only to figure out how to get past the partygoers, so she could escape through the front door.

As she crept toward the staircase, the clacking of metal-soled shoes echoed against the stone floor, and she ran back behind the door to the library. A servant appeared out of the darkness near the larder door. Rhoswen had never noticed an entrance there before. Once the waitman had disappeared into the larder, she stole across the foyer and into the dark, hidden hallway.

Only the occasional wall sconce illuminated the passage, and she hurried along its length, her calves tensing against its uphill slant. She scanned for places to hide in case someone appeared, but there were no nooks or doors to aid her. Finally, the hall ended at a short spiral staircase. Hearing no tell-tale clacking of servants' shoes, she crept upward.

At the top of the stairs was a long walk-in closet filled with brooms, rags, and a few large bags of flour and sugar, which one would not want to lug up and down the staircase regularly. A few poorly hidden bottles of wine peeked from behind the sacks. She hoped her uncle wasn't watching the staff as closely as he was watching her.

No door closed off the arched entrance to the closet. Rhoswen could hear the clanking of spoons in pots and authoritative voices barking orders. She inhaled the smell of meat as it wafted toward her on a current of warm air. *I am beside the kitchen.* The breakfast room was just around the corner, but it opened onto the Great Hall, as did the stairs she had originally planned to take from the cellar foyer. She risked being seen any way she went.

Cursing, she peeked around the archway in time for a strong draught to catch her hair. She jerked back out of sight as a waitman passed nearby on his way into the kitchen. The breeze that accompanied him smelled of grass and wildflowers. He had come from outside. She peered around the archway again. Seeing no one near enough to stop her, she darted out in the direction of the cool air. A narrowing crack in a doorway she had known nothing about revealed the darkening sky outside. She lunged for the door and slipped out into the night without a backward glance.

She broke into a sprint, but as she rounded the castle toward Keaton, she was forced to stop short. Round-topped rectangles of light spilled from the thousand-candle chandelier onto the grass through the tall, arched windows of the Great Hall. She gave them a wide berth, disappearing into the darkness beyond their borders. Finally, she descended the hill toward the drakiary, her feet flying through the long grass that whipped at her riding boots. She ran—away from the threatening advances of her uncle and cousin, away from a gathering of sycophantic aristocrats, away from the protection of her brother—and toward an ill-advised meeting with a group of D'Erenelleans her parents had told her she could not trust.

Realm it.

"Has she returned?" Badrick growled at the guards outside Rhoswen's door.

"Not long ago, your majesty," one guard replied. "Her waiting-woman just left her for the night."

"Lorelle, yes?" Badrick verified.

The guard couldn't hide his surprise at the king's knowledge of a servant's name. "Y-yes, your majesty."

"Find Lorelle," Badrick ordered, "and tell her that is not the last time she'll look in on Rhoswen before the night is through. I want to make certain Lady Stanburh's every possible need is tended to. Is that clear?"

The guard nodded once. "Yes, your majesty," he replied in bewilderment. Badrick stared at the pair until they both took off down the hall to find Lorelle.

Alone, the king knocked on Rhoswen's door. The absence of a reply enticed him to peek inside. Met with the breeze from an open window, he knew instinctively that the room was empty, but he moved farther inside and ran his palm along the abandoned bed to confirm it. He crossed to the window.

Torchlight outlined the nearest doorway into the arena, but the night obscured the gray outlines of the drakiary and everything around it. Whoever had flown to Rhoswen's window to retrieve her from the castle had moved quickly. He smirked at her poorly masked deception and closed the window, latching it, so it could not be used for reentry. *See you soon, Niece,* he mused.

LIX

Keaton

Rhoswen knocked on the door to Darr Beval's quarters before she could think better of it. Her head swam with thoughts of her parents' deceptions, her father's accusations, and the suspicious new Rider who had appeared in service near Stanburh—seemingly out of nowhere—at the time of an unusual Descent. She felt like she only knew half of every story; nothing made sense anymore.

Darr Beval let her in, and she took a seat across from Darr Thorndon and Aelfraed. They stared at one another, uncertain of where to begin.

"So," Darr Thorndon said, "after an inexplicably panicky outburst from the dragons, we lugged an unconscious royal through the halls of his castle and are now meeting up in secret to discuss how best to protect the Heir to our realm. Who would like to start the conversation?"

Everyone turned to look at Rhoswen. Apparently, *she* would be the one to start. Heat radiated up from her gut like a cauldron over fire. The group already knew she was the Heir, and now Aelfraed was also aware of the portal system—the last secret she held from the very Riders her father insisted she could not trust. Although she didn't expect her father was lying to her, he wasn't explaining himself either, and she resented how much of her life had been shaped by similar omissions.

How could these men, who have worked so hard to protect me, not be my allies? she asked herself, eyeing the open faces around her. She should have tried to speak to Thane before coming to Keaton. *Oh, I hate this,* she thought.

LX

Aethelburh

Rhoswen would hate this, Thane mused. Guests milled about the Great Hall with goblets poised in their fingers. Thane stood at the edge of the hall in his long-tailed black suit with white lapels and over-starched collar, cuffs, and vest. It was ridiculous that Gethin had been allowed to skip the event and leave Thane to play the semi-royal lackey in his stead.

A familiar woman approached, wearing a gown of iridescent fabric that shifted between light green and pale blue with each step. The dress splayed at her ankles and tightened around her knees, hugging her curves as it made its way up to her shoulders. Thane followed the lines of the gown to her blue-green eyes. Her features were somehow both delicate and strong, and her golden hair flowed in large, loose waves around her face and neck. Thane could only guess at her age; she held herself with a poise that denoted greater maturity than her unblemished skin. A group of young men crowded around her. Thane had not noticed this posse the last time he had met her, but he could understand why she attracted such a following: she was breathtaking.

Met might have been too strong a word to describe their previous encounter. This fetching woman had sat, unintroduced, beside his sister at the dinner party on their first night in Aethelburh. As she approached, she looked up at Thane through her long, dark eyelashes.

"You must be Gethin's cousin, Thane of Stanburh—am I correct?" Her voice was unexpectedly deep, but it was also clear and smooth, and it added to her allure. He reached to take her hand, her eyes traveling from his face down to his purple knuckles. "That is quite the bruise for someone of the royal family, even if you are technically a household removed, Lord Thane."

"Just Thane." He chastised himself for his forgetfulness. He had already modified several greetings to minimize the use of his right hand and had managed to divert attention from his knuckles with a wide smile and whatever compliments he could muster on short notice. This woman, however, had beguiled him utterly.

"Don't royals usually get someone else to do their dirty work?" she teased.

"You said it yourself: I am a household removed," Thane replied.

The woman laughed, and a few of the young men around her tittered. They were clearly less than enthusiastic with her newfound interest but eager to maintain her favor for when she undoubtedly tired of this new distraction.

"You are quite the topic of conversation," she continued. "What makes you so special, besides your lineage?"

The question caught Thane off guard. "Wouldn't you like to know?" he heard himself reply, much to his immediate horror. He cursed his reversion to juvenile wit. "Forgive me, I didn't catch your name," he said.

The woman affected a look of mock indignation. "News of my arrival did not precede me? Bring me the trumpeter!" she demanded with a theatrical flourish of her hand. Her admirers fluttered around her. "I am Ethelinda of Alston," she said. "A shame your cousin couldn't have introduced us at the dinner party in Aethelburh. Where is he, anyway?"

"The prince has taken ill.... Ethelinda—that could be a dragon's name," Thane blurted, recognizing the old language version of "noble snake" before considering whether a lady would appreciate being told she shared the name of a reptile.

Ethelinda laughed. "Right you are. I think my parents wanted a Rider more than a politically ambitious daughter. Sadly, they were disappointed once again." She said it so cavalierly that Thane couldn't decide whether she wanted him to respond with pity or laughter. Thankfully, however, his manners finally caught up with him, and he thought up an innocuous response. "Did you train, Lady Alston?"

"Ethelinda, please." She nodded. "For a couple years, but I never tethered. I wasn't a very accomplished trainee, and I didn't work well with many of the dragons. There was one I thought I might tether to, but the connection must not have been as strong as I'd imagined."

The line sounded well practiced, and again, something in Thane's mind told him to sidestep the subject. "You must have developed good relationships with the Riders in that time, though?" None of whom were present, unlike their last formal dinner party.

Ethelinda nodded. "Oh, yes. One masterful trainer, in particular: Darr Beval. And handsome, even all these years later!" She giggled, and the men around her begrudgingly followed suit. Their number had begun to diminish as they tired of her prolonged conversation with Thane and wandered off, but a few dedicated members seemed moored to her side, glaring at Thane over her shoulder as if he somehow impeded their sole function of fawning over her.

"All these years?" he repeated. "He's not that old...."

A pouty little crease appeared between Ethelinda's brows. Thane's heart skipped a beat. For a moment, he considered joining her flock.

"Oh! Of course, you little thing. I almost forgot how new you are to this training business. You must be referring to his son, Darr Beval *Junior*. I was trained by Darr Beval—Senior, if you will. Just a stunning family all the way around," she mused.

"Darr Beval's father was a trainer?"

Ethelinda eyed Thane in a way that made him feel younger than his nineteen years. Her countenance darkened, but her voice remained light. "Indeed. One of the greatest! He retired from training not quite a decade ago, and his son took his place in Keaton when he left. Have you worked with him—Junior?"

Thane nodded. "Quite—" *a bit,* he stopped himself from saying. He remembered how little he knew of this woman and how equally little he could trust most of the guests in this room. Last he had seen her, she had been speaking in hushed tones with Gethin. Noble or not, her name still meant *snake....* "—a Rider, from what I've heard."

Ethelinda nodded and glanced around the room, likely for her next target. "How long will you be staying with your uncle? Until you tether?"

And my sister Moves us into another Realm.... "That is the plan. It'll be good to get back home." *Like, yesterday,* he thought.

"You're not considering freedom of transfer?"

He shook his head. "My parents are getting older. Someone has to inherit their responsibility of protection in Stanburh." It had always been Thane's plan and birthright. It still stung that he would never realize that destiny.

"Well, Thane of Stanburh, may you Ride well and be a better Rider than your trainer's father."

That recaptured Thane's attention. He and Rhoswen were putting a lot of trust into Darr Beval, and if the Rider did not hail from good stock, Thane felt he should know about it. He grabbed Ethelinda's elbow. The look she cast on his gentle grasp was hard to read—it lingered somewhere between desire and disgust. Her posse, however, grew unmistakably incensed. He dropped his hand and begged her pardon. "Please, before you go, tell me what you meant by that."

"The war," Ethelinda whispered, watching him for signs of recognition. When none came, her eyes widened and eyebrows arched. "You don't know," she said, her tone revelatory. "That explains it.... Well, perhaps I shouldn't be the one to tell you."

War? Surely Thane would have heard about a war if it involved his father's generation. He stepped closer to her and was enveloped by the scent of her floral perfume. The hair on his arms prickled to attention, but he forced himself to ignore the sensation. "Please," he said in a low, confidential tone, "tell me."

Ethelinda stared at him, her eyes shifting back and forth between his. It felt as though she could see *through* him. He suppressed a shiver. "Not here," she whispered. "Come see me at Alston. We can speak freely there." And with that, she spun on her heel and walked away, her followers filling in around her like a thick cloud of smoke.

Thane's head swam, and a knot formed in his throat. He tried to clear it with a muffled cough, but as he reached to cover his mouth, his purple knuckles flashed before his eyes, and he tucked his fist back behind the gentle grasp of his left hand. He was so distracted that he jumped when a man with a serving tray of small tarts sidled up beside him. "Delwyn," Thane exhaled.

"Inspect the tray as if you are considering taking something, milord," Delwyn whispered, his expression insistent.

Thane flashed him a confused look but did as he was told.

"In the spirit of *friendship*," the waitman continued, "you should be careful, milord. She is dangerous."

"Ethelinda?" Thane asked, contemplating the contents of the platter. He hadn't eaten for half the day, and everything—even that which he could not readily identify—looked enticing.

Delwyn hushed him. "She is the Lady of Alston, made acting head of the territory when her father retired. She may seem innocent enough, milord, but don't be fooled. She is cunning."

Nothing about that woman strikes me as innocent, Thane thought. "Thank you, Delwyn," he replied at normal volume, selecting a few morsels from the tray. "I appreciate your recommendation."

Delwyn inclined his head and turned away to serve the rest of the party. Thane buzzed with sudden restlessness. He felt like running from the Great Hall and down the valley to the drakiary. Every passing moment made Aethelburh and its inhabitants seem less and less welcoming. And his sister was alone in Keaton, now with at least one Rider of questionable lineage, who had participated in a war he knew nothing about....

A plump woman within ten years of Magge's age with a bright-red mane and more freckles than not eyed him from a few groups away. Seeing that he was no longer occupied, she bounced up to him, curls bobbing. It was the woman in pink from the first dinner party. As she came within curtsying distance, Thane glanced over the top of her head, searching for a means of escape. Servants everywhere still circulated with trays of appetizers. He forced his grimace into a smile. It was early, and there was no end in sight.

"You shouldn't have done that," Lorelle whispered to Delwyn as she refilled their trays in the kitchen.

"I know," he replied. "But he returned my bracelet to me. I… felt I owed him."

She surveyed his face and grinned. "He bribed you with it!"

"Don't sound so proud of him," he replied. "It's not behavior worth praising."

"He's learning how this place works."

"Whose side are you on? I would have expected you to agree with my warning to him."

"Was that a tweak?" she countered. "Was that warning mandated?" He shook his head. "We can't choose sides," she reminded him. "And our beliefs have nothing to do with the way we *legitimately* tweak this realm." She considered saying more but had other pressing questions. "Any word on the dragons' strange behavior?" Again, he shook his head. "When do you Run?"

"In a few days. You?"

"Tonight, after the party. I… actually did have to tweak something," she added, unable to hide her distaste. "So pay attention because I won't be here to watch what happens in the wake of your meddling, and you will have to explain yourself if something comes of it."

Delwyn swallowed. "Perhaps I'll luck out."

"In this realm?" Lorelle snorted and slid a full tray of appetizers toward him. "Doubtful."

LXI

Keaton

Rhoswen couldn't stall any longer.

Somehow, Aelfraed interpreted her reticence as something more than feeling overwhelmed. "Rhoswen, step outside with me for a second. You gentlemen will excuse us?" The Riders stared at the pair in confusion as they exited the room and pulled the door shut behind them.

"What is it?" Aelfraed asked softly, the lantern over Darr Beval's door highlighting his kind gray eyes.

Rhoswen felt close to tears. She had never been so at odds with her parents' judgment, yet she felt so strongly opposed to her father's opinions that she didn't know how to believe them. Her eyes lifted to meet the caretaker's. She knew she trusted Aelfraed—even her parents had before they'd heard of his connection to Darr Beval—but she didn't know how to divulge her conflict without offending him. "It's hard to explain…."

He smiled. "Give it a try anyway. I'll do my best to understand."

Aelfraed seemed to comprehend everything from how to alleviate the tension in a room of alarmed Riders to the inscrutable language encoded on obscure stone-keys. But… if Darr Beval couldn't be trusted, and Aelfraed trusted him, then Aelfraed couldn't be trusted either…. *Right?* How could she make him understand that if she shouldn't even be communicating with him?

"I was given some information today that… contradicts what I had been led to believe—or *allowed* myself to believe. I don't know what is real now. The source is usually a good one, but the information *feels* wrong." She looked up at him, blinking away tears. "This isn't making any sense, is it?"

Aelfraed's face assumed an expression of deep concern. "It is hard not to trust a source that is usually sound. But remember: even the wisest of us can be led astray by emotion and its distortion of memory. Especially if we don't have all the information necessary to make informed judgments."

"That's *my* problem," Rhoswen muttered. "I don't know enough to disprove my source's beliefs."

He nodded. "Could your source be experiencing the same problem?"

She shrugged. "I suppose it's possible."

"But you believe strongly to the contrary of what you have been told? You feel it in your gut that *your* impression is the right one?"

She nodded.

His gray eyes sparkled in the dim light. "Heirs have a strong intuitive sense, you know. Can you usually trust your gut?"

Rhoswen thought back to her sense that Lorelle was hiding things from her. While she didn't have confirmation of this, she had chosen to keep the waiting-woman at arm's length. If nothing else, it was the safest route—and what her gut had told her to do. "I think so."

"If your gut happens to be wrong this time, can you correct your mistake or at least minimize it?"

Rhoswen pushed her bangs behind her ear. She had already shared so much with these men. If Darr Beval were on Badrick's side, much of her advantage would already be lost. And if her uncle reclaimed his maps, neither of them would be able to control the portal if she maintained possession of her compass. At worst, it would be a stalemate.

But she was the Heir. And if the dragons wanted her to Move, she had to trust that they would find a way for her to do so, even in the face of such a grievous error. She considered their earlier uproar when her safety was threatened. Wouldn't they have kept her from working with Darr Beval if he didn't have her best interests at heart...?

She finally nodded at Aelfraed.

He smiled. "Then, having all that information, you must make the wisest decision you can and hope for the best." He paused for a moment, watching her. "You can either come back inside with me, or I can escort you to the castle. We won't stop you from leaving. What would you like to do?"

Rhoswen took a deep breath and exhaled in resignation. "Will you help me explain the portal system to them?"

Aelfraed smiled. "I'll do my best."

No longer burdened with whether to share her tale, Rhoswen enjoyed watching the Riders' expressions change throughout her telling of it. But their mystification about the portal and horror at her uncle's marriage plans for her paled in comparison to their poorly concealed delight at Thane punching Gethin. That had devolved into all-out hysterics.

"The biggest problem is we don't know how to close the portal behind us," Rhoswen said once they'd settled down.

"Perhaps you need more keys," Darr Thorndon suggested.

"Like this?" Rhoswen pulled out the newest stone-key from Stanburh and handed it to Aelfraed, so he could translate it for her. She knew carrying that key with her was even riskier than trying to escape the castle undetected; had she been discovered and searched, she could have exposed the entire portal system. But much like whatever had told her not to trust her father's opinions or Lorelle's behavior, she had somehow known that she could bring the key to the caretaker without incident. She only hoped she could get it back to the castle with similar ease.

"'Forger of belonging,'" Aelfraed translated, and his eyebrows crumpled together.

"Thane thought these riddles could point to where the keys were found," Rhoswen offered.

"'Harbinger of duplicitous creation' and 'extension toward otherness'… those were found in Aethelburh and Keaton, right?" Darr Beval asked.

Rhoswen nodded.

"The castles are rough copies of each other," Darr Thorndon said, piecing it together. "If Keaton was designed to replicate Aethelburh—the 'harbinger' of the drakiary's creation—Keaton would be an 'other extension' of the original castle."

"But 'forger of belonging?'" Rhoswen asked. "That came from Stanburh."

"You went to Stanburh with that portal?" Darr Beval asked, eyes wide.

Rhoswen nodded; she had neglected to mention that part, lest it should lead to a discussion of her father's concerns. "What could that phrase have to do with Stanburh? It doesn't sound good."

"It doesn't necessarily have to be *bad*. In the most basic sense, the word 'forger' could point to the creation of something. It could mean Stanburh creates a sense of belonging," Aelfraed offered. "It doesn't have to point to a sense of belonging that is not genuine."

"But she's the Heir," Darr Thorndon said. "Her childhood home may *feel* like where she belongs, but it actually isn't." He grinned. "I love riddles."

Rhoswen considered this. Her earlier meeting with her parents hadn't embodied any of the comforts of home.

"It's as good a guess as any," Aelfraed said with a shrug.

"That's all he's good for," Darr Beval teased, "a decent guess."

Darr Thorndon punched his Riding partner in the arm.

"So, what do we do now?" Darr Beval asked, massaging his new injury. "Work with the portal until we figure out how to close it?

Aelfraed shook his head. "As Rhoswen didn't feel comfortable escaping here through the portal tonight, we don't have that option."

"And that was part of what tonight's meeting was supposed to be about?" Darr Beval asked.

Rhoswen nodded. "Not only that, but my uncle posted sentries outside my chambers. He could walk in at any moment to check on me and find me missing. I can't stay here much longer."

"Well, that considerably shortens this meeting," Darr Thorndon muttered.

Aelfraed handed the stone-key back to Rhoswen with a finality that suggested the meeting was not just shortened; it was adjourned.

"I have one more thing to ask," Rhoswen blurted out. "A Rider by the name of Denver has shown up in Dallin. He is newly tethered to a young green named Kipling. My parents received no word of his assignment to the area, and they don't trust the king, so they wanted me to inquire after him with Riders I trust." She smiled at them. "So, I'm asking you." The last of her doubt toward these men slipped from her shoulders like a heavy backpack released to the ground. She knew in her gut that these men could be trusted with her secrets—and her *life*. Confiding in them felt so right that her uncertainty simply dissolved. It felt both strange and uplifting.

The Riders exchanged bewildered glances. "Whence does this Rider hail?" Darr Thorndon asked.

"A small town in the south called… Hazlitt," Rhoswen remembered. "I'd never heard of it."

"In the south, villages and towns change names like the wind," Darr Thorndon said. "It's a convenient place to hail from when you want to hide your past."

Rhoswen's eyes widened. "Are you saying none of you know who this Rider is?" When they all shook their heads, she said, "I thought all Riders came through Keaton…."

"They do," Darr Beval replied. "And if this man and his dragon are young, we would know who they are."

"But we don't," Darr Thorndon agreed. "So, either he is going by another name, or he didn't come up through Keaton."

"How would that be possible?" Rhoswen asked.

"Good question," Darr Thorndon replied with a glance at his partner. His darkened countenance reversed the surreal unburdening Rhoswen had just experienced, and the heavy stress of uncertainty fell back across her shoulders.

No one was comfortable with the Heir walking back to the castle alone, so Darr Beval escorted her.

Their walk to Aethelburh began in silence but for the sound of the grass swishing past their boots. There was far too much to say to make any sense of it in the short walk up the hill.

But Rhoswen appreciated the quiet. Not talking to Darr Beval meant she couldn't blurt out anything regrettable about her father's apprehensions before she had a chance to speak to Thane. She might have decided to trust the Rider, but she still wanted to understand why he was the subject of so much angst, and Thane was better at finding out such things.

"A gold piece for your thoughts?" Darr Beval finally asked.

She sighed. "It wouldn't even pay for half of one."

"Yes, you have some pretty overwhelming things to consider," he said with a nod. "You're faced with more responsibility than a—*young lady* your age should have to deal with," he said, faltering at what to call her. "You're training for a new profession in new surroundings—and suddenly, that vocation has become *much* more convoluted than for the average Rider.

"On top of that, it's possible that your own *uncle* is leading a faction of unknown size against you. And you *live* with him. So, at your age, with your limited life experience, you must figure out whom to trust while struggling night and day to protect yourself from harm."

"Perhaps I should pay *you* for my thoughts," she muttered.

He chuckled. "Take the meeting we just had: you had to decide if the Riders you're sharing secrets with have your best interests in mind."

"You knew?" she asked, feeling as though she had betrayed him.

He sighed. "None of us blames you for it. You're right to be cautious. You still have to protect yourself for a good while yet—Deowynn isn't even pregnant. Your dragon has yet to be *born*...." The Rider looked up at the dark bulk of the castle growing nearer to them with every step. "This would be challenging for someone *my age*."

"How old are you anyway?" Rhoswen blurted. Her cheeks flushed.

Darr Beval laughed at the question. "Thirty-three."

It seemed another lifetime to her. He had learned so much in those extra years. She was just a kid—*almost* of adult age—and faced with an adult task. He would always be sixteen years wiser. So would Darr Thorndon, who seemed older still than Darr Beval. And Aelfraed... well, he would always be decades ahead of them all.

Darr Beval was right: she had lived a very sheltered life—more so than she had ever imagined—and was now forced to draw only on her instincts and the lessons her parents *hadn't* hidden from her to help make decisions that someone twice her age would struggle with. When he put it like that, her situation almost seemed unfair.

She felt another pang of resentment at having been led to mistrust these men, whom she knew in her heart were allies. She needed their wisdom and protection, and nothing about any of them felt threatening in the least. A sudden desire to share her burden with Darr Beval swept over her. She wanted to confront him, ask him why her father might feel the way he did, but how to approach the subject? Before she could find a way, they were entering the main doors of Castle Aethelburh.

They had expected to find an empty foyer with the party in full swing at the rear of the castle, but already, the gathering had dwindled to an unimpressive state. The waitstaff bustled to and from the dining hall, clearing dishes as guests lumbered toward the main entrance to take their leave. Badrick was nowhere in sight. *Did he leave my brother to see out the last of the guests?* Indeed, Thane was edging a group of chatty young men across the Great Hall. For his sake, she hoped that was the last of them.

As she and Darr Beval turned to head up the nearby staircase, Rhoswen met Lorelle's wide-eyed gaze. The waiting-woman could not have expected to see her charge outside of her rooms, let alone *entering* the castle from somewhere else. Composing herself, Lorelle looked away, as if she had not seen anything out of the ordinary.

Rhoswen went up ahead of Darr Beval, her confusion mounting. Lorelle's behavior had been strange of late, but now, rather than reporting Rhoswen's escape to her uncle, it appeared the waiting-woman intended to keep her illicit departure from the castle a secret. *Why?*

At the top of the staircase, Rhoswen remembered the sentries posted outside her chamber door and held out a hand to halt Darr Beval's progress. She peeked around the corner. The sentries were gone. Her heart leapt into her throat.

Darr Beval leaned in close. "What is it?" he whispered in her ear, his breath warm against her skin.

Rhoswen glanced at the Rider, eyes wide. Her voice came out in a grave whisper. "The sentries I told you about. They're gone. My uncle knows I am not in my chambers!"

"Yes," said a smooth, cool voice at the top of the landing, "he does."

Rhoswen froze. She watched, not breathing, as her uncle slid out from the shadows. Beside her, Darr Beval's body tensed. They both bent at the waist, and Rhoswen realized too late that she should have been curtseying; female bows were reserved for dragons. She bent her knees a little to compensate. The last thing she needed to do was slight her uncle after deceiving him. "Your majesty," they mumbled in unison.

"Darr Beval, didn't the sentries alert you to Rhoswen's condition? She is to rest this evening." The king sneered. "Or perhaps you… *avoided* them when you came to collect her from her chambers."

Darr Beval said nothing.

"He didn't collect me," Rhoswen blurted. "I was having a hard time resting with all the noise from the party, so I went down to have a peek at the festivities."

Badrick glared at his niece. "Past the guards who were ordered to keep you inside to rest?" He turned toward the Rider. "Festivities to which Darr Beval was not invited?"

"I came with Aelfraed for additional texts," Darr Beval improvised. Rhoswen felt the poor caretaker was far too often used as an excuse for their mistakes. "We ran into Rhoswen on our way in. As neither of us were aware of the party being held here this evening, Aelfraed returned to Keaton, and I escorted Rose back here to resume her rest."

"Rose?" the king parroted.

"We try not to be too formal down in the arena," Rhoswen said.

"But my dear, we are not *in* the arena. We are in the hall of my castle—outside the room you were meant to have stayed in for the duration of the evening—rather than galivanting about with some Rider *twice your age*—who is *also your trainer*." Badrick made a tsk-tsk sound behind his teeth and glared at Darr Beval. "*So* like your father."

The Rider bristled beside her. Rhoswen felt a surge of conflicting emotions. Not only had she done nothing to impugn her honor, but her uncle's concern for it was bewildering and suspect. And Darr Beval's inexplicable reaction to her uncle's accusations.... What was going on here?

Whatever this is, I can't let Darr Beval pay for my mistakes. "Forgive me, your majesty, but my restlessness has finally turned to exhaustion. Darr Beval was right in escorting me back to my room when I should have been lying down. I fear I may have used my status as your niece to bully the guards into letting me out, but I see the error of my ways." She looked to Darr Beval. "Thank you for the well-intentioned escort." She turned back to her uncle. "I hope you can forgive my excitement and poor judgment, your majesty." She curtsied and waited for his reply. Darr Beval's still-stiff posture increased her uneasiness as the silence dragged on.

"Get to bed," Badrick finally snarled. "I will have a word with Darr Beval before he returns to Keaton."

Rhoswen's gut knotted. She wanted to apologize to Darr Beval or protect him in some way, but she could not risk disobeying her uncle further. She curtseyed once more and walked down the hall to her room, abandoning Darr Beval to his fate.

Thane escorted the last group of hangers-on toward the castle entrance as they regaled him with a story about the trials and tribulations of having their linens artfully monogrammed. He nodded at the speaker and motioned subtly to the doormen to open the doors. As the storyteller took a breath between rapid sentences, Thane smiled and bid them farewell, ushering them all out. It was not the most well-mannered thing he had ever done, but the group seemed unfazed by it and were still thanking him as the doors shut. He winked at the doormen, his heavy eyelids practically doing the job for him.

Exhausted as he was from all his patient smiling, he needed to find his sister before he collapsed. Throughout the evening, his mind had vacillated between Rhoswen and Ethelinda; between the open portal in his sister's room and the meeting down in Keaton; between Delwyn's words of caution and the invitation to visit his new, mysterious, and beautiful acquaintance. He turned away from the castle doors and exhaled, but his over-starched vest and fitted jacket held him stiffly upright. Thankfully, they also concealed much of his surprise when the king, who had long ago slipped away from the party, spoke behind him.

"Is that the last of them?"

Thane turned to face his uncle. "Yes, your majesty," he replied with a nod.

Badrick stood at the bottom of the spiral staircase. "You held your own surprisingly well," he said.

No thanks to you, Thane thought. "Thank you, your highness," he said with a stiff, little bow that was not as low as it should have been—not that he could have bent much further. "How is the prince? You must have gone to check on him."

Thane's insinuation of abandonment did not elude his uncle. "Resting peacefully," he replied tersely. "You're probably eager to check on your sister," he added in a tone that made the hair on the back of Thane's neck stand at attention.

"I am," he admitted. "Did you happen to look in on her?"

A nasty smile played across Badrick's face. "Well, I tried. You see, Rhoswen visited Gethin before turning in for the night, but when I went to check on the two of them earlier, they were nowhere to be found." Badrick ran his finger over a vein in a nearby marble pillar and glanced at Thane out of the corner of his eye. "Gethin eventually returned to his room, I am happy to say. Rhoswen, however.... Well, I am not entirely certain what your sister is up to."

"I'm sure she can't have gone far." Thane kept his voice even, trying to sound more relaxed than he felt. Rhoswen had no reason to visit Gethin, and from the way the king was sneering, Thane knew it had been a mandated action. Nothing good could come of that, especially if she were now missing.... And if she wasn't guarding the portal.... "If that will be all, majesty...?"

"Of course." Badrick swirled around, turning his back on Thane as he made his way into the Great Hall. "Good luck in your search, Nephew," he called over his shoulder.

Wasting no time with a bow his uncle would not see, Thane headed up the staircase, his gait measured. When he was out sight from the foyer, he bolted upward, two stairs at a time.

Thane plowed through the door to his sister's room, and it slammed into something hard—Rhoswen. She stumbled forward, away from the door. "Rose? Are you all right?" he blustered.

She rubbed at her back. "Relatively...."

"I'm sorry." He stared at her in confusion. "Uncle Badrick just told me you were nowhere to be found."

"What? When? I just spoke to him."

They reviewed their separate conversations with their uncle.

Thane frowned. "He was just trying to worry me."

"Well, we have plenty of reason to worry," she replied. "He knows I wasn't in my room all night."

"Realm it," he said, moving to the edge of her bed. He tried to slouch against it, but his suit held him upright. He unbuttoned his jacket. "You don't think he found the portal, do you?"

"He couldn't have." Rhoswen told him about visiting their parents, her escape to Keaton, the meeting, and Darr Beval's reaction to Badrick's comment about his father. "What's going on around here?"

"You remember that woman who sat beside you at the first dinner party? I met her tonight. She used to train here. She mentioned Darr Beval, but when she did, she made a comment about how he still looked good for his age."

Rhoswen's face crumpled up in confusion. "For his age? He's still young."

"Right," Thane replied. "I didn't understand it either. Turns out, she trained under our Darr Beval's *father*. But she made a dark comment about him—Darr Beval *Senior*—as she was leaving. I think he might not have the nicest reputation." He wondered how that reputation might have played into this mysterious *war*.

"That could explain Darr Beval's reaction to Badrick's comment. Do you think Father's hatred might be directed at the *senior* Rider?" she asked.

He shrugged. "It's possible. It would certainly explain his warning."

"So you think our Darr Beval is trustworthy?"

Is anyone? Thane wanted to scream. *Our own parents lied to us about your identity for almost two decades!* He wondered whether the war was just one more thing their parents had hidden from them for his sister's sake—although he had no idea how or why that would be beneficial. If he didn't know about it, chances were neither did Rhoswen. Still, he didn't want to get her worked up before he knew more.

Darr Beval already knows everything anyway, he reminded himself, but the thought provided little comfort. "If I didn't, would I have let you share so much with him?" His voice sounded more confident than he felt.

"So, what do we do about Father's misgivings?" she asked.

Thane yawned. He was desperate to get to bed so he could stop thinking about everything he had learned tonight. His mind needed a rest. "Let's sleep on it," he replied and slipped out the door.

LXII

Detroit

"So, he took me to the metro park," Emmelyn told Josie, who was watching her with wide-eyed, unblinking interest. Josie had volunteered to work doubles for two days to cover for a sick co-worker, and they hadn't seen each other long enough to talk since the date. "The one with the big manmade lake and the beach."

"I know the one," Josie said with a keep-going flap of her hand.

Emmelyn smiled.

Everyone had been ambling toward the parking lot, tugging on lightweight jackets and slipping back into their sandals as Emmelyn and Jeremy had made their way to the beach. They'd dug their toes into the sand, as the setting sun washed the sky in oranges and pinks and flashed golden sparkles across the surface of the water to a backdrop of silhouetted trees.

"This is much better," Emmelyn had told him as they'd sat, hips touching. A few youthful squeals had still emanated from the play structure farther down the beach as food vendors packed up and their last customers chatted about the next day of work. As the sun had continued to dip lower in the sky, shifting its hues to violets and indigos, Jeremy had found Emmelyn's hand and woven his fingers through hers, the fear of being guilt-tripped by mothers or bothered by the Exchange again a thing of the past... or so she'd hoped.

"It is better," Jeremy had agreed. He'd set his shake down beside him, twisting it back and forth to seat it in the loose sand before doing the same with Emmelyn's cup. Finally, he'd looked into her eyes and snaked his fingers around the side of her neck to pull her mouth toward his.

Josie squealed with glee. "HOW WAS IT?"

Emmelyn winced. She was fairly certain all of their neighbors would extrapolate far more from that screech than was necessary—or even accurate. "It was… great," she said with an embarrassed shrug.

Josie groaned. "I need DETAILS!" she demanded.

Emmelyn was about to apologize for denying her best friend's wishes—partially because she and Jeremy hadn't gone past making out and partially because she enjoyed her privacy—when she found herself outside of the Exchange again.

Already? she thought and headed inside. *I suppose I need to apologize to these people, too….* She felt sheepish as she remembered her bad attitude the last time she had seen the Crew.

"You look happier," Inzay called to her, her perpetual smile beaming on her face.

"I'm sorry," Emmelyn yelled back. "I didn't mean to be so rude to you last time; I was just upset."

"Well, yeah!" Inzay commiserated, waving her off. "You were on a *date*!"

Today, Kyle and Bernadette were also present. She would have to apologize to Odore and Randy separately.

"So, how did it go?" Inzay asked, shoulders hunching excitedly.

Does no one care for privacy anymore? "It was great," Emmelyn replied, taking a seat on the couch.

She had reached the part of the story on the malt shop bench when she caught a flash of gray in her peripheral vision. A familiar dark braid disappeared around a group of bodies, and Emmelyn excused herself, ignoring the Crew's vehement protestations.

"Lorelle!" she called at the top of her lungs, her voice breaking. She caught up to the waiting-woman and touched her arm. Lorelle turned around and smiled. "I didn't think I'd ever see you again!" Emmelyn hollered.

"You never know with this place," Lorelle yelled. "How are you?"

"More importantly, how are *you*?" Emmelyn asked.

"Oh, I'm fine," Lorelle replied. "I have another Arbiter now—are you still Transferring for Emile?" she asked before she could say something disparaging.

"Yes, but I'm not sure I trust him," she yelled back.

Lorelle nodded. "Things are changing here, Emmelyn. Just do your job and keep your head down."

Emmelyn thought of the women who came to WE Dress; they didn't just accept what life had thrown at them, and she was not about to either. Nor was she about to let some insane annihilation theory destroy her realm because the Datists were sick of doing research. "That's not really how I work," she insisted. "What is Emile up to?"

Lorelle shook her head. "My team merged with another already at work in D'Erenelle. They had similar goals.... Apparently, Emile has other ideas about how the realm should be... adjusted. He got a whole new set of Runners and Transfers for it." She shrugged. "Who knows what way will work out best?"

The waiting-woman's words proved that Emmelyn had only the vaguest understanding of how anything worked in the Exchange. Worse yet, trying to ask questions about it in a deafening bar proved almost impossible. "I think *you* would know, Lorelle. You're there, and Emile's here. And you're relieved to be Running for someone else. I don't want to Transfer for someone who's doing harm to a realm just to make a buck." *Or worse.*

Lorelle's eyes grew wide, and she pulled Emmelyn over to a pair of chairs in the circle of her own friends. She leaned in close. "You don't have a choice."

"I could request a change."

"You can't do that."

"I could slip a note into your Transitor. Maybe your Arbiter could help me," Emmelyn suggested.

Lorelle's brow furrowed, and she shook her head. "Absolutely not, Emmelyn! Not only can my Arbiter not help you, but you would get me into serious trouble. Running is hard enough in the *realm*—I don't need the Exchange to be difficult, too. You could get us exiled with a move like that!"

"Okay, okay," Emmelyn replied. "Just explain this merger of groups to me. What's going on?"

"I think you know more than you should already." Lorelle stood. "I have to go. I'm sorry. Please be careful." She sped toward the back of the bar, obviously not interested in being pursued. Emmelyn respected her wishes and returned to the Crew and the rest of her story.

Vonn entered the Exchange through the portals at the back of the nightclub and practically ran into Kyle, who was about to leave through them. After a harried greeting, Vonn ordered a drink at the bar and continued to the Crew's usual circle, where Inzay and Bernadette were also getting up to leave.

"Tell Emmelyn bye for me," Inzay yelled in Vonn's ear as she passed by.

"Me, too," Bernadette yelled in the other and departed behind Inzay.

"She's here?" he called after them, but they didn't hear him. "Good to see you, too," he mumbled to the empty circle of chairs before selecting one for himself. He leaned back and sipped his Welsamarian gin and tonic, watching out of the corner of his eye as two women from his realm and a familiar Luthean made out in their overflowing chair one circle over.

He thought back to his discussion with Rehlia. He had let her down—or rather, Emmelyn had let him down, which let Rehlia down. He wondered which of his friends had said something to Emmelyn.... Regardless, he couldn't scold her for being sympathetic toward Emile; nor could he confront her about it because he couldn't explain how he had discovered that she had extended her condolences to the Arbiter. He had gotten himself into enough trouble without having to divulge his forbidden relationship with Rehlia. He took another sip of gin and closed his eyes, letting the oddly twangy rock music of Xixex thud around him.

Vonn had met Rehlia six years after he was inducted into the Exchange. She, too, hailed from Welsamar, and they quickly discovered they had more than a realm in common. He enjoyed her company and their discussions of realms, even if her side of the conversation was often stilted. He understood that she couldn't share everything with him—already, she divulged more than she probably should. And she understood that their relationship could come unglued at any moment. Still, he wasn't ready for this to be that moment. He hoped Emmelyn's loose tongue—and, let's face it, *his own*—hadn't scuppered things between them. He cared deeply for Rehlia.

As the ladies had promised, Emmelyn returned to their circle of chairs, her wrist still inked with red stamps. *So, she hasn't done her Transfer yet,* he thought, pleased that she could stay a while. "They said goodbye," he yelled to her as she sat down. He frowned at her empty hands. "No drink?"

"I've been a little preoccupied," she called back to him. "They *all* had to go?"

"Everyone but us seems to be on the same schedule today," he replied and nodded at the bar. "Shall I get you something?"

"I don't think so." She looked unsettled in a way he had never seen her.

"All right, what's going on?" he asked, setting his drink on the heavily ringed coffee table. "If it's about your sudden appearance here the other night, I wouldn't be too concerned about it."

She stared at him. "Why do you say that?"

Clearly something else troubled her. "I did a little research," he replied anyway. "While not many can do it, and it's not something you want to broadcast, it's not unique to you."

Emmelyn nodded. "Well, that's good to hear."

"But not what's bothering you," Vonn said. He scooted forward. "What is it?"

Emmelyn shook her head. "Just a discussion I had with Lorelle."

Suddenly, Vonn understood how Rehlia felt when he hid information from her after abusing her secrets. "Is she all right?" he prodded.

"Yeah," Emmelyn replied, leaning in toward his ear. He met her the rest of the way, letting her breath ruffle his hair. He tried to focus on her words through the tickling sensation.

"I don't trust Emile," she explained. "I asked Lorelle to help me switch to another Arbiter, but she refused—and for good reason, I get it." Emmelyn sighed. "I just don't have a good feeling about whatever Emile is up to."

"Lorelle was right—*as you know*," Vonn added when Emmelyn leaned back to flash him the I-already-said-that look, "but you don't even know what you're protesting. I mean, what has Emile done besides a couple triples?"

"A *couple* triples?" Emmelyn scoffed. "That's practically all I do."

"What?" Vonn tried not to look startled.

"Oh, yeah!"

She looked so frustrated and helpless. It made Vonn want to protect her from all the things she feared—but neither of them truly knew what those things were.

"It doesn't necessarily mean he's doing something wrong—" he began.

She silenced him with an icy glare. "Lorelle said her team merged with another in D'Erenelle because they were 'politically well aligned.' That's why I stopped being her Transfer. She got a new Arbiter, and Emile got a bunch of new Transfers and Runners for his team. She said Emile has different beliefs about the way the realm should be adjusted." Her gaze softened with despair. "I think your theory about the factions was right… and I think I'm on the wrong side of it."

Vonn had only known one other Transfer who cared so much about her—*rather helpless*—role in Exchange politics. Given a Transfer's limited power within the G'Ambit, few bothered to learn more than the procedures of their job. But not Emmelyn. She wanted to understand how her Transfers would affect the realm—realms, plural, if her concerns were founded. He admired that about her, even if she took a dangerous stance. Before he could commend her—and then warn her off—Denver showed up behind her, ever the grim specter.

As they performed their cool exchange, Vonn watched the stamps fade from Emmelyn's pale skin. She was thin, and her arms were slender; he was certain he could encircle her wrist between his forefinger and thumb. Her brown hair had grown an inch or two since she'd been inducted into the Exchange, and the new length suited her. His eyes followed the layers up to her face, which he realized had turned back to him. Denver was long gone. "Sorry. Did you say something?"

Emmelyn smiled at him, and his breath hitched. She was no Welsamodel, as Exchangers had coined his people, but she was stunning in another way. The realization took him by surprise.

"Maybe I should just be a nuisance to Denver and Emile. Make my frustration known in a more toddler-esque fashion," she suggested.

Vonn squinted at her. "The Exchange doesn't take kindly to rabble-rousers. You could get yourself exiled for intractable behavior, and then how would you make a difference around here?"

Emmelyn's face brightened. "You think I can make a difference?"

He felt desperate not to disappoint her. "Maybe. I just don't know how yet," he admitted as gently as one could when yelling over Xixen rock.

She deflated a little and stood to complete what he expected would be another triple. "We'll see," she replied and bid him goodbye. "Oh, and thanks for researching my weird appearance here the other night!" Then, she smiled and left the circle, unwittingly taking a piece of him with her.

LXIII

Aethelburh

Rhoswen was the first to reach the breakfast room. After a short and fitful night, she had given up trying to sleep, thrown back her covers, and pulled on her leathers before her waiting-women even arrived. She poured herself some vine water and stood with eyes half-closed, absently nursing it until it grew cool.

Out of nowhere, a hand reached past her for a mug on the shelf near her head. Rhoswen jumped and turned to find her cousin, who looked bored by her jitteriness. "Sorry," he mumbled. She didn't know whether she was more unnerved by his soundless entry—a skill he shared with his father—or the fact that he had apologized. He *did* look half asleep.

"Are you well this morning, my prince?" Rhoswen asked, stifling a yawn. She waited for Gethin to finish pouring his mug of vine water so she could top hers off.

"Alive, no thanks to you." He glared at her. There were dark circles under his eyes, and the cut on his eyebrow had dulled to a ruddy brown. "Do you honestly believe I don't know what you were up to last night? That wicked beast could have killed me! Just what you wanted, right? Get me out of the way so I can't inherit the realm from my father? You'll be lucky if I don't have you executed for treason." Without another word, Gethin stormed from the breakfast room.

Rhoswen went cold from head to foot. She was already on thin ice with Badrick, and if the king required convincing to act on such delusions, Gethin could accommodate. Before she could crumple into a tear-streaked ball on the floor, a low laugh sounded from the doorway.

"Gethin would make a lousy parent," Thane said. "Even toddlers recognize empty threats. What kind of an idiot does he think you are?" He sounded like their father. It was both comical and comforting, even in the wake of Gethin's frightening declaration.

"You really think it's an empty threat?" Rhoswen asked, her voice quavering.

Thane walked up to the buffet beside her and filled a mug with vine water for himself. Then he peered into her cup and topped it off. Her hands shook slightly as she held the mug, and he steadied them with his own. "Of course it is. Who's going to indulge him? Only the king can execute someone for treason. Do you honestly think he's going to tell his father how you duped him when it would make him look so much the fool?"

Rhoswen took a deep breath to steady herself. "I suppose he did disobey Uncle Badrick's orders last night… " she said before taking another sip of vine water.

Thane's eyes smiled over the rim of his own mug. "He just wanted to scare you," he said.

"I hope you're right."

He grinned. "When am I not?"

She wrinkled her nose and took a swipe at him, but he darted out of reach.

They loaded up their plates with assorted meats, cheeses, fruits, and breads. Thane grabbed the jug of vine water and brought it to the table. It would be—at the *very* least—a two-cup kind of day.

"So, tell me about this woman you met last night," Rhoswen said around a mouthful of fresh bread with fruit preserves baked into it.

"Not much to tell," Thane replied, his tone cavalier.

"Well, it seems like you had quite a discussion with her."

"Not really," he said. "She seemed to appreciate that we couldn't talk at the party, so she invited me to her estate to finish our discussion in private."

Rhoswen let out a whoop. "To her *estate*?! You failed to mention that last night!"

Thane gestured for her to keep her voice down. "It's not like that," he insisted. "She is the Lady of Alston. All she has is an 'estate.'"

Her jaw dropped. "And an *entire territory!* You were invited to Alston Manor by Lady Alston? *That's* who was sitting beside me at the first dinner party?"

He nodded.

"Will you go?"

He shrugged. "Delwyn warned me off," he admitted, not looking at her.

"What?" she asked, setting down the half-eaten slice of bread.

"He saw me talking with her and said she was dangerous." He shrugged again. "What if he's right?"

"What if?!" she spluttered. "He made a point of coming to you in the middle of a party to tell you that, and you're questioning him?"

"But I don't know her!" he countered. "In spite of our 'friendship' with Delwyn, I don't know if we can trust him. He could be trying to spoil our alliance with someone of power outside this castle… or she could be what he says she is."

Rhoswen narrowed her eyes at her brother. "This is what I meant about bribery making poor friends! Lady Alston knows who you are, Thane. What if Delwyn is right? What if she's trying to get you away from me, so Badrick can get to me more easily? She *was* one of his guests. Gethin personally escorted her to her chair! Who knows what side she's on?"

"I don't think any of last night's guests have strong allegiances to anyone but themselves. Did you get a feeling about her at the dinner that first night?" he asked.

Rhoswen thought back to that wretched meal. "I was so distracted by the dying Aethelia flowers and our cousin's incessant questions…." Ethelinda had sat beside her. Why hadn't she sensed danger if Delwyn spoke in earnest? "I didn't find her any more threatening than our uncle's glances that night. Still, if Delwyn bothered to say something—"

"But *you* usually have a sense about such things," Thane countered. "And our uncle had us separated last night and didn't try anything, right? If he'd been using Ethelinda against us, you'd have felt it. It's too big a risk, and he knows it. Anyway, Gethin might have walked her to her seat because she's beautiful."

Rhoswen didn't dignify the comment. "I wasn't in the castle enough yesterday for our uncle to have tried anything, and he clearly checked my room while I was gone. Last night could also have been a ploy to give us a false sense of security, which is a generous term for what it gave me." She sighed, hating how paranoid this place was making her sound. "You can't honestly be considering her offer…?"

"I just want to get clarity about what Father said," he replied.

Rhoswen failed to mention that Thane hadn't known about their father's misgivings until *after* he'd made a date with this woman. He was Rhoswen's only line of defense within the castle walls. Already, their rooms were a veritable realm apart, and the only other men who would protect her were a castle away—if they *could* protect her. The whole thing made her feel more uneasy than ever—and she had eaten semi-poisonous flower petals with her necrophilic cousin.

"See if you can get more information about her from Delwyn," she suggested. "In the meantime, we have to figure out this portal system—oh! And tell our parents about that new Rider in Dallin."

He nodded. "Let's get to Keaton."

A waiting-woman with dark, braided hair walked through the hall, her metal-clad soles ringing against the stone. The prince paused to watch her gray frock swing back and forth around her hips.

"Don't be uncouth."

Startled, Gethin hunched his shoulders as he spun around to face his father.

"How did it go?" the king asked.

"Fine," Gethin replied. "Rhoswen looked terrified."

"Of you or of your threat?" Badrick asked with an amused sneer.

Gethin scowled. "I was more than convincing."

"Is there such a thing?" Badrick rolled his eyes. "As long as she thinks you have the upper hand—*that* is what counts. *That* is real power."

The words hit Gethin like a spark, igniting a flash of memory.

He saw himself back in his room, the way it had looked well over a decade ago. He was cradled in his mother's arms, his knees scratched and bloody. A fight with another boy, in which he'd thought he'd had the upper hand, had ended with a violent push that had sent him sprawling.

"Earning the love and trust of others because you have learned how to deserve them—*that* is real power," his mother had cooed, dabbing gently at his knees with a damp cloth. He'd winced a bit but never took his eyes off her face. "Love is not something that can be taken by force or fear; imposed loyalty is fleeting."

As the image of his mother faded, his father's face came back into focus. Gethin took an instinctive step backward.

"Are you incapable of paying attention for the span of a single question?" the king snapped. "You should have known that Rhoswen's little book theory was a farce. At least we were able to use your stupidity to our advantage." With a contemptuous grunt, Badrick turned and strode away from his son. "Try to reserve what little remains of your concentration for your 'more than convincing' charade, will you?" he called over his shoulder. "Or I really will marry you to her."

Badrick cursed as he padded back to his chambers. *"More than convincing,"* he scoffed. "Another task botched."

As he rounded the corner at the top of the stairs, he was met with a scrawny messenger, who looked as horrified to have come face to face with the king as Badrick was angry to have been interrupted in his musings. "What is it?" he spat.

"Y-y-your request, sire. Your m-m-men have been located," the messenger stammered. He held out a piece of parchment with the five names Badrick had given him. Beside each, a location was scribbled. Badrick folded the parchment and secreted it in his pocket. The messenger was still standing nearby. "If you wish to be paid, go see Delwyn," he barked as his doormen opened the entrance to his chambers.

"Of c-course, s-s-s-sire, I th-th-thank—" the man stammered as he bowed.

Before the messenger could finish, Badrick slammed the door in his face. Inside his room, enshrouded by the familiar darkness, his shoulders dropped, and he allowed himself to slump into his favorite wingback chair. "My *angel,*" he cooed. His voice cracked with pain before turning angry. "You have ruined us. We are undone."

He rubbed at his eyes and slid his hands down over his mouth. "When you left.... *You always leave.* That's what you women do, isn't it? You *leave*.... And I could not do what needed to be done without you, Orla. You were my guiding light. My balance. Without you, my path changed. Without you, Gethin's path ended. He has enough of you in him not to fight it... and I don't have enough of you in me to let it go."

He pulled out the parchment the messenger had given him. "They aren't far. And with Gethin as useless as he is, I will need all the help I can get." He paused, the anguish reentering his voice. "I *had* all the help I ever needed. But you left." He heaved a ragged sigh. "You *both* left. D'Erenelle is all I have."

LXIV

Keaton

Although Rhoswen had predicted rain three days ago, the sun was shining, which meant they'd spend a good portion of class outside. Thane and Rhoswen's waitstaff were at the ready when the pair returned to their rooms after breakfast. They were armed with heavy roughs and various accessories to protect their young flesh from rough dragon hide. This was not just kenneling practice; they would *finally* be training on the backs of dragons—dragons who did not belong to their parents.

Rhoswen let her mind wander as Elsie and Lorelle strapped thin pads on the inside of her thighs, over her rear end, and at her shoulders, knees, and elbows. The senior waiting-woman kneeled to inspect Rhoswen's shins. Her Riding boots came up too high to wear the inner-shin guards, and Rhoswen had to argue with Elsie before she could leave her room without padding below the knee.

When she finally stepped into the hall, her brother was also making his way out of his room. He looked top-heavy and awkward in his dark-green tunic that swelled around multitudinous pads. A full head taller than she, his legs were long enough to accommodate the inner-shin guards, which made him appear even more ridiculous. They surveyed each other and laughed as their eyes met.

"How are we supposed to move in all this?" Thane called to her as they waddled down the hall like toddlers in thick winter gear. "I'm not even sure I can bend enough to sit astride a saddle."

"I think this is less about agility than avoiding injury," Rhoswen replied, her thigh pads swishing noisily against each other.

Thane looked down at her unpadded lower legs as they met at the end of the balcony. "Well, we should be fine then—except below your knees," he joked.

She could only stick her tongue out at him.

Down in the drakiary, Riders found themselves surrounded by chattering groups of well-padded, excited students. Their eagerness proved infectious. Rhoswen grinned at Thane as they parted ways to join their respective classmates.

Unable to coax more information from Delwyn since the party, Thane had suggested they coordinate a meeting with the Darrs and Aelfraed for that night. Rhoswen had been tasked with alerting Darr Beval, who was too overwhelmed with student appeals to talk to her, and her eagerness morphed into a niggling anxiety she couldn't make sense of.

You're right to feel anxious, a voice nexed from behind her. *I feel it, as well.*

She turned to see Darr Beval's beautiful tawny looking down at her. Fleta bent her head low and allowed Rhoswen to stroke her snout. *I have all day to confirm with him,* Rhoswen nexed back with inexplicable uncertainty.

But something is nagging at you. It wasn't a question; the dragon knew exactly how Rhoswen was feeling.

What's going on? Rhoswen asked suspiciously.

I can confirm with him for you, Fleta offered, ignoring the question.

With a nasally puff in the air that silenced the trainees surrounding Darr Beval, Fleta nexed the change of plans to her Rider. He blinked a bit at his dragon's intervention. Rhoswen thought Fleta's tone sounded about as anxious as she felt. *What's happening?*

If she had inadvertently nexed the question, no one answered it. Darr Beval nodded once to Rhoswen and again to his dragon before returning his attention to the students. "Fleta's right," he improvised, as he quieted the group. "It's time to begin. We are skipping lecture because today, we *fly!*"

Squeals and hoots of excitement rose among the students, and Darr Beval had to work hard to quiet them again. "All right, all right, settle down, or we'll never get to it! Now, this is not just a matter of jumping on the back of a dragon and taking off. You've all been preparing diligently for this, but those of you who haven't passed all your skills tests will only be watching today." This silenced what little whispering continued amongst the trainees.

"This is called a mass-flight. You watched Maven and Aeduuin perform single flights the other day. Single flights can help strengthen a relationship between dragon and trainee, or they can prove a discord between the two. A mass-flight, however, is for less experienced trainees, who haven't connected at any level with a dragon. The flight pattern is much more simplistic, so multiple dragon-trainee pairs can fly at once. Still, there is a procedure to follow, which you will see demonstrated by the elder trainees first."

Students tittered with excitement. At that moment, another Rider whom Rhoswen had never met released his trainees toward the stalls. They moved in groups of four, carrying huge saddles between them. They all wore rough leather gloves like the pair Rhoswen kept in her back pocket. After carefully lowering the saddles to the ground in front of their stalls, a select trainee from each group approached the stall door and carefully opened it. He or she then bowed low for permission to saddle the dragon inside. Once granted, the trainee motioned to the rest of his or her group to approach, and they bowed, as well.

"Not only does riding a dragon require permission for the Rider, but it also requires permission for those who will help saddle the beast," Darr Beval explained. Several of the groups began disappearing inside their stalls to prepare their mounts.

"Look over there," Darr Beval said, pointing to the last two stalls at the end of the row. "See how one trainee has remained outside each of those two stalls? The dragons within have rejected their assistance in preparing the saddle. They will switch stalls and begin the permission process again, with the hope of being accepted." It took a little longer for the dragons to decide than for Darr Beval to explain it, but both trainees were eventually deemed worthy and entered their new respective stalls.

"Thank D'Erenelle," Darr Beval mumbled. "Sometimes, one or both will not be accepted at all, and we'll have to completely reorganize the groups to find a better combination. As you know, dragons are fickle, but they are also as prone to peer pressure as we are. If one of their kind rejects a trainee, that can be enough to sway another dragon's opinion. It can take all day to find the right combination, and there is no guarantee the same lineup will be accepted the next. This is why tethering is such a momentous occasion—and why it makes Riding out much easier."

Riders moved along the line of stalls, approving each group for their flight. One by one, trainees sitting astride saddled dragons emerged from their stalls.

Laila raised a hand to ask whether tethered Riders had to go through this process every time they Rode out. "It seems vastly inefficient in light of a Narxon Descent," she noted.

Her forethought impressed Rhoswen, and she couldn't help but hope that Laila would be on her side after she tethered. *Perhaps I should befriend this girl....* Her stomach flipped—the thought of befriending someone for the sake of strategy made her ill.

Darr Beval shook his head. "No, that's why we have stable hands. They have good relationships with most of the dragons and can have them saddled in no time without the rigors of gaining permission. We train this way, however, to help familiarize the dragons with all the trainees, so they can forge relationships that might lead to tethering." He pointed to the entrance of the arena. "Now, watch."

The group followed Darr Beval's gaze to where a trainee and dragon stood, ready to take off. More saddled dragons were lining up behind the pair. Darr Beval warned his class to "stay put no matter what" and made his way up onto Fleta's waiting back; Rhoswen hadn't even noticed the tawny was saddled. Darr Beval indicated the various Riders around the arena, who were also mounted and at the ready. "All Riders not working the stalls must act as Failsafes," he told his students.

Rhoswen looked back at the first pair waiting to take off. Without any prompting from the instructing Rider, the dragon took a few quick steps forward and lurched into the air.

"They take off whenever the two of them are ready," Darr Beval explained, his eyes never leaving the pair. "No other Rider can tell them when to go; they have to feel it."

Across the arena, on the back of a tawny named Letha, a slim Rider raised his hand. His limp blond bangs were brushed all the way to one side and threatened to fall into his eyes. He tossed them back from his face with a sharp sideways jerk of his head.

At the Rider's signal, Darr Beval turned back to his class. "Darr Galorian has chosen to watch that pair. Because so many fly at once, a single Rider on the ground volunteers for each pair and watches them for any sign of trouble. This is why we need so many Failsafes."

Another dragon-trainee pair stepped up to the edge of the arena and wasted no time in alighting. The beast—a green with a gorgeous blueish hue that Rhoswen had never before seen—leapt into the air, and she and her trainee moved together seamlessly. Unlike the first couple, who had seemed to do well enough, this pair's takeoff looked effortless.

"Naida and Nixie have been flying together for a good while," Darr Beval explained. "This will be their last mass-flight. Next, they will begin performing single flights to test their connection."

Rhoswen thought she heard Laila heave a wistful sigh. It reminded her that her own dragon didn't even exist yet, and she wondered how she could possibly fly a whelp into the next realm when everyone here was practicing on dragons of adolescent age and older.

More pairs took to the air, and with each new set, a Failsafe's hand shot upward to claim them. Rhoswen was glad she was not a Failsafe—about a dozen trainees flew above them, and she could barely keep track of who was who.

Somehow, the flying lesson concluded without incident, and the trainees came back down on their beasts, pair by pair. Some landings looked a little rougher than others, but they suffered no crashes, and no Failsafe ever had to leave the ground. Everyone applauded, and Darr Beval concluded by narrating the procedure for unsaddling the dragons.

"Well now," he said, beaming at his students. "Are you ready to give it a try?"

The response was more mixed than Rhoswen expected. While some were still as eager as before, others expressed more hesitation now.

Darr Beval laughed. "Not so fast. When I said '*we* fly,' I meant *them*." He gestured over his shoulder at the older students. "You still have some things to master before you can take to the air yourselves. Today, you will experience everything they did—the permissions, the saddling, the rope tying, and the riding—but not the flying." Sounds of confusion mingled with whispers of relief and disappointment. "You can't fly dragons until you feel comfortable on their backs. So, today, you will ride them around the arena—*on foot* only."

Darr Beval jumped down from Fleta's back, deaf to his students' varied responses, and led his group up to the stables. Other Riders around the arena did the same. Throughout the drakiary, stall doors stood open, and dragons of every color and disposition peeked out of their enclosures. Rhoswen's heart raced.

The students began breaking off into groups of four, and Rhoswen turned to find herself face-to-face with Laila. She wore her brown hair in two girlish braids, but her angular features gave her a refined look. "May I join you?" Rhoswen asked.

Laila looked delighted. "I was about to ask you! I'm Laila Kinsey of Radbourne. This is Golda and Haylan. They're twins." Rhoswen recognized them both. Haylan was taller and much stockier than his waiflike sister, but they had the same blond hair and freckles. Rhoswen introduced herself.

"You're the weather girl," Haylan said, "from Stanburh." He was not mocking her—it was a statement of simple fact; he clearly meant no offense.

"I am," Rhoswen said with only a moment's hesitation. *Better than being the king's niece...!*

"We're from Stanburh, too," Haylan said. "Well, the outskirts. We don't have a fancy title like you. We're just the Barlows."

"Don't say that," Rhoswen replied. "Titles don't mean anything. And anyway, sensing the weather isn't that special. Surely you all have much more impressive talents of your own. I know you're really smart," she said, turning to Laila.

"She *is* very smart," Golda affirmed, patting the girl on her shoulder.

Laila beamed. "Haylan is good with animals," she said. When he tried to shrug off the compliment, she added, "He's a natural healer. Even Aelfraed noticed. He's taken Haylan under his wing for additional training in dragon care."

Rhoswen remembered Darr Beval's comment that Aelfraed had never found an apprentice. She wondered if the caretaker believed Haylan would not tether or simply felt he had the aptitude to learn more. *Why train a non-Rider apprentice if we're going to Move?*

"Well, Golda is good at everything she does," Haylan announced with pride, "but especially mindwalking."

Rhoswen started a bit. In Stanburh—at least her corner of Stanburh—calling someone a mindwalker was usually an insult. Most were frauds and only used their supposed skill as a way of making money or gaining power. Some of them had no psychic ability at all, and they used tricks to make their *walkings* more believable to gullible patrons. Here, though, Haylan had spoken the word in veneration, as if it were a prized talent. Rhoswen could appreciate Golda's apprehension as she placed a hand on her brother's arm.

"Hush," she said, "I don't want the realm to know...."

"Are you really a mindwalker?" Rhoswen asked. Golda nodded.

"An accomplished one, too," Haylan added, dodging a slap from his twin. Laila giggled.

"Don't brag," Golda admonished. "Some people feel very strange about it because they think I'm *walking* through their minds all the time, but I honestly don't." Her voice was sincere and almost pleading. "I try not to do it unless I'm asked."

"*Try* not to? It comes so easily to you that you have to block it out?" Rhoswen asked. This was a far cry from the hacks she had heard of back home. And these two were *from* back home.

"Told you she was accomplished," Haylan said, crossing his arms in front of his chest. Rhoswen adored his pride in his sister.

Golda nodded, ignoring her brother. "But I promise I'm not *walking* your mind now. I can see everything on your face." She smiled. "Sometimes, it's not necessary to *walk*." Rhoswen smiled back.

The Riders hollered for quiet and directed their groups' attention to Darr Galorian. He stood at the front of the assembly of trainees, his arms spread wide above his head. His voice was not deep, but it was clear. "Rather than assign each of your groups to a dragon and hope for the best," he began, "you will form a rotating line of groups and pass in front of the stalls together until you are selected by a dragon. Once selected, your group will step out of the line and stand in front of that beast's stall. The line will circle until every group is claimed. Are we clear?" Everyone nodded and muttered their assent. "Fall in, then," Darr Galorian said, and Riders began ushering their groups into a line with a decent space between each foursome.

"How will we know we've been selected?" Golda whispered to Laila, who shrugged. Rhoswen realized she didn't know either. Certainly, *she* would know in a way that the rest would not, and that posed a potentially dangerous situation. Her skin prickled.

Once every foursome was in place, the line began passing slowly in front of the dragons until it reached the end of the stalls and circled back around for another pass. The dragons chattered incessantly—arguing, passing judgments, giving compliments that the trainees couldn't hear or appreciate, even gossiping about unrelated topics as they watched the procession from the corners of their eyes. Rhoswen's head swam with the mental clamor.

As her group approached the center of the stalls, she heard Rusalka nexing her claim on them to her dragon neighbors. Rhoswen had to bite back a smile as they neared the tawny, who trumpeted skyward, her eyes alight. The four stepped out of line together in front of her stall, equally enthusiastic.

As the procession continued, many selections went uncontested, and the line dwindled. But a handful of beasts lingered in their decision making, muttering their concerns or having all-out arguments over foursomes, while the remaining students circled endlessly in the line. A couple of groups had to reorganize their members until two suitable combinations were found. Rhoswen thought the rationales were petty and sounded more like the product of a grudge between dragons than a dispute over the actual group members. Finally, when every group stood before a stall, the incessant chatter died down. Rhoswen rubbed her temples.

"Are you all right?" Haylan asked her. She smiled and gave him a quick nod.

Laila looked up at the tawny. "You have history with this dragon," she remembered.

"We get along rather well," Rhoswen admitted with a smile at the beast, who nodded and blew air through her nostrils.

"Maybe you'll tether to her!" Golda suggested.

"She can't," Laila replied. "She's Elmina's dragon."

"Oh. Why are we riding someone else's dragon?" Golda asked.

Darr Beval was passing by as she asked the question. "Because not enough of the young beasts wanted to practice with trainees today. We do whatever they want," he answered with a grin and continued walking.

Oh, yes, you are indentured to us, Rusalka snorted.

Rhoswen gave her a playful, chiding glance before returning her attention to Golda. "Golda, can you *walk* through the minds of other creatures or just our kind? What about dragons?"

Golda shook her head. "No, just us. And dragons are different. That's nexing. I'll only be able to do that with a dragon if I tether." She gazed wistfully at Rusalka, and Rhoswen wondered what kind of dragon would be a good match for her—a structured creature or one who was more carefree like herself.... You just never knew.

Darr Galorian beckoned for quiet. He instructed the groups to select their first volunteer and begin the permission process. Rhoswen's good rapport with Rusalka earned her the vote. She bowed before the tawny, who put on a splendid show for the others—all while nexing about how much fun they were going to have. Rhoswen tried not to giggle as her fellow groupmates went through the same—fairly unnecessary—process. Rusalka explained that by having the dragons select their groups, the members were pre-approved. Still, it was important to practice for when a stable was short of hands and dragons needed to be saddled by others in a pinch.

As no one appeared to have any trouble convincing their dragons of their suitability to saddle them, Darr Galorian continued his instructions. "There are already saddles in each stall. It will take the four of you to lift them. Get them in place and secure them the way you were taught. Riders will come around to inspect your work, but I'm certain your dragon will make it clear if something isn't right."

The last line was said with a bit of a smirk at the other Riders, and Rhoswen really didn't care to find out what happened if they made a mistake. *You'll tell me if we do something wrong, won't you?* she nexed to the tawny.

You won't, Rusalka nexed back.

The girls proved stronger than Haylan expected—a miscalculation they agreed never to let him forget—and they lifted the saddle onto Rusalka's upper back with ease. Then began the process of knotting the billet strap into place. Rhoswen's breathing intensified as she tried to focus on the ropes instead of her cumbersome arm pads.

You're doing fine. Just make certain your knots are secure.

"It's a good thing you know Rusalka," Haylan said as he tied a knot at the dragon's left flank. "This is going really well."

"She's a beautiful tawny," Golda said from the opposite side. Rhoswen couldn't see her over Rusalka's back.

They are lovely, Rusalka nexed. *You would be wise to befriend them.*

I shouldn't be selecting friends like a wartime strategy, Rhoswen argued. *That sounds like some horrible thing my uncle would do.*

What's so horrible about caring about the type of company you keep? I'm not telling you to run with thieves and murderers because they'd make convenient allies in battle, Rusalka replied in genuine bewilderment.

You're right, Rhoswen assured her. *They are lovely, and I'd be honored to have them as friends.* That seemed to please the dragon.

Darr Beval walked in to inspect their knots just as they were giving them a good, final tug. *They did it right,* Rusalka nexed, as if he could hear her.

"Looks good to me," Darr Beval said, ending his inspection with Rhoswen's knot. "You're first to ride?" She nodded. "Do you want to inspect the knots yourself?" Rhoswen shook her head; she trusted her group. "Then climb on up."

She forced her leg to bend against the thick, rough leather as she lifted it to the bottom stirrup. As she finally hauled herself astride, she could see Darr Beval out of the corner of her eye; he was fighting the urge to assist her, though clearly she did not need the help. She had done this on her parents' beasts more times than she could count… although with far more ease than she was doing now with roughs.

"Good then," he said finally and moved on to the next stall.

"They act as if half of us don't have Riders for parents," Laila said after Darr Beval left.

"Half of us don't," Haylan said. Laila tried to apologize, but he stopped her. "We don't have the practice you and Rhoswen do, but that's why you're going first." His tone was always so matter-of-fact, like nothing could ever offend him because the realm was the way it was, and that was that. Rhoswen admired that quality.

Darr Galorian instructed the mounted trainees to wrap their hands in the pommel loops and give their dragons' sides a gentle squeeze with their legs.

A dragon nexed in agitation nearby. *If that was a gentle squeeze, I don't want to know what you'd be doing in a Descent....*

Rhoswen bit her lip to stop herself from giggling, but Rusalka, who had also heard it, rumbled with laughter.

You ready? Rhoswen asked the tawny.

Whenever you are.

Rhoswen squeezed her knees together, just for show, and Rusalka shifted into a standing position. Rhoswen tightened her grip on the loops, trying to steady herself at the pommel instead of squeezing harder with her legs.

Use your feet, Rusalka nexed. *There are toe holds on these saddles. Didn't you use them with your parents' dragons?*

Rhoswen rooted around for the toe holds and slid the front of her boots into the small alcoves on the top stirrups. She pressed into them a little and raised herself off the saddle to test her balance. *I don't think I had access to them,* she nexed with some surprise. She had never been on her parents' dragons alone; presumably, her parents' feet had been in the toe holds.

Rusalka nodded, having caught more of Rhoswen's thoughts than she had intended to share. The tawny stepped forward to exit the stall. Darr Beval glanced over at them from a couple stalls away but grew distracted when a trainee began to wobble in her saddle.

Rusalka nexed for Rhoswen's attention. Her groupmates were cheering behind her. She unwrapped one hand from its pommel loop and waved to them over her shoulder.

I need to wait for those two, Rusalka nexed, slowing to a halt. In front of them, a green shuffled in place, unable to convey his concern to the trainee on his back. The Riders nearby were struggling to figure out why the young beast wouldn't move—and ignoring their own dragons' nexed instructions. *The toe holds, you ninnies,* Rusalka chimed in with some other dragons. *The toe holds!*

"The toe holds!" Rhoswen blurted out before she could stop herself.

Riders and trainees all over the arena stared at her with furrowed brows and awed expressions.

Perhaps I shouldn't have helped, she thought ruefully.

LXV

Detroit

After the quick succession of her last two trips to the Exchange, Emmelyn had a decent wait before her next Transfer.

Okay, a normal *wait,* she admitted as the sun began to set on a week-long delay. *Maybe I'll make a night trip and wake up outside the club.* But that seemed almost too considerate for the Exchange's taste.

On the other hand, she had been on a few more dates with Jeremy since her last Transfer, and they hadn't been interrupted (not that she had wanted them to be). In fact, she had used the time to do some serious thinking, and now that she had a plan she was desperate to put into play, the Exchange wasn't portaling her in.

She wasn't keen to simply "pop" into the Exchange again either. After that first and only time that she had blinked and found herself drinking beer with the wrong set of friends, she'd decided not to try it again. If she even succeeded, and her friends weren't there to provide adequate cover, she could be found out in an instant. It might not be a power unique to her, but Vonn had said not to broadcast it, and she meant to take his advice, at least for the time being.

Nothing was more tempting now, though.... Until she remembered the Minister who had stared at her after she'd suddenly shown up in the club. She shivered.

Since her last Transfer, Emmelyn had racked her brain, determined to prevent herself—and her realm—from being helpless victims of the Exchange. Nancy, the reformed gambler and newest patron at WE Dress, had unwittingly provided inspiration.

"Beating the house is a matter of odds, and the odds vary from game to game," Nancy had explained as they'd waited for Lydia to take her back to the clothing racks. "But you can improve your odds if you pay attention.

Roulette, for example, can favor the player if the table is old and wobbly and starts privileging some numbers over others. When I was playing, I looked for dealers who were sloppy enough to flash the hole cards. I'm no card counter, but it occasionally gave me an edge. If you can find a weakness and exploit it, your odds of beating the house are better than someone who plays by the rules."

And from what Emmelyn could tell during her discussions with the Crew, the rules were a bit hazy to everyone in the Exchange. She grimaced at their pervasive culture of uncertainty. *Feels deliberate.*

Her greatest advantage, she realized, was that she Transferred for D'Erenelle, the most studied—and *prized*—realm. One popular theory in the Exchange called D'Erenelle the "Dominant Realm," meaning the energy generated by rule changes within it created mirrored instances of that energy in all the other realms. Given that such energy could create tears that attract Narxon, this interconnectedness proved rather significant.

It also made D'Erenelle the center of attention, not only in the *minds* of Exchangers but also in their *activities*: since Badrick and Orla's ascent to the throne, D'Erenelle became the most tweaked realm of them all, as the Exchange attempted to protect it from its own rulers' deficiencies. Many Exchangers believed the realm's demise would spell disaster, given its far-reaching influence. Emmelyn couldn't help but agree, and she felt she needed to act against those who seemed deaf to this possibility of doom.

On the bright side, D'Erenelle's popularity increased Emmelyn's chances of locating a Datist with some knowledge about, and likely interest in, D'Erenelle. However, she would need to recruit one who wasn't in league with the "other side." Another rampant idea, Annihilation Theory, provided the backbone of the countermovement within the Exchange and Emmelyn's motivation for breaking the rules. Its proponents wanted to allow every realm to die out of existence, thereby depriving the Narxon of food and driving them to extinction. Then, new realms could magically regenerate over time, never again to be plagued by the realm-hopping parasites.

Their proviso? They believed the Exchange would survive because, as a non-realm, it could not harbor Narxon, so the parasites would not prey on it when the other realms had disappeared.

The idea seemed reckless beyond belief, hinging everyone's existence on another *theory*. As far as Emmelyn knew, there was no hard and fast evidence that the Exchange *was* immune to the Narxon. *If the counter-faction is wrong…!* She couldn't bear to consider it. And she couldn't let it happen without the certainty that it would *work*.

All she needed was the help of a Datist to place a few bets in the G'Ambit for her. She would use the bets to call attention to the divisive politics that were not even supposed to exist in the Exchange and force the contention between the two factions into the spotlight. If the Ivers were serious about protecting the realms, they wouldn't ignore tweaks by the countermovement to bring a realm to a swifter conclusion. Instead, Ivers and Datists would be forced to investigate the idea's legitimacy before allowing it to take hold. Permitting the realms to perish without researching the possible fallout was unacceptable, and allowing a few Exchangers to take that dubious decision into their own hands was equally irresponsible.

Most importantly, by using the G'Ambit to bring this heresy into the open, no one would be implicated, her Datist-accomplice included.

Now, she just needed to be portaled back into the Exchange for a Transfer with enough timestamps to ensnare some help.

As the sky turned orange, her impatience got the better of her. She needed a distraction, and Josie was out on a date.

"Jere," she said into the phone. "You busy tonight?"

"Not anymore," he said. Sounds of a clanging battle ceased in the background. *Video game.*

"If you're doing something—" she began.

"Nope," Jeremy insisted. "I'll be right over."

"But we haven't decided what we're doing."

"We'll figure it out," he said and hung up.

She smiled at his eagerness and sped off to her room to change. Twenty minutes later, he was knocking on her door. "Coming!" she yelled. As she turned the handle, an anticipatory smile washing over her face—

—she found herself in the gray daylight of the deserted street outside Dissonance. For once, the unromantic Exchange with its sick and ironic sense of timing had not let her down.

Emmelyn practically skipped into the marble lobby. She cheerily accepted her Transitor and Janelle's grouchy greeting, smiled as she counted the stamps coloring her wrist, and bolted up the stairs two by two… (well, at least half of the way up).

First stop: the bar. She ordered a gin and soda to buy her time to survey the crowd. As Trevor placed her drink on the bar, Kyle came up beside her. *Perfect,* she thought. "Buy ya a drink, sailor?"

Kyle shot her the kind of look an embarrassed kid might flash his dorky father. "When did you get here?" he asked before ordering an Assalyan draft.

Assalya brewed excellent beer. She wished she could bring one back for Jeremy…. *Stay focused, Darrow,* she told herself. "Just now," she hollered, holding up her full glass as if that were indisputable proof of her recent arrival. She sidled in closer to him. "Who's that?" she asked, jutting out her chin toward a pair of guys at the other end of the bar. One was dressed in plain clothes and the other in cowboy gear.

"The Datist or the other guy?" Kyle asked.

"Which one's which?"

"Felix is the Datist. Red hair," he replied, his tone hard to read. He squinted. "Actually, judging by that outfit, I expect the cowboy is a Datist, too, but I don't know him. Why?"

"Felix looks nice," she replied.

Kyle stared at her, not even acknowledging the beer Trevor set down in front of him. "What happened to Jeremy?" he asked.

Although her relationship with Kyle was finally bordering on friendship, Emmelyn was a little surprised he cared enough to ask. "No, no," she yelled, "not like that. I just wanted to speak with a Datist." She actually didn't know how to explain her sudden fascination, so she gambled on his disinterest and offered no further justification. She won the bet.

"Okay," he called, his eyebrows askew. He lifted his beer to Trevor in a gesture of appreciation and returned to the circle without a second glance at her.

Rather than follow him, Emmelyn moved down to the far end of the bar just in time for the cowboy—if that's what he could be called—to vacate his stool. Now she understood why Kyle hadn't suspected the man was from Tallulahdur. Outfitted like Randy from his standard ranch-hand hat and vest to his wide, studded belt, the rest of him was on display, barely covered by revealing black leather chaps that gave his outfit a distinctly BDSM flare. She pried her eyes away as he disappeared into the crowd. It was an image she would never shake.

"This seat taken?" she managed to ask, trying not to think about the naked buns that had just sat there.

"All yours," the guy beside her yelled with a smile.

"Emmelyn," she hollered into his ear and extended a hand to him.

"Felix," he called back, shaking it. "You a Transfer or a Runner?"

With her fingers curled around her glass, her wrist displayed four bright-red stamps. "Transfer," she replied. "You?"

"Datist." He sipped his beer. Unlike the "cowboy," he wore a light-blue button-down shirt with the sleeves rolled up to his elbows and medium-wash jeans. If Kyle hadn't declared him a Datist, she might have thought him a Runner or Transfer who lived in her own realm.

"The first I've formally met," she admitted. "I'm new here."

He smiled. "What do you think of the gig?"

"I think we Transfers are getting the shaft," she exclaimed. "I don't care about the money, but I don't think it's fair that we get cut out of the G'Ambit when we're the ones passing all the intel back and forth."

It was a gamble, which seemed appropriate in the G'Ambit, but his response to her straightforward rebellion would tell her a lot. Would he be intrigued or dissuaded?

He flashed a surprised smile. "And how do you propose you Transfers should be involved? You have no pertinent or interesting information about the realms."

Intrigued it is. "We could add a little chaos to the mix." She flashed him a mischievous grin.

"I don't know if this place needs any more chaos," he replied.

"Really? This place seems like the epitome of calculated order to me. Except when triples are involved," she added with a shrug.

Felix looked over at her with interest. "You ever Transferred one of those?"

"Quite a few," Emmelyn yelled back. She took a sip of her drink. "From what I hear, that's not normal." He shook his head. "We Transfers may not have much realm information, but we know a lot about the goings-on right here in the Exchange."

"What does that matter?" Felix countered. "Anyway, it sounds like your Arbiter is already injecting plenty of chaos into your realm without your proposed help. What realm do you Transfer for?"

"D'Erenelle."

Felix's eyes widened. "Who's your Arbiter?" he asked.

Emmelyn hesitated. "I don't want to get anyone in trouble...." She leaned in closer to him. "I just don't know that what my Arbiter is doing is... *helpful* to D'Erenelle. Seems like there are two schools of thought about that around here...." She straightened back up. "But what do I know? I'm new."

"You don't sound new," Felix yelled, his expression tentative. But he was hooked; he hadn't touched his beer for almost the entire span of their conversation. "And what do you want to do?"

"That depends on you," she replied.

"On me?"

"On what you can tell me about those two schools of thought." She leaned in closer. "What do you know about the rumor that there are two factions emerging within the Exchange?"

"Just about everything there is," he replied. "It's no rumor; it's the driving force behind most of the activity within the G'Ambit nowadays."

"Can I gather from your earlier reaction that you want to protect the realms and the Realm Cycle? You don't buy into this whole Annihilation Theory nonsense, do you?"

Felix nodded. "I'm pro-realm. Annihilation Theory is bunk. Sometimes a realm can't be saved—and we have to accept that unpleasant possibility—but that doesn't mean the work we do to prolong a realm's existence isn't beneficial to the Realm Cycle at large."

Emmelyn smiled at their shared opinion and made a mental note of the moniker. "What if I told you that I have a pro-realm contact in D'Erenelle who just confirmed that she is no longer Running for my Arbiter?"

"This Runner was part of the Arbiter shakeup?" Felix asked. Emmelyn nodded. He looked around, as if to verify no one was watching them. "You really shouldn't know about that."

"But I do," Emmelyn replied. It was a half-truth. Most of her knowledge on the subject came from rumor and her own conjecture, but it was the best she could do, and it had given her the foothold with Felix that she needed. "And if I know *that,* what other kinds of information might I have that would be of interest to gambling Datists?" *Asking for a friend,* she inwardly joked.

Felix stared at her, sizing her up. She wondered whether there could be spies in the G'Ambit who tried to trip up gamblers—someone in plain clothes who helped out the Ministers. She took another sip of her drink to hide her uneasiness. She really had no way of knowing what additional information—if any—she could get that a Datist might find interesting. After their last fraught conversation, Lorelle might not want to speak to her anymore. Vonn, on the other hand, could probably be counted on for more gossip....

"What do you want in exchange for this kind of intel?" Felix asked.

"I have a few bets I'd like to place."

A look of realization came over his face. "Ah, so it *is* about the money."

"It's not." She stared at him, waiting.

He let her. "What if I want in on these bets?" he finally asked.

"I'm counting on it," she replied.

Felix narrowed his eyes. "You also seem to be pro-realm. If you're so certain your Arbiter is anti-realm, why are you protecting his—or her—identity?" He gave her a sideways smile. "You know I can look it up, right?" He thumbed his chest. "Datist."

Emmelyn resisted the urge to face-palm herself for not thinking of that. "Well then, it doesn't matter if I tell you," she replied. "Suffice it to say, it isn't *my Arbiter's* identity I'm interested in protecting in this little gamble."

"Yours?" Felix suggested.

She nodded. "Among others'."

"All right," Felix yelled in her ear. "What do you need to know from me?"

Yes! "Do you always place bets through the same Runner?"

Felix half-smiled at her. "You really are new, aren't you? I don't need a Runner. Most bookies are Datists. I place them directly."

Noted. "Gotcha," Emmelyn replied as Trevor approached them.

Felix downed his beer and ordered another. Emmelyn still had half a drink and declined. "I tend to bet on two realms," he continued. "D'Erenelle and Welsamar—are you familiar?"

She nodded. "I have contacts in both."

"How did you manage that as a novice?" he asked. When Emmelyn shrugged, he laughed. "You should have been a Runner."

"Not as much anonymity that way," she replied.

His raised eyebrows painted him impressed. "True. So, the only time I'd use a Runner would be to contact an Arbiter about backing my bet at the outset. Because I bet on those two realms, I'd use a different Runner—and Arbiter—for each."

"And shall I guess you won't share their identities with me?" she asked.

He shook his head. "You got it."

Realm it. She didn't want to find out that he sent bets through Lorelle and risk immediate exposure. By the same token, she didn't figure Lorelle played the G'Ambit.... "Can you at least assure me that both Arbiters are also pro-realm?"

Felix considered her question for a moment before deciding it was fair to ask. "Sure, I can vouch for them. What's your first bet?"

"I'll tell you next time," she replied. The delay would either cement his desire to participate or give him the chance to change his mind. If she weren't whisked away by the Ministers during her next Transfer, she would know he was still interested—and hadn't ratted her out. "How will I contact you, so you know I'm here?"

Felix smiled in a boy-you-*are*-green kind of way. "I'll know, and I'll find you."

"Right," Emmelyn replied and pointed at him, "Datist."

"Right." Felix took another swig of his beer and stood, bottle in hand. "Until next time, then."

Emmelyn nodded and watched him leave before she, too, stepped away from the bar and threaded through the crowd of bodies swarming the dance floor. *How am I going to keep him away from the Crew the next time I'm here?* she wondered.

She approached her circle of friends, who wasted no time in interrogating her.

"Who was that?" Inzay asked.

Emmelyn waved her off. "A Datist named Felix. Kyle knows him."

"Not well," Kyle protested with more than his usual defensiveness.

"What did you want with him?" Vonn asked.

"Yeah," Inzay interjected. "I thought things were going well with Jeremy."

"Oh, they are," Emmelyn insisted. "It was nothing like that. I was worried about Lorelle. I just wanted to make sure she was all right. He, uh, knows her. She was... a bit off the last time I saw her." She nodded at Vonn as if to say, "You remember." He didn't nod back.

Kyle was staring at her, and she realized the narrative wouldn't make sense to him: how could she have known to ask Felix about Lorelle when she didn't even know who Felix was a few minutes ago? *Realm it!* She prayed Kyle would keep his mouth shut for once.

"Well, is she?" Inzay asked. "All right, that is."

"So it would seem, but he mentioned something about a friend of hers.... I couldn't quite make out the name," Emmelyn lied. "Might you know it, Vonn?"

Vonn looked less than thrilled to be called out. Thankfully, as the primary source of gossip within the group, he was expected to have an answer, and he didn't—*couldn't?*—disappoint. "The only one I know is a waitman named Delwyn," he offered.

"Delwyn," Emmelyn repeated, "that must have been it. Thank you."

Vonn gave her a curt nod, his expression souring. If the rumor about his having an Arbiter girlfriend were true, Emmelyn would need to be careful about what she shared with him, lest it should get back to her. And now, she had to be careful with him *and* Kyle. So much for asking for particulars about Delwyn.... She would just have to wing it.

She glanced at her wrist. "I think I'll grab another drink," she announced. "Can I get one for anybody else?"

LXVI

Keaton

"I believe that green wants his trainee to use the toe holds," Rhoswen told the see of eyes around her. *Improvise!* "Rusalka behaved the same way when I wasn't using mine. I just sort of figured it out—on accident." She shrugged.

The Riders continued to stare at her. The trainee looked down at his saddle, located the toe holds, and slipped his boots into them. His green trumpeted happily, and other dragons joined in. Rhoswen saw Darr Beval gaping at her, and she instantly regretted her decision to intervene.

He glanced at his fellow Riders, who seemed to hesitate somewhat, but as trainees continued to move their dragons along—whether intentionally or not—everyone's attention reverted to the matter at hand. Darr Beval locked eyes with Rhoswen and nodded once before turning away. Fleta exhaled noisily at Rusalka.

He wants us to keep our heads down, Rusalka translated.

I think I sort of understood that one, Rhoswen nexed back.

Not long after they had entered the arena, Rusalka grew bored with their path around its circumference. She wandered out of step with the others, and in no time, the perfect line along the outside of the arena frayed into multiple lanes. Some dragons walked beside each other to chat, while others weaved in and out of the slower beasts around them. *Should we have upset the procedure this way? I don't need any more attention drawn to me,* Rhoswen nexed.

This is good, Rusalka insisted. *You all need to learn how to maneuver, and you were never going to in a straight line. They would have told us to do this anyway; I just sped up the process.*

This meant some trainees plunged into intermediate riding conditions the moment they entered the arena. Rhoswen felt guilty, but they seemed to do pretty well, and no Rider had to come out to save anyone.

Want to fly? Rusalka asked.

"What?!" Rhoswen blustered in surprise. A few heads turned toward her, and she smiled weakly at them. *No! Rusalka, what are you thinking?*

Just a joke, the tawny nexed, but Rhoswen could tell that she would have taken off from that very spot if Rhoswen had acquiesced. *Maybe later,* the dragon mused.

Later?

Well, you do have that meeting planned for tonight....

Other dragons snorted in amusement.

Are they eavesdropping? Rhoswen asked.

It's a dirty little dragon habit. We all do it.

That made Rhoswen laugh out loud. She cupped a hand over her mouth and avoided making eye contact with the trainees around her. *Are you all suggesting I begin my flying lessons tonight?*

A mix of snorts, some more approving than others, sounded around her. Trainees glanced around in confusion.

Why not? It's not like you haven't practiced with your parents, Rusalka nexed.

Rhoswen hesitated. *But I've never flown by myself before.*

You're doing fine now. What do you think the next step after this exercise is?

Maybe I should wait to learn it in class....

Is that what you're doing with the portal?

That stopped Rhoswen short. *I'm sorry?*

Rusalka blew an impatient burst of air through her nose. *You're not going to learn how to use the thing in lecture, my dear. What are you waiting for? You're overthinking that little puzzle. It's like any good song.... It has a certain ring to it. We don't have time to waste. You need to master these skills now before –*

A couple dragons trumpeted their disapproval, and Rusalka fell silent. Various beasts cast disgruntled glances in the tawny's direction, earning more confused reactions from trainees and Riders throughout the arena.

This is going well, Rhoswen nexed sarcastically. *I'm sorry; I hope you're not in trouble.*

I nex too much, Rusalka replied grumpily. The dragons that had been glaring at Rusalka looked away, but the trainees on their backs remained noticeably baffled. They kept glancing at Rhoswen, their confusion bordering on agitation. *Uh-oh,* the tawny nexed suddenly.

Rhoswen felt a series of strong tugs on the right side of her saddle, and a moment later, Darr Beval was sitting behind her. Even through her roughs, she could feel his chest against her back and the lines of his legs and arms following her own as he reached around her to steady her hands with his. Her grip tightened on the pommel loops, and her cheeks flushed as he whispered in her ear.

"What in the realm are you doing?" The tickle of his warm breath did nothing to calm her. Rusalka rumbled with apparent glee at Rhoswen's reaction.

"I'm *sorry*!" she whispered back. It seemed like every part of their bodies was touching. She could barely speak—or think—or breathe. The weight of her roughs suddenly felt hot and oppressive. "We-we were discussing the agenda for the meeting tonight, and—and all the dragons were listening in—"

"Well, unless *all the dragons* want to blow your cover, they'd be wise not to draw any more attention to you than they already have. That stunt with the toe holds was conspicuous enough!" Darr Beval hissed.

Rusalka broadcast his admonition, and a few dragons grumbled ruefully. Others rumbled in arrogant agreement.

"We're all sorry," Rhoswen whispered back, glancing at him over her shoulder.

Darr Beval let go of her hands and sat back a bit. He shook his head, and a small smile curved his lips. "That never fails to amaze me," he muttered before swinging a leg over and making his way back down to the ground. "We're good here. Just a little idle gossiping among beasts, I think. Let's speed 'em up!" he yelled to the arena at large, moving his arm in a broad circle. Darr Galorian instructed the trainees to give their dragons another squeeze with their legs.

Rhoswen looked around. All the saddled dragons were in the arena space now. *Won't we crash into one another?* she asked Rusalka.

Well, we won't let that happen. But we'll only intervene if we must. The idea is for you all to learn how to steer. The chaos is good training for when we're battling Narxon. Give 'er a squeeze, my dear!

It was only for show, but Rhoswen did as she was asked, and Rusalka sped into a jog. She wove in and out of the dragons around her, mostly per Rhoswen's instructions, although once or twice, she had to zig or zag away from an obstacle Rhoswen hadn't seen in time.

That's all right, Rusalka assured her. *We both have a set of eyes for a reason. You're going to miss things, and so am I. We tether because we are two halves of a team. You'll learn soon enough.*

Supportive grunts arose from a couple of nearby dragons, but most were too busy dodging one another to pay attention. The arena ride had, indeed, deteriorated into mild chaos.

Rusalka issued a derogatory snort and nexed to Rhoswen, *At least you're staying on.* She motioned with her head to their right and sighed.

Rhoswen glanced in the direction Rusalka indicated. An imbalanced trainee lurched to the right as his dragon made an abrupt turn, and he slipped from the saddle, his pommel loops the only thing keeping him from crashing to the ground. Darr Galorian hollered, and the dragons all came to an abrupt halt. A few trainees were flung forward, stopped by the pommel slamming into their guts. Rhoswen had enough notice to brace herself with her toe holds to keep from sliding forward.

Sorry, Rusalka nexed. *We have to stop when someone falls to avoid trampling the trainee.*

A Rider helped the lad to standing and checked him for injury, but nothing seemed hurt, aside from his pride. Once the young man was mounted again, Darr Galorian instructed everyone to bring in the dragons. The trainees nudged their toe holds to usher their beasts into the stables.

You're getting good at this, Rusalka nexed.

Thank you, Rhoswen replied with a smile.

Back in Rusalka's stall, Rhoswen's group applauded her ride.

"You were wonderful!" Golda squealed. "Can I go next?"

Rusalka blew air through her nose to show her approval, and Golda bounced in place. Rhoswen's foot had barely left the bottom rung of the laddered stirrup before Golda hurried astride. Rhoswen ensured the trainee's feet were secure in the toe holds, and a Rider came by to check their progress. Finally, Darr Galorian began the procedure anew, and before they knew it, Golda was riding around the arena on Rusalka's back.

Haylan's focus was trained on his sister, but Laila used the time to pepper Rhoswen with questions. "How did it feel? You seemed completely comfortable out there! Was it as easy as you made it look?"

"You've practiced on your parents' dragons, haven't you?" Rhoswen asked.

Laila nodded.

"Then it will be just as easy for you. And look at Golda! She doesn't have our experience, and she seems to be having a wonderful time!" Rhoswen pointed at their groupmate, who was waving at them from Rusalka's back.

Haylan inhaled sharply, his brows knitting together. "Be careful!" he called, as if she could hear him over the din. "Hold on with both hands! Watch what you're doing! Pay attention!"

Laila and Rhoswen giggled.

When Golda returned in one piece, Haylan bid Laila go next so he could finish admonishing his sister, but he couldn't get a word in—Golda rambled on about what it must be like to fly if riding on the ground was so marvelous. Rhoswen laughed at them as she watched Laila—and Thane, she realized, as he passed by on the back of a young red. Both were holding their own among the other trainees.

Soon, Laila returned. She was a little flushed, her braids loosened by the wind, but clearly invigorated. "That was fantastic!" she exclaimed and began a fevered discussion with Golda about their experiences.

Haylan did not appear to share their enthusiasm. Even after watching three successful rides, he stared up at the saddle, his breathing quick and unblinking gaze intensely focused. *He's not just worried about Golda's safety,* Rhoswen realized.

Rusalka shifted in place. *That one is skittish,* she nexed.

Rhoswen patted Rusalka's hide and went over to where Haylan stood by himself. His frame doubled in size with the bulk of his roughs, yet he was eyeing the saddle as if it might bite him. "You know the best part about training?" she asked him, her voice low.

"What?" Haylan asked, not taking his eyes off the mount.

"They don't just throw you on the back of a dragon and send you flying on your first day. They ease you into it. You learn about dragons and their care so you understand them better; you practice tying knots so you can trust you will be safe on their backs; and you grow comfortable riding them on the ground before you even think about taking to the air. Before you know it, you're flying through the sky, and you can't even remember why you had to go through all those steps in the first place."

Haylan glanced at Rhoswen. "You've flown before."

She shrugged. "Never alone, but I came back to tell the tale dozens of times."

Haylan exhaled. "Make sure my feet are secure in the toe holds?"

Rhoswen smiled. "Will do."

Haylan climbed up into the saddle, and Rhoswen had just started checking his boots when Darr Galorian came by to inspect the knots. "Good to go," he said and walked back out.

"That's it? He doesn't want to check anything else?" Haylan protested.

"If the knots are secure, you're secure," Rhoswen assured him, patting the toe hold that hugged the toe of his boot.

Darr Galorian yelled to the trainees to begin, and Haylan glanced down at Rhoswen.

"Until the next Ride, Haylan," Rhoswen said with a smile.

Something changed in Haylan's face when Rhoswen used the phrase only exchanged between tethered Riders, and a subtle shift in his posture gave him a more determined look. He squeezed his legs against Rusalka's side, and the dragon winked at Rhoswen as she lifted herself to standing and stepped out of the stall, Haylan sitting tall on her back.

Golda and Laila called out their well wishes as Haylan and Rusalka departed, but he didn't wave or turn back. In no time, he was outmaneuvering the other trainees around him, most of whom appeared to be the more apprehensive members in their groups. Still, Haylan could have held his own among the earlier trainees. He rode with focus and confidence. The girls beamed when he returned.

Laila and Golda were still fawning over Haylan when it was announced that the afternoon would culminate in single flights for the older students. Darr Galorian instructed the younger trainees to unsaddle their beasts, bow their exits, and take the rest of the day off. Rhoswen's group patted Rusalka and thanked her for showing them such a wonderful time.

It was my pleasure, Rusalka nexed to Rhoswen. *They're a good team.*

Yes, Rhoswen agreed. *Thanks for all the advice.*

Rusalka winked again and bid the others farewell with a playful snort.

LXVII

Ahndalar

"I have no idea what she's up to," Vonn said. He paced at the foot of the bed, his quick, barefooted turns rasping out a *shhhp* sound against the slate tile floor. "But she's going to get us all in trouble if she's not careful."

"I don't know about that," Rehlia replied. She hadn't seen him this worked up about anything since they'd started dating… or whatever this clandestine togetherness could be called.

"Oh really? Why would she suddenly begin talking to Datists? What could a Transfer possibly need to know?"

"Doesn't your friend, Kyle, date Datists?" she asked.

"Occasionally," he admitted. He paused his pacing to look at her. "But Emmelyn has a boyfriend in her realm. That's not what this is about for her."

That was news to Rehlia. "She has a boyfriend?"

"Well, she's dating someone," Vonn said dismissively. He took up pacing again. "She said she was asking about Lorelle's wellbeing, but then she asked for the name of Lorelle's friend in D'Erenelle because that Datist had mentioned it." He looked away from Rehlia and rubbed his hands over his eyes. "I didn't want to get involved, but she trapped me. I gave her Delwyn's name. Can you keep tabs on whether she tries to do anything with that?"

Rehlia was grateful to find him forthcoming about Emmelyn. She also appreciated that he had given her something actionable, even if he had only done it to maintain his reputation as the quintessential gossip.

But her satisfaction was tempered by his shirtless request that she protect his new crush from the perils of the Exchange. *It's my job,* she reminded herself. *Emmelyn appears to be on the right side of this, even if she's going about it in a dangerous way. And she could prove valuable….* "I'll see what I can do," she assured him. *All this for a woman who does not even return his affection,* she mused.

He flashed her a helpless look. "How can I stop this madness?"

"Try to figure out what she's up to," she suggested. "Maybe you can talk her out of it."

"I'm getting the impression no one talks Emmelyn out of anything once she's set her mind to it."

"Even if it threatens her safety?" She raised an eyebrow. "Or her exile?"

The color drained from his face. "Do you really think it could come to that?"

Rehlia felt the bitter constriction of her heart at his barefaced concern for the Transfer. "I will try to help avoid it."

"Thank you," Vonn breathed in relief. He crossed to the bed and took her up in his arms. "How could I possibly thank you for protecting my friends?"

Don't fall in love with them, Rehlia thought. She forced her lips into a seductive smile she knew he couldn't resist. "I'm sure you'll find a way."

LXVIII

Detroit

"We're taking it slowly," Emmelyn insisted.

"How many dates has it been?" Josie asked. "Fifteen?"

"Last night made an even dozen, if you must know," Emmelyn replied. "I don't believe in that ridiculous three-date rule. It's too prescriptive… and fast."

"It's the only way to keep 'em coming back for more," Josie countered with an insinuating bounce of her eyebrows.

"Clearly not." Emmelyn wiggled her eyebrows in response.

Josie laughed and chucked a pillow at her.

"What's going on with your new man?" Emmelyn asked, catching the pillow before it hit her in the face. She held onto it for future ammunition.

Josie adopted a dream-like expression. "Dominic? Oh, he's… *something else.*"

"That good, huh?" Emmelyn asked, wiggling her eyebrows again.

"Oh yeah," Josie said, waggling hers back.

Emmelyn threw the pillow at her. "Apparently, *you* believe in the three-date rule!"

"You better believe it!" Josie replied. The two broke into a fit of laughter, and Josie couldn't wipe the silly grin from her face.

In truth, Emmelyn was still struggling to reconcile her two lives. She knew she could have a happy, *normal* life with Jeremy in her realm. But she was beginning to realize, as she set her plan into motion in the Exchange, that she could not give up her Exchange life, even if Jeremy would never be a part of it. She certainly wasn't about to abandon her plan—she couldn't just sit by and allow Emile and other anti-realmers to threaten the existence of the realms and their inhabitants. But she hated being unable to confide in anyone about her fears as she set things in motion, Jeremy—and Josie—especially.

Moreover, she wasn't even sure she could live that "happy, normal life," knowing these other realms—and a threat to them—existed, if she couldn't be a part of the Exchange. She wondered if exile included a memory wipe....

Exile *had* to include a memory wipe.

Unless that knowledge was penance for exile.

Her gut knotted fiercely.

Josie was still rambling on about her most recent date with Dominic. Emmelyn was happy to distract herself with her friend's giddy delight. "So, when do I meet him?" she asked.

"This weekend," Josie replied. "I'm bringing him to Dissonance with us."

"We're going to Dissonance this weekend?"

Josie stared at her in dismay. "Didn't Jere tell you? See? The three-date rule *is* real."

After telling her best friend to shut up (there wasn't another pillow within reach), Emmelyn picked up her phone. She had missed a text from Jeremy:

Dissonance Friday with the crew. You in?

The crew. The knot in Emmelyn's stomach tightened—*remarkably*. "Ah. Yeah, I guess he did." She texted back in the affirmative and received a smiley face for her effort.

Josie rolled her eyes. "Loser."

"Shut up," Emmelyn snapped playfully.

By the time Friday rolled around, Emmelyn still hadn't returned to the Exchange, and she felt more than a little unsettled.

"What's with you?" Josie asked as they readied themselves. As clubbing was now becoming a regular thing—something Emmelyn *never* thought she'd say—she and Josie had gone shopping for new outfits. Josie was struggling to zip up her new dress and finally shuffled over to Emmelyn, zipper first, to appeal to her for help.

Emmelyn zipped it up and fastened the hook-and-eye at the top. "I'm just antsy," she replied.

"Ohhh, is this your version of 'third-date' night?" Josie teased.

Emmelyn searched for a pillow to throw. "No," she replied finally, coming up empty. "I don't know; I'm just... eager to see him, I guess."

"Awww," Josie cooed.

Emmelyn renewed her search for a pillow.

"You look fantastic," Jeremy said, giving Emmelyn a kiss as she came through his front door.

"Thanks. So do you," she said.

"Awww," Josie cooed again from the doorway, her arm wrapped around Dominic's waist. Emmelyn shot her an I-will-cut-you glance, but it was ignored for introductions.

Dominic was tall with dark hair and those hard, Eastern Bloc features that some women found irresistible but were not Emmelyn's catnip. He looked great with Josie, though, and the two seemed smitten with each other. Emmelyn hoped it would last.

Dominic did not have the accent to match his looks. "Hey, man," he said to Jeremy. "Nice place."

"Thanks," Jeremy said. "Pretty sure I won't hear that once Nate and I get our new apartment."

"Your what?" Emmelyn and Josie asked in unison.

Jeremy laughed. "We just found it today." He glanced around at the grand foyer of his parents' home. "It's time."

"Is it?" Emmelyn asked. "I didn't realize you were eager to get out on your own."

Jeremy shrugged. "Nate more so than I—you know how awkward it is with his folks these days—but I'm good with it."

Nate's parents' marriage was on the outs, and their constant arguing was hard on him. He did anything he could to stay away from home.

"Where is it?" Josie asked.

Jeremy described the new construction not three blocks from the university. "We move in a couple weeks," he announced. "Surprise!"

"Congratulations, Jere," Emmelyn said, giving him a kiss on the cheek—or so she tried; at the last minute, he turned his head and changed the quick peck into something that lasted long enough for Leo and Claire to witness as they walked through the door.

"I may never get used to that," Leo joked.

Claire smacked him on the arm. "I think it's lovely," she said.

Dissonance was crowded by its normal standard, which Emmelyn would have already considered crowded. They had passed several clubs on their way, all of which had lines out the door, and Dissonance was no different. Once inside, the group split in two—some to find seating and the rest to find drinks—but only the beverage team succeeded. All the chair circles were occupied, and the counter was standing room only.

"They actually removed the bar stools," Nate marveled as he leaned against the bar, funneling drink orders to and from the red-headed bartender.

"Let's dance," Jeremy suggested in Emmelyn's ear, abandoning the drinks idea.

They made it through several songs—or what felt like several songs, since they were almost indistinguishable—but they barely had room to move. No one was willing to leave for fear the other clubs would be too full to accept them. *This place has* got *to be above occupancy,* Emmelyn thought, as someone bumped into her shoulder again.

"This is ridiculous," Jeremy yelled in her ear. Trapped on all sides by the bodies of other immobilized clubgoers, they could only sway back and forth. "You wanna get out of here?"

"Not enough cars," she replied. He was standing behind her, and she had to lean backward to yell in his ear.

"Would be if anyone else wants to leave," he hollered. "Let's ask."

"If we can find them," Emmelyn joked. She looked around as they extricated themselves from the dance floor.

Neal came up behind them and put his head between theirs. "We found a place to sit in the back!" he yelled to them and began steering them like a human shield through the crowd toward the back of the bar. The group cheered when they were reunited and lifted their glasses high into the air to toast their success at finding an empty ring of seats.

"Shall I get us something then?" Jeremy asked Emmelyn, resigning himself to remain at the overpacked club. Even in the back, there was no room to move.

She nodded and took a seat. The dim lights in this part of the club, along with their proximity to a huge tower of speakers, made it impossible for her to track her friends' conversation. Her attention strayed to the back wall near the restrooms. In the Exchange, portal doors to other realms would appear in that wall.

She suppressed a groan. Felix would have had ample opportunity to turn her in if that were his plan, but she wasn't being portaled into the Exchange to find out. She was *one* plane away from where she wanted to be, yet the risk of exposing her portaling abilities made her shrink from using them.

Unless....

Can I choose where *I pop into the Exchange?*

She got to her feet and gestured toward the bathrooms. Claire and Selma stood, as well, and followed her through the door labeled "*she.*" Even the bathroom was packed. A woman vacated a stall, and Emmelyn went inside.

When she was done, she adjusted her outfit but did not open the door. She closed her eyes and thought of the Exchange—specifically its bathroom, which was identical to this one. To differentiate the two, she envisioned her Exchange friends outside in their usual circle of chairs—which, admittedly, felt a bit weird in this setting.

Then, she began to consider what would happen if someone were using this stall on the Exchange side.

Panicking, she decided against popping into the Exchange. She reached for the latch on the door, but as her fingers curled around the sliding metal lock, the crash of running water in the sinks and the slurred discussions of strangers gave way to muffled music filtering through the bathroom door. No way she could be in the crowded nightclub of her realm anymore. She slid back the lock and stepped out of the stall. Claire and Selma were gone.

She called both of their names, but neither girl answered. Actually, *no one* answered. The bathroom was quiet but for one other person in a stall, who jostled the toilet paper in its holster rather than respond. Emmelyn washed up, pulled open the bathroom door, and looked to her right.

A Runner was stepping through the black void of a portal door and into another realm.

She'd done it.

She walked back into the club—past the now-empty circle where her realm friends were sitting—and strode up to the bar to look for Felix. He was not far from where they had met a week ago.

"Hi," she yelled in his ear, catching him off guard. Lucky he was there at all. She smiled and mouthed her apology.

"Emmelyn," he called, "what are you doing here?"

"Ordering a drink," she said with a nod to Trevor. *Does the bartender ever take a day—or a shift—off from this place?*

"No," Felix persisted, "I mean, I didn't know you were coming."

Emmelyn felt the bottom drop out of her stomach. She had forgotten that Felix would be watching her comings and goings to meet back up with her. Her current visit would not have been documented in the system. It wasn't *lucky* that he was here; it was a *terrible* coincidence. *I knew this was a bad idea!* she chided herself. "Maybe it was a last-minute thing," she said, keeping her left hand below the bar to hide her unstamped wrist.

Felix might have protested, but Trevor came over to take her order. She asked for a water—it would be strange for her to walk out of the bathroom in her realm smelling of alcohol before Jeremy had bought her a drink. *Sure, now I'm thinking!* She turned back to Felix. "So, how does this work?"

He still seemed uncertain about her presence in the Exchange, but he reached in his shirt pocket and pulled out a click-top pen and a slip of parchment stamped with the same red-circled E as her wrist. Well, the same stamp her wrist *would have displayed* had she been legitimately portaled here. Emmelyn watched as he prepared to write the bet with a modern pen on this ancient-looking paper. Someday, she would have to ask why they only used parchment. "What's the bet?"

"D'Erenelle's Runner, Delwyn, is pro-realm," she replied.

His face dropped. "We don't bet on that."

"Don't or can't?"

He shrugged. "Why would we? Runners are supposed to be neutral players, doing as their Arbiters prescribe, regardless of their political views."

"You believe that?" Emmelyn asked. "After the Arbiter shakeup in D'Erenelle?"

Felix shook his head. "Those are the Arbiters' politics," he insisted, "not the Runners'."

Emmelyn flashed him a dubious glance. "Do you honestly think Emile required a whole new set of Transfers and Runners because his team's politics were of no consequence to his plans?" She wondered if she had said too much, but she figured he would have looked her up by now. She slipped her unmarked wrist between her knees.

Felix stared at her. "Look, I know Emile is your Arbiter, but how do you know all this?"

Emmelyn shrugged. "I've done my research. It's almost a sure thing," she lied. She knew *nothing* about Delwyn. But she hoped, by virtue of his being on Lorelle's team, that he was pro-realm.... "Do you want to place the bet or not?"

"I can't imagine anyone would bet on it...." Felix considered her offer for a moment before shaking his head and scratching something on the parchment. "But it's new and different—and mildly scandalous, since no one is supposed to have *opinions* around here—so someone might find it intriguing," he yelled. He clicked the pen shut and stuffed it and the parchment back into his shirt pocket. "I obviously can't use an Arbiter's backing on this. Who's going to front the cash?"

Emmelyn hadn't thought of that either. "How much?"

"You tell me," Felix replied. Emmelyn reached into her purse to pull out her wallet, but he stayed her hand. "I'd have to switch out your realm's money for GE credit," he yelled. "I could do it, but it's a hassle—especially if we win, and I have to convert it back...."

Emmelyn's eyebrows furrowed together. "Credit? What do you need money for? Everything here is free."

He chuckled. "Everything in the Exchange is free because we all work here. But we don't *live* here. The Datists, Arbiters, Universals—we all have lives outside this building, and they require money like in any other realm. You get paid for your job in *your* realm. Reduction of tuition costs?"

Emmelyn blinked. He *had* been researching her. The idea made her skin crawl. "Yes, as you clearly know—but I don't get paid *here*—at least, I haven't yet—wait, what are you talking about?" she babbled, flustered by her lack of privacy and the truth about a building she had believed to be an entire realm until a second ago. "Every time I come here, I walk in off a street in Detroit."

Felix gave a dismissive wave of his hand. "That's just what your portal looks like because it's tethered to that club. If you weren't a Transfer, you could walk out those doors into Geltis Exadon. That's the name of our realm here."

Did he mean non-realm? Emmelyn had been told the Exchange was a non-realm since her first Transfer, but Felix seemed to imply that the Exchange was just a *building* within a non-realm... or *realm*.... "Geltis Exadon?"

He nodded. "Datists often jokingly refer to it as the 'Greater Exchange.' The Exchange runs our realm in pretty much the same way it does all the others."

Emmelyn held up a hand, her mind reeling. "So, you're saying the Exchange is just a building in a realm called Geltis Exadon, and only those who work here on a daily basis get paid for the privilege?"

"Well, sure." His brow scrunched quizzically. "What would you need GE credit for? You said it yourself: everything is free here, and you're only here on occasion."

Emmelyn didn't bother to enlighten him about how intrusive those occasions often felt.

He considered her for a moment. "Runners get a stipend to start, but like Transfers, they aren't paid—that is, until they retire. Packages are pretty lush if you Run or Transfer long enough. Anyway, the kinds of folks recruited to those jobs aren't the type to do it for money. Look, you're worried about this whole anti-realm thing, aren't you?"

She nodded.

"Exactly. One peek behind the curtain, and you're invested in the well-being of these realms, even at personal cost. You didn't think about payment until now, did you? You're one of the brave and selfless souls who puts her needs above others' for the good of the order. Could you back out now?" She leveled him with an of-course-not glare, and he replied with a told-you-so smirk.

"So, we *are* selected for our personalities," Emmelyn replied.

Felix shrugged. "It's a part of it. There's an artificial intelligence algorithm that uses rule changes in the realms to judge good candidates.... You're a bit atypical, though."

She blinked. "Am I?" *Why does that sound like a bad thing?*

"Most Transfers are the... easygoing types. They want to help, but they don't care about more than what their job requires. No one I know of has attempted whatever it is you're doing now."

Emmelyn ticked through her list of suspicions about the Exchange: the deafening music, the exclusionary betting ring, the distance between Runners and Arbiters, and a litany of unanswerable questions among its herd of complacent participants.... *Why am I the first to question this? And why was I even recruited? Felix could learn more about me than I care to consider.... Surely, the algorithm knows what type of person I am....*

The Datist peered at her again. "You really won't tell me what you're up to?"

His question snapped her from her reverie. "It's better if you don't know. Plausible deniability."

He snorted in disbelief. "Yeah, *right*.... But you're positive this is a sure thing?"

"Ninety-five percent," she replied with more confidence than the percentage implied. She couldn't make Lorelle her first bet, or the waiting-woman would call her out on it. But if she botched the outcome of this one, she might not get to place another.

"Well, what about the winnings?" he asked. "I could front the cash for you, so I don't have to bother with yours, but—"

"They're yours," she interrupted. "The winnings. You can have them."

"All of them?"

She nodded, wondering how much he could win on such an obscure gamble.

He looked surprised. "It really isn't about the money for you, is it?"

She shook her head.

If he were going to press the issue, he thought better of it. "I guess I have bet to place then," he declared.

Out of the corner of her eye, Emmelyn thought she saw a cowboy hat approaching the bar. *Randy?* There weren't enough people here to provide her adequate cover. She had to get back to her realm—*now*.

She slid her untouched water away from her. "I have to go. And next time, pay better attention to my Transfer orders. You could have missed me." Before he could reply, she slipped off the stool and rushed toward the back of the club. She was already envisioning her friends in the bathroom in her realm as she reentered the same stall as before. All the deafening chaos of the women's room in her realm's Dissonance surged back around her. She opened the stall door and approached the sink.

As she washed her hands again, she scanned the reflection in the mirror for Claire's and Selma's feet. Both were recognizable below stall doors. She announced her departure to them and set about chastising herself for her recklessness until she rejoined the group.

Jeremy was standing amidst the circle of chairs, a bottle in each hand and a weary look on his face.

"What is it?" Emmelyn asked, accepting a beer and taking too large a swig from it.

"Typical," he yelled in her ear, "as soon as I get our drinks, they all want to leave."

Emmelyn was eager to get away from here—both "heres." "Fine with me."

LXIX

Aethelburh

After riding practice, Thane and Rhoswen walked back up to the castle, their boots swishing through the tall green grass.

"You did really well," Rhoswen told him.

"As did you. We can *fly* these beasts, Rose. Half the trainees out there hadn't even seen a dragon up close before they arrived here, and we've flown on them."

"Flown *on* them," she reminded him. Haylan's humble words still rang in her ears. "But not *flown them*. It's one thing to ride with your folks. It's another to fly a beast by yourself."

They stepped inside the castle and moved toward the kitchen for a late lunch. Rhoswen had only glanced at the buffet when an unfamiliar waitman approached them, bearing a silver tray with a folded letter on it. He offered the tray to Thane. "A correspondence for you, sir," he said.

Thane, apparently, did know him. "Thank you, Garrick," he said as he lifted the note from the tray. He flipped over the letter and broke the teal wax seal on the back. A piece of it fell to the floor, and Rhoswen grabbed it up before the waitman could. The round glob of wax had been pressed with a flower-shaped seal. "Who sent it?" she asked.

"Thank you, Garrick," Thane said again. Ignoring the waitman's attempt at further discussion, he grabbed Rhoswen's wrist and dragged her out of the kitchen to the nearest spiral staircase. She waited to protest until they were behind the closed doors of her brother's chambers.

"What is the matter with you?" Thane demanded.

"I could ask you the same thing!" she replied, rubbing her wrist.

"I'm not going to discuss anything personal in front of servants to the king."

A fair point, Rhoswen mentally conceded. "Sorry. Who sent it?" she asked again.

"Ethelinda."

She thought her eyes might bulge out of her head. "The Lady of Alston?"

He nodded, skimming the letter again.

"So, is that a formal invitation for you to visit her?"

"Yes. She is inviting me *today*—for dinner."

Rhoswen's eyebrows lifted in surprise. "That's short notice. Isn't that unusual protocol for aristocrats? Don't they plan such things well in advance…?"

"Usually," he replied. "But I don't know how far away Alston is or how to get to her—"

A knock on the door interrupted them. "Lord Thane?" a voice called from the hall. It was the waitman Thane had tried—apparently in vain—to dismiss. Thane crossed to the door and opened it.

"Forgive me, sir," Garrick dissembled, "but the carrier is waiting outside for a response to the letter. He is also willing to ferry you to and from Alston if you so choose."

Rhoswen clenched her teeth to keep her jaw from dropping.

"Would you be so good as to send for Delwyn please? I have need of him before I can make a decision to travel," Thane asked.

Garrick bowed his head. "Forgive me, milord, but Delwyn has taken a brief leave of absence. May I be of assistance to you?"

Thane stared at the waitman and then shook his head. "I will have an answer for you in a moment." He shut the door before Garrick could respond. "Now I can't talk to Delwyn about Ethelinda," he began in a desperate whisper.

Rhoswen's eyes widened. "What is there to talk about?! He warned you about her from the start!"

"But what if the Riders really *can't* be trusted…?"

Rhoswen shook her head. "*No*. I refuse to believe that. Plus, they know everything now." She eyed him, her brows furrowing. "Besides, that isn't why you want to go."

"We need to know what Father was talking about…." Thane trailed off, lost in thought.

Rhoswen exhaled noisily. She didn't believe for a moment that this was the reason Thane wanted to visit Ethelinda, but clearly nothing she said would talk him out of it. *He is an adult,* she reminded herself, realizing at the same time how close she, too, was to majority. It was time for her to protect herself. "I'll just go down to Keaton."

Thane nodded. "All right, but I want you there before I leave. And don't go anywhere else—especially back to this castle—without an escort." He cracked open the door to tell Garrick he would be down presently to take the carriage to Alston. Then, he turned back to Rhoswen. "Let's get you down to the cellar," he whispered.

In the hidden maps room, Thane set up the maps for a portal to Keaton. "Get the trinkets for the supply room," he instructed.

"No," Rhoswen snapped, fishing through the box. She couldn't keep the frustration from her voice. "Not after riding practice—it will be swarming with students and Riders."

"Aelfraed's room, then," he suggested.

She shook her head. "Remember what happened last time?"

"Well, where do you suggest?" he asked.

Rhoswen adjusted the map and stabbed her finger at a room in response.

Thane's face screwed up in confusion. "But we don't have a trinket for that—" he began, stopping short as Rhoswen pulled out a bag from the box. She emptied the contents onto the table.

"These are the miscellaneous ones we didn't know how to use," she said, struggling to soften the edge in her voice. "I'll try them." She poked through the trinkets and held up one that looked like a flat, spikey blob of metal, as if someone had cut the edges of a coin into haphazard points.

"What is that?" Thane asked.

"I don't know. I've never seen anything like it. But he has so many... *things* in his rooms. Maybe this resembles one of them."

Thane sighed. "You need to figure out how to transfer the map into that room while the portal is open so you can close the portal off to this room and remain in Keaton." He looked aggrieved. "We don't know how to do that. If something goes wrong—"

"I'll figure it out," she interrupted. After Deowynn had told her that she shouldn't fear the maps changing while she used them, she never bothered to contemplate what could happen if a portal closed around her while she was inside it. Her brother seemed to consider it now, and he appeared less than optimistic about the concept. Her flesh began to prickle. She shifted her focus back to her anger instead of her rising anxiety. *It's my risk alone. He made his choice.*

Thane squinted at the room where Rhoswen had placed the metal object. "You think his chambers will be safe?"

"What about *your* safety?" she exploded. "You need to be at this meeting tonight as much as I do, and instead, you're gallivanting around with a woman who can't be trusted!"

"No, *you* are the most important part of this meeting. I will go find out what I can from Ethelinda and try to get back in time." His voice was aggravatingly level.

"*Try*?" Rhoswen repeated. "You know this isn't about Darr Beval's trustworthiness anymore."

"Look," Thane snapped, his tone fraying with sudden frustration, "you may be the Heir, but you don't know everything. Mother and Father have made certain of that. I'll be realmed if we enter this battle with only half a plan and three allies because our parents can't be bothered to help us. *Someone* has to figure out whom we can trust, and I have an opportunity to do just that, so I'm going to take it."

Thane's outburst surprised her as much as his sentiment. Rhoswen could appreciate his disillusionment with their parents' omissions, but it wasn't a justification for his reckless decision to visit Ethelinda. She'd had enough of his false altruism. "Go, then!" she barked more loudly than she had intended.

Thane glared at her and shoved her compass into place. The portal opened, and he nodded at the empty room beyond. "Start without me if I'm late," he said coolly and disappeared into the overflow library, locking the shelving behind him with a *click*.

Rhoswen listened to his footsteps fading away. Her breath quickened. Even if she did have a portal at her disposal, she had never been locked inside this room, and her anxiety only doubled her anger. She reached for a bookend, but its heavy, grounding weight could not prevent a swell of rage. She hurled the carved marble at the wall where the break in the shelving usually was. The bookend ricocheted onto the floor, chipping off a fragment of marble that skittered into a dark corner. She scowled and turned back to the room on the other side of the open portal.

Darr Beval's chambers. *He could walk in at any moment,* she realized, and her heart skipped a beat, instantly dispelling her anger. With one final glance, she removed her compass from the map. The portal snapped shut, leaving her in darkness but for the oil lamp on the table.

She situated two maps of Aethelburh and three paperweights on the floor in front of the portal wall. Then she reorganized the trinkets and set her compass back on the map. The wall shimmered open. The small closet that she'd found the other day on her way up from the cellar proved unoccupied. The familiar brooms and slumped bags of baking goods sat around the edges of the room, barely visible in the meager light from the arched entrance to the kitchen. *Here we go,* she thought.

She locked the portal open with the Aethelburh key, pocketed her compass, and knelt in front of the maps. Bracing herself on one arm, she reached over the parchment and began dragging the pair of maps into the portal. The trinkets vibrated against the uneven stone floor. As she edged more and more of the maps into the portal, she realized she was holding her breath again, and she forced herself to take a quick gulp of air. Soon, she was entirely in the portal. The walls began to pulse with a faint glow, and her heartrate increased.

She stood up and took several steps backward into the maps room. The portal opening grew taller, as if it knew what she intended. *Thanks,* she thought with no small amount of bewilderment. Then, she ran forward and leapt over the maps into the narrow nook on the other side. Without much space to jump into, she had no way to slow herself down before she crashed into a shelf and knocked something onto the floor. She froze as the object rolled, waiting to see whether the commotion had drawn any attention, but no one came to investigate. Behind her, the portal continued to pulse. She dropped to her hands and knees and dragged the maps through the rest of the way. The portal's glow dimmed and resumed its normal appearance. *Thank the realm,* she thought with a sigh.

She groped in the dim light from the kitchen for a few odds and ends from the shelves to weigh down the map and carried the paperweights back into the maps room.

She removed her textbooks from her Riding bag and replaced them with the box of trinkets. Then, she stared at the maps of Keaton. There was no way to conceal them in the bag without folding them, and she had no intention of creasing them—the rolling ends were troublesome enough. With a shrug, she snaked the parchment tube diagonally into the bag, letting it stick out of the top, and clamped the lamp shut.

Back in the closet, she replaced her compass on the map, removed the Aethelburh key, and closed the portal. As she eased the last of the map materials into her bag, the clacking of metal-soled shoes neared the kitchen. There was no time to restock the shelves with the items she had used as paperweights. She threw her bag over her shoulder and bolted out of the closet, only slowing her pace to a walk as she moved through the Great Hall toward the entrance of the castle. She knew Thane wanted her to use the portal so she would be out of the castle before he was. But it occurred to her that she needed to be seen leaving to avoid arousing suspicion about her absence. With a polite nod to passing staff, she slipped out the main doors and into the sunshine. The sun had begun its descent through the sky, and she squinted at her lengthening shadow as she started down the hill toward Keaton.

"Cousin!"

Perhaps being seen wasn't such a good idea. For a brief second, Rhoswen considered breaking into a run, but she restrained herself. "My prince?" she inquired, turning toward him.

"Are you going back to Keaton?" Gethin asked as he caught up to her.

Think fast. "Yes—to study. There is rumor of a test tomorrow, and some of us are meeting up, just in case."

Gethin eyed the two rolls of parchment protruding from her bag. "What are those?"

Rhoswen felt faint. "Maps," she replied, unable to think of a convincing lie.

"Why do you have maps? Where did you find them?"

She hesitated as she searched for believable answers. "They are realm maps. Thane and I realized we didn't have a full understanding of the layout of the realm, and there might be questions about that on the test tomorrow. Freedom of transfer, you know...."

"And where is Thane?" he asked.

Realm it all! "He went down ahead of me," she improvised.

"Freedom of transfer?" Gethin repeated. "What does that have to do with Aelfraed's recent lectures on the Heir?" Before Rhoswen could reply, he dismissed the questions with a wave of his hand. "I have news. I had hoped to tell you together, but you can pass it on to Thane. My father has just told me that I am to take some time away from training to visit your parents."

Rhoswen's jaw fell open, and she was certain her eyes were about to pop out of her head. "I'm sorry?"

Gethin looked as if he had just eaten the last bite of her favorite dessert—in front of her. "Yes. He thinks, with my mother gone, your parents may have a balancing effect on me."

Rhoswen couldn't help but stutter through her reply. "W-why would you need b-balancing from my parents?"

"To help me ascend the throne or fly out with the Heir Whelp."

"Fly out with the Heir Whelp," Rhoswen repeated dumbly.

"Yes. As you mentioned last night, the Heir has yet to be chosen, which means I still have time to redeem myself in the eyes of the queen dragon—either as Heir to the next realm or as ruler here."

That concept startled Rhoswen even more than the idea of her cousin's stay in Stanburh preventing them from portaling home. Could she be unseated as the Heir if the rightful prince balanced himself?

"How long do you plan to stay with my parents?" she asked. She had tried to keep her voice even, but the question was transparent.

Gethin flashed her a devilish smile. He was clearly pleased to be causing her discomfort. Rhoswen doubted any amount of parental influence could offset such cruelty.

"We have made no definite plans, but my return will be contingent upon whether my father wants to proceed with my case against you for what transpired in Deowynn's stall the other night. I won't be anywhere near you for a while, so he may delay sentencing." He laughed. It was not a pleasant sound. "Obviously, it would be awkward for me to stay with your parents while you were being executed back here!"

Rhoswen willed back hot tears of fury and terror. Her uncle was a madman, using his revolting son as a pawn in a game he shouldn't even be playing. But was he only using *Gethin* as a pawn, or had Ethelinda also been put into play when she summoned Thane away from the castle? And *Thane.... Enough,* she thought. *This is too much.*

A chill shivered down her spine like a lit fuse and then heat radiated upward throughout her body in a flash. Blood boiled in her ears, and her jaw clenched tight. She felt like she was on fire. She glared at her cousin and swallowed hard against the heat rising in the back of her throat. When she spoke, she almost didn't recognize her own voice; it came out in a deep and eerie growl from behind her gritted teeth."If what you say is true, then I can put myself in no greater peril. So, I will make my point in a way that you will understand: *if you endanger my family in even the slightest manner, there will not be a realm far enough away for you to hide in, and your father won't be capable of saving you from the Descent I will rain down on you."*

Gethin paled, his smile dropping from his face. The dark scab on his brow contrasted with his now-clammy flesh, and his breath hitched in his throat. With an ungainly twirl, he sped back up to the castle, his cape twisting around his ankles and tripping him up.

Rhoswen watched him leave, her body tensing against a flood of emotion. Her nerves buzzed, and her heart pounded against her rib cage. Her breathing turned ragged, and she took a deep breath, holding it until Gethin was inside the castle. When the air finally exploded from her lungs, tears streamed down her face. She turned and fled down the valley toward Keaton, the sharp edges of the heavy trinket box bouncing painfully against her hip. The exchange with Gethin replayed in her mind, and she began second-guessing the wisdom of threatening the prince. It would not be hard for him to poison Badrick against her—that process was well underway already. Her feet hammered against the ground and sweat broke out over her body.

Now, everyone's *lives are in danger,* she thought, *and it's all my fault.*

From the window of his study, King Badrick watched his son and niece depart from each other in opposite directions. He sipped at a small metal chalice of dark root liquor, his back to the door, and awaited his son's inevitable and tiresome entrance.

"You would have the patience for this, Orla," he muttered to the empty room around him. "I fear I never will." The corners of his mouth lifted in a bitter smile. "Of course, if I were a patient man, I wouldn't be in this situation, would I?"

The prince entered right on cue. "I told her," he announced, his voice shaky.

Badrick continued to sip his drink. Its boozy warmth slid down the back of his throat and into his gut, but it did nothing to tame the coldness coursing through him.

"I told her," Gethin repeated, his voice louder but still uneven.

Still, Badrick said nothing.

Gethin walked around the room to stand in front of his father, keeping the desk between them. His face reddened with anger. "I told her, and—and she threatened me," he persisted.

The king took another sip, staring over the rim of his cup at his son.

Gethin's voice stopped shaking as it grew loud with outrage. "She threatened *both* of us! She said if we harmed her family in any way, she'd rain a Descent upon me, and you wouldn't be 'capable of saving me.' *Capable!* That's a threat to your safety, as well!"

The king rolled his eyes. He found his son's outbursts exhausting, and Badrick wasn't even the one expending the explosive energy. *Perhaps if he put a little more effort into doing things properly, Gethin could spare himself some of the exertion,* Badrick thought. "Well, it sounds like she really took the prospect of her execution seriously, Gethin."

The prince spluttered in offense.

"Oh, please. She wouldn't have had the gumption to threaten you if she had honestly thought you were serious," Badrick said, refreshing his cup from a glass cannister on his desk.

"As a matter of fact," Gethin replied, "she said it was precisely *because* she had nothing to lose that she was able to threaten me, so she must have taken me pretty seriously."

"*As a matter of fact,*" Badrick mocked, "she would also have nothing to lose if all your threats rang *transparently* hollow."

Gethin's brow furrowed, which must have tugged at the scab above his eye, as he lifted a hand to it.

Badrick snorted. *Pathetic.* "She is going to Keaton, I see. Did she tell you her plans?"

"What plans?" Gethin asked, dropping his hand to his side.

"If you would stop worrying about your face and actually do what you are told, perhaps you would know *what in the realm she is up to!* She had maps. Did she tell you what they were for?"

"To study," the prince grunted.

"To study *what*?"

Gethin's brow scrunched again and then quickly released, but he kept his hand at his side. "That's the part that didn't make sense. Something about Freedom of transfer...."

Badrick set down his chalice and rubbed his temples with both hands. "Pack your things. You do me no good here, and I'll be realmed if she can communicate freely with her parents."

"What?!" Gethin blustered. "You were serious about sending me to Stanburh? I thought that was just a line to unsettle her!"

Badrick ignored the question and continued. "You will gain access to their correspondence, track their behaviors, and report their movements back to me. To accomplish this, I suggest you make yourself as likeable and seemingly trustworthy as possible. I know this will be quite a feat for you, so it might behoove you to begin practicing *now*."

Before Gethin could protest, Badrick grabbed up his chalice and hurled it at his son's head. The prince ducked, and the metal cup clanged off the muntins in the window behind him. Its contents spilled across the floor in a dark, wet streak. Apparently, no longer concerned with his eyebrow, Gethin scurried from the room, slipping on the root liquor in his haste.

Badrick turned back to the window. Rhoswen was long since out of view, but he could still envision the maps sticking out of her bag....

Slow footsteps clacked in the doorway behind him. "Excuuuuuse meeee, siiiiire—"

"What is it, Baul?" the king seethed, closing his eyes. *When is Delwyn coming back?*

"A letter for youuuu, siiiiire...."

The king stormed over to the man and snatched up the parchment from his outstretched tray. "That'll be all, Baul, and if you utter one syllable on your way out of that door, I will have you fed to the dragons." Badrick had already broken the unstamped wax and was well into the letter by the time Baul had shuffled out the door. "WHAT?!" he roared. "BAUL! Bring me the Pentagraphs—and do it quickly, or the dragons will be the least of your problems!"

The prince almost tripped onto the landing at the top of the spiral staircase when his father began yelling one floor below. Gethin couldn't really fault the king for his frustration: Baul moved like a tar-covered snail in the dead of winter. What the prince didn't understand was why his father was using his son's waitman at all when he had a much speedier servant of his own. *Probably to inconvenience me,* Gethin thought. He found his footing as his father's orders tore across the Great Hall and up through the balcony:

"Bring me the Pentagraphs!"

A chill shot upward from the base of Gethin's spine, stiffening the hair on his back, neck, and arms.

The Pentagraphs were an institution synonymous with the great war. Since the truce, the king had occasionally called upon a member of the group to carry out an unsavory errand or two, but Gethin couldn't remember the last time his father had called them all together. If he meant to assemble the five of them, something serious was going on. Gethin raced back to the balcony's edge to see what could have elicited such a demand. From this angle, he could just see into his father's study, where a letter flailed in the king's gesticulating hand.

To hear it told, the realm had recently celebrated Gethin's second birthday when war had broken out. The young prince had learned little of the battle in his early studies, but his tutors' carefully worded tales had been colorful enough to inspire interest in his father's five high-ranking allies. Back then, Gethin would run around the castle grounds, playing out heroic deeds—gaining an imaginary reputation that would propel him into the ranks of the five. In his childish fantasy, he might even oust one of the other members, his extreme bravery casting shame upon the lesser man, whom the prince would then replace.

He'd tear about, battling this and saving that, until his mother caught him defending the honor of a waiting-woman against an evil basket of dirty laundry. When Orla had explained that these "valiant defenders," as Gethin knew them, were, in fact, terrible men whose actions were more cruel than courageous, the prince had been left to wonder at the validity of his tutors' lessons.

As Gethin had taken his studies into his own hands, he'd searched for published reports of the war but had little luck. Only an obscure reference or two had remained in the annals of the cellar library: dingy, scrawled accounts tucked away into the pages of old, forgotten books. Most were unsigned letters, detailing events in harried shorthand, as if someone had been desperate to chronicle all that had taken place but hadn't had the courage to circulate it. What he'd read had made his skin crawl and his gut churn. It turned out, Gethin had too much of his mother in him to stomach the gruesome acts that the five henchmen performed on the king's behalf... much to his father's chagrin.

Now, Gethin resented that weaker portion of himself, even if his mother would have felt pride at knowing her son could not execute Pentagraph-level atrocities. His father's sneers only perpetuated his feelings of mediocrity.

The prince stepped away from the balcony and climbed the stairs toward his chambers. Baul had already set out his empty bags but had not yet filled them. Gethin went to the nearest drawer and pawed through it. He'd thought his father's story about sending Gethin to the Stanburhs was part of the ruse; in truth, it appeared, he would follow a letter announcing his arrival tomorrow.

That meant he would have just enough time to pack before his father's meeting with the Pentagraphs.

The king usually met with them after nightfall, when they would not be detected entering or leaving the castle. The Pentagraphs lived a strange dual life. Their existence was both highly public—for their appointed positions of power in the realm—and private—to protect their royally sanctioned dirty dealings.

Gethin certainly would not be invited to attend this clandestine meeting. *But if father needs the Pentagraphs for something, I'll be realmed if I don't find out what that thing is.*

LXX

Keaton

By the time she reached Keaton, Rhoswen's breathing was jagged with a mix of fear, anger, laughter, and pain. Her hip hurt from where the trinket box had banged into it. She forced a deep breath past her constricting throat and entered the arena through the side door. Riders and students stood around the fence, their attention directed skyward. The single flights were well underway. Rhoswen walked briskly around the arena, wiping the tears from her cheeks and avoiding everyone's eyes.

She slipped up a flight of stairs and into a distant lecture hall far from the arena. There was no door in its stone archway, but the room was so remote, she felt she could chance it. By now, most students would either be heading to a late lunch or watching the flights.

Rhoswen moved toward the back of the room to an empty section of wall adjacent to the doorway and kneeled on the floor. Her hands shook as she slid the maps from her bag and overlaid them at the compass roses. She used her bag and the box to keep the ends from curling and arranged the trinkets as best she could. *Change of plans,* she thought, taking a deep breath.

She placed the compass onto the stack, and the wall opened to the secret maps room. Inside, she found the scroll she wanted and then slipped back out to reorganize the maps on the floor. By the time everything was in place, she realized how much the distraction of the maps had calmed her. Still, she needed reassurance; she only hoped she would get some. She slid her compass onto the map of Stanburh.

It helped that her reception was a warm one. Although her entrance through the kitchen wall now left her parents unfazed, they seemed as thrilled to see her as if she had been absent for years.

They progressed through the obligatory assessment of her wellbeing and moved into the sitting room, where a fire roared in the hearth. The weather in Stanburh was damp and chilly, and everything had a gray cast to match the sky. Rhoswen eased herself into a cozy chair—*and* the reason for her visit. "Have you learned any more about Denver?" she asked.

Allistair shook his head. "None of my remaining contacts in the south have heard of Hazlitt. If it existed, its name was a fleeting one—so much so that they can find no trace of it. The closest they came was a place called Helewis."

"But only about half of its residents use that name. The rest call it Linden now," Magge said.

"I don't understand," Rhoswen said. "Has Stanburh always been Stanburh?"

"For as long as my family has kept it," Allistair said with a nod.

"The north is more established than the south," Magge explained. "They're still redefining their borders down there, changing town names, and instituting territories. The south isn't as densely populated either, and the sparseness causes the towns around each lord's stronghold to be rather ill-defined. It weakens the lords' power to maintain their domains. And the royal family is too far removed to enforce anything."

"Hazlitt could have been the name adopted by a town for such a short period of time that half its residents weren't even aware of the moniker before it changed again," Allistair added.

"But then why give that name for his hometown?" Rhoswen asked.

Allistair shrugged. "For the same reason the names keep changing: politics. Perhaps he has ties to those who adopted the name, even if it didn't stick for long. Or perhaps it changed after he left—if it ever existed."

"'If it ever existed?'" Rhoswen repeated in disbelief.

Magge's eyes narrowed with skepticism. "It would explain why we haven't been able to find it. Did your source have any knowledge of him?"

Rhoswen shook her head. "Not of anyone named Denver or a green named Kipling," she replied, careful to exclude any pronouns. Her parents weren't the only ones who could omit details.

Magge glanced at her husband. "He could be using false names for himself and his dragon...."

"Well, that must be it. *All* Riders have to come up through Keaton, right?" Rhoswen insisted.

"We're still looking into it," Allistair replied. His expression darkened the way Darr Thorndon's had when she had asked him the same thing.

Rhoswen tried to use his reaction as an opening. She did not like this pattern of lying, even if by omission, and she wanted to make one more effort to curb it. "Father, what you're suggesting doesn't make sense, and it makes me think there is a lot more going on here than I know about. If you won't tell me your suspicions about Denver, I wish to know your concerns about Darr Beval."

Allistair's brow furrowed. "You should not be associating with that man!" he bellowed, his gaze uncompromising. "He is not to be trusted, Rhoswen. The details don't matter; the message is the same."

It seemed he'd brook no further discussion on the topic. *Unless....* "I ask because my life and my status as Heir have been threatened."

"What?" Magge exploded, coming to her feet. She turned on her husband, eyes alight. "I told you, Allistair. I told you this was too danger—"

Allistair silenced Magge with a glance that Rhoswen had never seen exchanged between her parents before. It startled her. "What are you talking about?" he asked her.

Rhoswen explained Gethin's threats and his impending arrival at their door. Her parents were not thrilled about either concept. "He says it's to balance him, so he can assume his place as regent or Heir."

Magge scoffed. "He couldn't."

Allistair agreed. "It's to cut us off from communicating with you." Rhoswen's stomach knotted at the thought. "But it also means his threat is hollow. Badrick wouldn't dare execute you with his son in our care." A brief silence ensued, the counter-threat left unsaid.

"Do you think Badrick knows you are using the portal system to visit us?" Magge finally asked.

Rhoswen shook her head. "We don't believe so, but we can't be sure. Gethin saw that I had maps with me as I was leaving the castle today. I brushed it off as a part of my studies, but there's no telling what he'll say to his father...."

"Or what memories it might trigger for him." Allistair leaned back in his chair, his expression thoughtful. "What does Thane think of all this?"

"Yes," Magge said, "where is Thane?"

Rhoswen told them about the invitation from Lady Alston, but something about the way Allistair's already-dark expression closed off at the mention of Ethelinda's name gave her pause, and she decided to leave out the part about Thane's interest in the Darr Beval mystery.

Magge looked beside herself with worry. "He went alone?" she asked, her voice restrained into evenness. It made her question even more unsettling.

Rhoswen nodded as her shoulders hunched in self-defense.

"What were you two thinking, Rose?" Allistair asked, his neck muscles taught with stress. He turned to his wife. "I had all but forgotten about that wretched woman. We should have warned you."

"You should have warned me about a great many things," Rhoswen said, trying to keep any inflection from her voice and failing miserably. But before anyone could say more, they were interrupted by the entrance of a familiar young man through the front door.

"Lady Rho—*milady*?" his voice stuttered in disbelief. A stable hand of around twenty-five stood in the doorway in a grungy white shirt and brown trousers. His tan skin was streaked with dirt, and his brilliant dark-blue eyes, wide with surprise, popped from behind his scraggly black mane. Macon.

The Stanburhs did not keep many servants. The maids and the stable hands made their own schedules, as long as the drakiary was continuously staffed. Given the amenable working conditions, the Stanburhs enjoyed little turnover, fierce loyalty, and an abundance of familiarity with their servants. Many lords would not conscience such friendliness, but it suited the Stanburhs entirely well… except in situations where their privacy—or secrecy—was compromised.

"I didn't know you were coming to visit," Macon continued, not moving. He looked frozen in place, like he was holding back a flood in the doorway.

Suddenly, the head of a well-dressed royal waitman in familiar gray livery peeked around from behind Macon. His face, too, was awash with surprise. Rhoswen swallowed thickly. She didn't recognize the man, but he certainly recognized *her.*

"Good to see you, Macon. Just a brief visit," she replied, eyeing the waitman.

"Ah—a messenger for you, Lord and Lady Stanburh," Macon said with a small incline of his head. He added, *"from Aethelburh,"* and his face pinched with unease.

Rhoswen turned to her parents—who betrayed *no* signs of concern. A portal to Keaton stood open one room away; a royal servant had stumbled upon a guest of Castle Aethelburh, who could not have arrived here before him; and there was no telling whether this waitman would report back to Badrick—or what he might say if he did.

Allistair took the parchment from the waitman, broke the royal seal, and scanned the note. "Well, Rose, it looks like the prince should have hopped on the same dragon you did," he improvised. "Your cousin is also coming to visit." Allistair handed the message to Magge.

"Is he?" Rhoswen asked in mock surprise. "For how long?"

"It doesn't say," Magge replied. "He arrives tomorrow."

Rhoswen nodded at the waitman. "Well, I could have saved you the trip, had I known. My apologies."

The waitman gave her a tiny bow, but he looked as though he were struggling to make sense of their explanation for her appearance in Stanburh. "Not at all, milady."

"Macon," Allistair began, "see that the king's waitman has a good meal out in the servant's quarters before he returns to Aethelburh, will you?"

"Of course, milord," Macon said with a tiny bow to both Allistair and Magge. "Good to see you, milady," he added to Rhoswen.

"You, too, Macon," Rhoswen replied. She stole a quick glance at the waitman, but his face was hard to read.

Once the door closed behind them, and the servants could be seen through the window a good distance away, everyone exhaled at once.

"This is not good," Magge said.

NEW Long Run!

Realm: D'Erenelle
Buy-In: $200GE
Termination Rights: Yes
Bet: Prince Gethin of Aethelburh will be wed to Lady Rhoswen of Stanburh, as instigated by King Badrick to prevent Movement.

LXXI

Aethelburh

It was well after lunch when Delwyn ambled into the kitchen. His expression betrayed his surprise at finding the room occupied; Lorelle was finishing up a snack before the cooks could converge on the kitchen to prepare dinner.

"That was fast," she said between mouthfuls. She had been working overtime to earn the privilege of her next absence from the castle in advance. In the process, however, she had forgotten to eat lunch.

"I found my Transfer and left," Delwyn replied. He stepped up to the high table where lay a small spread of fruit, cheese, and bread.

Lorelle hovered her knife inquiringly over a crusty loaf. He accepted her offer with a nod, and she slid the blade through the bread in two passes. As she handed the slice to him, she noticed dark circles under his eyes. He seemed unnerved about something—although, that was a normal look for Delwyn.

"Thank you," he said, reaching for a piece of cheese.

"You left early," Lorelle replied. She was baiting him for information, but she tried to stifle the inflection in her voice to keep his guard down.

"It was time for me to go back."

"I just figured you'd wait until you knew."

"Knew what?"

Lorelle did not look at him. She continued cutting more cheese for them so she could wrap up the rest of the block. "You left before the carriage returned to Alston. How could you have known what Thane would do?"

His eyes grew wide. "What are you talking about? Are you saying he *didn't* go to Alston?"

After the kind of day she'd had, Lorelle felt she could really do with a good laugh, and watching Delwyn work himself into a lather in his flustered and frantic way would suffice. But she worried it could escalate to something that would draw attention, and she couldn't let that happen, especially for her own amusement. "Calm down, Delwyn. He went."

He exhaled in relief, his wide eyes closing as he steadied himself. "Why did you do that?"

"Because you were reckless." She popped a chunk of melon into her mouth, swallowed the juice, and spoke through the flesh. "You shouldn't have meddled, and you shouldn't have left before you knew what result it had."

"I thought he summoned the carriage," Delwyn said.

Lorelle shook her head. "She sent it for him."

"You jest," he insisted, his mouth falling open.

She shook her head again.

The waitman's exhalation was ragged with frustration this time. "That was close," he said. "You were right; I shouldn't have meddled. But I honestly thought he summoned the carriage."

"He could have used one of the king's. Why would he call for one of hers?"

Delwyn rubbed a hand over his face. "I wasn't thinking."

"Maybe you were thinking that you didn't want to find out if you had affected his decision—that you wanted to wait one more Run before you had to report the outcome of your interference."

He looked at her, his mouth lifting into a weak smile, but his eyes remained troubled. "That really *would* be reckless."

"It would." She extended a hunk of melon to him, which he gingerly liberated from the tip of her knife. "You'd have had more to report if you'd waited, too."

His eyes widened. "What's going on?"

"The king has called for the Pentagraphs."

"Here?" He looked ashen.

"Yes."

"*All* of them?"

"Mm-hmmm."

"*Why?*" His voice came out in a choked whisper.

"I don't know," she said, her tone flat despite the anxiety she felt creeping up from her diaphragm. "There are rumors circulating about the Heir, but I can't get as close to the king as you can, so I don't know if that's what set him off."

"When do they meet?"

"Tonight."

Delwyn fidgeted his discomfort. "We'll have to see what that means before we can report back anyway...."

"We?" Lorelle asked.

He nodded. "There have been developments in the Exchange, too. Now that we're on the same team and working in the same location, Rehlia has decided to stagger our returns. We'll Run each other's messages, so we can both take off less time here."

"You mean, co-Run? Thank the realm!" she breathed in relief. It was getting harder and harder to explain her recurring absences, especially the extra ones corresponding to her recent change in teams; she'd considered inventing more dying relatives. "Sounds like the Exchange is improving!"

Delwyn flashed her a weak smile. "I'm not so sure." He shifted from foot to foot in a signature display of antsiness. "Rehlia added an extra note to my Transitor." He passed her a scrap of parchment, and his face scrunched up apologetically. "I didn't know it was for you; I know we're co-Runners now, but I think you might have preferred I hadn't read that. I'm sorry."

Lorelle eyed the scrap. Her name was clearly printed on the reverse of the message. She held it up for him and raised an accusing eyebrow.

"I didn't see that until after I'd read it," he explained sheepishly. "I'm new to this whole co-Running thing."

She nodded, ignoring the fold in the parchment that would have kept her name on the outside and the private message secreted within. *There are tradeoffs with everything….* She scanned the note. "I'm in trouble," she said, bewildered. She had never done anything in the Exchange for which she had been reprimanded.

"Not you, really. Emile is the one in trouble."

"But I did his bidding. It's my fault." She read it again, her chest constricting with guilt and regret.

Before her switch to Rehlia's team, Emile had ordered her to coax Gethin and Rhoswen together. The less-than-romantic arrangement had made Lorelle's flesh crawl, not only because she did not want to force such a detestable match on Rhoswen but also because it seemed to her a gratuitous action that could not possibly benefit the realm. *But Runners don't have the luxury of acting on their opinions,* she had reminded herself. She had no choice; if Emile had tricked the Ivers into passing down the missive, then it was her responsibility to execute the action, no questions asked.

But the Ivers *hadn't* passed down the missive.

Emile had passed it down *himself*—in the form of a *triple.*

A triple that was likely being used for nothing more than generating a bet in the G'Ambit. *A triple that Emmelyn had Transferred quite unwillingly,* Lorelle remembered, her anguish mounting.

"You couldn't have known," Delwyn said. He grimaced at a sudden memory. "They're betting on it. It's running long."

She cursed. Rehlia had not cancelled the missive when Lorelle joined her team, which made the action look legitimate. In reality, however, Rehlia had not known about it; as an illegitimate triple, Emile had never logged it into the system. Only after she had completed the task and reported it had Rehlia realized what Emile had done. By then, it was too late. And now a bet on her unsanctioned tweak hung over them like a bad portrait.

She ruefully remembered the ill-fated conversation.

"Your majesty," Lorelle had called after the king, as he'd strode away from the withdrawing room where Gethin babbled in semi-consciousness. She'd dipped into a low curtsey when Badrick turned a snarling grimace on her.

"I'm so sorry to bother you, my king," she'd dissembled in the direction of the floor. "I just wanted to know if you preferred to keep Prince Gethin and Lady Rhoswen together—to reduce the number of guards—considering the way things are going." Her stomach had knotted instantly, and she'd had to hold her breath to keep from dry heaving.

"'The way things are going,'" the king had repeated uncertainly.

"I don't mean to presume, your majesty," Lorelle had continued, "but their interaction with each other.... Well, I didn't realize it wasn't common knowledge, given the public nature of their display...."

"You'll have to forgive me," the king had replied with a sneer, "but I don't speak rambling waiting-woman."

Lorelle had had to bite down on her pride—and her tongue. "Prince Gethin and Lady Rhoswen. Are they not intended for each other? Or is that perhaps their own intention? Clearly, there is an attraction between them.... I just thought—"

The king's face had gone blank as he'd considered this idea. "Are you the only one who believes this?"

Lorelle had not anticipated the question, but it had seemed promising at the moment. "I can't imagine so, my king," she'd lied.

He'd nodded. "I had no intention of putting a guard on my son's chambers."

"Oh! My mistake. Please forgive me, your majesty," Lorelle had pled, slowly backing away to give him the chance to stop her.

"Wait, uh—"

Lorelle had halted and waited for permission to stand. "Lorelle, your majesty," she'd offered into the growing silence.

"Lorelle. Stand up," he'd ordered, eyeing her again. "I must go speak with my son for a moment. After I've left him and Rhoswen is ready to settle in for the evening, send her to Gethin's chambers for a brief visit."

Lorelle had nodded and curtsied again, backing away from the king until he had turned away from her, and she could proceed with her duties.

A chill overtook Lorelle from head to toe, and her blood cooled in her veins at the memory. She shivered and balled the message in her fist. *I'm so sorry, Rhoswen.*

DATIST Archives

To: Gullveig, Runner

Lord Twyford's proposition is amenable. Notify him and make the necessary arrangements before you tether the portal to the Two Fords. Keep it inconspicuous – in the back of the establishment perhaps?

While you are in Salton, pass on the enclosed message to Lord Twyford's servant and Runner, Talena Illisan. Arbiter Emile Illisan has bartered for her return to Welsamar. She should leave immediately of her own accord. If she does not, confiscate her key.

LXXII

Tendalar

Galladar.

Emile's least favorite holiday.

His opinion contrasted with most of the population of Welsamar *precisely* because of the holiday's gratuitous nature. Welsamar experienced two seasons: a warm spring and a cool fall. Spring's move into fall was Galladar; fall's move into spring was Geddalar.

There was *no* reason to celebrate either.

Both transitions were so gradual that you only realized they had happened when you needed to put on a button-down shawl cardigan or take one off. Memorializing either imperceptible shift was utterly pointless. Most people relished the time off for a day of festivities; Emile considered it yet another obligation to go home to the family – or be chastised for several holidays to come if he didn't.

Jerold was already at the party by the time Emile arrived at his sister's house. Given his mother's reaction to his return, one would think the lad had been away from home for three seasons or better, not several weeks.

"Emile! Look who's home!" Talena exclaimed by way of greeting. She was beaming, her arm around her son. They stood in the lush gardens behind their expansive home, surrounded by countless guests, most of whom were not related to their family. Emile yearned for a holiday without the rabble. "You know, he Rides in Sullinar now," she added. Emile was uncertain whether the announcement was meant as a barb for his imagined absence from their lives or as an opening for obligatory praise from her fawning acquaintances within earshot.

Regardless, Emile knew the story well. As one of the farthest cities from Tendalar, Sullinar would be the least scrutinized. It's the reason he'd picked it. "So I heard," Emile replied, kissing his sister on the cheek. He shook Jerold's hand. "Congratulations, my boy." Jerold tipped his head in appreciation, and Emile swept his arm out to the side. "Walk with me. Tell me about your new home."

They moved away from Talena, and Emile smiled at passersby as if his conversation with his nephew were nothing more than casual catch-up. Still, he kept his voice low. "The ruse appears to be working."

"Thank you for educating me on Sullinar. I wouldn't know what to tell them otherwise," Jerold said. He sounded sheepish.

"You're lying to them for all the right reasons," Emile tried to reassure him. "How *is* your new home? A rustic delight?"

"The customs are simple enough. None of the conveniences of Welsamar, though," Jerold replied.

"I expect not! Everything smoothed over with the Stanburhs?"

"Ravinger doesn't seem to think so, but they've been quiet since our introduction.... He says that's even worse than their being inquisitive."

"He would know," Emile replied. "They have a history."

"Since you mention it," Jerold began, "I have some questions about history. And as I can't ask my mother...."

Emile's eyebrows flattened. "You most certainly cannot. I told you what I know, Jerold."

"I doubt that very highly." Jerold stopped walking and faced his uncle. "You're an Arbiter with an endless supply of historical data at your fingertips...."

"History belongs in the past," Emile replied, his voice smooth. He smiled at another idiot-friend of his sister as they passed. She wore an overlarge lime-green velvet top hat with light-pink lilies of blown glass along its rim. A tragic accompaniment to her deep-fuchsia dress.

"The past makes the present," Jerold insisted. "Look, I took you up on your offer to Run for a reason. I need to understand a few things, or this arrangement does me no good."

"I would submit that you know everything you need to, to make this arrangement work—"

"For *you*, perhaps. If you want me to keep up this Sullinar charade, you'll answer my questions."

"That charade is no favor to me, I assure you," Emile said. "I wanted you dead to this realm from the start." He eyed his nephew. He could never have guessed the lad could be so heavy-handed. The only other time his nephew had reacted so vehemently to anything was at Wallen's naming ceremony, when he had suggested the Rider visit home without his dragon. *Intriguing.* "What is it you want to know?"

"Where did my mother Run?" Jerold asked.

"In D'Erenelle, as I told you."

"*Where* in D'Erenelle?"

"I will only answer that if you do something for me," he replied. Jerold snorted in disapproval, but Emile cut him off before he could protest. "If you want your key to continue letting you into Welsamar, I'd suggest you agree to my terms."

It was a lie, but he figured a compelling one, as Jerold had no idea that Emile required *possession* of the key to alter its functionality. *One of the Exchange's greatest failings,* Emile lamented and arched an eyebrow to keep from rolling his eyes. "Or would you prefer I tell your family what I told the Exchange about your honorable demise?"

"What do I have to do?" Jerold asked without hesitation.

So, you're desperate for this information. "Ask your questions first," Emile said. "If the answers are that important to you, you'll take the risk." He kept his expression blank as he watched his nephew.

Jerold hesitated only briefly. "All right. My mother?"

"She Ran in Salton."

"Where the portal is?"

Emile nodded. "She was a servant of Lord Twyford's. He is the benefactor of the tavern that facilitates the portal."

"That would explain the tavern's name. Does he know about the Exchange?" Jerold asked.

"He does. Years ago, a Runner brokered a deal with Twyford to tether the portal to the Two Fords so the Exchange could have protected access to the northern end of the realm."

"What did he get out of it?"

"A bar with a disappearing door in the back." Emile stared at his nephew.

Jerold raised his palms in surrender. "I'll admit that one was pure curiosity." He sighed. "Look, when you told me Diron wasn't my father, I realized I didn't know a part of myself that makes me... *me*. My mother obviously doesn't want me to know about my birth father, and I couldn't ask my—*Diron*. So, when you offered me the position of Runner in the very realm where I was conceived, it seemed like the ideal way to get answers. I'm just trying to figure out who my father is. Maybe Twyford would know."

I should have guessed. Emile shook his head. "*Lord* Twyford cares nothing for the politics of the Exchange or others' lives. When he lost your mother as a servant, I'm sure he simply found a replacement without a second thought. I cannot imagine he knew anything about her, let alone whom she was carrying on with. He is reputedly not the friendliest of men, Jerold; I don't want you pushing your luck with him. He has been gracious enough to safeguard the portal all these years, and we cannot jeopardize the security of the Exchangers who use it."

"'Gracious?' I figured he would get something for his trouble," Jerold prodded again.

"And I figured you would find fulfillment in your new double life." Emile shrugged his shoulders. "Who knew?"

Jerold tilted his head to the side. "How do you tether a portal to a spot in a realm anyway?"

"It's an in-depth process," Emile replied. "But it is made much easier with the help of a witch, and the Runner who brokered the deal with Twyford was a very powerful one."

"A *witch*?" Jerold asked in disbelief. "Is she still alive?"

Emile narrowed his eyes. "Are you looking for her or your father?" When Jerold didn't answer, he pressed on. "Why this sudden preoccupation with finding a man who probably doesn't even know you exist? He didn't raise you. What answers could he possible give? Diron is a good father to you, is he not?"

"He is," Jerold insisted. "But I have never related to my family in the way they do to one another. Something was always... *off*. I thought becoming a Rider would provide that missing piece—and it did... mostly. I just want to understand where I come from."

Ah, the plight of the bastard, Emile mused. "I see. Well, perhaps you need another task more than answers. Now, for my half of the bargain." He fished something out of his pants pocket and held it out to his nephew. A red marble sat motionless in his palm. "Watch Emmelyn, will you? If she becomes troublesome in any way, pop this into the Transitor with your message. I'll know what to do."

"Troublesome?" Jerold asked, his brow furrowing. "What kind of trouble?"

"You'll know it when you see it. Just be on the lookout."

Jerold nodded and secreted the marble into a pocket of his leathers.

"And as for this quest you're on: don't let it interfere with your job," Emile warned. Then, he smiled and steered his nephew back toward the party. "Remember: I brought you into the Exchange. I can just as easily take you out of it."

LXXIII

Aethelburh

When Delwyn found Lorelle again, he was fidgeting so much, he was practically shaking. Lorelle couldn't bring herself to question him, though. She was on her hands and knees, scrubbing at the root liquor that the king had spilled on the floor of his study. She splashed a rag into a bucket and slammed it against the stone. Water sloshed across its surface well beyond the area of the dried and sticky spill.

Delwyn jumped back a little to stay out of the line of fire. "Are you all right?" His voice quavered like the rest of his body.

"I should have realized!" she chastised herself.

"I'm sorry?"

She wetted the rag and slapped it messily against the floor again. "Emile. *That realmer!* This explains the Arbiter merger. He needed all new Runners and Transfers because his existing staff started figuring out that his triples were illegitimate. *Poor Emmelyn….*"

"Who?" Delwyn asked.

"My old Transfer. Never mind. I'm just trying to piece it all together…." She finally calmed down enough to ask him about the source of his nervousness.

"The meeting tonight," he began. "If the king is calling for his Pentagraphs, then it might only be a matter of time before he asks me to do something awful, and I end up feeling the same kind of remorse you're feeling about Rhoswen."

"Did I hear the Lady of Stanburh mentioned?" Garrick's smooth voice asked as he strolled into the study. He had clearly been skulking outside the door, or they would have heard him coming. A second pair of clacking footsteps grew louder as Sherman ambled in behind him.

They were an odd pair. Garrick was—similar to his name—*garrulous* in a sort of Narxon-may-care kind of way, whereas Sherman was meek and thoughtful almost to a fault. They formed an unlikely friendship, but no one else on the staff was closer. *That is, if anyone could truly be close to Garrick….* Lorelle found him obnoxious and far too gossipy to take into her confidence. But that did *occasionally* come in handy… when he wasn't spying on *her*.

"Sherman here tells me Rhoswen visited home today. Why didn't the prince just go with her to Stanburh?" Garrick asked, eyeing the trail of water seeping ever closer to the rug.

Lorelle scrunched up her face in confusion. "What are you talking about?"

Garrick ran the toe of his shoe through the water, smearing it away from the carpet, and nodded at Sherman to do the storytelling.

"I saw Lady Rhoswen at Castle Stanburh when I delivered the message that Gethin would be arriving there on the morrow," Sherman explained, his voice quiet. He hailed from a small town in the south, where they spoke softly and used antiqued phrases like "on the morrow." Lorelle thought it added a quaintness to his already sweet demeanor.

"You're sure you saw Lady Rhoswen, not someone who looked like her?" she asked him. He must have just gotten back. It was almost dark outside, and she needed to get this liquor cleaned up before she couldn't see well enough to distinguish it from the dark stone.

Sherman nodded. "The stable hand recognized her. Lord Stanburh said she flew in on a dragon, presumably with one of the Riders of Keaton."

"It's the only way she could have beaten him there," Garrick added. "Lady Rhoswen was with Lord Thane before I delivered him into Lady Alston's carriage, and Sherm was long gone by then."

"Who took her?" Lorelle asked.

Sherman shrugged. "I didn't see a dragon from Keaton there."

"Her parents might have picked her up," Lorelle suggested.

"From the way Sherman told it, it doesn't sound that way," Garrick said. Sherman shook his head in confirmation.

"I was just in Keaton," Delwyn said with a glance at Lorelle, "and I didn't see any Riders coming or going—"

"That's because none of them did."

King Badrick stood in the entrance to the study. At the sound of his voice, the servants bent low, their lips clamped tight and eyes directed at the floor. Badrick bade them all stand up. "I did not give any of my Riders permission to take Lady Rhoswen to Stanburh, and they would not have gone without my leave. You must be mistaken," he explained, his eyes sweeping their faces, uncertain of which of them had claimed to see his niece.

Sherman nodded his head agreeably, giving himself away. The king eyed him for a moment before storming from the study with a flourish of his cape. The waitstaff bowed in his wake. At the last moment, before disappearing from view, he called for Delwyn to follow, and the waitman rushed out after him.

It took another moment before anyone in the study dared breathe or even move. Finally, they unbent themselves, huddling together to resume their conversation in hushed tones.

"Since when does the king walk in and have a chat with his servants?" Garrick asked the others.

Lorelle tossed the rag back in the bucket with a splash. "Since he wants to know what the servants know," she whispered back.

The king strode away from the study and the barely concealed shock of his servants. His waitman's shoes clacked behind him, growing louder with every step. Badrick turned to face the man, his cape swirling around him, and Delwyn had to stop short to keep from running into him.

"You found someone to help us in Keaton?" the king asked.

Delwyn nodded, his shoulders still hunched up around his ears from his abrupt halt. "I have, your majesty."

"Then you will confirm whether a Rider took Rhoswen to Stanburh today."

Asking Delwyn to find a spy in Keaton, although unprecedented, was not an action outside the realm of possibility for a man like the king. But admitting uncertainty of whether his Riders were acting autonomously around him—*that* was new. The last time the king mistrusted his own Riders like this was during the unspoken war. The return of such a mindset signaled a shift that he—or Lorelle—would need to report on their next Run. *This will complicate matters....* "Of course, your majesty. I will return to Keaton at once."

"You've already spoken to your man today?"

Delwyn nodded again. "He had little to report, sire."

The king sneered. "See that he has more to report by tomorrow," he replied and dismissed Delwyn with another abrupt turn on his heel.

As Badrick moved away from his study, he could hear Delwyn's clacking footsteps fading away and a door at the rear of the castle opening and closing. The Great Hall fell silent, the king's own padding footfalls inaudible.

He already knew who would have taken Rhoswen to Stanburh without his permission; it didn't take a spy to figure that one out. Thankfully, he would speak with a Rider tonight who could take care of the problem. He scowled, his frustration getting the better of him.

There is only one thing to do about you, Darr Beval.

LXXIV

Keaton

Rhoswen stepped back through the portal into the classroom just as a pair of giggling students stumbled in through the adjacent archway. Their arms were wrapped around each other, lips locked and feet stumbling, as one tried to walk backwards and the other forwards. The couple lost their balance and crashed into the padded arm of a nearby loveseat. They scrambled against the smooth leather as they groped their way to the cushions, laughing and shushing each other.

Rhoswen squinted at the pair in the dim light, her pupils sluggish. Even the dark-gray twilight of Stanburh had been brighter than this. She fell to her knees in front of the maps, placed the trinkets gently into their case, and as she lifted the box to put it into her bag, the maps rolled up on themselves. The sound of crinkling parchment tore through the room, and the creak of leather ceased as the couple froze and a familiar voice demanded her identification.

Rhoswen jumped to her feet and peered at the heads of the lovers where they peeked up over the back of the couch. "Aeduuin? Sterling?"

The young men untangled themselves and jumped off the couch to stand apart from each other. "Rhoswen?" Aeduuin asked. "We were just, ah...."

"Looking for a quiet place where you wouldn't be disturbed?" she suggested, stepping forward to situate herself more squarely between them and the maps.

Aeduuin rubbed a hand across the back of his neck. "I guess we had the same idea you did, huh?" He looked nervous. Behind him, Sterling was blank faced with shock.

"Your idea might be more fun than mine." She wondered how she could get them out of here so she could pack up the maps. "I just needed to be alone for a while," she hinted.

"Of course," Aeduuin blurted, but he didn't move toward the door. Instead, he stepped closer to Rhoswen, his expression uncertain. Her skin crawled as he drew nearer the maps. "Rhoswen, I don't know how to say this… " Aeduuin muttered.

"It's fine, Aeduuin," she blurted, uncertain of what she was sanctioning.

He was still shuffling toward her. "You know… trainers really aren't supposed to have… *intimate* relationships with trainees."

Something about the statement lodged in her heart like a thorn as she remembered she was supposed to be in Darr Beval's sitting room right now. "Aeduuin, I won't tell any—"

He wouldn't meet her gaze. "It's just that… I *think* you've done me a favor before, and I can't really ask you—"

Rhoswen's heart pounded in her chest, and she choked as her lungs refused to take in air. *How could he know about my help with Corliss?!* Her mind raced over the details of that day, but she couldn't conceive of a time when Aeduuin had become aware of her presence within the green's stall. His focus had been entirely on the dragon. *Who would have told him?* She thought about Thane's trip to Alston. *What if it isn't Darr Beval's* father *we should be worried about…?* She felt as if the thorn were twisting sideways in her chest. She glanced up at Aeduuin.

"I mean, I *shouldn't* ask you for anoth—"

But he didn't have the chance not to ask her for another favor. Roars and screams arose from the arena below, stopping him midsentence.

Sterling had moved through the arched doorway to look out a window on the other side of the hall. "A dragon is falling through the sky—he was hit by Narxon! There's a tear! It's a Descent!"

Aeduuin raced to the door, his terror mirroring Sterling's as he watched the scene unfold. Rhoswen took one step to follow but stopped herself. She couldn't abandon the maps.

"I have to help them," Aeduuin yelled. "Come on!"

"You can't!" Sterling was about to launch himself out the door after Aeduuin, but he stopped and looked back to Rhoswen. She was frozen in place, waiting for him to go so she could pack up, but he wasn't leaving.

"We have to stop him. Are you coming?" he asked.

"Yes," she replied, but neither of them moved.

Even in the dim light, Rhoswen could tell from his scrunched features that Sterling was sizing her up. Aeduuin's foolish bravery had set a precedent, and Sterling was waiting for Rhoswen to prove herself in the same way. His scrutiny made her feel unworthy, and the sensation drowned out her concerns about the maps.

"Absolutely," she said and followed him to the door. They sprinted through the hall and bounded down the stairs after Aeduuin, the bellows and screams growing louder as they ran.

She sensed the pull of the trinket box and maps—the very things that could one day provide her an escape route from her uncle's madness. Was she a fool to leave them behind, unguarded in a public space that anyone could—and likely *would*—walk into?

And that's when her hand fled to the vest pocket that normally bulged with her compass. Her heart clenched, and she gasped as her fingers fell flush against the fabric. *My compass!* She'd left it in the rolled up maps.

The compass her father had warned her all her life never to lose.

She'd left it behind.

"I'll be right back," she called to Sterling, turning on her heel.

He grabbed her arm. "We have to help! Don't be a coward!"

He had voiced it. That label was the reason she had followed him without her belongings in the first place. She wanted to protest, to tell him that she was braver than that, to promise to return after she'd grabbed her things, but he was dragging her along, unaware that the objects' importance far outweighed the fear he assumed she harbored toward the Descent. She could only nod and speed back into a run beside him.

What have I done?

Beval watched as the young red dragon screeched and flailed through the air, his hide marred with a widening ashy swath where the Narxon had grazed him. The lack of healing rain only prolonged his agony, and Failsafes flew out to rescue the trainee from his back before he could buck the lad from the saddle.

Fleta lurched upward toward the first ink-black intruder. Beval felt the tawny's gut rumble beneath him before her jet of fire turned the Narxon to a shower of ash. Beval cocked his head back. The tear was so massive that smoke-dragons pushed themselves into the sky, fully formed, to race toward the ground unimpeded. *Thank the realm it's high up,* he nexed to Fleta as her wings beat at the air.

Merry and Thorndon had sped ahead of them to take their place at the rear of the tear. Another smoke-beast was pushing its way out, bending the edges of the sky with its inky bulk. Beval had to give his head a shake to refocus his eyes. *I've never seen so much distortion. How are we going to do this?* he asked Fleta.

The tawny seemed as disturbed as her Rider. *We need another dragon on our side of the tear to burn them as they fall through, or I won't be able to get close enough to cauterize it. I'll put out the call – hang on!* She shifted her weight and turned sideways in the sky, narrowly missing the edge of a smoky wing and a line of Merry's fire.

As Fleta circled back toward the front of the tear, Beval thrust his boots down into the toeholds to demand another change in course. Fleta veered upward just in time to miss a young green bolting toward the gash. Corliss.

Fleta nexed to the beast, chastising her for her involvement, while Beval hollered to Aeduuin to land. The young pair careened off to the side and out of Beval's line of sight. Fleta approached the tear once more but was forced to hover a good distance away to avoid being hit by the Narxon emerging from it.

"What were they thinking?!" Beval yelled.

They're trying to help, Fleta nexed back, her tone more perturbed than charitable. *Someone has met my call for assistance,* she added.

Who?

As if in answer, a huge red flew in from overhead and incinerated the black smoke-beast prying itself through the opening in the sky.

No.

Beval felt his stomach knot and his heart chill. He knew that red. He had known Godelief all his life. As the red took her place in front of the tear, Beval steeled himself to gaze at her now-visible Rider. The man was clad all in black, only a shock of blond hair outlining his head. His features were indistinguishable in the warping from the tear, but Beval could have identified the man through any amount of distortion.

His father.

Beval Senior had retired from training at Keaton almost a decade ago, much to his son's relief. Beval had been recruited to replace his father, and the only reason he gave up freedom of transfer to take the position in the king's drakiary was because he knew his father would no longer be teaching—or residing—there.

For Beval Senior, however, retirement was not an all-encompassing status. One job he refused to relinquish: he remained second in command to Badrick as the leader of his group of hired assassins, the Pentagraphs. If Beval Senior had been summoned here, it was because the king had something terrible for him to do.

As if we need to add to this chaos, Beval thought.

Godelief broke off her jet of fire just long enough to prepare for another burst, and Fleta began her count-off with Merry. As another Narxon pushed its way through the tear, Godelief blasted the opening, and Fleta and Merry's streams met at the top of the gash. They worked their way down toward the plume of ash Godelief was creating while a lower swarm of dragons rushed to catch little, burning tendrils that slipped past her destructive blaze.

Beval's eyes watered with the heat and smoke, and the distortion of the sky made it hard to follow the dragon's flames as they closed the tear. Still, Fleta and Merry aligned their jets flawlessly, and a scar began to form where the sky once gaped. Beval beamed with pride at his tawny. There was a reason he and Thorndon were Riding partners, and it wasn't just because the men got along so well; their dragons were a formidable pair in a Descent.

But as far as Beval was concerned, that partnership topped out at *two.* Despite the heat radiating from the fire around him, Beval's skin pimpled with gooseflesh at the thought of his father's involvement in their cauterization.

As the pair reached the midway point, they signaled Godelief to retreat to reduce the heat warping their view of the tear. The red descended, joining the others below, who burned the Narxon that escaped Fleta and Merry's efforts at closing the gap.

Finally, the pair pushed out their last fireballs and sped away from the explosive plume where the flames met in midair. When the fire dissipated, both dragons swung back around to inspect their work. The scar was holding.

Barely.

Is it bulging? Beval asked Fleta. He blinked to focus his gaze. Without the rain, smoke and ash continued to build up around them, making it hard to distinguish the silvery scar from the dark-gray skies. Out over the trees, Beval could just make out the injured red as he dove out of sight and presumably into the nearby river. He was followed by two more dragons, who also disappeared as they trailed him. *Where is that realmed rain Rhoswen predicted for today?* he wondered.

Something's not right, Fleta agreed. She went silent as she consulted her partner. *Merry says the back of the tear looks wrong.*

Beval didn't know what that meant, but he didn't like the sound of it.

Godelief flew up beside Fleta. "That doesn't look like it's going to hold," Beval Senior called to his son.

Beval bit back a sarcastic reply and inclined his head in greeting. "Father. Suggestions?"

"I've seen this once before," his father yelled, "recently, in Upwood. The tears are becoming strange… less predictable."

More good news. "What did you do?" Beval hollered back.

"Nothing. The rain came, and it stopped bulging." Beval Senior glared at the greedy storm clouds.

It already has. Look! Fleta called Beval's attention to the scar.

Its swelling had ceased, even without the advent of rain, but Beval mistrusted this inexplicable good fortune. *If you can call anything relating to a Descent fortunate,* he thought as the young red screeched in the distance, his wounds continuing to fester.

What if it doesn't rain? he nexed to Fleta. When she didn't answer, he asked her a different question. *The tears are changing? What does that mean?*

The tears never change without cause, the tawny replied. *And they never change in isolation.*

What do you mean? Beval asked again.

Fleta paused before answering. *Something always changes with them.*

Acknowledgments

Were I to fully express the depth of my gratitude to everyone who helped with this book, I would require another publication of equal size to *An Heir of Realms*. I hope, then, that those I mention here will understand the necessarily abbreviated nature of my acknowledgments. It is no meager reflection on the size of their contributions or my appreciation for them.

I will start with my beta readers: Catherine Gernaat, Jason DeSantis, Dorene McLaughlin, R.P., and Darren Todd. You opened my weary eyes to the diverse viewpoints a reader might have when venturing into this story, and your wisdom not only improved the tale but bolstered my courage in telling it. I can't thank you enough for the time you took to read and comment on it, especially Cathy, who labored through it twice. I've read this book a time or two myself, and I appreciate the effort you all put in to make it better. Thank you for caring enough to do so.

To R.P., whom I have deemed my Publishing Adviser Extraordinaire: you carried me under your wing and told me not to look down. Thank you for helping me navigate the rocky waters of self-publishing; your tips, tricks, and hacks, along with your straightforward approach to the process smoothed the entire experience (and my feathers on multiple occasions). While I'll never understand why you bothered to share your wisdom with me, I will be forever grateful for your time, effort, patience, guidance, and interest. I hope I proved worthy of your tutelage.

To Darren Todd, a truly fabulous editor: you not only corrected my eerily consistent mistakes for over five-hundred draft pages but took the time to teach me how to fix them, all without compromising my voice. You have improved my writing in leaps and bounds, and I find myself smiling when I write something in a first draft that you had once corrected in a hundredth. You polished this rock to a gem, and I appreciate what it took you to do so.

To those who brought the cover art to life: Moo, Gramma, and Rob Carlos. Leave it to my mother to come up with so complex and unorthodox a cover design that I had to hire out custom artwork! Thank you, Moo, for your creative vision that never fails to inspire awe… a couple kinds of awe…. And if Moo can conceptualize it, Gramma will make certain it's anatomically feasible. Thank you, Gramma, for ensuring this fabulous idea could become a reality and for taking the frightening trip into my head to bring my thoughts to the page. And I couldn't have found a better dragon expert to bring this series to life (mostly because Moo found him): Rob. You and I rarely found ourselves on different wavelengths during this project, but you made certain that all my needs and desires were met, even thinking of a few that I wouldn't have considered. Your meticulous attention to detail has changed the course of this series, even beyond the art, and I appreciate your thoughtfulness and incredible skill. Thank you, all of you.

To my bosses at Stoney Creek Advisors, LLC, William A. Waggoner II and Peter Mitroff: you gave me the freedom and support I needed to complete this story, all while maintaining your belief in my ability to complete my day job, too. No one could ask for better employers, and few could be lucky enough to count them as friends. Thank you for giving me room to breathe, faith to soar, and trust to accomplish more than I thought I could. Thank you for everything. Truly.

To my CF teams—both my former pediatric group in Kalamazoo and my current adult-clinic heroes at the DMC: you have helped keep me alive to realize my dream of becoming an author. You are kind, caring, courageous, generous, wise, and occasionally goofy—all my favorite traits in people but especially awe-inspiring in medical staff, who've seen some things and still never tire of helping others (at least not as far as I can tell). Thank you for all you do—for *all* your patients. My love and gratitude to you all.

To my mentor, Tim (TL) Lentz: you transitioned me through some important realizations in my young life and helped me to hone my dreams at an early age. You believed in me when my clay was at its roughest, and you helped shape me into something that held promise. I thank you for your passion, your support, and most of all, your guidance. While I won't do you the disservice of saying you made me what I am today, I will most certainly credit you with softening my edges and broadening my mind, both of which I so dearly needed. Thank you for the effort that took. I can't image the patience it required.

To my dearest friends: Kristin Pirozzo, Lindsey DeBoever, and Gail McCormick. You never failed to ask how the writing was going, even when you feared a long and unedited reply. Thank you for asking, for listening, and for showing excitement and support. You provided welcome distractions from my writing, even when we were talking about it. I hope you still want to read it after all that, and I hope it's worth reading, too. You certainly deserve it. I love you!

To my aunt, Tracie: you fostered my love for dragons from an early age and never stopped. (Translation: this is all *your* fault.) Thank you for indulging my many whimsies these equally many years—and for never telling me to grow up. Love you!

To my family—Granny, Grampy, Uncle Tim and Ellen, "Ninja" Jo, Jack, LaVonda, and my cousins: thank you for showing interest and enthusiasm and for believing I could do it, even if it took ten (plus) years. If you haven't always believed in me, you've faked it well, and it means so much to have you behind me in everything I do. I wouldn't be who I am today without you, and I am so fortunate and appreciative. I love you all.

To Bill, perhaps one of the most patient men I have ever met: you have loved and supported me in even my most trying moments (which may very well be all of them). I don't tell you enough how much I appreciate you, but I love you for your kindness, your understanding, and your dancing. Especially your dancing. Thank you for always dancing for me.

To my best friend, Jennifer (Jupes) Peace: you believed in me back when I started this series a decade ago, even when my drafts were frightening at best (and you offered to read them anyway!). You have believed in my every endeavor and, whenever possible, taken an active role in each. Thank you for always being there, for sharing, for asking, for listening, for boosting my spirits and supporting me, for laughing with (and at) me, for giving me the courage to skirt the ledges and then talking me off them, and for loving me in spite of myself. I don't know what I would do without you. I love you and always will, even when we're old, deaf, and reintroducing ourselves to each other from our close-set rocking chairs in the nursing home. I'll see you there.

To my parents, Moo and Did: I would be lost without you. Not a day goes by that I am not thankful to have you as my parents, my guiding lights in this life and probably the next (who else would take me?). You have supported this dream and everything that led up to it without fail or hesitation. You never doubted (at least not openly), you never questioned (except to help me improve), and you always loved (in your special, *special* way). You are the best example I could follow, and I thank you for not judging me when I fail to meet your standards. You keep the bar high, but I couldn't reach for it if not for your shoulders. I love you with all my heart. This one's for you.

A Note from the Author

A sincere thank-you to everyone who has taken the time to post reviews and positive feedback on Amazon, Goodreads, and social media outlets. If you haven't yet, please share your opinions to help other readers connect with this book. I *so* appreciate your effort and time.

www.facebook.com/Heather.Ashle.Author
www.twitter.com/realmriders
www.instagram.com/realmridersseries
www.heatherashle.com
www.realmriders.com

And please follow my Amazon author page and join my newsletter via my website for updates about the second novel in the Realm Riders Series, *A Transfer of Realms,* to be released (hopefully!) before the end of 2024.

I can't wait to share this tale with you!

Heather Ashle

About the Author

Heather Ashle began combing bookstore shelves at an early age, accumulating more titles than she could read in one lifetime. She connected most strongly with stories about dragons and magic, as their immersive and fantastical themes created a welcome distraction from Cystic Fibrosis (CFF.org) and the hours of daily treatments required to keep her alive and reading.

While her education took place as much in the halls *between* classrooms, where she walked from class to class with her nose in books, her studies officially culminated in two English degrees from Oakland University. She started writing the *Realm Riders Series* in college and has nearly completed books two and three of the series. She is excited for the approaching release of the second book, *A Transfer of Realms*, and hopes her tales can provide others a whimsical reprieve from their own life challenges.

Learn more about Heather's authorial journey from her blog and sign up for updates about future releases via www.heatherashle.com.

Made in the USA
Monee, IL
12 June 2025